Wildalone

Wildalone

KRASSI ZOURKOVA

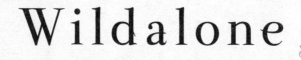

WILLIAM MORROW
An Imprint of HarperCollins*Publishers*

P.S.™ is a trademark of HarperCollins Publishers.

HarperCollins books may be purchased for educational, business, or sales promotional use. For information please e-mail the Special Markets Department at SPsales@harpercollins.com.

A hardcover edition of this book was published in 2014 by William Morrow, an imprint of HarperCollins Publishers.

FIRST WILLIAM MORROW PAPERBACK EDITION PUBLISHED 2015.

Map on pages vi and vii by Danae Blackburn

Excerpt on page 269 from Friedrich Nietzsche, The Birth of Tragedy, trans. Ian Johnston (Arlington, VA: Richer Resources Publications, 2009), accessed online August 22, 2014. https://archive.org/stream/BirthOfTragedy/bitrad_djvu.txt.

Art used throughout by Marina99/Shutterstock, Inc.

Designed by Lisa Stokes

Library of Congress Cataloging-in-Publication Data has been applied for.

ISBN 978-0-06-232803-8

15 16 17 18 19   OV/RRD   10 9 8 7 6 5 4 3 2 1

Wildalone

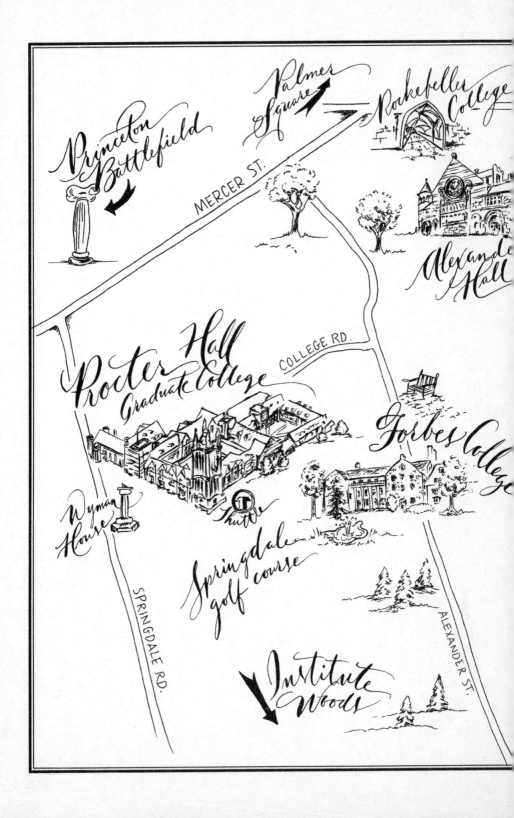

Princeton Battlefield

Palmer Square

Rockefeller College

MERCER ST.

Alexander Hall

COLLEGE RD.

Procter Hall
Graduate College

Forbes College

Wyman House

Shuttle

Springdale
golf course

SPRINGDALE RD.

Springdale
golf course

Institute Woods

ALEXANDER ST.

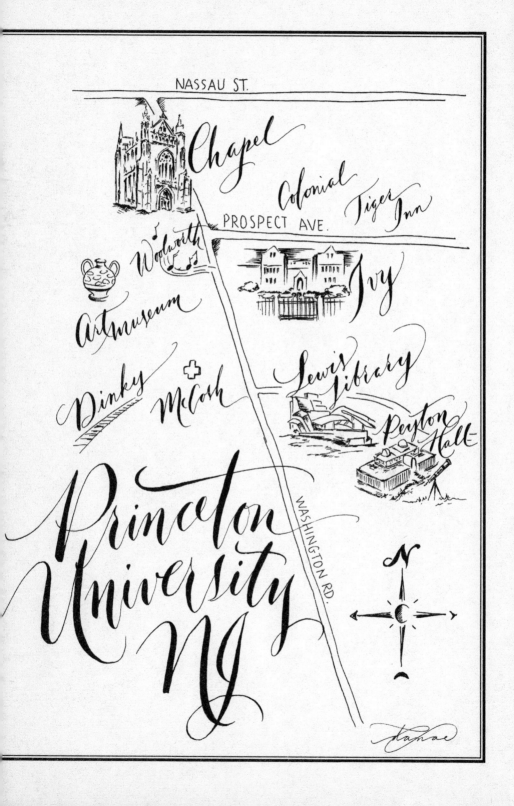

Prologue

IN 1802, AT the Rila Monastery in Bulgaria, the monk Rafail carved the last of six hundred and fifty miniature figures on a wooden cross, allegedly losing his sight after twelve years of work on the piece.

In the early 1990s, while going through sealed archives marked as "Threat to Ideology" by the former Communist government, researchers found a collection of religious artifacts. Among them was a scroll taken from the monastery library at Rila, dating back to Rafail's time.

Based on the following account found on the scroll, it has been suggested that when the monk began work on his masterpiece, he may have been already blind.

Monastery of St. John of Rila, this fifth day of the month of August, in the year one thousand seven hundred and eighty-nine, as spoken to our Lord by one of his humbled servants, transcribed it is thus:

I am told that this is being written at the light of sixteen candles, and I trust the eye of the stranger who counts them, the hand that puts quill to parchment, recording my words—for trust is the only path left to the blind.

I was blinded for what I saw. But by mercy of the One high above all things, was what I saw worth it!

Legends are sung of the Samodivi; grim, lush legends. But no legend unfolds these ravenous beauties in words as they unfolded for me in moon-woven flesh, one silver night, outside these monastery walls.

A woodcarver by craft, I had journeyed to Thrace and back, going from door to door, selling the fruits of my hands—reproduced church relics—to anyone who would pay a trifle for them. A late hour caught me deep inside the forest and I headed to seek shelter with the monks. As my feet neared the end of a long day's labor, I saw a figure cross my path: a girl still, but already ravishing, her white skin ripe like the skin of a lily cut from the stem just before blooming. A thin dress enveloped her, sewn from moonlight, weightless—a spiderweb—hiding nothing of her body as she stepped toward me.

I was not a holy man then, and I had tasted beauty on my travels—beauty as rare in the darkness of our world as a man without regrets among the dying. But I had never, not once, laid sight on a creature to rival her. With a luminous smile, she lured me through the trees, onto a lawn where her two sisters already waited. They closed a circle around me and rushed into dance—stunning, flawless—as the moon poured its jeweled envy over them. Their toes barely touched the ground, but it pulsed under them with the distant beat of drums, as if somewhere, far off, the mountain's heart had been set ablaze. They took me into their fury, into the curve of their locked arms, and I struggled to keep up, fighting the blood that invaded my veins further with each step—until a spasm seized my chest. I saw them smile, saw their eyes flash triumph as my body collapsed at their feet. Slowly, the others dissipated back into the night, but she stayed and held me, spilling her hair like heavy gold all over me . . .

Woe, they say, shall befall the traveler who happens upon the Samodivi, the one who beholds their dance under the full moon. But blessed be a human of such woeful fate: when she bared her skin for me, when she placed her breast within my hands and her hungered lips opened into mine, there was no woe, no torture left in this entire world—not even death itself—that my soul would not have welcomed. Time vanished when her white legs parted over me, quiet, soft like snow whose touch a man never forgets once he has been drunk on it. I took her with my eyes, my hands, my mouth. Took her desperately, mad with an ache that tore through bones and sinews; an excruciating ache that wouldn't cease, not even when she had me force my way inside her. If she had asked, I would have begged. Died. Killed. Been damned for her. I would have done anything, and done it many times over.

But she asked nothing. Her face bent over mine and she kissed my eyelids, closing them before a sudden pain singed the sockets where my eyes had been. I heard her laughter—free, innocent, the laughter of a child—and felt her lips press once more, this time against my chest. Yet before her fingers could dive in to claim my heart, the cry of a rooster echoed over us, announcing the dawn—

Then silence.

The monks found my body where she had left it, and I was carried into their holy dwelling whose walls I would never leave again. The sights of the world have since been taken from me, and with them—most of its burdens and its blessings. By divine whim, my skill with the wood was left intact, and my fingers now carve with a new fervor: the last joy and last sorrow left to me from among those I had once known, before I came to know . . . her.

I shall grow old in darkness and in darkness I shall leave this earth, all its treasures still vivid inside my scarred eyelids. But until then, every night, within that same darkness she dances for me—breathtaking as she was back then—and she abandons her beauty to my madly aching heart, the heart which her fingers failed to reach but which she stole, she stole nonetheless . . .

The darkness softens. I hear the beat of her steps. Her skin falls on me. Then the rest of her; her quick lips on my mouth. I see her, all of her, as the eyes of a mortal never could. And from then on, for a while at least, death holds no meaning.

Part I

CHAPTER I

What Hides in the Hills

I HAVE LEFT everyone I love. For good.

My mind shoved the thought back into a corner and tried to focus on counting dollar bills, expecting them to decompose any second from the impossible humidity of summer in America. "Good luck here, sweetheart." The driver of Princeton's airport shuttle took the money and thanked me with a wink. "You'll need it." Then, to prove the point, he drove off through the alleys of an empty campus.

Deep breath. Ignore the falling dusk. They know you're coming, somebody will show up soon.

I sat down on the larger of my two suitcases and waited. The evening was soaked with heat, with an almost liquid smell of grass so vibrantly green that its juice seemed to find a way straight into my lungs. I could reach out and touch it—smooth, thick as a Persian rug, the grass of a university whose name had become legend, even in my tiny country halfway across the world. Princeton was the one school that had always remained elusive. No flashy photos in brochures. No self-advertising. An enigma, tucked into its own pocket of the universe.

Now all around me, among the lush tree crowns, lay strange gray-stone buildings lifted out of a movie about medieval knights: the sharp corners of walls softened by arched entryways; the roofline punctuated by towers whose zigzag fortresses eavesdropped on the secrets of cloistered courtyards; the iron-barred windows gaping for air, letting out streaks of light saturated to the color of freshly peeled oranges. And over all this—an odd silence. Not of absence, but of something about to happen. Of a fever about to begin.

"It must have been a long flight from Bulgaria. Sorry I kept you waiting!"

The voice had a German accent and belonged to Klaus, the student who had volunteered to pick me up. We shook hands, then he pointed at a golf cart parked nearby.

"I was going to show you around, but maybe we should head straight over to the dorm. You'll get a tour tomorrow anyway."

Forbes, one of six residential colleges at Princeton, turned out to be far removed from everything else, isolated at the south edge of campus. Annexed to the school in 1970 as an experiment in coed housing, the former inn looked nothing like the neo-Gothic buildings we had passed on the way: a bulk of red brick nestled awkwardly behind a few old trees, with a façade whose slate roof and grid of white-pane windows gave it the air of a sanatorium rather than a college dorm. On the Internet, I had seen open terraces and a large veranda adjacent to a pond—but none of this was now visible from the street. The golf cart swerved into a paved driveway, up to a varnished portico where the U.S. flag and that of Forbes flapped their perky twin greetings.

We followed several secluded corridors, then Klaus unlocked a door and wheeled my suitcases in. "It's a bit dark right now. But don't worry, you'll get a lot of light during the day. Your room overlooks the golf course."

On the wall across from us, a window reached almost to the floor. I opened it and inhaled the dark air—still humid, yet already waking the lungs with the first fresh touches of night. Sounds invaded the room: a faint rustle of wind in leaves, the echo of sticks broken by invisible feet, syncopated calls of a nightbird. And water, whispering things into the black sky.

Stepping out on the grass took me only a second.

"Technically, you aren't supposed to use it as a door." Klaus showed me a sticker on the glass that warned this was not an egress. "And I would try to stay off the golf course; it's not school property. You may also want to lock the window latch. Even when you're home."

Home. I looked at the dorm room that had the impossible task of replacing my home: it held nothing but a few pieces of furniture, passed down by the ghosts who inhabited it briefly each year. Mute carpet. Crippled ceiling. Pale cinder blocks, desperate to mimic bricks but doomed to the anonymous vibe of a motel. It was the smallest room I had ever seen.

"I have to say it's a bit strange." Klaus leaned against the chair while I pushed my luggage into a corner. "Lucky for you, but strange."

"What, that one can reach everything in this room just by standing in the middle?"

"No." He smiled politely, and I realized how spoiled my own joke had made me sound. "That they would let you live all by yourself."

"They?"

"The powers that be in Admissions."

I turned around and looked at him. How much did this guy know? Was he testing me? Hinting at things that were supposed to be long forgotten yet still lurked somewhere, in an old Princeton file, pointing to me as the last person who should be left all by herself on this campus?

I kept searching his face for clues. "Why wouldn't they let me?"

"Because most of the first-years have roommates." He smiled again—a vacant smile that assured me he knew nothing. "The foreign students especially. We are paired up with Americans, to ease the transition."

"I think I'd rather transition solo."

"You say that now, but the place will get to you, trust me. This isn't some big European city like the one you come from; it's the middle of New Jersey. Fields, forests, and factories. You'll be bored out of your mind."

"From what I hear about Princeton, I'll be too busy to worry if I'm bored or not."

"That's exactly the problem. Too much solo time with the books can drive anyone crazy."

"Not someone from the Balkans. We are crazy already."

He struggled for what to say next, careful not to risk crossing the line at which ethnic stereotypes stopped being funny. I wanted to tell him that it was okay, that I had lived my entire life around people who said things to your face, no filter needed. But I followed his example and kept my thoughts to myself, trying to imagine four years of this. Of small talk with strangers.

"Speaking of expatriates, there should be a list in your welcome package."

Our eyes met over a large envelope he had given me earlier. It wasn't hard to guess what would be on that list: names of other Bulgarians who were attending Princeton. Or who already had. The only question was how far back in time the powers that be had decided to go.

I rummaged through the stack of sheets and found the list, all the way at the bottom.

"You should be proud; few countries come even close. A Bulgarian or two every year—that's quite something."

I scanned the names while he spoke. Twenty or so, each with an e-mail address and a phone number. Next to them—the class years, starting from 1994 (the first Bulgarian to graduate from Princeton after the fall of Communism). It was an impressive list, yes. But Klaus was wrong about one thing: there hadn't been a student every year. The number missing in that column was 1996.

"It makes sense that there are so many of you, actually. The 'YES' man is said to have been very impressed with Bulgarians."

"The what man?"

"The 'YES' man. Dean Fred."

I still had no idea whom he was talking about.

"Fred Hargadon, Princeton's dean of admissions. They say he owns the unofficial trademark to that 'YES' on the letter."

It was the one acceptance letter I would never forget, the only one that didn't start with "*We are pleased to inform you . . .*"—just a simple "*YES!*"

"I don't recall seeing his name on it."

"Because he left in 2003. Used to handpick each student here for many years, knew everyone by name. Rumor has it his resignation brought the whole school down in mourning."

It might have. But for me that resignation had been perfectly timed. If the man who remembered names so well had stayed at his job only four more years, my application to Princeton would have had a very different fate.

After Klaus finally left, a door clicked shut in the hallway behind him. Then everything settled back into silence: Forbes was deserted. For now, I was probably the only living soul in the place, summoned a week early for preorientation with a few other foreign students elsewhere on campus.

I pulled a set of sheets out of my suitcase and began to make the bed, trying not to look over at the page whose content was supposed to make me proud. "Don't hesitate to call any of them; they'll be more than happy to talk to you," Klaus had said about the names in that column. But he didn't know that the only person I wanted to call was not on the list, someone from the class of 1996 who had never made it to graduation but who, just like the others, had been handpicked by the "YES" man—back in 1992.

Later that year, a tragedy had quietly unfolded on the dark hills of this same college campus, leaving no ripple, no trace, every detail meticulously locked into the safe vaults of things past. Yet the secret had remained hidden, deep inside those hills. Stubborn and unconcerned with time, it had waited patiently—knowing, all along, that one day it would be brought back to life.

THE DAYS BEGAN TO VANISH into one another with mechanical, hurried precision. Unpack. Settle in. Set up phone account. E-mail account. Bank account. Cafeteria plan. Memorize campus geography. Dash to events. Learn names, link them to faces. Connect. Socialize. Barely checked off, each task fueled the next as if a giant clockwork had been set in motion, requiring every tooth on every wheel to fall, quickly and elegantly, into place.

I tried to keep up with all this, with each detail that makes a new place feel unmistakably foreign. Nodding for yes and shaking my head for no— the opposite of what I was used to. Waiting for a green light to cross the street and having to remind myself, at the white flash, that it wasn't the color but the image that counted. And food, unlimited quantities of food everywhere. It was easy to pile up too much on my plate, or to pick the wrong thing and then feel guilty for wasting it. Not to mention the tricky foods, the ones that only looked familiar but weren't: feta cheese turning out to be tofu, cilantro disguised as parsley. No matter how odious the taste, I couldn't just spit it out in front of everyone, now could I?

But worst of all were the mornings. For a while, I woke up convinced I had heard my mother's voice from the kitchen. Then one day the sound of the alarm carried nothing except its own voice, and it hit me for the first time: the distance from home and the panic that comes with it.

When the word *America* had first dropped from my lips the previous summer, my parents warned me not to even think about it—without an explanation, or a hint that their voices hid much more than fear of sending an only child away from home. We argued for months. But to study abroad had become my dream, and they gave up once I threatened not to apply to college if they forced me to stay in Bulgaria.

That fall I took exams, wrote essays, filled out financial aid forms—all my friends were doing it. Lucky to have been admitted to the most elite high school in the country, we had spent years studying English, being taught in English, virtually drowned in English from the moment we entered the class-room. And with it came a craving for the real thing, for a life in that magnetic continent across the ocean where not just the language but everything else we saw on TV and read about in books would become ours—real, tangible, natural like breathing.

Now I was already here. But nothing felt natural about it, and to even catch my breath seemed a luxury. Within a week of arriving at Princeton, I was drained—from lack of sleep, from stress and the incredible speed of every-thing. Then, just when I thought things couldn't get any worse, they did.

"Theodora Slavin, yes? Pleased to meet you, very pleased—our new piano prodigy who is loaded with talent like a machine gun. I don't envy anyone who stands in your way."

Guns were an odd topic for a welcome reception at the music depart-ment, and the man who brought them up (blue velvet jacket, unruly hair, the unshaven charm of a boy refusing to grow up even in his fifties) didn't exactly fit my idea of faculty. Yet he knew about my piano background and had to have seen my file, so I ran with his metaphor:

"Is Princeton really a battlefield?"

"Yes, and not only Princeton. But don't worry, you're uncovering the rules of combat as we speak. My job is to make sure you strike with every shot. Your job"—he winked as if to soften the impact—"is to resist the urge to do the opposite of what I tell you."

I still couldn't figure out who he was, but luckily he reached out for a handshake. "Nathan Wylie, your music adviser. Do we call you Theodora, or is there a shorter version?"

"Just Thea. Pleased to meet you too. Although I believe I am assigned to Professor Donnelly."

"Correct. Sylvia is your go-to for all things academic; she can propel you at school better than anyone. But in terms of stage track record, we figured you'd need a villain more than a fairy godmother. By the way, here she is—"

He waved a woman over just as she was stepping through the door. Even if the halo of short brunette curls and the red lipstick might have fooled you from a distance, everything else about Sylvia Donnelly—the composure of her heavy walk, the inquisitive eyes that scanned the crowd without hurry, the strain of authority in the air while she waited for one of us to speak first— made it clear that she had been teaching much longer than Wylie, possibly even longer than any other professor in the room.

He introduced us and turned to her. "Perfect timing, by the way. I was just telling Thea that you and I have agreed to share custody."

"Then it bodes well for us that she isn't running for the exit already. I can imagine what other things you must have told her." After a thorough look at me, the scrutiny in her eyes softened up. "Tell me, dear, how has it been so far?"

We started chatting about the trip from Bulgaria and my first impressions of life on campus. Wylie had excused himself to take a phone call.

"Try not to be intimidated by Nate. His sense of humor is peculiar, but also quite refreshing once you get used to it."

"It doesn't bother me."

"Good. That's the one ally you can't afford to lose."

"Because he is my adviser?"

"That too. But he also happens to be department chair. Which means he can align things for you, so long as—"

The rest was lost. Wylie had come back and his face promised nothing but bad news. "They've postponed the Paderewski concert; Moravec is ill. Francis needs to fill the gap right away and asked for the usual: a showcase of students across the department. I told him no way. I'm sick of potpourri."

"Of course you are; so is everyone else. But the concert is this week. We'll never find a replacement."

"Then we need to come up with an alternative by tomorrow morning." He fixed me with his eyes, as if remembering only now that I was still there. "Actually, I think I just did. What if we opened the season with a shocker? Say, by showing off one of our newest students?"

I had no idea how to react. Could he possibly mean me? There had been a mention, in a handout somewhere, about Princeton's Paderewski Memorial Concert—an annual affair honoring the Polish pianist and politician. That year's concert, by the famous Czech pianist Moravec, was supposed to be on Friday and I had planned on going. Now Wylie seemed to think I should be the one onstage.

Donnelly's reaction took a few seconds: "You aren't serious, right?"

"Why not? We can afford a risk, for once."

"This isn't risky, Nate. It's reckless. Thea is only a freshman; we can't put her through a solo recital yet."

"A freshman who looks better on paper than many of our seniors combined. And you've heard her demo; you know what she can do."

The "demo" was a recording I had submitted as part of my college application; it was never meant to outlive the admission process. Practicing for it had taken months, and now they expected the same performance on less than a week's notice. There was no way. *A solo recital at Princeton.* It was an unbelievable opportunity, a chance I wouldn't have dreamed of. But it could also turn into a grand fiasco. Who cared how I looked on paper? So far, everything in America was proving much harder than I had imagined. Even my English—impeccable on transcript—was already failing me miserably. For years, I had been cramming my brain with rules of grammar, idioms, and Latin word roots; I had read Shakespeare in the original and scored higher on the SAT than Princeton's admission average. But a chat with native speakers had nothing to do with the intricacies of linguistics. It felt like watching champions play table tennis while you stood on the side, forced to swallow Ping-Pong balls.

Wylie, however, wasn't giving up. "Come on, Sylvia, think about it. Everyone loves young talent, so people are bound to be curious. In fact, the younger she is, the better. Plus, we get to keep the Slavic spin of the evening, which means fewer ticket returns."

She nodded, just barely. Now they were both looking at me.

"I promised to be the guy finding you gigs, didn't I?" And there he was, joking again. "We got down to business a lot sooner than usual, but what the hell. So are we on?"

On? My mind was spinning with fear and I only managed to say how grateful I was to be considered for this.

"You aren't *considered*—Friday is yours if you want it. All I need is a yes or no. But you have to tell me now."

"I haven't touched a piano since I left Bulgaria."

"You've got four days and classes haven't even started yet. With your technique, snapping back into top form shouldn't be a problem."

It was as if we were discussing a bike ride around the block.

"Professor Wylie, I've never carried an entire concert at a place like this."

"Of course not, no one assumes you have. Is that all?"

I stared at him. What else did he expect me to say?

"Fantastic then, it's done! You'll have plenty of time to doubt yourself later." He turned back to Donnelly, as if I had once again ceased to exist. "Revised announcements will go off to press tonight. We can give the ticket office a green light tomorrow."

"And the program?"

"What about it?"

"Given the timing, I think we should let Thea choose it herself."

He made up his mind instantly, the way he seemed to decide on every-thing else. "Fine, go ahead."

Still in shock, I asked to play all Chopin.

Wylie wasn't thrilled. "I get it, I do—'the Chekhov of the keyboard' and all that. But give us a tour de force, not a tear fest."

Donnelly came to my rescue: "Let her do it, Nate. I like the idea: the music of one Eastern European played by another, both voluntary exiles to a life in the West."

They argued briefly about the pros and cons of an entire evening dedi-cated to Chopin, then Wylie agreed to let me have it my way. And so it was settled. Whether I wanted it or not, Friday was mine and there was no turn-ing back.

BY NOON THE FLYERS WERE all over campus, crisp white against a collage of colors on bulletin boards. Only from up close could one detect the thin bor-der in Princeton's signature black and orange, framing the date—September 14, 2007—and the two names placed side by side, as if a magical typo had linked me to one of the most gifted men to ever touch a piano:

THEODORA SLAVIN PLAYS CHOPIN

I adored his music. Many great composers had come before him: the indulgent complexity of Bach, the unleashed ornamentation of Mozart, the thunderous genius of Beethoven who had all Europe on its knees. But only Chopin managed to bring out the piano's full ability to create extraordinary sound. He considered grandiosity vulgar. Loud playing—offensive. A frail man with a velvet touch, he devoted his life to a single instrument. And the result was phenomenal. "Everything I hear now seems so insignificant that I would rather not hear it at all," wrote a well-known pianist after hearing Chopin play live. "That was beyond all words. My senses have left me."

Donnelly, of course, had guessed right away why I wanted to play Chopin, and how in his "voluntary exile to the West"—leaving his native

Poland, barely twenty-one, to brave the music salons of Paris—I saw my own. Now the proverbial window of opportunity had opened for me. And a foreign world waited, eagerly. A world ready to be charmed but unforgiving if you failed.

At Forbes, I became a celebrity overnight. People had seen the flyers, so suddenly everyone knew my name and that of the obscure European country I had come from.

"You've put the Balkans on the map," a guy said to me at breakfast, meaning it as a compliment and not realizing it could just as easily pass for an insult.

"Thanks. Although my country has been on the map for thirteen hundred years."

"Yeah? Cool!" He grinned under his baseball cap. "What was there before, vampire castles?"

"No, that's Romania. Still the Balkans, but a bit farther north."

"Whatever you say. By the way, I'm a bit north of you too. Room 208." My blank look elicited an even wider grin. "In case you ever get, you know, bloodthirsty and stuff. Give me a shout. Or just come over."

Normally, I would have shown him how Balkan vampires react to casual hookup invites. But that morning I didn't care. I was exhausted, hadn't slept at all. My mind was in overdrive, trying to predict each disaster waiting for me at the concert—as if anything could have warned me of what was actually going to happen, that the piano wouldn't be my only worry Friday night.

To "snap back into top form" on time, I went to one of the practice rooms in Woolworth, Princeton's music building, and didn't leave it except to sleep and eat. Playing for hours at a time was second nature to me—I had grown up doing it since I was five years old. My parents themselves were not musicians. They hadn't even attempted an instrument. *How come then?* The question used to fascinate people, as if there were a secret formula they could apply to their own kids. *How did she get hooked on it so young?*

Having heard the answer many times, I spiced it up by insisting that a certain childhood incident had stayed clear in my mind. The truth was, I only wished it had. As with every story repeated by one's parents over and over, imagination had embellished the details until it was impossible to tell where fact ended and fiction began. But on one thing everyone agreed: there had been an old piano at our house. A piano that had remained silent for years.

Supposedly, a great-grandfather had brought it in from the scrapyard. A dentist with a passion for "resurrecting things" (picking up discarded junk and adapting it to home use), he had seen the salvaged piano as the vertex of a quest, a chance to show off his carpentry skills—or so the story went—by proving to the world, and to himself, that even a broken soundboard couldn't ruin a piano. It was the soundboard, the piano's "heart," that took the vibration of strings hit by hammers, amplified it, then carried it out into the room much like the diaphragm of a loudspeaker projects an electric signal to the ear. For weeks, our house had echoed with the sound of carpenter tools. When finally even the tiniest crack in the spruce wood had been fixed, a tuner had inspected the two-hundred-plus strings and confirmed that their tonality was, once again, pitch-perfect. Thus, Great-Grandpa had won: the piano had been resurrected. Unfortunately, nobody at home could play it. But he must have figured that someone, on a yet unsprouted branch of the family tree, was bound to pick it up sooner or later.

And it happened. I found the piano shortly after my fifth birthday, in the locked room down the hall from my own. Late one night, I heard someone cry in there. Too scared to come out of bed, I waited for the crying to stop. Which it did—just before my mother walked in to fix my covers while I pretended to be asleep.

The minutes ticked on. Who could possibly live in that room? I had often wondered what was inside. A passage to a secret garden? A hidden treasure? Or maybe the room was full of ghosts? I rolled between the sheets, eager to find out but also afraid of the dark, of everything that waited in it.

"Fear has very short legs, it can't get too far," Dad had once said to me. "All you have to do is go after it, pull it by the elbow, and look it straight in the eye. That's how you make it disappear."

So I took his advice. Jumped out of bed and walked into the hallway. A beam of light spilled out of the mystery room: somebody had left the door ajar. I pushed it open, peeked—there was no one; only the moon sneaked in through the windows. On the right, three identical wooden chests lined the walls, silenced by buckle-shaped locks. On the left waited a piano. I came closer and started pressing the keys—

"What are you doing here, Thea?"

My mother carried me out before I could tell her that I wasn't done yet, that I wanted to play some more. Back in my room, she made me promise to never—never!—go through that door without permission.

And this was where everyone's memories began to diverge. I had ended up by the piano a second time—but how? Had the lock given after so many years? Dad was convinced I must have come in through one of the windows, but I had no recollection of either a window or a door. All I remembered was being already there and pressing the keys—the ones I liked best—until a tune emerged under my fingers. A tune that made me feel warm and safe, as if I were under the covers, falling asleep—

"Fine, I give up. Since I don't want you doing this behind my back, from now on you are allowed to play. But on one condition." My mother always had conditions, for everything. "Once you start, quitting is not an option."

And so the door was locked once more, while the piano earned a place in the living room and never left it. The story, of course, had to be filtered for the ears of strangers. There was no mention of the crying I had heard that night, nor of a second condition my mother imposed on me: not to play that tune again. The rest was short and lovely. *Our girl and the piano found each other.* But how about the locked room? What was in it? *Oh, you know, unsafe things. Whatever we had to put away when we childproofed the house.* With that, curiosity was quenched. My parents were told how lucky they were to have me, and the conversation moved on, having exhausted its brief detour.

Over the years, I kept my promise and didn't quit. My lessons had started right away, and before I learned to read the alphabet I already knew how to read music. At first, playing for others terrified me; then I grew accustomed to the adrenaline and even began to enjoy it. But what I truly loved was play-ing for my parents. Making them proud. And seeing on their faces something that had rarely been there before: a smile. Once, I overheard a neighbor refer to them as "broken people." I didn't know what he meant, but it occurred to me that everyone else's parents seemed younger, more energetic, happier. I never mentioned it or dared to ask questions. Instead, I hoped that whatever had done the breaking would be erased by my music as I became better. So I continued playing—stubbornly, every day, until my wrists would start to ache, then to throb, then to turn numb with pain from the long hours of practice.

"This will open doors for you," Dad would tell me, with a brief knock on the piano as if it were itself a door. Meanwhile, the only door I craved to see open was the one to our house, on the other side of which children my age played games instead of piano sonatas. I began to feel trapped, chained to the keyboard. And whenever my friends did something I couldn't be a part of, playing became the equivalent of punishment.

"You are restless, you want answers. But music is not something a child can fully understand," my piano teacher warned me, being the only one to sense that something was wrong. "So don't expect to fall in love with it quite yet. For now just master the technique. Tame the keys, teach instinct to your fingers. One day you'll begin to hear the music. To really hear it. Then the universe, too, will begin to listen."

Hear it? Every piece demanded to be heard hundreds of times, maybe thousands, until its sounds would haunt me even in my sleep. I didn't argue with him back then, but now wished I had asked him questions—about that elusive age at which one stopped being a child and became worthy of the cosmic ear. Did eighteen cut it? It'd better. Because, with my first concert in America only days away, I dreaded finding out what might happen if the universe decided to listen before you were ready.

I CLOSED THE LAST MUSIC score on Friday afternoon feeling strangely calm, as if an old friend had promised to be at the recital. "It's just you and me, psycho," I whispered to Chopin's picture on the cover. Then I left to get ready.

Alexander Hall was one of the most formidable buildings at Princeton. Reigning over an entire lawn by itself, the brown monolith rested undisturbed, surveying the campus with its cyclopean eye of a rose window.

Inside, the concert hall was just as overwhelming. Massive stone arches loomed throughout the balcony, descending over the seats with the weight of a Roman cathedral.

After so many concerts and competitions, I knew that stage fright was normal, part of what being a musician was all about. Even Chopin, the undisputed genius, had dreaded giving concerts, avoiding it whenever possible. "The crowd intimidates me, its breath suffocates me, I feel paralyzed by its curious look and the unknown faces make me dumb," he had once written, and I knew exactly what he meant. All it took now was one glance at the enormous hall, streams of people rushing in, and the doubts began. *What if I snap under the pressure? If Wylie has miscalculated the risk?* Then there were also accidents. Tripping over the floor-length dress. A muscle spasm while you played. A sudden itch. Cough. Sneeze . . .

The stage coordinator put an end to my self-torture: "It is time."

I stepped out into the applause. Across the stage—black, shiny, waiting—was the grand piano. Everything became quiet while I sat down and adjusted the bench. Over the next two hours, these people were going to receive my music in exchange for a brief acceptance. For an acknowledgment that, because of my one talent, I was welcome. I belonged.

The preludes began—compelling and rich, gathering speed, spilling into the restless 8th and the mere thirty seconds of the flashy 10th. I tried to think only about the music, and not about measuring up to the sound that other hands before mine had drawn out of this same instrument, on this same stage. The trick was to not let your eyes escape into the rows of seats where hundreds of other eyes flashed back their judgment, at least not while you played. So I kept mine glued to the familiar black and white of stripes racing up and down the keyboard. Soon the hardest part was over. I had decided to close with three nocturnes and my favorite one—the open-wounded B-flat Minor—was saved for last, before the intermission. I could play it with eyes closed.

It was in the moment of silence before this last nocturne that I first saw him. A tall boy, possibly my age, strikingly beautiful even from a distance, under the glimmer of the exit sign. He walked in through the door closest to the stage and remained there, arms folded over his chest, all of him sunk in darkness except the eyes—tiny pools of reflected light that refused to let go of me.

My fingers fell on the keys and disappeared in the music, in its dark anguish. I had to concentrate on the piano and could no longer see him. But every nerve in my body felt his presence, felt watched by him—the only person in the hall still standing—as if he wanted me to notice him. To know he was there. And to play the last nocturne only for him.

After the final notes I looked up, back toward that door—

He was gone.

The applause came to me distant, dulled, as if obscured by the layers of a dream. Who was this guy? Not only had he arrived late—he hadn't bothered to hear me finish the piece, dropping by probably not so much for the music but because his ticket would have gone to waste. And why did I even care? The insolence of latecomers was nothing new to me. They felt entitled to rush in, fret, demand their seats, argue with ushers, and even prompt the dreaded "wave" (an entire row getting up to let them pass) just because they had paid money for those tickets. It inevitably ruined everything. The mood. The magic. The flow of music in the room. Yet this time there hadn't been a single stir. He had walked in quietly and nobody had turned. Nothing had given him away except his eyes and a dark silhouette. Could this be the shift my piano teacher had once promised me, that abstract ear of the universe? A universe reduced to a single person. To a stranger who obliterated everything else . . .

The intermission slipped by fast, with my two advisers rushing over, ecstatic, to wish me good luck with the rest. When I returned onstage, I saw the hall already waiting. But there was no one at that door. Nor in the aisle. Nor anyone who looked like him in the nearby seats.

The second half had only études—mostly from Opus 10, the set Chopin dedicated to his main competitor, Franz Liszt. The dazzling 1st softened into the dreamy 3rd and the much darker, haunting 9th. Then came Opus 25—a deluge of sound, storm upon a storm. The audience went wild and it gave me a moment to run backstage for a sip of water. When I came back, the applause continued, but the door to my left stayed closed. Only seconds remained before the clapping would stop. Before it would be time for the last étude.

I sat at the piano. Took a breath. Looked at the door. Lifted my fingers and placed them over the keys. Another breath. The shut door. Slowly, I lowered my right hand into the hesitant notes of the most stunning, most intimate of the études: the Nouvelle Étude in F Minor from 1839. Its first measures were still unfolding when I saw the dark figure walk in, as if he had waited outside for the music to begin. And again he stayed at the door, anonymous in its shadow, eyes locked on me in anticipation of the sounds.

I had no idea who he was or why his presence had such an effect on me. But of one thing I was now absolutely certain: he wasn't a latecomer. Twice already, his entrance had been timed purposefully, with precision. As if he had seen the program, recognized the piece that mattered most to me in each half of the recital, and decided to hear only that piece, nothing else.

As I made my way through the étude, I imagined the crowds after the encore: everyone rushing to get home, the evening already reduced to a memory. What were the chances that I might run into him there? That a stranger who hadn't even shown his face would decide to stay behind and try to meet me?

Still, I kept wishing that he wouldn't leave. Just before the last notes, when I lifted my eyes from the piano, I saw him reach toward the stage to drop in its corner a single white flower.

Then he walked out through the exit door and disappeared.

"THIS IS WEIRD. GUYS HERE don't do things like that."

The girl who had decided to give me a crash course in American dating was just doing her job. Her name was Rita and she was my RCA (short for "residential college adviser," the third-year student who lived in Forbes for free and was in charge of me and nine other freshmen down the hall). To cement the team spirit, she had brought everyone to my concert. Now, as the two of us headed back to the dorm, she dug into the only piece of gossip I had produced so far: a long-stemmed rose.

"I mean, a guy might go out of his way to give you a flower if he's already dating you or for your birthday. But to lurk by the door and stare at you like that—no way."

I glanced back as we walked. Far behind, the rose window of the concert hall bulged its lethargic blue stare, awake for a few minutes longer before the building would be shut down for the night. Two arched exits still beamed their light across the lawn. But there was nobody left; the doors were already closed.

"And how come you didn't see his face?"

"Everything except the stage was dark. It always is."

"I don't know, sounds kind of creepy. Maybe you have a stalker, Tesh!"

It was her affectionate nickname for me; she had Hungarianized it. The family had moved from Budapest to New York when she was only five, which meant she had lived in the U.S. long enough to qualify for the RCA role that typically went to Americans. *Only those who know how to fix everyone else's problems* was how she had put it. Now she seemed intent on fixing mine.

"Look, let's not overthink this. I don't have a stalker. He was there to listen to Chopin, not because of me."

"And the flower was for Chopin, not you?" She smiled, having added one more to her collection of verbal victories. "Tesh, no offense to your dead composer, but from what I've seen, men nowadays don't think with their ears. Nor with their brains, for that matter."

"Sure. Around you men probably lose the capacity to think at all."

She ignored the comment, but I was right—with her willowy figure, long black hair, and eyes the color of dark chocolate, Rita looked like she belonged on a catwalk. Next to her I was the washed-out twin: blond, pale, and watery-eyed.

"So let me get this straight: I'm the one who turns heads, whereas you get noticed only because of the piano?" Her laughter echoed high above us, multiplied by the vault of Princeton's most prominent arch, Blair, where I had once caught an a cappella group's performance and, for half an hour, had forgotten everything else. "If I didn't know you any better, I'd think you were the queen of hypocrites. When was the last time you looked in a mirror?"

I had never worried much about my looks—until my first week at

Princeton. *You're so dressed up, is it your birthday?* I would hear this so often that I started changing outfits five times before I could leave my room in the morning. "Dressed up" seemed to capture anything outside the American fashion uniform of jeans, T-shirt, and sneakers. In my case it simply meant "all black"—a look that would have barely passed for casual in Bulgaria, where girls wore sky-high heels and miniskirts even to the supermarket.

"Tesh, seriously. I know you have all this piano stuff going on, but try to break out of your shell every once in a while. Come to parties, drink, chill out, whatever. Everyone's been asking about you."

"Who is everyone?"

"The guys in our RCA group; don't tell me you haven't noticed. They blush like schoolgirls as soon as you show up, all enigmatic with that foreign accent and those skinny black outfits of yours. It's kind of funny, actually. They've nicknamed you 'Triple B'—Badass Bulgarian Bombshell."

"*Badass* . . . is that a good thing?"

"Are you kidding? It means you have the whole package: looks, attitude, sex appeal. There—" She stopped and turned me around, pointing at my reflection in one of Dillon Gym's windows. "Gorgeous face, legs up to here, boobs any girl would kill for, and those full lips—I'd be dropping flowers onstage too, if I were a guy!"

"Wow, thanks . . ." I smiled, trying not to sound self-conscious. "It's nice to hear these things from a girl, for once. With guys you never know who has an agenda."

"They all do, I'm sure. But now with that new admirer of yours, none of them stand a chance. If I'm sensing correctly, the bar just got raised tonight?" She wasn't giving up on the latest gossip, not so easily. "Let's see . . . He needs to be erratic. Appropriately mysterious. Bonus points if he broods over nineteenth-century music. Oh, and God forbid he should show his face—that alone would disqualify him before he even speaks!"

"Except I doubt I'll ever see him again, Rita. I don't even know his name."

"But he knows yours, and Princeton is smaller than you think." She stole one last peek at the flower. "Never mind what I said before, the guy is probably perfectly normal. On the off chance he makes another weird appearance, though, I want to know about it."

"You sound just like my mother."

"I prefer *chaperone*, thank you."

Both of us laughed. The promise to report any stray flowers or weird appearances was on the tip of my tongue when someone called Rita's name and a group of people surrounded us. We had finally reached Forbes.

CHAPTER 2

The Room of Breathing Clays

WE HAD ONLY one weekend before classes would start, so the goal was to get the most out of it: rush from one meet and greet to the next, bond over food, party all night, then come home with a roster of new friendships. And not just any friendships. Upperclassmen, preferably athletes, who might single you out from the freshman pack and bring you into their coveted circle, which in turn meant you would be going to postgame parties, formals, and any other bash open only to the sufficiently popular.

There was, of course, a science to all this. To maximize the return on everyone's time, it was wise to move in groups, avoid one-on-ones and not linger. Names were thrown around like confetti. Introductions were brief. Conversations ended abruptly, having barely started.

"Nice to meet you. I guess I'll see you around?"

"Yeah, you too."

"Cool."

"Bye."

I deviated from the rules only once, chatting up a Russian girl at a party with the hope that we might become friends since we had so much in common. But she quickly excused herself, saying that hanging out like this, just the two of us, wasn't in our best interest.

"What do you mean?"

"We'll get stuck in our Eastern European bubble. When instead we should be talking to Americans and learning how to become more like them. That's why we're here, right?"

Right. Except I felt no need to become somebody else, and wanted to spend my time with whoever seemed most interesting to me—American or not.

Unfortunately, the one person I was dying to meet didn't happen to be around. He had entered my life briefly, leaving it without a word, and his flower was now the single piece of evidence (a quickly fading one) that he had been real. With more than seven thousand students at Princeton, the odds of running into him again were slim. Yet no matter where I went, part of me anticipated his presence.

The concert had been a success, and Donnelly took me out to lunch on Sunday to celebrate the review about to appear in Monday's issue of the *Daily Princetonian*. A trusted source, as it turned out, had given her a sneak preview.

"Listen to this—" She opened a yellow folder before we had even headed over to the restaurant. "*Foreign talent is always a breath of fresh air, but last Friday a student from Bulgaria served everyone an oxygen tank*. It sounds like something Nate would say. In fact, I wouldn't be surprised if one of his numerous fans wrote it."

"Professor Wylie has fans?"

"He's a bit of a rock star. You didn't know?"

I shook my head, ashamed that I hadn't found the time to read more about my adviser online.

"You should hear him on the electric guitar; it bends the limits of everything you've been taught about music. Naturally, students love him. And you lucked out when he decided to take you on."

I was sure I had; the concert had proven this. But it had also proven that Wylie viewed me as his newest pet, and I dreaded how far he would go in "finding me gigs." Or what could happen if one day he overestimated me.

I told Donnelly that I was grateful to both of them.

"My pleasure. But this was just warm-up, honey. The real test will be New York. Nate is already pulling a few strings to get you there, although it's far from a slam dunk." My puzzled face made her laugh. "Meaning 'a sure thing.' Not much of a basketball fan, are you?"

"I'm not really into sports."

"Well, this will have to change here. Everyone is into sports. Besides, you and our athletes share one thing in common: you don't need to worry about grades. The piano comes first, and the school understands that."

"Understands . . . as in fewer classes?"

"No, as in flexible curriculum. There are easier courses whose sole purpose is to give students like you a break: Physics for Poets, Rocks for Jocks. Those two should get you through the science requirement, unless you hate geology."

I wanted to ask what she meant by "students like me"—I was not a jock—but we had already reached the restaurant. The place turned out to be much pricier than I had expected. Its glass wall overlooked a sidewalk patio directly on Nassau Street—the main shopping and dining artery that divided the north end of campus from the town of Princeton. Once again, I regretted not having done a simple Internet search. When Donnelly's e-mail had mentioned lunch at the Blue Point Grill, I had glossed over the name, unaware that in America the word *grill* signaled upscale ambience and thirty-dollar entrées. Now she, of course, fit right in with a brown pantsuit and coral brooch pinned to the lapel, while I sulked next to her, hoping that my black jeans and turtleneck could pass for edgy college chic.

"Mrs. Donnelly! We were starting to worry that you had forgotten us this week."

The waiter showed us to our table and I tried to decipher the menu while the two of them exchanged pleasantries. It was a maze of seafood dishes, referring to at least a dozen kinds of fish I had never heard of before. When she ordered the sea bass, I asked to have the same.

He grinned in my direction. "May I interest you in any of our delicious starters?"

"Excuse me?"

Donnelly sensed that I needed help. "Would you like a soup or a salad, dear?"

"No, just the main course would be fine, thank you."

I was going to need quite a few restaurant trips in America before a meal would stop being an exercise in embarrassment. Luckily, Donnelly didn't seem to mind. She loved the place, calling it her "weekly indulgence," but I found it hard to believe she had the means to come here so often. Back at home, my family went to an upscale restaurant only on special occasions—two, maybe three times a year. Most other families could afford even less.

"So where were we?" She unfolded the napkin and placed it in her lap—another American custom. I copied everything she did. "Ah, yes, classes and grades. The bottom line is to manage a decent GPA. It doesn't have to be great, just decent."

"I need higher than decent to keep my financial aid."

"That's the last thing you should worry about, especially with reviews like the one you just received. Your campus job, on the other hand, is a bit of a problem. I heard they've assigned you to the dining hall two nights a week?"

"I don't mind working."

"It's not a question of whether you mind. There are only so many hours in a day, and you can't be washing dishes while you should be at the piano, practicing. Have you talked to anyone about it?"

"My award letter said this was part of everyone's package, no exceptions."

She frowned, taking off her jacket and pulling up the sleeves of her beige blouse, as if to prepare for a battle with the food that hadn't been served yet. "First of all, it isn't *everyone*—only those who can't pay their own way. And second of all, there are always exceptions. The whole thing is absurd anyway."

"Why?" There was nothing absurd about earning pocket change when you needed it.

"Because somebody took a great premise and flipped it on its head. With the ton of money they are giving you each year, do you think a thousand or two more would have made a difference?"

"Probably not."

"Certainly not. Money isn't the point here. The point is that a job teaches humility in a way books can't, at least that's what we trumpet all over the brochures. But I don't see how we get there by having kids on financial aid serve food to their rich classmates. If anything, the lesson is more needed the other way around."

This was a new angle for me. I had always accepted as a given that there would be rich students at Princeton, and that I wouldn't feel equal to them. At least not in terms of wealth.

"Anyway, I'll see what I can do. Unfortunately, the semester is starting and the Financial Aid Office will probably give me a hard time. But by spring at the latest we should have this fixed." She sounded so confident that I wondered if there was anything she couldn't fix, once she put her mind to it. "How do you like the sea bass?"

The food had just arrived and I was taking my first bite. "Delicious, reminds me of my mother's cooking. Except for a flavor I don't recognize. Not exactly thyme."

"It's rosemary." She savored the dish, eyes closing in approval. "I have a garden at my house, and the one herb I always want fresh is rosemary."

Rosemary. Or thyme. We all had an herb that could take us home.

"Now, let's talk classes. We should reshuffle quite a bit." She took a chart out of her purse and a red pen flew through the page, circling a few boxes. "You don't need this literature class. They read a book a week and it will eat up too much of your time." A quick X in three of the boxes got rid of the excessive reading. "Definitely keep Composition, but one music class is not enough. I'd say two, even three—to beef up your résumé early on. Which means that either Greek Art or French 101 has to go."

The tip of the pen froze over Monday's schedule, ready to strike either class as soon as I made my choice.

"Professor Donnelly, I'm not sure about the trade-off."

She shrugged. "Everything is a trade-off. You'll get more use out of the language than the art history. But you already have Bulgarian and . . . what was your other language? Russian, right? So if you want to take art instead, go ahead."

"I meant the trade-off between that and music."

The pen dropped on the table. "Not sure I understand."

"There are other things I'd like to explore."

"Exploring is fine. But I can't let you jeopardize the piano."

"How would this jeopardize it?"

"Easily. Music doesn't tolerate being pushed to the side—either you drop everything for it or it drops you. So, while endless sampling of the liberal arts may work for anybody else, for you things are different."

Things had always been different for me, and I loved it that way. Yet it wasn't the kind of "different" Donnelly had in mind. Had I stayed in Bulgaria, my entire future would have been mapped out for me: competitions and concerts all through high school, then admission to the National Academy of Music, then more competitions and concerts, endlessly. It was a great future if you loved music (which I did). But I had come to America to choose my own future. And this time the piano wasn't enough; I wanted everything. Whatever I had been missing out on, all my life.

When I tried to explain, Donnelly wouldn't let me finish. "Thea, I get all that. I've been through it myself, believe me. What I don't get is how exactly you propose to do it."

"Do what?"

"Fulfill the prerequisites for the major on time, qualify for the Performance Certificate, keep your stage appearances, while all along scattering yourself across the board like this. I don't think it can work."

I felt short of breath just listening to her list. "Professor Donnelly, I thought I had more time."

"More time for what?"

"To decide on my major at Princeton."

The window was exactly two years, I was sure of it. In American colleges, you could try majors and switch them even halfway through the ride. Whereas in Bulgaria the decision had to be made by the end of high school. There was no such thing as applying to a college or university in general, only to a specific department. And if the department said yes, that was it.

"You aren't serious, are you?" The twist in our conversation had drained the smile off her cheeks. "Or are you actually telling me that you might major in something else?"

"I've thought about it."

"And?"

"I need to take classes outside of music before I can make up my mind."

She looked at me as if my face had become a snapshot of the apocalypse. "Fine, then, we will revisit this once the semester is over. But in the meantime I wouldn't put it on Nate's radar, if I were you."

I promised her not to. She handed me the chart, French 101 and Greek Art still intact on it. Yet this was only the first of eight semesters at Princeton, and the fight was far from over. It was possible, of course, that I might major in music. But I was done sacrificing my entire world for it. I was eighteen years old. I wanted to live. And if this meant no longer being Wylie's protégée or having to endure Donnelly's grim silence, then so be it.

FINALLY, MONDAY CAME. MY LONG-AWAITED, much imagined first day of school in America. Like my great-grandfather, who had worked so hard on resurrecting his piano that in the end he probably found those to be the most stunning sounds ever produced by a musical instrument, I had played the day up in my mind beyond proportion. Walking into a Princeton classroom had to be a rite of passage, an entry into something wonderfully new—or so I thought when I left Forbes in the morning.

Shame, then, that the moment was ruined almost instantly. My first class happened to be Greek Art, and within minutes of entering the lecture hall I was already mortified. Other students seemed to have read dozens of pages that I didn't even know had been assigned. They answered questions, recognized images on slides, and kept laughing at the professor's jokes about the origins of Greek mythology. Meanwhile, I was sinking in my seat. How was it possible to be so behind already?

The answer was simple: orientation week. I had been obsessing over preludes and nocturnes while everybody else had tracked down the syllabus for each class and started reading. I could hear Donnelly's voice in my head: *Everyone except you and the athletes, dear . . .*

When the lecture ended, I hurried to leave, grateful not to have been called on to join the discussion.

"Miss Slavin, could you stay a minute, please?"

Professor Giles threw the words across the auditorium like a casual afterthought, without registering the question mark or even glancing in my direction. Austere in his tweed jacket, he had an unexpectedly deep, nuanced voice for a lean man in his sixties. It was because of this voice that, as I would soon find out, most girls in the class found him irresistibly charming.

"Glad to see you in Greek Art." His eyes scanned the room, making sure the last student had left. "My family attended your concert last week. Everyone thought it was quite the triumph."

I thanked him, relieved that the reason he wanted to talk to me had nothing to do with class participation. But the relief didn't last long.

"May I ask what made you decide to take my class? First-years typically start with Art 101."

"I love art history. And Greek Art was the closest it got to home."

"Home?"

"I meant my country, Bulgaria."

"Ah, yes. Right at the heart of Eastern Europe, next to Greece." He sounded disappointed. "It never ceases to amaze me, the musical talent in those Balkan lands of yours. Carries a certain . . . restless quality. A subtle unrest going so far back in time one could say it practically runs in the blood."

Could. Or was he actually saying it?

I forced my eyes to stay on his. "You've heard other Bulgarians play?"

"I have, I most certainly have." He lifted a sheet of paper and stared at it, as if trying to reclaim his mind from a distant memory. "Miss Slavin, I hope you would indulge me with a slight departure from the syllabus."

"A departure?"

"Of sorts, yes. Your first paper is due on Friday, and I always leave its topic open: choose a Greek vase and tell me which myth you think it depicts. Everyone has a favorite, so giving students a choice helps fire them up. In your case, however, a certain vessel struck me with its particular . . . shall we say, resonance?"

The sheet landed on the desk, no longer upside-down from where I was standing. And two figures emerged on it, delicate like cutouts from an elaborate cartoon: a man holding a lyre and another man waiting for the sounds.

"The vase is on display downstairs. You won't have any difficulty finding it."

Princeton's art museum, of course. In Bulgaria, it was unheard of for a university to have its own art collection, let alone an entire museum. But then again, with tuition at $33,000 a year, why would Giles have us write from photographs when the originals were only steps away?

I took the page from him. Maybe I should have been suspicious. Maybe it should have occurred to me that grading curves had rules (treat students equally) and that "departures" didn't happen lightly, on a whim. But for the moment, I convinced myself that everything made sense: class homework involving music was assigned to me by a professor who had heard me play. He had admired my technique. My inexplicably restless talent. And as for everything else that ran in my blood, he obviously had no clue at all.

THE OPEN PAPER TOPIC TURNED out to be a mixed blessing: it fired everyone up, but mostly with stress. By midweek, the usual "What's up?" had given way to "Did you pick your vase yet?"—a question I answered briefly, skipping the fact that my vase had been chosen for me.

And not just the vase. One particular Greek myth stood out in my mind because, as Giles had said, the gift for music in the Balkan lands did go back in time. Way back, actually. Only hours from my home, in a region known as Thrace, the mountains had once echoed with the song of a man described in legends as the greatest musician who ever lived, the "father of all songs." His lyre was believed to have charmed the anger out of beasts, coaxed trees and rocks into dance, and even diverted the course of rivers. More than two thousand years later, people in my country still knew the story of Orpheus by heart. His love for Eurydice. Her death from a snakebite. And his descent into the Underworld, to claim her back. Touched by his music, the gods agreed to let his wife live again. On one condition: that he wouldn't turn around to look at her, on the way out into the world of the living.

I could have filled the required pages easily, without treasure hunts in museum basements. But Giles had insisted, from the first slide he had flashed in our lecture hall, that no photograph stood a chance against the breathing clay.

Princeton's collection of "breathing clays" hadn't made it to the main floor galleries, so I followed the map to the lower level. Thursday was the only night of the week when the museum stayed open late—at a quarter to ten, the place was deserted. I had wanted to be there alone and look for the vase undisturbed, but now wished I had come earlier, with the others. There was too much silence. It rose from the gray carpets and crawled up the walls, leaving its invisible imprint on everything.

The first two display cabinets held mostly fragments. Clustered at random, the pieces peeked through the glass with the shy stare of creatures locked for centuries inside a tomb. I stopped in front of the third cabinet: its vessels were intact. There were warriors, gods, heroes, kings, each trapped in a pose of irreversible defeat or triumph. But the image I was trying to find had nothing to do with heroic battles. It had to do with music.

Finally I saw it—at the end of a shelf, strikingly odd with its inverted shape that the Greeks had called a *psykter* (round belly, no handles, neck much shorter than the foot, as if the potter had sat at the wheel in the blur of a hangover). I leaned closer and the two figures played out their story. The musician's head fell back in sadness. He dropped the lyre. Emptied, the air ached for sound. Still under the music's spell, his companion bowed, while high above them a full moon—the glass reflection of a track light—pierced the black-clay night.

"The time is now nine forty-five and the museum will be closing in fifteen minutes."

Everything startled me at once: the flash of a shadow across the glass, a rustle at the back of the room, the echo of speakers asking all visitors to proceed to the nearest exit. I looked around but there was no one. The security guard had probably decided to let me have those last remaining minutes to myself.

I had brought a book—Ovid's *Metamorphoses*—and opened it to the part on Orpheus and Eurydice. Giles had wanted a subtle unrest, but the story of the musician from Thrace, of how he led his wife away from death, had more unrest than anyone could have asked for. A living man, lost in the Underworld. Walking in darkness, among deaf rocks and dead shadows, knowing that even a single mistake will cost him the life of the woman he loves. Then the gods raise the stakes and the sound of Eurydice's steps begins to fade, even though she is following closely, still within reach. *Will he or will he not turn?*

Slowly, the words crept across the page, guiding my eyes in long-forgotten rhythms:

> They made their way in silence up a steep
> and gloomy path. With only steps
> to climb before their feet would touch
> earth's surface, he panicked that he might again
> lose her and, anxious for another look,
> he turned. Instantly, she slipped away.
> He stretched his arms to her, despaired,
> eager to rescue her, to feel her body,
> but they held only air. Dying
> a second time, she didn't blame him,
> didn't complain—of what? of his great love?—
> just spoke a single word: farewell.
> He couldn't hear. And with no other sound,
> she fell from him again, becoming shadow.

The rest was his brief life without her, a life filled with nothing but sorrow. Consumed by grief, he swore never to love again. And not even the most seductive of women—the immortal maenads, possessed by the god Dionysus—could tempt him to break his vow. Enraged when Orpheus spurned them all, they ripped him to pieces.

"The time is now nine fifty-five . . ."

I closed the book just as the ceiling lights went out, leaving only the cabinets visible—illuminated from the inside, a deep amber of hidden bulbs that made the vases glow, stirred back to life after a long slumber. Suddenly, the entire place resembled a tomb. Dark, eerie, as if I had descended into a corner of the Underworld myself. My imagination ran wild. I couldn't wait to go back to my room. Start writing. Attempt to capture on paper the uncapturable: the music and soul of Orpheus, whose tragic tale was now flashing through my mind like a film reel. If the musician on the front of the vase was indeed him, then another scene from his life might very well be on the back. His death, maybe? The cabinet was locked, so I tried to see past the glass, as far along the vessel as I could—

"It must be a maenad, back there."

I turned around and froze. Someone was watching me from across the room, leaning against the wall between me and the only exit. It took a second to recognize the silhouette: my "stalker."

I did my best not to sound nervous:

"Beg your pardon?"

"That vase you were just looking at. Its other side must be a maenad, taking her revenge on the doomed musician."

Something about his voice got to me. I wanted to keep hearing its sound. Warm. Quiet. Disarming like the sound of a piano when your fingers are barely pressing on the keys.

I turned back toward the glass; it was easier to talk to him this way. "Why do you think so?"

"What else would it be? A sad lyre player on a Greek vase—your best bet is Orpheus, having just lost Eurydice. The only thing left for him now is to get torn to pieces. So that must be the back, no?"

He had read my mind again—from a distance, just as he had done in Alexander Hall. The concert flyers did mention I was from Bulgaria, which explained why he would bring up Orpheus. Yet how had he found me here? It was too much of a coincidence for him to be at the museum this late, especially on a night when everyone went clubbing (Thursday and Saturday were the notorious party nights at Princeton). He had to have followed me into the galleries, only to watch me in secret until now.

The thought made me uncomfortable and I kept looking at the vase, away from him. "You seem to know a lot about Greek mythology."

"Only parts of it. The myth of Orpheus holds a special . . . fascination in my family."

"A dismembered musician somewhere down the family tree?"

"Yes and no. Long story."

I waited for him to explain, but he didn't. The room was filling up with silence and I hurried to say something—anything—before the mad beating in my chest would have echoed all the way through to him:

"Are you in Greek Art? I don't remember seeing you there."

"No, that's too epic for my taste."

"What is your taste?"

He paused. Then his voice became even quieter: "I think you know."

I didn't, not yet. But no one had ever talked to me like this—cryptic, soft, as if our intimacy was a given. It made me want to trust him, which scared me even more. "Actually, I don't know anything about you."

There was a loud clicking sound, then the room became fully dark: the museum was already closed. I sensed a shift in the air, a cologne's vague mix of moss or bark with crushed petals, and realized he had come up to me, so close his chest brushed mine every time he breathed. I heard my voice finally take a risk:

"Thank you for the rose."

He said nothing; maybe he was nervous too.

"Do you play the piano yourself or are you just a music fan?"

"I do play. And your Chopin is stunning." He said it slowly, as if each word was meant to sink through me and remain there. "Will you write about Orpheus?"

"I think so."

"You should; that's the most desolate myth of the Greeks. The man who lost his love because he was too weak."

"Or because he loved her too much?"

"It's the same thing, really." He lowered his face to mine. "Security will be here any second."

My pulse went wild from the touch of his cheek, from its unfamiliar, intoxicating warmth—

"Theodora . . . Comes from Greek, doesn't it?"

"Yes, but no one calls me that. Just Thea."

"I will find you soon, Thea."

He let me slide past him, up the single flight of stairs leading back to the main gallery where the lights were still on. When I reached the top, I turned around. But the darkness was empty.

THAT NIGHT, BEFORE I STARTED writing, I read the end of Ovid's tale again—*the most desolate myth of the Greeks*. The death of Orpheus.

It began with the poet of Thrace seated on a hill, matching tears and songs to the tune of his strings. As the wind scattered a woman's hair, her voice rose through it: "Behold, sisters, behold the one who scorns us!" A spear was hurled, but it fell without wounding him. Next came a stone— charmed by the music, it dropped at his feet to beg forgiveness. As the fury raged closer, a clamor of drums drowned the soft voice of the lyre. Finally deaf, the stones grew red with blood.

The first to be torn apart were the birds, the beasts, the innumerable living things that followed the poet, enthralled by his song. Then the maenads gathered on Orpheus—like hounds circling a doomed stag in the amphitheater's arena. Mute for the first time, succumbing to his fate, he stretched out his arms to them, and the spirit breathed out through that mouth to which stones listened, whose voice the wild creatures understood—and vanished down the wind.

The birds, lamenting, wept for Orpheus; the beasts gathered in despair one last time for him; the trees, shedding their leaves, mourned him with bared crowns. They say the rivers wept too, swollen with their own tears; and the water nymphs—the naiads—with disheveled hair, put on somber clothes.

The poet's limbs were scattered through the land, his head and lyre thrown into the river Hebrus, bound for the Underworld—and (a miracle!) floating in midstream, the lyre whispered mournfully; mournfully the lifeless tongue murmured; mournfully the banks echoed in reply. The ghost of Orpheus sank under the earth, only to recognize all those places he had seen before. Searching for the fields of the blessed, he found his wife and held her in his arms. There they walk together to this day, side by side—now she goes in front and he follows her; now he leads and looks back as he can do, safely, at his Eurydice . . .

FRIDAY PASSED WITHOUT A TRACE of the mystery stranger. As did Saturday. But he had promised to find me, and this became my secret. It changed everything: the quiet alleys, the secluded courtyards, eerie buildings peeking out from behind pallid trees—every place on campus turned vibrant with color when I imagined it as the place where I might see him next. "Apparently I was right, you have a stalker," Rita would have said, before launching her own investigation as to why anyone would follow me into a deserted museum and talk to me in the dark. Which was exactly why I decided not to tell her any of it. There was no need for him to be labeled "weird" again; I didn't want the word lodged in my mind. Whoever that guy was, he understood Chopin's music and loved the story of Orpheus, just as I did—if this meant he was weird, then so was I. And I didn't worry that he would keep stalking me. I worried that he wouldn't.

On Saturday night the RCA group voted down Rita's proposal for a trip to the movies and ended up party hopping through the dorms instead. "Guys, you should save your energy for the Street tomorrow," she kept warning us, but nobody cared. We rushed from one spot of blasting music to the next, high on adrenaline from finally being out at night in college. By noon the following day, all of us were going to regret it.

The Street, as the first few blocks of Prospect Avenue were known, was the liveliest (and often the only) hub of nightlife at school: a strip of land running parallel to Nassau Street in the northeast corner of campus, where Princeton's eating clubs opened their doors—and their free beer taps—twice a week, on Thursdays and Saturdays. Everything about the Street had a strict nomenclature. To give us a leg up in the game, Rita handed everyone an aspirin after brunch and prepped us on the basics.

"Eating club" was a fancy name for a cross between a dining hall and a fraternity house. The clubs were not affiliated with the school, which washed Princeton's hands of the alleged wild parties, excessive drinking, and anything else that went on in them. The current count was ten clubs, and at the end of sophomore year you had to pick one, just as you had to pick a major. But there was a catch: picking a club didn't mean the club would pick you. Five out of the ten ran a lottery, and according to a wide consensus, Vegas paled in comparison to what you had at stake when your name was pulled out of a hat (or wasn't) at your club of choice. The other half were openly elitist. Priceless member spots were awarded in a process known as "bicker"—a fraternity rush spiced with the pinch of a job interview, a bacchanal, and a political campaign, all in one. "Bicker week is like the Dark Ages: things lose their shock or shame value," Rita had summed up succinctly, leaving it up to us to imagine the rest.

And then there was Ivy. The oldest and most exclusive of the clubs, it reveled in its own legend: the unmatched aura of a name, the undisputed splendor of one-hundred-plus years of history, and a pervasive rumor (which was most likely true) that even a perfect human being, lavishly cloned in God's own image, would be turned down by Ivy absent a pedigree involving royalty, a head of state, or, at a minimum, a billionaire. Ivy was the fabled fortress of privilege. The magnificent outlier. The ultimate spoiled child who made up rules and refused to account to anyone for it. Ivy was the vein that had always pulsed at the very heart of Princeton.

"If the thought of bickering there so much as breezes through your mind, you must talk to me immediately. Especially the girls."

Rita said it in one breath, but we could tell she was serious. Someone managed a timid *why*.

"Because the place is ruthless. It will chew you up and spit you out— all for daring to think, even for a second, that you are worthy of such a fine establishment. A friend of mine was so brainwashed from bicker that for weeks she subsisted on almost nothing but tea, to 'fit the Ivy mold.' Until she ended up in a hospital bed and had to take the rest of the year off to recover."

"They asked her to go on a diet?"

"Oh no, asking is not their thing. Someone had been gracious enough to point out, before escorting her to the door, that while she was overall suf-

ficiently pretty, and certainly a daredevil when the occasion called for it, several members felt she could benefit, if you will, from being rather skinnier."

There was a tense silence.

"Okay, I hear the sound of mental scales weighing pounds." Rita jumped
from her chair, having guessed perfectly well what many of us were thinking.
"I will impose detention if you buy into any of that skinny nonsense. Now
let's go, the parties have started."

For one week only, Sunday was the day that mattered on the Street. It
was the official opening of the eating clubs, an afternoon when the entire
place—even Ivy—was up for grabs. All doors stayed shut, but the few yards
separating those doors from the sidewalk became the scene of a wild celebration: Lawnparties. It was a sea of sound and color. Girls in sundresses. Guys
in whatever the closet had happened to spit out. And everywhere—crowds,
the excited commotion of crowds packed around buildings, raising beer cups
to live music of which I could hear only the bang of drum sets and the wail of
throats too close to the microphone.

Rita kept the group together, navigating us through a maze of lawns and
backyards. I was glad to be out, instead of sulking in my room with fantasies
of a stranger about whom I knew absolutely nothing. But, as it happened, I
couldn't escape the thought of him for very long.

"Tesh, I keep forgetting, there's someone I want you to meet." Rita
grabbed my hand and pulled me across the street. "He's been pestering me
ever since he heard you play last Friday."

I almost tripped on the sidewalk. *Ever since he heard you play.* Was I
finally going to meet him? The real him this time, not a vanishing shadow?

We headed to a building whose redbrick walls and white Ionic columns
created the effect of a Greek temple slapped in front of a city hall. As we made
our way through the crowd, she kept asking people if they had seen Ben and
explained to me that this was Colonial, one of the clubs accessible to anyone
with a Princeton ID. The guy, meanwhile, was nowhere to be found.

Ben . . . Benjamin? I let the name swirl around in my mind, trying to
imagine it belonging to him. A nice name, for sure. But not mysterious
enough. Bennett? Or Benedict, maybe?

"There he is!"

She waved at someone and I felt my heart skip a beat. Unfortunately, it turned out to be a sophomore from Forbes whose endearing, gap-toothed smile flashed at me before he confessed that my concert had left him speechless.

"*Awe-stricken*, I believe, is how it was described to me. You've inflicted a spell on our poor Ben, Tesh!" Rita didn't bother to conceal the matchmaking tone. "Who, by the way, dabbles in violin himself."

"Poor Ben" turned absolutely red. "Can't say I've got the talent for it. But I'm addicted to classical music. Really beyond repair."

We went on to talk about the challenges of string quartets (his favorite), and whether any impact was lost when arranging piano pieces for the violin and vice versa. He had a sweet, unobtrusive way of showing his extensive knowledge of music—theory, history, the entire who's who of classical repertoire—and I caught myself wishing for more chats like this one. Still, I couldn't shake the disappointment that he wasn't someone else. All weekend, I had been waiting for a guy who would follow me into an empty museum yet not even ask for my phone number. Maybe he just saw me as a girl who happened to play the piano and like ancient pottery? No wonder the promise to find me had slipped from his mind, just as my own promise to join Ben at a Schubert recital in two weeks slipped from mine as soon as I said good-bye and headed back to Forbes.

The first thing I did in my room was to check e-mail. A message was waiting for me, yes, but not the one I had hoped for. It was marked urgent, with a subject line *Tomorrow A.M.*, and I sensed right away that something was off. For a second time, I had been singled out. And again for no apparent reason. On its face, the note seemed class-related: my Greek Art professor had graded the papers. If I didn't mind an early rise, he wanted to meet me in the art museum at eight o'clock Monday morning.

THE MINIATURE NICKEL KEY SLID into the lock and turned to the right— once, then a second time.

"Extraordinary, isn't it, what a handful of clay can become?" Giles was standing in front of the cabinet, exactly where I had stood four days earlier. The museum was closed on Mondays but he had access to it, and the only thing that struck me as extraordinary was his decision to summon me there for a private visit. "Each of these pieces is simply earth, baked into shape and given some color. But lend an eager eye to it, and an entire world comes to life after thousands of years!"

"In Bulgaria that world never really died. I was raised on these myths."

"And is this why you took liberties with your paper, Miss Slavin? Normally, my students write about what they see on a vase, not what they imagine might lie hidden on the back."

His comment caught me off guard. "I thought the invisible would be more interesting."

"Fair enough. And your description of the angry maenads killing Orpheus was definitely vivid. But if you are going to hand in a guess, then it'd better be correct. Or at least brilliant."

Clearly, mine had been neither. "I wrote about Orpheus because I love music."

"Love of music—this would certainly be the more obvious explanation. Yet your use of the myth fell short. A reiteration of what others have said a thousand times already."

I took a deep breath. "Professor Giles, I'd be happy to revise the paper if you think it can be fixed."

"Fixed?" Something lit up his eyes, as if he had just caught me dipping my spoon into a forbidden jar of honey. "That depends."

"On what?"

"On whether you have anything fresh to say. Otherwise we are just dragging the same story back and forth."

"From the empty into the void."

"Pardon me?"

"In Bulgaria we have a saying: 'to keep pouring from the empty into the void.' To talk in circles and not say anything of substance."

"Then why did you do it?"

"Do what?"

"Drown me in five pages of void and empty."

Enough was enough. This man derived some sick intellectual pleasure from provoking others, and now I had become his target: the one to receive both the special attention and the special ridicule. I had encountered such teachers before. But while I was looking for a polite excuse to leave, he reached toward the cabinet. His careful fingers opened the glass door, held the base of the vessel, and turned it around.

It was a simple image, much simpler than my paper had guessed. No hurled stones. No dismembered beasts. No packs of raving women carrying out an ambush. There were two figures—only two—but otherwise the scene was exactly what I had described. A musician falling back: slumped shoulders, legs bent, limp hand about to drop the now mute lyre. And descending over him with fury, hair spilling in the dark, gown folds no longer vertical but fluttered in the chaos of her speed—a woman. Snatching his arm. Pulling his curls so violently that his head was snapping back, away from his collapsing body.

"You can see for yourself—" Giles pointed at the vase. "The death of Orpheus has always been described as a group murder. And yet, this painter clearly had something else in mind."

"Just one maenad?"

"Exactly. While reading your paper, I kept hoping that you would drop the plural."

One maenad or many—what difference did it make? "Maybe she is a stand-in for all the others, to simplify the composition."

"Could be. But do you really think the answer is so obvious?"

He opened his briefcase, took out my infamous five pages, and handed them to me. Right at the top was a big red *A*.

"I don't understand. I thought you didn't like my paper?"

"You see, Miss Slavin, it more than satisfied the class requirements. Smart. Well-written. Thoroughly researched. What it didn't satisfy was my personal curiosity."

"About what?"

"About whether you'd live up to another paper I read a long time ago. By far the most unique piece of writing ever handed to me."

"On this same vase?"

"This very one. Unfortunately, battle scenes tend to be more popular among art students, so a musician invariably goes unnoticed. But one student noticed him. And suppose I were to tell you that she saw the single maenad on the back—through the locked glass, through the clay—as if she had been armed with X-ray vision?"

The accusing stare was all over me again. What possible response was he waiting for? Then a suspicion began to creep in, and with it—the question of how long ago that other piece of writing, the one so similar to my own, had been handed to him.

"If I recall correctly, it has been exactly fifteen years."

I felt the room spin around me, swiping up everything in a whirlpool of gray.

"Miss Slavin, is yours a common last name in your country?"

"Not really. Not at all, actually. Why?"

"Would you happen to have a relative who attended Princeton right about that time?"

The key flipped inside the lock, returning the vase to its peace which had been disturbed, briefly, for a second time in fifteen years. And in this final moment, while his back was turned to me, I had one last chance to turn my own back on the past—to run up the stairs, drop that class, and never talk to Giles again.

My last chance to escape the still breathing footsteps of Elza Slavin.

CHAPTER 3

Unseen, at Night

IN THE LEGENDS of my country, no creature is more beautiful or more cruel than the *samodiva:* the young witch of the forest who dances under a full moon, lures men with promises of love, then takes their lives. Folk superstitions claim that *samodiva* powers run in certain families, but I never believed this. Or at least I tried not to. Because it would have meant that the madness of these creatures ran in my own blood.

Once upon a time, beyond nine lands into the tenth, three maidens of unwitnessed beauty, three samodivi, *lived deep within the forest. Their milk-woven skin was whiter than the mountain snow; their topaz-blue eyes were clearer than the morning dew; their waist-long hair had a golden shine so pure that the sun itself turned cold with envy. And this is why, away from evil-bearing eyes, the* samodivi *came out only in the night, bathing under an age-old oak tree, dancing endless dances, drunk with moon—until a rooster's cry would send them hiding from the dawn, back inside a cave that neither man nor beast could enter.*

The book, an English translation of Bulgarian legends, was the only one I had brought with me to college. At first it stayed at the bottom of the suitcase. Then, as Forbes became flooded with unfamiliar faces and I felt even more alone in the crowded hallways than I had in the empty ones, I took the small volume and kept it by my bed. It was a reminder of home, of an old tale linked to my family. And of Elza Slavin.

To call Elza a "relative" was safe but wrong: she had been much more, an earlier version of me. I found out about her only months before my flight to America. Until then, the details of her brief time at Princeton had been kept from me, as had all other signs of her existence. For my sake, the family scraped her off our lives like the scab of a wound. Relatives were sworn into silence. Friends and acquaintances drifted away, together with the past. My parents muted their own hearts, burying in three buckled chests everything she had owned or touched. Then a lifelong vigil began. Suffering quietly. Keeping constant watch. All along, they probably imagined how their little Thea, still a toddler when the tragedy hit, would grow up a happy and healthy girl, sheltered from prior events. And for fifteen years the secret hibernated obediently—a bird embryo locked inside the eggshell—without a hint dropping from anyone's lips. Then the surface cracked.

All it took was the distraught face of my grandmother, Baba Mara, who saw me twirl in her flower garden one April afternoon. We had just finished lunch. Next to her, my mother had dozed off on the long, cushion-covered *mindehr*.

"What's wrong, Babo?"

The old woman sat there frozen and—was I imagining it?—teared up. Only moments earlier, she had been chatting away.

"What happened?" My white cotton dress doubled up as a handkerchief and I wiped her cheeks. "What is it? Tell me."

She clenched her calloused hands. "You remind me so much of her."

"Of whom?"

"My girl . . ."

"What girl?" I assumed she meant my mother at my age.

"My long-lost darling girl—"

"Thea, that's enough!" A frantic hand grabbed my elbow. "I close my eyes for a minute and what do you do? You manage to upset your grandmother!"

"I didn't do anything. We were just talking about how she—"

"Whatever the two of you were up to, I won't have it."

"What's with you, Mom?"

Nothing, apparently. Just a migraine. And it was getting late, so she wanted to hurry and drive home before dark.

The good-byes were quick, the brief hugs—awkward. When we reached our house and I wouldn't stop asking questions, I was told that Grandma was imagining things. That it might even be dementia.

But secrets don't give up so easily once they have come to light. Later that evening, I went to say good night to my parents and heard crying on the other side of their bedroom door. As far as I knew, my mother never cried. She didn't smile much either, but she certainly never cried (Dad and I joked that she was the iron soldier in our family). Now I stood in the hallway, amazed at how well I knew this sound. Every nuance of it, its inexplicable desolation: the crying I had heard in the ghost room, all those years back.

Once again, I was told not to worry. Mom was upset over Baba Mara's health, nothing more.

"Then how about the locked storage room? You were crying in there too, the night I found the piano."

"We all have our moments, Thea. And not everything needs to be shared, even with family. So let's drop it. Please."

For the first time, I began to suspect that someone might have played that piano before me. Someone my parents still loved but had kept a secret all my life.

Determined to find out more, I drove to Baba Mara's house the next day, only to discover that she had neither dementia nor any desire to discuss the odd incident.

"Forget what I said or didn't say, Thea darling. Is it true what I hear, about you going to America?"

"Well, yes, but how did you . . . did Mom tell you?"

"Of course she did! I should be very angry with you right now. Such an achievement, and not a word to me yesterday?"

I had asked my parents not to announce anything until I had chosen a school and was ready to tell people myself. Yet, all of a sudden, my mother had spilled the news overnight. Had she used it as a warning? An added reason why the long-lost girl was not to be mentioned in front of me again?

We talked at length about America. What fascinated Baba Mara most was that colleges there were mini towns, with everyone living on campus, sometimes even in the middle of nowhere and with no trace of civilization in sight. Meanwhile, my thoughts were elsewhere.

"Grandma, you still haven't told me who I remind you of."

"What an obstinate child! Everyone reminds us of someone—today one memory, tomorrow another. But it's not the past that counts, especially when you have such a future ahead of you!"

As I sat in the car and watched her wave from the gate, I couldn't stop thinking about that mysterious girl from the past. She wasn't supposed to count, yet clearly did—otherwise what would be the harm in telling me about her? And if my immediate family wouldn't do it, was there anyone else I could ask?

I ran the list of relatives through my mind, a list whose unusual brevity I had so far taken as a given. An aunt in Vienna. Two estranged cousins (our parents were not on speaking terms). Three dead grandparents. It was odd how Mom and Dad had managed to distance themselves, and me, from everybody. I couldn't point to a single family reunion, a full house at Christmas, or a birthday when it hadn't been just the three of us. But I did recall something else: the name of a small town, a few hours away, where Baba Mara had once claimed to have a cousin of her own.

That weekend, under the pretext of a last-minute trip with friends, I packed a few things and hit the road.

WHAT TSAREVO LACKED IN GLITZ it made up for in seclusion, managing to stay under the radar as a sliver of privacy for those in the know. All along the

Bulgarian Black Sea coast, towns rivaled one another with golden beaches, archaeological sites, and ultramodern hotels. Tsarevo was not one of them. Tucked in a negligible bay about two hours north of the Turkish border, it had no claim to fame of its own. The sea had gnawed away at the beach until barely any sand was left, the archaeologists never flocked there, and the hotel magnates slashed any semblance of luxury out of their construction budgets. My parents avoided it too, when we vacationed at the Black Sea each summer. But until now I had never questioned why.

The city hall (a massive yellow building looming over the town square) was as good a starting point as any, so I walked in and committed the sin of disturbing the clerk's midday snooze with a question.

"Oh, one of those." His voice left no doubt how he felt about people who had nothing better to do than trace family roots. "The name?"

I spelled Baba Mara's maiden name.

"*Zlateva* with a *Z*, right?" At snail speed, he paged through a large register, then reluctantly informed me of a retired schoolteacher who had gone by that name years ago. "Stefana Zlateva. I don't know if she's still alive, though. And even if she were, I wouldn't put too many eggs in that old basket."

"Why not?"

He lifted a finger to his forehead. "Rumor was, she had a plank unscrewed up here."

I thanked him for the address and left.

Number 1 Smirnenski Street looked more like a boutique hotel than a single-family home. Then again, so did most of the houses in Tsarevo, the owners having long ago poured their life savings into accommodations for the phantom tourists that the fall of Communism never brought.

I rang the doorbell. The woman who opened was tiny, bent over with age like the top of a hook. With one hand behind the waist to help unfold it and the other shading her face from the sun, she looked up. Squinted. Those eyes—two embers of mischief—were the only part of her that had managed to stay young over the years.

"The noontime knocking brings a guest!" Her voice zigzagged between highs and lows, the way old people's voices do once they become too frail.

Then the mischief sharpened into recognition: "For heaven's sake, look who's back after all this time!"

"I don't believe we've met before."

"But of course we have! I prayed to see you once again before I die."

The clerk was right, she didn't know what she was saying. "Could you spare me a minute?"

"A minute? I have heaps and heaps of minutes, child, if the Lord should wish it so."

We sat down in the garden, flanked by a fig tree on one side and a pomegranate on the other.

"You missed your old friend?" Her eyes rolled in the direction of the fig tree. "Told you this fig was good enough, told you better not go running to the church so much. But you wouldn't listen, Elza *samodiva*."

"You take me for someone else. I am the granddaughter of Baba Mara."

"And so you are! My cousin's beloved grandchild, Elza. Still the same—" She looked me up and down. "No, younger!"

It was possible in theory that two women could have dementia producing an identical delusion. In reality, the odds were close to zero. Baba Mara had only one child: my mother. And my parents had only me—or so I had always thought. But if there was anything lucid in what I had heard so far, if Baba Mara did indeed have another grandchild, then it meant that at some point, back when I had been too young to remember or possibly before I was even born, I must have had a cousin or a sister.

The word slipped out automatically and the old woman's face lit up.

"Yes: sister! That's what the *samodivi* are—all sisters." She crossed her ankles and began to swing back and forth on the bench. "Coming out at night, on the full moon . . . all beautiful, and all alike. Dancing by the cemetery, at the church above the sea. God have mercy on anyone who sees them!" Then her voice dropped to a whisper: "But don't worry, I haven't told anyone about the sisterhood. Your secret has been safe with me."

I repeated that she had the wrong girl, but my words didn't reach her.

"And the way you moved, the way you danced by that fig tree! White beauty in the moonlight . . ."

She closed her eyes, lifted her arms in the air and started singing:

The samodivi haunt the night
haunt the night
dressed in white.

Go see their dance and by surprise
by surprise
lose your eyes.

She hummed the same lines over and over until I began to feel a strange unease. That tune sounded familiar. Not so much a memory, more like the distant ripple of a dream. A nursery rhyme heard long ago when someone had lulled me to sleep with it, strikingly similar to the first tune I had played on a piano.

I jumped from the bench but she grabbed my wrist, cutting off the song as abruptly as she had started it:

"I warned you many times: don't go near the church! I knew it would be by the church cemetery that they'd get you. The *samodivi* don't know mercy. And they don't forget."

The garden door banged shut.

"Well now, Mother, I leave for five minutes and you already have a visitor?"

The man looked like a fisherman returned from sea: tan skin, a navy striped T-shirt, hair and beard unkempt, turned half blond by sun and half gray by age. He froze, as if having just seen his death.

I came to his rescue: "My name is Thea. I'm trying to track down any relatives who may have known Baba Mara and . . ." Somehow, the name Elza refused to come out. "And the rest of my family."

"Ah yes, I remember you—the little toddler everyone was fretting over. But that was what, fifteen years ago? Look at you now!"

I didn't know what to say, how to begin talking to someone who was related to me yet a complete stranger. He looked just as uncomfortable. His face had relaxed a bit from the shock, but only barely, and he was now starting to sweat in the midday heat.

"So, Thea, good to see you all grown up. Your mother and I are second cousins, which makes me . . . your uncle, sort of?"

The old woman beamed a smile at him. "Didn't I tell you our Elza would come back?"

"You did, Mother, you did." His eyes warned me not to say anything. "Let's go. It's time for your lunch already."

He took her inside and returned alone a few minutes later.

"She isn't well, makes up a lot of things. And when she does, arguing doesn't help. It just exhausts her."

"I can imagine." What I couldn't imagine was why she would make up those things in the first place. "By the way, I owe you an apology—I should have called first. Everything has been last minute."

"Nothing wrong with last minute. You are family."

I slid to the end of the bench to make room for him—for his buff yet already vaguely worn-out body, and the invisible cloud of machine-oil vapors that engulfed the air around him. "My parents never mentioned I had family here."

"It was probably for the best." Then he clarified: "Less family, less headache."

"I want headache. It gets a bit lonely, being an only child."

"Only child? Is this what they told you?"

At last, someone had come out and said it. I tried to process the thought. But the word *sister* remained abstract to me. Unthreatening. Like a genetic disease that could only afflict others since it wasn't supposed to be part of my DNA—until now.

"I once had a sister, didn't I? Elza, the girl your mother took me for."

He stared down, wedging his heels deeper into the earth. "Maybe I shouldn't have told you."

"No, I'm glad you did. And I already suspected it anyway, that's why I came here. No one speaks to me about her, so I was hoping you might."

"I can tell you what I know, but I'm afraid it isn't much."

"It doesn't need to be."

He leaned back on the bench, ready to sink into the past. "You were almost three years old. You don't remember her at all?"

"Just a lullaby she must have sung to me; that's it."

"From what I recall, she wasn't allowed around you much. Your parents worried that you'd begin to . . . that she might damage you. Too much nonsense going on."

"What kind of nonsense?"

I felt a sudden, almost irrational need to know. But pressing him was a bad idea—what if he changed his mind and stayed mum, like everybody else? Down in the dust, a string of ants curved its thread around the edge of his shoe. Finally, his eyes lifted.

"I saw your sister only a few times, and very briefly. I was working on the ships—traveled nonstop, so I was never here. You look a lot like her. Everything about that girl was very . . ." He shook his head, as if the adjective he had in mind was inadequate. "Airy. Not air-headed, not at all, but . . . what's the word . . ."

"Ethereal?"

"That's it! Moved lightly. Spoke lightly. As if she could be blown away like a dandelion."

"Do you know what happened to her?"

"Yes, *that*." He continued to avoid my eyes. "I was here when it happened. Wish I hadn't been, though. There was some talk about a boy that summer—I never met him but heard he was a handsome one, the type girls always fall for. They said he broke her heart. Not a chance, if you ask me. The boy hasn't been born yet who can walk away from a creature like her."

"She was that beautiful?"

"Beautiful? Ha! The most perfect girl I ever saw! All she had to do was smile at a man and he was ready to die for her. Down at the ships, everyone was at her feet. She'd come to the docks, flash her pretty face, and those fools would talk about nothing else for days. Me they called 'the witch's cousin.' Most of them took a few punches for that one!"

"Do you think that she was really . . ."

"What, a witch? I don't believe in witches."

"Then why did people call her that?"

"Something must have snapped, inside that head of hers. She started walking by the sea, all alone, often even way past sunset. God knows what she was up to out there. Then one night she went missing and turned up by the old church, almost no life left in her. Your parents took her back to Sofia and we never heard from them again."

"So you don't know if she is still alive?"

"I always assumed she was. But from what you're telling me, it doesn't seem to be the case." He fidgeted with a rip on his jeans, above the knee. "I warned you I'm not much help. And neither is my mother."

"She called me *samodiva*. I know the legends, of course. But what do they have to do with Elza? And with the local church, and cemeteries, and fig trees?"

"That's where they found your sister, by the church graveyard. A fig grows right there. As for my mother . . . she hasn't had her wits for years. Believes a lot of things."

"What things?"

"That the *samodivi* do exist. There's a story linked to our family. Have you heard it?"

"No."

"It isn't very old. My great-aunt, Evdokia, lived in a region that's now in Turkey. After one of the many Balkan wars moved the border, everyone fled to our parts here, chased by the Ottoman troops. Evdokia had a newborn, but a crying baby is the last thing you want while hiding in the forest. So imagine waking up in the middle of the night, and over you—a man in a turban, holding your child against the tip of his yataghan. *All infidels must be slain, in the name of Allah!* When the blade goes through, it's as if your own heart is cut in two. Then horror erupts. A massacre. Even the moon, up in the sky, bleeds. Until suddenly, as if dropped straight from the heavens, white figures begin descending through the trees. Young girls. Frail. Luminous. The kind of incandescent beauty one encounters only in fairy tales. With quick precision, they tear off each turbaned head in sight—*crack! crack!*—necks breaking like twigs, spurting red fountains as the bodies fall, twitching, on the soaked ground. Once all is done, the creatures vanish. But before they do, they fall into dance, inviting only one human girl into their circle: the one bent in tears over her dead child. Later, those who survive would recall how Evdokia saved their lives. How, mad with grief, she summoned the *samodivi*."

"Summoned them?"

"I've heard that anyone born with *samodiva* blood can call on them like that—" He snapped his fingers. "No spell, no nothing. Just wish for them at night, and here they come."

I could see now why my parents had kept me in the dark all those years. *Born with* samodiva *blood*. Was I? Was my sister? It sounded like a harmless superstition. Folklore. Fairy tales. But once the seed had been planted in my mind, it became impossible to weed the questions out.

"Are you saying that even I could . . . that some sort of witch power runs in our family?"

"I'm saying it's all rubbish, stuff old people make up to tickle their aching bones. You'd love to have superpowers. I mean, who wouldn't? But I'm sorry to tell you that's just a pretty tale. Evdokia wasn't a *samodiva*. Otherwise she'd still be alive, roaming our shores at night."

"How did she die?"

"Pneumonia, shortly after getting here. I've seen her grave with my own eyes."

"At the church cemetery?"

With a quick nod, he changed the subject: "How long are you in town? You're welcome to stay with us."

"Thank you, but I've booked a hotel. Driving back early tomorrow."

"I see your parents don't keep such a close watch anymore."

"They don't have a choice, really. I'll be leaving for America soon."

"You too?"

It was the final secret I would find out from him about my sister. That fateful summer, she had bragged about going to college soon, ticket already bought and everything. There had been frequent mentions of New York City. Then the incident at the church had happened.

"I've often wondered if she ended up going or not," he said, glancing at me before my silence reminded him that I knew even less about Elza's fate than he did. "And this whole college thing . . . Your folks must be a mess now.

After losing one child, they probably never thought the second one would leave too."

"Maybe that's why they had me in the first place? Insurance against loneliness, once Elza grew up."

"Don't dwell on it. People have children for all sorts of reasons, even later in life. Gives them a chance to fix everything they did wrong the first time." He smiled and stood up from the bench. "I'm sure they did their best to keep you out of trouble. And yet—here you are."

As we were saying good-bye, I asked if he had a picture of Elza. He went to check in some old albums but came back shaking his head.

"Sorry, no luck. The good news is, though, you can just look in a mirror. When I saw you standing here earlier, I thought it was her ghost, I swear."

"Am I . . . ethereal?"

"I sure hope not!" He chuckled. "You're a real girl, flesh and blood. Make sure it stays that way."

I thanked him and promised to send them a card from America. But I wasn't done yet. I had one more stop to make before leaving Tsarevo.

THE CHURCH WAITED, PATIENTLY, ON the bare rocks above the Black Sea. A sunset sky bled all over it, bursting off the windows in deep pomegranate hues as if the entire building had been set on fire from within.

I sat in the car.

What now?

Walk up the hill . . . Open the door . . . Go in and light a candle . . .

Or just drive off and never come back?

Not that it mattered. I felt betrayed—by everyone, especially my parents. And now that the truth was out, nothing could change it or give me a clue what to do with it.

I had a sister.

Possibly a crazy one.

Was she still alive? If not, how had she died—an accident? A suicide? Or something even worse, sealing everyone's lips for so long?

I left the car by the road and headed uphill. A path led to the entrance, curving only once, halfway up, to avoid contact with the old fig tree whose crooked branches sagged into the ground—an impenetrable dome of fruit, bark, leaves. *The way you danced under that tree, white beauty in the moonlight . . .*

I shut the voice out of my head: just an old woman, spicing up her story with the stuff of legends. But other voices took its place. Acquaintances. Strangers. People who knew more about my past than I did. I could imagine their conversations. Years of hidden glances. Gossip disguised as pity, heads shaking as soon as I would turn my back:

"That poor family. Trying their best to keep at least the younger daughter from sliding off the deep end."

"Why, what happened to the older one?"

"You haven't heard? She was into witchcraft. It's a shame, really. To be so smart and yet get caught up in *that* sort of thing!"

"And the Slavins didn't know?"

"They must have. Why else rush to have a second child fifteen years after the first one? Saddest part is, the problem might even be genetic . . . But let's hope for the best. So far, little Theodora seems to be turning out just fine."

As I climbed higher up the hill, I could hear waves hurling their fury at the rocks below. The air was densing up with salt, with cries of seagulls, with an odor of dead clams and seaweed (baked by day, rotting off by night). From a distance, the church had an austere, minimalist charm—almost a natural extension of the rock. But up close, the simplicity was striking. The walls seemed thrown together by chance, out of whatever materials had happened to be lying around. Stones of all shapes and colors balanced under the spell of an invisible hand, ready to collapse back to nature's chaos.

The front door was locked, so I circled to the back, where a terrace opened out above the sea. It was impossible not to feel small against such vastness of water. But I also felt its indifference—the crushing indifference of a world whose territory began where my home ended. Somewhere in that world, thousands of miles away, *abroad* already waited. The dream. The unknown. My bet on a supposedly fantastic future. Now, for the first time, I wondered if I was ready for it. How could I be, if I no longer even knew who I was? "Ghost child" (a term I had seen in a book, once): someone raised in the shadow of a dead sibling. All my life, without realizing it, I had been a substitute for another girl. Getting her hand-me-downs. Her piano. Her looks. Whatever else allegedly ran in our blood. I probably acted like her. Spoke like her. It had been just a matter of time before America, too, would beckon . . .

Distracted by these thoughts, I didn't notice nightfall. The distant hills had disappeared. The dark was quickly creeping in. I stepped back from the railing, turned around, and walked over to the next corner—

It took a second to realize my mistake, but by then it was too late. In front of me, directly at my feet, was the graveyard. Crosses. Tombstones. Thistles. Swaying at me, blocking my way out.

Don't go near the church, it's by the cemetery that they'll get you!

I hadn't listened, and now had walked into a trap. Suddenly the wind was gone. The sound of waves had altogether vanished. The air turned so still I began to hear my breathing. Terrified, my eyes traced the darkness in a semicircle, back to the middle of the terrace. And there, ineffably real against the black canvas of the sky . . .

a girl—

dressed in white

thin, so thin she appeared almost weightless

facing the sea, feet barely touching the ground, arms lifted in the air, slowly moving—

I ran through the graveyard, stumbling, fighting the urge to look back for proof that I wasn't being chased, then shortcutting downhill—away from the path, from a black shape that could only be the fig tree.

As soon as my feet reached asphalt, I dived into the car, slammed the door, and released my panic on the pedal.

HOW DO YOU TELL THE two people you love most that you just lied to them? I dreaded the return home, the inevitable face-off. Not that I needed excuses—the penchant for secrets apparently ran in the family. Besides, given what I had uncovered, my parents had much more to explain than I did. But none of this made things easier. The drive back from Tsarevo. The first steps into the living room. The alarm on their faces when I admitted that I hadn't been on a trip with friends, after all. And finally the hardest part, the one about my sister.

I wanted to know everything and they gave in reluctantly, as if each detail would feed me poison. Elza had been their pride. The perfect child. A brilliant little devil, very early on. Learned to read when she was three. Started piano at five. English at seven. Went to the best high school. Won awards. Then a full scholarship to America.

So far—a lot like me. But this was just the surface.

"What happened to her?"

My mother said it first: Elza left for college and never came back.

"I need to know what really happened, Mom."

The two of them locked eyes—accomplices for life, trying to outwit grief. Then the vast quiet of their sadness poured out, the dam suddenly released after so many years.

Elza used to write home once a week, called every Sunday. Then for two weeks in November—nothing. My parents had given it a few more days before they called the school and were assured that their daughter was attending to her schedule, as shown by scans of her ID in cafeterias and academic buildings.

On the tenth of December, two weeks before Christmas, a phone call delivered the distressed voice of a university official. Something terrible had happened: Ms. Slavin's body had been found on a nearby hiking trail. Not a sign of violence, thank God. And no, there was no doubt as to the girl's identity. The school was going to take care of the funeral arrangements (or air transport, if the family preferred to bury her at home) as well as other incidentals, including round-trip tickets for the parents.

"So you went to America?"

My mother shook her head. "We received another phone call, Thea."

That second call had brought news of the strangest kind, a turn of events beyond comprehension:

Elza's body had been stolen from the funeral home. Overnight. Just like that.

"We are deeply sorry, Mrs. Slavin, but despite the joint efforts of university security and town police, at present there are neither leads nor suspects."

The newspapers proceeded to speculate about a possible break-in, but the funeral home was found safely locked in the morning, exactly as it had been left the night before. Not to mention the obvious—why would anyone abandon the body by a hiking trail, only to bother with stealing it back later?

"The school reiterates its condolences. Our office will update you immediately on any progress, but for the time being we suggest you postpone your trip."

More calls had followed. Many more. But none of them brought a single answer. To this day, my parents had no idea who—or what—had taken the life of their girl.

THE YEARS HAD WASHED THE Polaroid out to a nondescript beige—everything except the eyes. For a brief moment, they had bewitched the camera with the dark blue of winter seas. Then, gradually, the sky had withdrawn its storm. The waters had breathed out and cleared. And now these same eyes streamed their pale luminosity down on you as if, in the last second before she forgot ever having seen you, Elza had reached every corner of your mind, all the way to the bottom.

That evening I lay in bed, staring at the girl who would have been my best friend. We did look alike. If we had been closer in age, we probably could have passed for twins. Yet I didn't see it in me, the spell of that stunning creature whose name still lit up the eyes of everyone who knew her. She had been ethereal, a dandelion: the flower of wishes. Of all flowers, this was the only one that began bright and ripe (like the sun), then paled to a weightless silver (like the moon), letting you blow it off into the wind—a constellation of scattered seeds—so that your wish would come true. Like every girl, she must have had her own wishes. The piano. The faraway school. The boy who maybe (or maybe not) had dared to break her heart . . .

A knock on the door made me slide the picture under the pillow—my father had come to say good night. But instead of the usual peck on both cheeks, he just stood by my bed, saying nothing.

"Should I not go, Dad?"

"Not go? So that's what we've come up with now—defeat?"

"I'm serious. I don't want you and Mom dealing with this a second time."

"There won't be a second time. Because you *are* coming home for Christmas."

"Of course I am." Although I wondered if, by then, his hair would be even whiter; whether people aged visibly in four months if you didn't see them. "I meant everything else: seeing me off, not having me around, worrying about me."

"Parents always worry. That's part of the predicament."

"You'll worry less if I am here."

"How did this get into your little head?" He sat down on the edge of the bed. "Of course you're going. We'll worry much less if we know you are happy."

"I can be happy anywhere. No need to follow in my sister's footsteps."

His hand rested on my knee—a hand so big and warm I often wanted to curl up inside it, like a Lilliputian. "It's fine to follow someone else's footsteps, Thea. So long as you don't follow someone else's dream."

I looked around, at everything that wasn't going to fit inside the two suitcases. "My dream right now is to lift all this and plant it in Boston, with you and Mom in it."

He tried to smile. "Your room will still be here when you come home for winter break. As will your mother and I."

"But I thought you guys were against America?"

"Not against it, just . . . wary of it. Of one school especially."

"Which one?"

The frown was instant. And very, very deep. "Princeton."

In a flash, the past few weeks came back to me: the stress of choosing a college, my parents' unexplained aversion to Princeton. Ever since the acceptance letters came, they had insisted on Harvard and I accused them of name snobbery—"Harvard is Harvard" seemed to be the mantra in Bulgaria, a no-brainer for anyone lucky enough to get in. But the deadline to decide hadn't come yet. I still had a week to change my mind.

"Dad, do you think we'll ever find out what happened to her?"

"No. And I don't want you trying. You are going to college, not on a ghost chase into the past."

"Why not? I was thinking what if—"

"There are no ifs, Thea. We did everything we could. And so did the police, the school, the press, our embassy. The case went even higher up the chain—and nothing. Trust me, it becomes a downward spiral very quickly."

"Why?"

"Because you love her, and you want to know. You search obsessively. Press articles. School records. Nothing you haven't seen already, yet you still go through the files a thousand times. *What if I missed something? There has to be a clue* . . . Years go by. Then one day the Internet pops up and becomes your daily drug. *Just five more minutes, one more search.* Until you start to realize that you aren't getting any closer. That you never will."

He looked devastated. At that moment I knew: I would be going to Princeton. Maybe my father was right, and there was no hope of ever finding out what happened to Elza. But how could I be certain unless I tried? Everything that I considered mine—my family, my home, the life I was supposed to leave behind—had crumbled, a scaffold built on lies. And in its place? Suspicions. Warnings. Fears that, just like my sister, I might become . . . what exactly? Unhinged? Delusional? A freak? Witch? Monster?

"So, no detective games. Promise?" He gave me a kiss and headed for the door.

"Dad—" When he turned around, his face was finally at peace. "What's the story with the *samodivi*?"

THE AIRPORT IN SOFIA LOOKED like any other: white marble, steel, everything drenched with light through a glass ceiling, as if the entire terminal was designed to give those who stayed behind the illusion of being headed somewhere, into a sky of their own.

I had traveled abroad before for music festivals and competitions, and loved every minute of it—even the fuss at the airport, with my parents snapping pictures while I showed off the boarding pass as an official license for the next adventure to start.

This time was different. I forced myself to walk through security. Then passport control. Then down a hallway toward the gate. And I kept turning back—over and over, to catch a glimpse of the two figures quickly subsumed by the crowd, reduced to a pair of moving dots (their hands, still waving).

What a blessing she is, this little girl. Yet the Slavins will always remain broken people.

Years had passed since I overheard these words. But it was only now, on a plane to America, that I caught on to their meaning. There were probably all kinds of broken people. People who had lost a love. A home. A dream. And then there were also the wrecks, those who had gone through a loss more than once, their soul patched and torn and repatched until it resembled a quilt: each square a distinct color, proof that the heart would stay warm, ready for the next breakage.

Now, for the first time, I felt broken too. I tried to think of college, of the new life waiting for me there. Yet all I could picture were Mom and Dad, going back to an empty house. It had crushed them, back in May, to find out I had decided to go to Princeton. And not just decided, but made the arrangements without telling them—written to the school, booked the plane ticket, everything. It was their worst nightmare; fate laughing in their faces after eighteen years of struggle to avoid exactly this: me becoming like Elza. I tried to explain that I was different, that the past didn't scare me and Princeton was as safe a school as any other. If by being there I could solve the mystery of her death—why not? Or even if I couldn't, at least they would make peace with the place and finally take that canceled trip from long ago, only this time for my graduation . . .

To get through the ten-hour flight, I started reading the book of legends. Its cover showed a girl in white standing by a well, looking up at the moon. *Once upon a time, beyond nine lands into the tenth . . .*

The tale of the *samodivi* had them swimming in the black waters of a mountain lake—naked, innocent like children absorbed in the oblivion of games. After the bath, once they got dressed again, came the magic of their dance, the hypnotic swirl of the *horo:* a circle of intertwined arms and flashing feet whose beat sent shivers through the forest.

Never before had mortals seen the wonder of such beauty. And of those ill-fated ones who did, of those doomed roamers of the night who set brave foot upon the moon-soaked samodivi *meadows, not one laid eyes upon the dawn again, not one reached home to tell a tale of lovelorn sorrow.*

Now a vagabond would fold his knee under the dome of oak-green branches. Now a thief would claim the fallen oak leaves as pillow for the night. A merchant, having chased elusive trades all day, would tie his horse around the rigged oak bark. Or a monk, astray, would hum his prayers to the oak roots, touching cheek to earth as summons for the mystic lull of sleep. But it was just as well: an equal end was destined for them all. An end of threefold joy and tenfold horror . . .

"What's the story with the *samodivi,* Dad?"

He had turned pale, the defeated pale of a man who has suffered quietly for a long time only to realize that a disease has been eating him from the start. "Why are you asking, Thea?"

I summed up what I had learned in Tsarevo, without mentioning my church visit.

"Old Stefana, still living in her loony world! She used to fill your sister's head with folktales too, which is why we didn't want you anywhere near her. But the son at least could have shown some common sense."

"He only told me what he knew."

"And you believed all this?"

"Why wouldn't I?"

"Because people have nothing better to do. They get bored, and they let their sick imaginations wander."

"Was Elza's imagination sick too?"

No answer.

"And, Dad, does any of this really run in our family?"

He sat back down on the bed, reaching for my hand as if his touch could convince me even if his words failed. "Nothing runs in our family, no matter what anyone says. Your sister was a perfectly healthy girl. And so are you."

"Yet she believed the *samodivi* legend."

"She was fascinated by it, then started to believe it, yes. But not because of family lunacy. The whole thing was a school project."

I almost laughed. *All students are to dance at full moon in a church cemetery. White garment optional. Extra credit if carried out within vicinity of fig tree.*

"Why would any school assign such a project?"

"It wasn't assigned, she volunteered. Your sister had two passions: piano and archaeology. Each summer at the Black Sea, she would drag us out to see the ancient settlements. Town walls, churches, all kinds of ruins. The older and more decrepit, the better."

Which explained her frequent escapes to the church in Tsarevo, but not the figure I had seen there.

"In those first years after Communism, looters began to smuggle our antiques abroad. Elza and her school team signed up with the Ministry of Culture to compile a central database of artifacts. They opened Communist archives, warehouses, entire rooms of artworks labeled 'highly privileged' and sealed for decades. There, she found a scroll that eventually consumed her mind."

"What kind of scroll?"

"The written confessions of a monk who was allegedly blinded by *samodivi* in the forest. Elza loved bizarre stories and wouldn't stop talking about it, about how this man might have been the master of the Rila Monastery cross."

"The famous one?" It was one of Bulgaria's most treasured relics. A wooden cross carved with hundreds of elaborate, miniature gospel scenes.

"Yes. She became convinced that this monk had received mysterious powers from the *samodivi*. That he made the cross only after he was blinded."

"What if it was true?"

"That's not possible, Thea."

"Why not?"

"Because these creatures don't exist. Some disturbed man wrote a piece of fiction and your sister went too far with it."

"Do you happen to have a copy of this fiction, Dad?"

"This fiction is in the past. And you promised me not to go there."

He seemed upset, so I didn't insist—either that night or in the next few months before I left for America. All my questions about Elza, especially about her life at Princeton, received the same answer: *None of this matters anymore.* Her letters from school? Destroyed. Her possessions? There had been no point in keeping them. And the three buckled chests? He took me to the locked room and opened them, one by one. All three were empty.

I didn't believe for a second that my parents, the two most sentimental people I knew, who kept even ticket stubs from my concerts neatly arranged in albums, would discard what had been left behind by their first child. More likely, Elza's things had been removed from the house and locked up elsewhere, safely out of my reach. Perhaps with time, after I had spent a few semesters at Princeton, Mom and Dad might finally let go of the fear and allow me access to my sister's life, including the alleged "fiction" that had consumed her mind with tales of monks and forest witches.

For now, another piece of fiction had found its way into my hands, and I continued to read about the *samodivi* while everyone around me on the plane slept. The words had the playful rhythm of a fairy tale. Yet Bulgarian fairy tales often read with the bleak echo of omens:

> *Stepping softly from their bath, laughing and aglow with star mist, the maidens would begin to sense the hidden stare of a traveler. They'd tempt him, draw him out, then gift their blameless bodies to him. Until a strange beat would imbue the night. A pulse of suddenly awoken rhythms. The beauties would begin their dance, the moon unleashing madness on them. And breathless, raving, free at last, they'd lock the man inside their deadly circle . . .*

The rest was a terrifying feast. An indulgence of cruelty. The witches dance their prey to the verge of death and, just as his heart collapses in its first convulsions, they descend on him with the hunger of beasts—taking out his eyes, his heart, tearing off his limbs in an outburst of vengeance.

Then the unthinkable unfolds: the youngest of the three, Vylla, falls in love. He happens to be a young shepherd, a gifted pipe player, a drifter without a care in the world. Like everyone before him, he stumbles upon the *samodivi*. Hidden in the darkness of the forest, he watches the moon infuse its wild rhythms into their dance. But before Vylla's eyes fall on him, before she detects, somewhere down in her savage heart, the first beats of a strange new longing, the night has already revealed to him (or the wind has already whispered, or his own heart has already guessed) a secret never before known to a mortal man: the secret of where Vylla's power lies, and how to steal it—

The secret of how to capture a *samodiva*.

CHAPTER 4

Captive

MY GREEK ART professor didn't believe me when I told him how little I knew about Elza. In a way, he was right: I had spared him the crazy part, the one about the *samodivi*. But as for the real details of her life, including those last few months at Princeton, I truly had no clue at all.

He didn't either, or maybe he preferred not to talk about it. When I tried to get more out of him, he mumbled that speculation never did anyone any good, especially speculation about the past. "Bygones aside, Miss Slavin, I would like to continue our banter on the Orphic myth." And with a vague remark that he had something else to show me, he asked me to stop by his office around five on Friday afternoon.

Unlike him, though, I couldn't brush bygones aside. All summer, I had fantasized about how, once at school, I would trace Elza's steps. Where she had lived on campus. What she had studied. Favorite professors. Roommate. Best friend. Maybe even a boyfriend, after her bad luck with that boy back home.

My list of action items was stapled to a campus map showing the administrative building most likely to have information on each. The Registrar's Office was the starting point. A self-proclaimed "steward of academic records," it kept not only enrollment data but also each student's course selections and grades. Next, the Financial Aid Office would know whether Elza had worked on campus, and if so, where. Undergraduate Student Housing could give me her dorm and, with any luck, her room number. From there, I would look to the residential college for specifics on her life at school.

The trick with all this, of course, was to ask questions without drawing attention to myself or the fact that I was trying to solve a crime. Because if word spread that the crazy missing girl's sister was now at Princeton stirring up trouble, the school would probably put me under special surveillance, to monitor my safety and state of mind the way Wylie was supposed to monitor my music career, Donnelly—my curriculum, and Rita—my social life. Not to mention that they would also inform my parents. And this, more than anything else, I had to avoid.

So far, Giles was the only one to have figured out my link to Elza—if it were up to me, I preferred to keep it that way. But getting strangers to talk required skill. And only a week ago, my first detective attempt had already backfired.

"Miss, I apologize, I must have misunderstood. Are you Elza Slavin or not?" The plump woman at the Registrar's Office had stared at me over her tortoise-rim glasses. "Because if not, there isn't much I can do to process your request."

"I am Elza's sister. Hopefully that counts?" My student ID barely elicited a glance. "She was class of '96, whereas I just started here and was curious about . . . about her life at Princeton."

"Curious?" A perfectly tweezed eyebrow curved up, to signal that she wasn't hired yesterday. "I'm afraid curiosity is insufficient grounds for access to someone else's files, even by a sibling. All student records, with very few exceptions, are confidential. It is school policy and, as such, is strictly enforced."

"What are the exceptions?"

"Directory information: name, dates of attendance, degree and major, place of birth. For members of athletic teams, we also list weight and height."

In other words, either statistics that didn't apply to Elza or basics I already knew.

"You wouldn't be able to tell me anything else? Not even what classes she took?"

"Only if she gave written permission. And 'written' means signed by Ms. Slavin personally."

By now, an ill-concealed impatience had sneaked into her voice. I decided to take a chance.

"What if the student never graduated?"

Judging by her unflinching expression, this didn't make a difference.

"Or if the person is no longer"—the word *alive* lingered at the tip of my tongue—" . . . no longer in the U.S. and won't be coming back?"

"The safeguards apply regardless. Naturally, our students' expectation of privacy doesn't end at the country's border."

"I see. Thanks anyway." I took back the transcript request form she had asked me to fill out earlier. It was only now that, all of a sudden, and probably for no other reason than to make sure I wouldn't bother her again, she decided to be helpful.

"For future reference, here is a copy of our policy on access to archived student files. You will see, in clause (b), that confidentiality terminates only upon death or seventy-five years after the file was created. If you still think your inquiry merits further review, you can write to the Dean of the College. Instructions are on the back."

I thanked her again, and this time I meant it. But my excitement was short-lived, as I sat down on a bench outside to read the handout.

A request for confidential information regarding a student who died within six years of matriculation must also be accompanied by a release signed by the next of kin.

Next of . . . what? I looked up the phrase on my phone—a legal term for who would have power over your affairs after you died. The order was: children—parents—grandchildren—siblings. Which meant that my parents' signature, not mine, would be required for access to Elza's files.

As if this weren't enough, within the hour my phone rang. The Office of the Dean of the College had been notified of my attempt to obtain records, and instead of me writing to them, they were now contacting me.

"Thea, it has come to our attention that you are the sister of . . ." The man needed a label for the precarious Elza situation, and I thought, *Just say it: the sister of that poor girl whose dead body was abducted from our campus fifteen years ago.* " . . . of Ms. Elza Slavin. My God, what a tragedy! And under such perplexing circumstances . . . or so I am told, as these events predate my affiliation with Princeton. Must be difficult for your family, no doubt?"

"Yes, my parents are scarred for life. But as for me, I don't remember Elza at all."

"Makes sense, given the age difference. It's still admirable, though, that you decided to attend the same university. I imagine this wasn't your only offer from a top-ranked school, and many in your place might have held a grudge against Princeton."

"I was actually glad that Princeton didn't hold a grudge against *me*."

"Quite the opposite. Our school will always be in your family's debt. Which is not to say that what happened was Princeton's fault, of course, but welcoming you as a student here was the least we could do."

I didn't like the sound of this. "Are you saying that I was accepted to Princeton because of what happened to my sister? Legacy . . . of sorts?"

Under the controversial practice of "legacy admissions" in America, applicants related to alumni, especially alumni who had given money or done other favors to a school, were twice as likely to get in.

"Look, Thea . . ." This time he took extra care with his answer. "I've seen your file—you have more than enough credentials to be admitted on the merits. All I was saying is that there happens to be prior history, and we need to be sensitive to it. Which brings me to the reason I called. I want to make sure that if you ever need anything, or run into roadblocks of any kind, you'd let me know personally. No point in following protocol, or talking to administrators who are unaware of the situation and can't be of much help. Like that lady at the Registrar's Office today."

"But she must have been aware, if she informed you of my visit."

"Not until you left and she ran a routine check for the name you had given her. Next time just call me, all right? It would simplify things." I was sure it would—by helping him keep tabs on me. "As for your sister's transcript, that's not a problem at all. I'll have a copy e-mailed to you."

"How about all the other files? Can I have access to them?"

"I don't believe there are any. Everything was handed over to Princeton Borough Police, as part of the investigation. But may I give you a piece of advice?"

"Sure, please do." Advice was always on offer when I was denied information.

"You've started a new chapter of your life. Coming to America. To Princeton. Don't spoil it with pursuits that will only upset you and lead nowhere. Try to bury the past and . . ." This sounded so close to "bury the dead"—the one thing my parents would never have a chance to do—that I could almost hear him blush. "Anyway, I think you know what I mean. Oh, and one more thing. I've asked Counseling Services to give you a call."

"Counseling?"

"Yes. From our health center, over at McCosh. You certainly aren't obligated to speak to them, but I suggest you do. Very informal, just a handshake, to make sure we cover all bases. It would be confidential, of course."

Which at Princeton was strictly enforced, as I already knew. What I didn't know was what "bases" exactly he thought he had to cover.

"Does the school view my interest in Elza as . . . problematic?"

"Your interest—no, not in and of itself. What could pose problems is interest from others. Despite the significant time gap, some repercussions are to be expected."

"Such as?"

"Well, the case appears to have been major news at the time. And people don't forget major news, especially at a quiet place like Princeton. Sooner or later, it's bound to come up in conversation."

"So what if it does? I have nothing to be ashamed of."

"Of course not. But I suppose your sister's death is, nonetheless, a very sensitive subject. We want you to be fully equipped to handle it, that's all.

Our job is to provide each student with a smooth college transition, and we try not to let anything stand in the way."

I was certain that, for the moment, his job required him to mute my suspicions and steer me over to a counselor. But I had my agenda too. And, like him, I wasn't going to let anything stand in the way.

SCHOOL SWALLOWED ME LIKE QUICKSAND. I tried to decode the mysterious urgency, class assignments crammed into deadlines that could be met only with lack of sleep and a racing heartbeat. Yet I had no point of reference. Back home, I had seen such life-or-death resolve on people's faces only when an ambulance or a fire truck was involved.

To top things off, I had to start my campus job—those cafeteria shifts Donnelly had warned me about. The Financial Aid Office had assigned me to the Graduate College dining hall, probably because of its proximity to Forbes. I had heard rumors about the place, about its indulgent beauty conceived almost a century ago when a famous feud exploded between Dean Andrew West and Princeton's then president, Woodrow Wilson. A graduate college was to be built. Wilson wanted it on the main campus, where everyone would blend in and the graduate students could serve as example for the rowdy undergraduates. West, however, had a different plan. He envisioned an opulent academic cloister, a minireplica of Oxford and Cambridge, where he would preside over his scholars-in-training and bring back old European traditions, far from the undergraduate hordes and from Wilson's reach. Soon, money followed. And West was able to realize his dream, erecting a Gothic campus gem that would be widely envied and emulated by rivals such as Duke and Yale.

Wednesday was my first day at work and, eager to see West's creation, I cut through the golf course. It meant breaking the rules, of course, as the golf club was private and its members didn't appreciate having to play around trespassing students. But the route up College Road would have taken much longer, and I had no time for idle walks.

After a few impeccably mowed hills, the campus map led me through a carved stone arch, a courtyard, and down a hallway that ended at a massive wooden door, wide open. For a moment, I thought I had mistakenly walked into a church. Then I saw long tables. Chairs. Salt and pepper shakers, positioned at perfect intervals among the seats. There was no one else in the giant dining hall and I tried to take it all in, to imagine how I was going to work— and others were going to eat—in a place that looked and felt like a Gothic cathedral.

Everything about Procter Hall was enormous, medieval, and beautiful. The heavy doors opened into a vestibule separated from the rest by thin wooden bars. The hall itself was absolutely overwhelming. Its walls began with rich oak paneling that held portraits of dead academics. Above them, arched windows rose uninterrupted in the white stone, letting the light pour down on the tables in abstract, whimsical shapes. Higher still, domed like the inside of an inverted ship, a carved beam ceiling closed its rib cage over twelve low-hanging chandeliers, suspended from buttresses with a gargoyle grinning on each. On the opposite end, a lavish stained-glass window dominated the entire hall, flaunting its intricate lace of sharp, bursting colors. And reigning over all this, high above the entrance, was an organ—the most magnificent one I had ever seen.

The job itself had nothing to do with beauty. Outfitted with rubber gloves by the exit, I took the tray from everyone who was done eating. Silverware went on the right. Dirty dishes—on the left. Food was tossed into one garbage can, napkins and trash into another. At first, my stomach cringed from the sight of what people left on their plates. Then I stopped noticing.

"The graduate students are an odd bunch," one of the girls on my shift had warned me. "Most of them are nice enough, but some are so socially challenged it's scary. Just ignore them. You don't have to indulge anyone's inept attempts to flirt."

"Like what?"

"Like tacky pickup lines. Tonight, for example, the entrée is baked chicken. If you end up serving behind the food line, you'll have to ask whether they want a breast or a leg. Which elicits some very weird responses from certain guys. Every single Wednesday! The same baked chicken—and the same guys and the same responses. It's pathetic."

Luckily, busing trays didn't involve a dialogue about body parts. A few students stayed behind to strike up a conversation with me. And yes, they were mostly guys, but all of them were genuinely friendly. The only question that felt borderline was the one about my accent—not because of the accent itself, but because being from Bulgaria acquired a different connotation when I was cleaning people's plates instead of sitting at the table with everyone.

Throughout the shift, constantly in front of my eyes across the vestibule, a grand piano hid under a cover. Princeton had many pianos, most of them in claustrophobic practice rooms or in common areas where the human hustle never stopped. This one was perfect: as soon as the dining hall closed at night, nothing would come between me and my music.

Later that evening, I grabbed a few score sheets from my room and sneaked out the window. A short gravel path led to the golf course, where a pond separated the golf club's property from that of Forbes and a fountain hummed its nostalgic splash out at the sky—the same sound I had heard the first night from my room. After the pond, one had to walk uphill, diagonally through the grass, toward the Graduate College and its Cleveland Tower, whose four white turrets poked through the silence, in a dreamy attempt to lift the entire building up into the air.

There was an absolute, breathtaking peace—the kind you can only wish for but never quite imagine until you happen to be in the middle of it. Not a single leaf moved in the scattered trees. The full moon had polished every blade of grass in liquid silver, its own astonishing circle suspended low above the tower, big and palpable as if someone had rolled it over as close as it would dare to get.

It hadn't occurred to me that Procter Hall could be locked, but it was. I turned to leave, resigned to the idea of having to play in the crowded Forbes lobby again—

. . . when I heard steps. Loud and heavy. Echoing from a stone staircase whose spiral began right outside the dining hall and disappeared underground, in one of the many corridors of the Graduate College. A dark mess of hair was already popping out, followed by the rest of a stocky, middle-aged man in black overalls.

"Good evening. Might you be a nymph, perchance?"

A what?! I glanced toward the exit, wishing I had never left my room.

"Profoundly sorry, did I frighten you?" His huge eyes kept blinking in my direction. "Of course I did, it being this ungodly hour and all. But please don't mind my misguided humor. I sensed you needed help?"

"Oh no, thank you. I was just leaving."

The eyelids finally froze as his stare fell on the music sheets in my hand.

"If I may—" He reached past me and slid a large key into the lock of the dining hall's entrance, turning it only once. "No lock should interfere when the night demands its music."

Something about his voice—a shade of laughter in its timbre—was strangely soothing. I asked if playing this late might disturb anyone.

"Disturb? Not at all. Sounds don't escape walls like these. Although I wish they did . . ." The sound of his own voice dissipated up toward the ceiling. "Happens only once in a few blue moons, a true nymph's music."

"I am certainly not a nymph."

"That's hardly for you to judge." He scratched his head, pulling out a few stray leaves whose shape reminded me of ivy before he stuffed them into his pocket. "Embarrassing, to say the least. Yet the vegetation around here needs constant pruning. Part of the job ritual, really."

I tried not to laugh. What needed pruning—badly—was his head. Mane, eyebrows, beard, all merged in a cloud of cotton candy spun out of tar instead of sugar. Princeton seemed full of such odd-looking types: frumpy graduate students, disheveled professors, too busy or distracted to bother with the basics of grooming. It was the Einstein look. More than a century earlier, the quintessential Princetonian had proven that not only time and space, but also the looks of a genius could be relative.

"So you are the invisible gardener? You've done wonders with this place."

A net of wrinkles caught his eyes as he started laughing. "I'm merely a janitor. Keykeeper. The tower, mostly."

"You keep the keys to Cleveland Tower?"

"Someone ought to. Being up there at night is rumored to have tempted a soul or two into a plunge."

"Suicides? At Princeton?"

My curiosity unsettled him. "Not anymore."

"When was the last one?"

"The last—" He hesitated, either searching his memory or sifting his words. "It must have been long ago. Long before anything that bears resemblance to the present."

His answer confused me, but it was the only one I was going to get. With a nod toward Procter Hall, he reminded me that I had come here to play, not to discuss suicides with strangers.

"Thank you for unlocking the door. I am lucky you happened to be passing."

"My deepest pleasure. By what name can I call you?"

"Thea."

"Theia . . ." The new vowel slipped between the other two, as if a long missing sound had completed a musical harmony. His eyelids closed, imprinting it to memory.

"And yours?"

"It's Silen. Like *silent* with a silent *T*."

He pulled an odd instrument out of his pocket (two flutes sharing a single mouthpiece), pressed it to his fleshy lips, and vanished down the staircase, leaving behind the trail of a melody whose hesitant, airy sounds had a vague resemblance to Debussy.

Unable to shake off the feeling that I had just dreamed this man up, I reached for the doorknob. And this time it turned obediently, letting me into the vast silence of the dining hall.

A FAINT EMERGENCY LIGHT ILLUMINATED the piano; the rest hid in darkness. Slowly, the music carried me—first to my home, to the living room where I used to play just like this, by myself, then to Alexander Hall and the silhouette I had seen there. *Your Chopin is stunning.* These words wouldn't leave my mind, bringing back his voice and the few brief things he had said to me. I wanted to play for him again. And I began to imagine him, sitting a few feet away from me, listening . . .

I must have been there for hours. My wrists were too drained to stay above the keys and my body felt incredibly, overwhelmingly tired. But I didn't want to go back to Forbes, not yet, so I closed the piano and put my head down to rest a bit.

When I looked up again, it took me a moment to figure out where I was—I had fallen asleep. Outside it was already dawn. Most of the darkness had lifted, and in its place a dense fog had fallen over everything.

I headed back through the golf course, barely awake, lulled—even as I walked—by the air's unexpected thickness.

"Why are you trying to vanish so quickly?"

The panic and the urge to run came a split second before the certainty that running could only make it worse: a guy had turned up next to me. Restless eyes. Tousled hair. Face still flushed from whatever he had left behind. Caught in my own thoughts, I hadn't seen the figure approaching through the fog. But he had seen me. And now he was smiling at me, knowing—as well as I did—that we were far from the world. Alone. Invisible. That no one would hear a scream from the golf course. Not through the fog and not this early.

Why are you trying to vanish? I had to say something. Anything.

"Why wouldn't I?"

"Because I am not about to let you."

That smile again. I stepped back. Then two more steps. He followed, as if a hidden force drew him in my direction. It felt paralyzing to watch him move. He was flawless. All energy. Agile like a wildcat whose swagger marks the bounds of a new domain.

"Are you afraid of me?" The thought seemed to bother him and he added, much more gently this time: "Don't be."

Suddenly I recognized the voice. The silhouette. No longer hidden or obscured by shadows, moving through the white air with a resolve I hadn't noticed in him before. We had finally met, my stalker and I. Not from afar, not in anonymous darkness, and not with museum security about to pop in any second. He was even more striking in daylight—beautiful with the dubiously perfect beauty of magazine spreads, the kind I could have sworn had been infinitely retouched, except he was now standing, disheveled and real, right in front of me. His face had an unnerving blend of strength and fragility. Intense, sinuous cheekbones. Full lips sending a chill at the faintest curve of a smile. Eyes an air-light blue that seemed easily wounded but likely could, just as easily, turn ice-cold in a flash.

"I haven't seen you in the fog before," he said, still smiling.

I hid behind a joke too: "Creatures like me come out only at clear dawn."

"Then why make an exception now?"

"Maybe it's a lucky aberration . . ."

It was impossible to look away from that face. But I had already seen the rest of him, and was acutely aware of it. The strong, smooth neck. The bare chest, as his shirt hung open above the jeans. And his skin—fine, almost translucent, making him appear susceptible to harm yet also immune to it.

"Your aberration seems to have caught me captive." His eyes searched mine, as if expecting a reaction I hadn't produced yet. "What are you doing today?"

"I have class, then piano practice."

"Skip them. Spend the day with me."

"I don't think I can."

"Why not?"

Because I don't put my life on hold for complete strangers. I bit my tongue. "It's not that simple."

"We can make it simple." He glided his eyes over my face—their insistent blue—down to my lips as if he were kissing me already. I couldn't react. Couldn't move. My heart was about to fly out if he leaned in another inch. But he changed his mind: "Do you live in Forbes?"

I nodded. A shadow slipped across his face.

"I will wait for you at nine, by the Cleveland."

"Not today. Maybe if—"

"I will wait for you." His fingers brushed my cheek—barely, making sure I wasn't a visual trick played on him by the fog. "I'm glad I found you."

Just as he had promised he would. But he hadn't found me, hadn't even looked for me. All he had done was run into me by accident.

I cleaned my voice of reproach before the words came out, simply stating the fact: "It took you a while."

"Yes, too long. Almost longer than a lifetime."

Then he walked away into the fog.

JEANS AND A GRAY T-SHIRT—THE usual for everyone else—had to do just fine. I was going to stop by Cleveland Tower and tell him that I couldn't drop school on a moment's notice. If he really meant to ask me out, the weekend was only two days away. But he didn't seem the kind of guy who took no for an answer, so the last thing I wanted was to show up dressed for a date.

"It's an art, Tesh," Rita had explained to me a few days earlier, while we were getting ready to go out ("it" being the tricky balance between glammed up and casual). "You need to look like a million bucks. But you also can't have a guy think you are trying too hard."

"Guys can think whatever they want."

"Except one of them, right?"

"All of them." I couldn't believe she was still dropping hints about the guy from the concert. "What is 'too hard' anyway?"

"This—" She pointed to the far end of my closet, where I had hung a couple of party dresses. "LBD? I don't think so. At least not for the Street."

"L what?"

"Little black dress."

I added it to my mental stash of acronyms, next to BLT, which had come up at lunch that day. Her index finger glided through the hangers.

"Ditto for any sparkle. Leather—maybe. But that's about it."

"Which means half my clothes are practically useless?"

"Sorry, but yes. This isn't Europe, where people dress to the nines. You must give the impression of having just stepped out of the Gap, yet still look hotter than everyone else who's doing it."

"So what do I wear then?" I was starting to sweat. Whoever said that dressing up for a party was half the fun clearly hadn't dressed at Princeton.

"Let's see . . . Show me your jeans."

I dropped them on the bed: three pairs, probably not brands she knew.

"The ones in the middle are too bland; you can use them for class. So either the dark wash or the skinny. I'd go with the skinny. It's sexier."

"Does everyone really wear jeans all the time, even to parties?"

"Pretty much." She reached into the closet for a black tank top and a pair of high-heeled sandals. "Perfect! Unless, of course, you want to use your forty percent on the legs. With legs like yours, I think you should."

This time I was completely lost. She started laughing.

"The killer equation: you never show more than forty percent of your skin. Jeans go with cleavage. Miniskirts need at least sleeves."

The art had started to feel like trigonometry. It still felt that way now, as I was about to head out to Cleveland Tower, with the same three pairs of jeans spread on the bed.

Badass, I tried to convince myself, staring in the mirror to decide if black eyeliner would be overkill or not. *Badass Bombshell.*

The clock above the bed ticked 8:40.

I threw on the skinny jeans and, a few seconds later, was out the door.

WALKING TO THE GRADUATE COLLEGE this early was like swimming against the current of a mountain rapid: everyone else rushed in the opposite direction, trying to make it to class on time. I had decided to skip the golf course and take College Road, to clear my mind before meeting him. It didn't work. The long walk only made me tense. I told myself that he might not show up; that his urge to spend the day with me could have dissipated, together with the fog. But he was there, right on time. Just as he had been for the two Chopins.

His effortless walk brought him over to me in seconds. I had never seen anyone walk like this: owning every move, as if he had absolute control not just over his body but over every inch of the world that surrounded it.

"Good morning, creature."

"Good morning, captive."

"Me?" He leaned in, over my ear. "I'm about to take you away. That makes *you* the captive."

"And what does it make *you*?"

"It makes me want to start your captivity right away."

I tried to look away from his face. To focus. To figure out a way to tell him that I couldn't stay. That I was late for class already.

"Let's go." He reached for my hand but I pulled it back.

"Go where?"

"You'll see."

"Why can't you tell me?"

He took a keychain out of his pocket and an open convertible beeped from the parking lot by the tower.

I was starting to see, yes. No wonder he acted as if he owned the world—just like those students Donnelly had warned me about, the ones who never served food to anyone. He had probably eaten at Procter Hall the night before. I might have even cleaned his tray without knowing. Now I was expected to drop everything and take off for a day, simply because a guy with a fancy car said so.

"I'm sorry, but I have to leave."

"All of a sudden, just like that?"

"I can't skip school. I told you this already."

"You can't or you don't want to?"

"Both."

"I see." Not a hint of hesitation. "These games are cute, but I don't play them. No need to put on an act with me. We both know school can wait."

"And you can't?"

"I don't want to wait. I haven't stopped thinking about you all morning."

All morning? I haven't stopped thinking about you all week!

"Do you even go to school here?" I had assumed he did, but most of my other assumptions about him were turning out to be wrong.

"What if I didn't?"

"Then I can see why it's not a big deal to you."

"Forget the why. Come with me." He looked at my lips again—as before, without any attempt to hide it. "I'll wait for the weekend if I have to. But I'd rather start being with you now. It doesn't need to be the whole day, I can bring you back sooner."

His voice had softened. Or maybe it was those words—*start being with you*—that made me change my mind. They sounded like a promise. The kind of promise I had fantasized about ever since I saw him in Alexander Hall.

He took my hand and headed back toward the car. It turned out to be a Porsche, black and shiny.

"I didn't realize my captivity would be so . . . high end."

He shrugged. "It's just wheels."

A select few in Bulgaria drove expensive cars on the streets of the capital. My parents had such friends, and even some of mine received the occasional permission to borrow daddy's pricey ride. Most of them loved to play coy—what impressed us ordinary humans was, of course, just "wheels" to them. But unlike anyone I had ever met who drove a car of this caliber, he sounded like he actually meant it.

"Where are we going?"

"Breakfast." He opened the door for me. "It's too far to walk, trust me."

Trust him? Based on what? But I ignored my fear and got in. Only the night before, I had spent hours at the piano imagining this very moment, and now had come close to ruining it. So what if I skipped a few classes? He was probably doing the same. Or skipping work—which was a bigger deal anyway.

The automatic locks clicked. I tried to think of something else, to act as if I hadn't just driven off with a guy I barely knew. Rita and all her talk about stalking! This was Princeton, everyone knew the place was safer than a police station. Besides, if I wanted a safe and sheltered life, what was I doing in a foreign country, all by myself?

We passed through several streets whose crooked old trees closed a tunnel over our heads. He drove as effortlessly as he walked, each move calculated to deliver exactly the effect he aimed for. I watched his hands on the wheel—the nails bitten down, strikingly flawed against his otherwise perfect looks—and realized that he probably had bad days too. Stress. Letdowns. Things that bothered him or didn't go his way.

Before I noticed, the houses had given way to woods. Smudged green, racing us on both sides of the road.

"Where are you taking me?"

A smile—slow and sure of its impact. For a moment or two, while my heart pounded its panic through my chest, I had mental flashes of what could happen next. Things this guy might do to me. Stuff I had seen only in movies.

He stepped on the brakes and swerved into the grass. I looked in the side mirror—the road was completely empty.

Was there any chance that pain hurt less if inflicted by someone beautiful?

A key turned, choking the engine off—

Then everything became absolutely quiet.

THE GRASSES SWAYED DREAMILY IN the morning wind. Tall. Thick. Reaching almost to my waist as he led me through them.

I was still embarrassed after what had happened by the car. He had held my door open, in disbelief that I refused to come out.

"No?" A glance at the trees behind him, then another one back at me. "What exactly do you think I'll do to you?"

As if what I thought mattered. We were alone, in the middle of nowhere.

"If you really suspect I'm a serial killer, you'd be much safer outside my car than in it."

I didn't find any of this funny. "Why did you bring me here?"

He walked over to the trunk, opened it, and came back with a blanket and a picnic basket.

"Breakfast. Do you believe me now?"

I slipped out of the seat. "Sorry, my imagination is too vivid."

"Vivid is good. But don't freeze up on me like that." He shut the door and, with the same assured smile, blocked my way until I leaned back against the car. "I don't cook for a woman just to drag her into the woods and torture her. Not against her will, anyway. So I need you to relax for me. Just relax. Can you do that?" His voice had the opposite effect on me. "I'm not going to do anything to you unless you want it."

There was something hypnotic about him, something that made any thought of resistance seem absurd. Even just hearing him talk about doing things to me made me want them, badly, whatever those things might be. And this scared me, more than any scenario I had imagined back in the car.

Our mystery destination turned out to be a field surrounded by trees, a place so secluded that the forest had to be crazy not to hide all its secrets there. The keeper—an old willow—dozed in the middle, crown drooping to the ground, long ago succumbed to gravity.

He parted the branches and spread the blanket in their scattered shade, waiting for me to sit down first. "This is my hideaway. I don't show it to anyone."

"Never?"

"Never. I come here when I want to be alone."

"Why make an exception now?"

His eyes traced every spot where the sun touched my skin. "Maybe it's a lucky aberration—"

He said the last word directly into my lips, opening them, tasting them—a deep, greedy, luscious kiss that could wipe out any instinct for self-preservation.

"What's wrong?" His lips still touched mine, even as he spoke.

"Nothing, I just . . . I felt dizzy for a second."

"Being with you gets me carried away. I should know better."

I don't want you to know better. "Maybe it's because I haven't slept much."

"Or because you haven't eaten much?"

He took out a bowl and a plate of matching porcelain, tore the plastic wrap, and placed them on the blanket. The bowl was full of blackberries and the plate had four crepes, rolled up in tubes.

"This should help." He lifted one of the crepes to my mouth.

I took a bite, trying not to make a mess all over his fingers. He fed me like a child, amused by it, by how I stole glances at him, my eyes already hooked:

Boots. Black and angular. Baring each crease of their thick leather. Dark jeans, loose on the hips despite the belt. His stomach, its muscles almost visible under the soft white fabric that covered them. And that T-shirt—the most striking one I had seen on a guy. It fit him perfectly, a cut so tight it forced you to imagine the rub of his skin against cotton when he moved, the V-neck deep and wide, exposing his chest all the way down the rib cage.

"Have these too." He pointed at the bowl of blackberries.

"I will, on one condition."

"Shoot."

"Tell me who you are. I don't know anything about you."

He leaned back on his elbows. "What do you want to know?"

"Where you live, what you do, what you like . . ."

His eyes got lost in the willow, narrowed by a smile (unless it was the sun falling into them). "How would knowing change anything?"

"Maybe it won't. But it will leave less to my vivid imagination."

He said nothing for a while, then reached for my hand.

"Come."

I followed him out into the field. After a few steps, he turned around and gave me a flower. It must have been caught in the green web surrounding it, hidden, invisible until now. The delicate petals were saturated with red, trembling at the slightest touch of air.

"I didn't realize poppies grew here in New Jersey."

"Nobody does. It's a secret."

At each step, as he opened the grasses to make way for us, I saw more poppies. All of them in wild bloom. Astonishing. Surreal.

Finally he stopped and turned to me:

"Knowing always changes everything. Be with me this way."

He remained still, mouth pressed to my ear, waiting. There was so much about him I wanted to know, and the way he evaded my questions promised nothing good. But at that moment, none of it mattered. All I could think of was his breath, fast and warm against my skin.

Be with me. . .

I kissed him—over the collarbone, where the shoulder curved into the neck. He absorbed my answer. Savored its meaning. Then poured over me as if I was about to slip away any second. I felt his kisses everywhere, through the clothes, as he kneeled on the grass and pulled me with him.

It was too sudden and I tried to slow him down. That didn't work, only electrified him more.

"Wait, I can't—"

"You can't what?" His hand went up my leg, I could feel its heat through the jeans. "Don't be afraid of me."

"I'm not."

"Then let me." He pulled the zipper open and my entire stomach turned, as if someone had twisted it inside me.

I caught his wrist. "Don't."

"Why not?"

"It's too soon. I've barely just met you."

His weight lifted off me. I thought he would be angry, but he took my hand and kissed it.

"Technically, you haven't met me yet. I'm Rhys. And you?"

"Thea. Your name means 'lynx' in my country."

"That explains why you're so afraid of me. And which country are you from, Thea?"

"Bulgaria."

His smile froze, as if he had sensed a predator approaching through the forest. "Of course you are."

"Why 'of course'?"

Just a shrug, no answer.

"How much do you know about Bulgaria?"

"Not as much as I should, apparently. But maybe we can fix this?"

He started asking about my home, the piano, and how I had ended up all the way in America. I skipped only the Elza part—the part I wasn't sure I would ever reveal to anyone. We lay like that for a long time, hidden inside the grasses, talking. Around us the forest was at peace, except for the occasional flap of a bird or swish of wind coiffing the branches. When I felt his hand on mine again, I realized I had been asleep for hours. The sun had started to set, and shadows of trees now stretched across the entire field.

"Why did you let me sleep all this time?"

"Because you needed it." He helped me stand up. "We have an entire evening ahead of us. Or at least I hope we do. If you don't have to be back yet, I'm taking you to dinner."

The restaurant was a small wooden house somewhere on the New Jersey shore. An old sign by the door had just one word: LOUISA's. There were four tables, all of them empty, and a woman at the counter (probably Louisa herself) grinned at him before flipping the Open sign to Closed, so that no one would disturb her special visitor.

"Have Barnaby play for us," he told her quietly on the way to our table.

A few moments later, she placed two dishes in front of us while Rhys poured the wine.

"Sorry, I forgot to ask. Do you like seafood?"

"Yes."

"It's their specialty. But that's not the reason I brought you here. Look—"

An old man had appeared through a side door and was heading to a table with all kinds of glasses on it. He poured water into all of them, then his wet fingers touched the rims. Hushed, delicate sounds filled the room with a haunting fragility I had never heard in music. Each tone drifted up and died in the air almost instantly, leaving behind a silence that made one's heart fold in on itself with aching.

"I knew you'd love this." His voice had turned soft again, the way he had spoken to me by the Greek vases. "Have you listened to water harp before?"

"No. It reminds me of Chopin."

"The melancholy Pole? Are you sure that's a good thing?"

Something about his tone bothered me, but before I could figure it out he had moved his chair closer to mine and was asking the man to play another piece.

By the time he finally dropped me off at Forbes, it was almost midnight.

"When can I see you tomorrow?" Quick and straightforward, like all his questions that day.

"I have class all morning, then I'm free until five."

"Meet me at one. Same place as today. "

He drove off without letting me say anything else. As the car muted its roar into the distance, I realized that his beautiful, strange name was still the only thing I knew about him.

CHAPTER 5

The Two Deaths of Orpheus

THE NEWS HAD hit Wylie's in-box first thing Friday morning, and he had e-mailed me right away: *Come by ASAP! Forget about school!*

But by the time I was done with class and saw his message, it was already noon. When I finally made it to his office, the itch to tell me had flushed his entire face.

"Where have you been? You've just won the lottery!"

Propped up on the floor next to him, an electric guitar made a ticking sound. It turned out to be a clock: quarter past twelve. Unless he kept our meeting short, I was going to be late for my date with Rhys at one.

"What lottery have I won?"

"The ultimate jackpot." He dragged the mystery out for a few extra seconds. "Carnegie."

A glossy booklet flew across his desk and I managed to catch it just in time. The cover had a picture of the most famous concert hall in America.

"Subscriber's guide to the current season. Page six. Bottom left."

I followed his instructions, too shocked to think. Page six had a calendar. One of its boxes was circled in red.

"November 23. You think you can swing it?"

"What exactly am I supposed to swing?"

Donnelly had warned me: Wylie loved to see his students succeed and was now pulling strings to get me into New York. But Carnegie, of all places?! She had called it "far from a sure thing." Apparently, when this man played puppeteer, things became sure in a matter of days.

"It's the annual 'Twenty Under Twenty' concert. Twenty students, all in their tragic teens—you get the idea. It used to be just Juilliard, but lately they've started to break the mold. This year the list includes two kids from Columbia, one from Stanford, and you."

And me. Once again, it had been decided—whether I felt up to it or not.

"What will I be playing?"

"On this I've got bad news and bad news. Which do you want first?"

It was a joke to him. I said nothing, just waited.

"The first bad news is, you don't get to choose this time. The concert is part of their European series, so the program has been set for months."

I looked at the circled box and the heading in it:

Tribute to Modern Europe: The Pulse of Spain

"And the other bad news?"

"Right. The other bad news is that the piece will kill you. Skinned, roasted, and eaten alive."

He handed me a few sheets of music. Dense clusters of notes raced down the front page.

"Have you played Albéniz?"

"No. I've heard of him, but I'm not too familiar with his music."

"Think of him as Chopin, born a Spaniard: took folk themes and turned them into salon music. Not my type of show. Still a genius, though, hands-down."

The title was a Spanish word, *Asturias,* and seemed to be part of something called *Suite Española.*

"Actually, it was your Chopin that sealed the deal."

"What does Chopin have to do with it?"

"One of the big kahunas came to your concert. Was absolutely blown away, especially by the études. Kept referring to you as 'The Maelstrom.' You know what that means?"

"A whirlpool?"

"Yes, but on steroids. A vortex so powerful it destroys everything in its way. Now this guy is convinced you're the only one who can manage the Albéniz. If it can be managed."

If.

For once, Wylie wasn't joking. He walked over to a stereo, pressed a button—and the music swept the room. Frightening. A flurry of sound. Faster than anything I might have imagined.

"All yours." He pulled the CD out and handed it to me. "Listen to it until it makes you sick. Drink it, eat it, breathe it—I don't care. But nail it!"

"What if it can't be nailed?"

"Then the failure would be mine as much as yours. And I don't fail." A quick pause, to make sure I understood. "Now let's agree on a strategy."

"Agree" simply meant that he laid it out for me while I listened:

I had to practice every day, from now until the concert. By midterm exams, I was expected to know the entire piece by heart because, as he put it, "all sheet music would fly out the window." Donnelly was going to be my first checkpoint, Wylie—my last. And for the next two months, starting immediately, I could forget about having a life.

By the time he let me go, I could also forget about meeting Rhys. The guitar-shaped clock was already striking the hour with a few deftly chosen chords, Wylie style: "One" by U2.

I RAN OUT OF THE music building, caught the next campus shuttle, and, miraculously, arrived at the Graduate College only ten minutes late. He was there but didn't kiss me. Didn't even smile. My apology for being late barely registered on his face.

"I thought you were blowing me off. Glad I was wrong."

"Why would I blow you off?"

"I don't know, that's the problem. You keep your distance and I still can't figure out why."

"Rhys, I've been looking forward to this all morning. But one of my professors held me up after class, and another one wants to meet at five."

"I'll have you back by then."

We started walking—first on Springdale, then left on Mercer where large houses lined the road. Farther down, a cluster of trees threw a thick shade over the sidewalk and he finally took my hand:

"Let's cut through here."

"Are we supposed to?"

"Are we . . . what?" He sounded distracted, preoccupied with something. "It's fine. Come."

I pulled my hand out of his but he continued walking.

"Thea, come on."

One of the first things I had learned at Princeton was that there were no fences, not even around private houses, yet this didn't mean you could pass through. Only two days earlier, while looking for Procter Hall on my way to work, I had mistakenly walked into the garden of Wyman House, the home used by the acting dean and his family. A woman had asked me sternly not to trespass and I had no intention of being scolded again.

"Are you coming or should I carry you?"

He smiled as he said this, waiting for me in the middle of a lawn surrounded by trees on all sides. All except one—the one across from us, where an enormous stone mansion dwarfed everything in sight. When I didn't answer, he headed back in my direction.

"What's wrong?"

"This is someone's house."

"So?"

"So . . . why can't we just take the road?"

My worry fascinated him, and the bad mood began to lift from his face. "It's fine, I promise. Just come with me. We're almost there."

I looked at the mansion: no signs of life. "Almost where?"

"Do I scare you this much?"

What could I say? I wasn't scared of him anymore. But maybe I should have been.

"How can I make you trust me?" He backed me up against the closest tree and leaned his hands on it, trapping me in between. "We don't have to go anywhere. In fact, the plan just changed—you win."

Winning against him was impossible. His lips were already down my neck and the words didn't matter.

"Rhys, wait . . ."

"Are you sure you want me to wait? I don't think you are." His hands left the bark and slipped under my clothes, over my bare skin—back, stomach, chest. "I don't want to wait either. I imagined you the entire night!"

I couldn't believe what I was doing. We were in someone's backyard, in plain daylight, a few feet from the sidewalk and all the cars passing on the road—but I didn't care.

When he began to unbutton my shirt, it sobered me up instantly. I pushed him away.

"What's the matter?"

"We can't do this here."

"Who cares where we are?"

"I do."

"No, you don't. We weren't here yesterday and you still acted this way. Why?"

"Because . . . you don't even know me."

"I don't need to know you." His stunning eyes were ruthless. "I need to *have* you."

He pressed me back against the tree with an insistence that he was unable—or unwilling—to control.

I doubted that my arguments would last much longer. "Then because I don't know you."

"You don't need to know me either. All you need to do is *let* me."

The words spilled over the madly pulsating artery on my neck. He pinned my arms up against the tree and slipped his hand into my jeans, without even bothering with the zipper.

"Rhys, stop." I said it with the last bit of voice left in my throat.

He froze while he still held me. I heard him take a breath. Then his body detached itself from mine and, without touching me or even looking in my direction, he walked away and disappeared through the trees.

WITH TWO WHOLE HOURS BEFORE my meeting with Giles, I went to the art library and tried to read. But the longer I stared at the book, the more upset I felt over what had just happened: the miserable walk back from Mercer Street, the anger at being left under that tree.

I don't need to know you.

And why would he? Getting to know every girl whose clothes he wanted to take off? A full-time job, for sure. Shortcuts, on the other hand, were exactly what sex was supposed to be: Casual. Anonymous. Easy. He was probably used to getting girls naked just by smiling at them, let alone inviting them on fancy car rides or picnics in the forest. So if I wasn't willing to reciprocate the extra effort, why waste any more time on me?

I left the library and went into the art museum for one last look at the vase in case Giles decided to bring it up again. Or at least so I told myself, while in fact part of me still missed Rhys. Not him exactly—the fantasy of him. Of our few moments by the Greek vases, when he had spoken to me in riddles about love.

The place turned out to be the opposite of what I remembered: no magic, no ghosts, just an unremarkable room with a few cluttered cabinets. Inside, each piece had a brief description. The entry next to the Orpheus vase read: *Psykter, Athens, cir. 500 B.C. [Acq. 1995].*

It took me a beat to process what I had just read—the brackets, the abbreviated word inside them—and to realize that the only trace of Elza I had discovered so far wasn't a trace at all. Giles was wrong. She couldn't possibly have written about the same vase. Either his age or the long stream of students had caught up with him, mixing up his recollections to produce the incoherent story he had thrown my way.

Princeton had acquired the vase in 1995. And by then, my sister was already dead.

"MISS SLAVIN, IF MEMORY SERVES me right, there is a creature similar to the maenad in the legends of your country?"

The question flew out at me as soon as I walked into Giles's office, before I had a chance to sit down.

"Yes, *samodiva*. In Bulgarian, *sam* means 'alone' and *diva* means 'wild.'"

"How interesting . . . a *wildalone*." The word rolled off his tongue so naturally. "Untamed and all by herself. Like the maenad on a certain vase."

We were back to my unforgivable error: writing the paper in the plural. It had offended him deeply, and I still didn't know why.

"In our folk tales, the *samodivi* never come out alone. They dance together in the forest."

"As do the maenads. Their name means 'raving ones.' And in your typical myth that's exactly what they are: a retinue of savage women, intoxicated by Dionysus in the frenzy of his rituals."

He opened one of the books on his desk and, oddly, didn't need to flip through it to find what he wanted:

> *"I have seen those frantic women, who dart in frenzy from this land with bare feet . . . seeking to gratify their lusts amid the woods, by wine and music maddened . . . with snakes that lick their cheeks. Crowns they wore of ivy or of oak or blossoming* convolvulus. *One plunged her wand into the earth and there the god sent up a spring of wine."*

He closed the book.

"Familiar?" His eyes lit up with a strange excitement. "*Bacchae* by Euripides, won him first prize at the drama festival in Athens. An entire tragedy about the maenads. Or, in this case, *bacchantes,* as they were known in Rome."

"I am sorry, but I haven't read it."

"Well, I assumed as much. Yet I still thought it might ring close to home."

He studied me for another moment, until it became clear that a vague nod was the only response he was going to get.

"Professor Giles, you wanted to show me something."

"Yes, I did." He hesitated, as if no longer sure it was worth the effort. "How well acquainted are you with the myth of Orpheus?"

"Other than what I wrote in my paper?"

"Everyone knows that part—his descent into the Underworld and the tragic mayhem that follows. I am more interested in the rest. In his life *before* he met Eurydice."

My brain struggled for details, but to my own embarrassment retrieved very little: "He was born in Thrace, to the Muse of poetry, Calliope. When Apollo gave him a lyre, the boy began to turn his poems into songs."

"Yes, yes, the music and all. But more to the point, Orpheus spent many years in the mystery schools of Egypt. Upon his return to Greece, he became involved in the cults of Dionysus."

"Cults?"

"Cults, rituals, mysteries, orgies—I have heard the entire thesaurus. Most of the negative labels were invented by the Roman Church, the orgiastic one being a particular favorite."

"Why would the Church invent orgies?"

"Funny, isn't it? There was sex, of course—after all, Dionysus is the god of nature's forces and of anything that produces life. Yet sex for its own sake, especially in its . . . well, its less common variations, was never a defining part of the rituals. Often they involved no sex at all."

"I don't follow. The Church just filled the gap with made-up stories?"

"Filling gaps was not the intent, I'm afraid. Quite the opposite. You have to understand, there was a time when the Dionysian religion was as widespread as the Christian one, a pagan rival that had to be quashed quickly. And proclaiming the Greek rituals a drunken orgy was the surest death knell. Even more ironic is that it became a case of the lamb devouring the sheep, since Christianity had borrowed so much from the Greeks."

"From their myths?"

"Especially from the myths. Dionysus, for one, is thought to be an archetype of Christ: both died in an act of sacrifice and were reborn, not to mention having the power to heal and to distill wine out of water. As for Orpheus, he is a Christian precursor too—of John the Baptist. John spread the teachings of Christ much as Orpheus spread the Dionysian mysteries. They both developed ideologies based on ascetic living and practiced rituals of purification with water—to the Greeks it was *kathairein*, or catharsis, to the Christians it is baptism. But my favorite analogy, one I am sure you can appreciate, is that John was beheaded at the request of an angry woman."

"Salome?" I had seen an opera about her. The princess who demanded John's head when the young prophet didn't return her love.

"Salome, yes, the most consummate witch of all. Or *wildalone*, as you might call her. Used her beauty as a weapon to get his head severed. After watching her dance, the king just couldn't say no."

I pretended not to notice the curiosity with which he looked at me as he said this.

"Anyway, the Christian appropriations from the Greeks are a topic for a different, and potentially endless, conversation. The point is, Dionysus was much more than a god of wine and sex. His rituals were part of a complex philosophy, a series of mystical initiations whose goal was to achieve rebirth. A spiritual rebirth, certainly. But also a physical one."

"How exactly did they do it?"

"This is one of the greatest enigmas of the ancient world. Hence the term 'mysteries.' The culmination of them all—the Mystery at Eleusis—lasted nine days and was arguably the most profound experience known to the Greeks. Unfortunately, everyone initiated into it was sworn to secrecy. And the secret remains untouched to this day."

He gave me that expectant look again, as if I had the uncanny ability to get his Greek mysteries decoded.

"Miss Slavin, I don't suppose you can think of a circumstance in which one of these creatures, one of your . . . wildalones . . . might decide to venture out on her own?"

My wildalones. I shook my head.

"Strange that you can't, because your sister described it so vividly. She developed her own—rather colorful, if I may say—version of the Orphic myth. I still have no idea how she came up with it. Perhaps growing up in those lands, on top of millennia of history, fuels the imagination in ways we, Western scholars, can only envy. But the fact remains: I hadn't seen anything comparable until then. And I haven't since."

"What was so unique about it?"

"Everything. How would you react to the proposition that before Orpheus went into the Underworld, long before he even met Eurydice, he was already dead?"

I thought I had misunderstood. "You mean his soul?"

"No, really dead. In the most common, physical sense of the word."

"I don't see how it is possible."

"You don't, not yet. But now imagine this: a young man dies, probably an accident—even the most brilliant musician is not immune from death. Everyone mourns him. Especially women, all the women who were charmed by his music but never managed to steal his heart. Then out of nowhere, in the middle of the wake, a mystifying rumor trickles out—rumor of a ritual. Secret ritual. Dangerous. Dark. One that would plunge you straight into the madness of Dionysus. If you only dare, you can achieve the two things you desire most: bring that man back from death and make him forever yours. All this, of course, at a price—your own life."

I stared at Giles. He sounded a bit delusional. Maybe one had to be, in order to climb so high up the academic pyramid? But I was curious about the rituals, so I decided to play along. "If you die, how is the man forever yours?"

"Giving up your human life doesn't mean you die. On the contrary, you are reborn as a maenad—immortal, possessed by the god. According to your sister, someone loved Orpheus enough to go through the ritual for him."

"Eurydice?"

"No, Eurydice comes much later. This woman is different and doesn't have a name—your anonymous wildalone. She is angry. Broken. Orpheus has never loved her, and never will."

"But you said she could have him forever."

"Aha! Here we come to the core of things: How do you own someone? And not just own them, but own them against their will. Any guesses?"

I had none. Couldn't even imagine it—owning or being owned.

"It all goes back to that same ritual. The woman becomes a maenad. And the man, he . . . he wakes up from death to find himself a creature of a very different kind. You can think of him as a demon, although not exactly in the traditional sense. Our modern concept of the demonic dates back to medieval times, when Christian scriptures linked the term to malevolent spirits. The Greeks, on the other hand, believed in a being known as *daemon*."

He wrote it down and circled the diphthong.

"Is there a difference? I mean, other than the extra letter?"

"They are like black and white. The Greek daemon was a benevolent creature, halfway between man and god. Your sister described him as a version of Dionysus: sensual, temperamental, prone to madness and even violence. In typical Dionysian fashion, he also had absolute power over nature and an unmatched gift for the arts. Music, especially. Which would explain why, through the rest of his time on earth, Orpheus achieved unsurpassed mastery of the lyre. The only problem is"—here Giles turned to a nearby projector and flipped the power switch—"even a daemon must pay a price for immortality."

A scene from a vase emerged on the opposite wall. It resembled the one from my *psykter*: a vicious maenad attacking a weak musician. But then I began to realize that this was a different kind of attack. She was forcing her mouth on his, pressing his hand over her bare breasts.

"Are they . . ." I wasn't sure that saying "sex" out loud was a good idea. "It looks like the maenad is raping him."

"Because that's exactly what she is doing. The ritual operates as a marriage vow, binding the daemon to the maenad forever. In essence, he has a debt to repay—since she gave up her human life to save him. And now every month, on the full moon, he must engage in the sexual rites of Dionysus with her. The two have become eternal lovers, whether the daemon likes it or not."

"What if he breaks the vow?"

"Here lies the irony, you see. Nothing in this world can do physical harm to him, with one exception: he is at the mercy of a single woman, a woman he probably will never love. If he breaks the vow, she will tear him to pieces. The Greeks called this *sparagmos,* and I used to share the majority view that such acts of violence were only symbolic, enacted as theater in the dramatic spirit of the rituals. Now, having read your sister's paper, I am not so sure anymore."

He switched the projector off, returning the wall to its varnished white.

"How do you know there is truth to all this?"

"I don't." The regret in his voice confirmed why he had been so eager to assign the vase to me: Who else, if not Elza's sister, to bring him the missing answers? "Nothing would thrill me more than to find proof—any proof— that what she wrote was actual historic fact. Yet for now I must dismiss it as mere speculation. Provocative, compelling—sure. But still nothing more than an afflicted girl's fantasy."

"Afflicted . . . you mean mentally ill?"

"Maybe not according to strict medical definitions. Unfortunately, however, I can't rule it out completely."

The thought that something had been wrong with Elza's mind sapped me of any interest in the Dionysian rituals.

"Professor Giles, I don't think my sister wrote this paper."

"No? Why not?"

"Because Princeton bought the vase in 1995. It wasn't even here when Elza was attending."

He savored the challenge. "You have a rare inquisitive mind, Miss Slavin. But I am sorry to tell you that the vase *was* here in 1992. It had been loaned to our museum by a Greek foundation, and your sister's paper became the reason I eventually lobbied the school to acquire the piece. We obtained funds quickly, although the logistics took years."

Without saying anything else, he took a few typewritten pages out of a drawer. The edges were dark with age.

"This is what I wanted to show you. I must say, I never expected it to see the light of day again."

I noticed Elza's name printed at the top, and had to fight the urge to grab the sheets from him.

"She writes very convincingly, you will see for yourself. But when I first read it, I thought it was better fitted for a creative writing class. Not so much art historical analysis, more of a dreamy garble. A recounting of make-believe cult practices."

Obviously, he had changed his mind—enough to save the dreamy garble for fifteen years.

"Then I looked at the back, at the copied illustrations. And the Dionysian practices were all there, exactly as she had described them. Everything already painted on the vases, over twenty centuries ago!"

He started to leaf through, pointing at each image.

"The mysteries of Dionysus—the drinking, the ecstatic frenzy . . . A maenad dancing . . . A maenad with Dionysus, in a sexual embrace . . . Maenads dismembering some sort of wildcat . . . And take a look at this—"

He flipped back to the first page. It started with a single sentence, separated from the rest:

I AM THE MAENAD AND THE DAEMΩN,
THE BEGINNING AND THE END

"Can you guess what this is?"

"It sounds like a quote."

"The quote of all quotes. I suppose you haven't read the Bible?"

"No. My parents grew up under Communism and we were not very religious."

"*I am the Alpha and the Omega, the beginning and the end.* Christ said it in the final book of the New Testament, the Book of Revelation. These are the first and last letters of the Greek alphabet. They have become a Christian symbol, a code for the belief that only through God can one achieve immortality."

"Just like in the Greek rituals?"

"More so than you think. A similar statement has been attributed to Dionysus, so I am not surprised to see it in a Greek Art paper. The better question is, why did your sister replace Alpha and Omega with 'maenad' and 'daemon'? It has to do with the ritual, obviously, but I can't pinpoint the exact link. It must be a pun of some sort. A riddle."

And now he, in turn, was passing that riddle on to me.

"What happens in the rest of the paper?"

"It flows beautifully. All the way to its tragic end."

"The death of Orpheus?"

"Not just a death. A suicide. The daemon breaks his vow, so that the maenad will kill him. Because what is immortality without happiness?" He let the question sink in, as if expecting it to haunt me even after all his other questions were gone. "When we humans lose a love, we wait for time to dull out the pain. And time obliges—they don't call it 'healer of all wounds' for nothing. But a daemon can never heal. In eternity, time simply doesn't exist."

It was a while before there was another sound in the room—he was getting up and his chair screeched against the floor. I took this as a sign that we were done and hurried to get up too.

"Enjoy the journey back. Back home, and back through time." He smiled and handed me the paper. "It is truly a mysterious part of the world, yours."

I asked if I could photocopy the pages, but he had already done it.

"You can keep the original. I figured you might want it in case you . . . for its sentimental value."

Before I could thank him, a phone rang on his desk and I saw all signs of emotion wash off his face as he reached to answer it.

I LEFT THE ART BUILDING in a daze, with the paper tucked inside my bag like a secret heirloom. But as soon as I reached Forbes and started reading, I realized that this was not the kind of heirloom I wanted.

THE TWO DEATHS OF ORPHEUS

by Elza Slavin

I had known her name for several months now. She had typed it herself, probably the way we all type our names: by habit, without thinking. Yet seeing it felt unsettling, wrong, as if I had put my own name on a school paper and then someone had erased me from the page, replacing me with her:

Elza.

Giles was right about her writing—powerful, and somehow dreamy. It engulfed you in a world of myths and visions and, before you noticed, it had carried you back into the bizarre darkness of its universe.

A universe permeated by death, intoxicated with it. I saw the madness of nocturnal rituals where people drank, danced, and copulated under a strangely detached moon. Among them was a young musician. Lost in sadness. Haunted by his doom. Ready to die—wanting to die—just like everybody else around him. In that world, death seemed to be the answer to everything. Death as a cure. As the ultimate ecstasy. A long-awaited end, then a rebirth. And above all, death as a sacrifice that would enable love to last forever.

From beginning to end, the paper was exactly as Giles had said. Except one thing: it didn't sound like a theory at all. Dreamy as her writing was, I knew—and this intuitive certainty frightened me—that what Elza had put down on those pages hadn't been a theory, at least not to her. She had written it with a chilling confidence, the way a surgeon dips the scalpel for an incision through the skin. And the suicide of Orpheus, each gory detail, was described as if she had been there and witnessed it.

All this, of course, had fascinated our art professor. To him it was just scholarship—brilliant, but still only an academic exercise creating fiction out of ancient pottery. To me, it was a glimpse into the madness of my sister. Whether that madness fit within strict medical definitions or not, Elza had died at Princeton. Maybe, by the time she wrote that paper, she had already *wanted* to die. Now I was no longer sure that these pages (an afflicted girl's fantasy, as Giles had called them) didn't have something to do with it.

And what if they did? A paper in itself proved nothing. It offered no leads I could follow, no insights into her life or who might have ended it.

None, except the vaguely disturbing hope that maybe the past wasn't buried as deeply as everyone said it was.

I opened the window. All the way—the room needed air. Then I slipped the paper among the Chopin scores at the bottom of my suitcase and turned off the light.

In darkness, places begin to feel alike. I remembered another dark room, not too long ago, where a guy had whispered to me before I even knew who he was, telling me that I should write about Orpheus. And something else, the first thing he had ever said to me: *It must be a maenad, back there.*

The singular.

How had he known?

I sneaked under the covers, curled into a ball, and tried to summon sleep under my burning eyelids.

CHAPTER 6

The Devil Himself

THE SCHUBERT RECITAL with Ben would have been a magical evening (tiny church off campus; violin music by candlelight) if I had managed to stay focused on where I was and not think about Rhys.

Almost a week had passed since the incident on Mercer Street, and I never heard from him. It was better this way—I had nothing to say to someone who would drop me without a word simply because I refused to have sex in public. He probably had nothing to say to me either. The kind of girl who could keep up with him was not a shy freshman from Bulgaria, and he must have figured it out right there, under those trees.

Still, I couldn't let go. Blaming him was the easy part. Yet what if it was my fault too? I felt insecure—not only with him, but in America. Expecting disaster at every step. Threatened by anything unknown, unfamiliar, foreign. Rhys was the opposite: nothing seemed to intimidate him. He didn't look much older than the students at Princeton, but acted older. Late twenties, maybe. A man, not a boy. A man who knew what he wanted and went for it, confident that he would get his way.

"Hey, are you all right?" Ben was waving at me, looking worried.

I became aware of the noise, hands clapping from all sides. The concert had ended, even the last encore, and I hadn't noticed any of it.

We headed for the Street. By the time we arrived, it was close to eleven and the insanity had started. Hundreds of students, most of them already drunk, zigzagged in groups back and forth, from one club to the next. Rita texted me from Colonial and we found her in the crowd—everyone partying, shouting, spilling beer from disposable cups. Ben and I were too dressed up for the place, but nobody seemed to care what anyone else did or looked like, so we all danced for a while until Rita grabbed my hand.

"Oh my God, Tesh, he's gorgeous!"

"Who?" I thought she was trying to sell me on the advantages of dating Ben.

"There's a guy who has been staring at you for the last five minutes. I bet it's your stalker! Don't turn, though, he'll see it."

I didn't need to turn—the stalker hadn't left my thoughts all night.

"He came in with the swimmers, but I doubt he's on the team. I've seen them compete a few times, and I definitely would have remembered him." She kept looking over my shoulder, across the room. "I'm surprised this guy would go to a Chopin concert, actually. He looks more like the lead of some Euro rock band. And, Tesh, much as I do hope you get to meet him this time, I think it's too early for you to be mixing with the Ivy crowd."

"Why Ivy?"

"The swimmers practically run that club. No one is allowed into their clique, and as far as dating goes—good luck counting on anything serious, no matter how sexy or cool you are. They commit only to the team."

"If that's the case, then why are you worried about me mixing with them?"

"Because I know you like this guy. And from what I've heard, their entire gang is not to be trusted."

"You never think anyone is to be trusted."

"Exactly. Most of the time, unfortunately, I turn out to be right."

"Wouldn't you rather trust people and turn out to be wrong?"

It was a reminder of how different Rita and I were. Although born in Hungary, she had grown up in America, where, from what I could tell, the smart thing to do was protect yourself against emotional impact from others. In my culture, we gave the benefit of the doubt until proven wrong.

"Tesh, I'm serious. There's nothing wrong with playing it safe."

"Actually, there is. I've been forced to play it safe all my life. Shouldn't everyone be entitled to a mistake or two at some point?"

She shook her head. "Your mistake just left, by the way. Too bad."

I turned around, only to see him walk out the door. *That was it? He wouldn't even come to say hi?*

The next half hour drifted through me without an imprint—I smiled, talked, danced, all as if an external force prompted my body to keep moving. When I headed out long before anybody else, Rita and Ben looked worried; he even offered to take me back to Forbes. I said I'd catch the campus shuttle, even though I had no intention of doing so. What I needed was a long, solitary walk.

I also wanted to call my parents and tell them about Carnegie. I had been putting it off all week, waiting to be in a better mood so that nothing would sour the moment of giving them the news. Now I simply sat down on one of the many campus benches and made the call.

It was 7:00 A.M. in Bulgaria. Dad had been up for a while, but my mother sounded sleepy.

"Huh? New York . . . what about it?"

"I'll be playing there in November, Mom. Carnegie Hall! Can you imagine?"

There was no answer—she probably thought she was still dreaming. I wished I could see her face, the change on it as the news sank in. But this was the curse of the telephone: I would never know.

Finally, Dad's voice came through from the second handset: "Thea, baby, that's terrific! Tell us everything! When? How?"

I gave them the details: Albéniz, Wylie, the crazy intensity of it all. On the other end there was silence again.

"Mom? Dad? Are you guys all right?"

Yes, of course they were. So excited. And proud of me. And happy. Then came the sentence that broke my heart:

"You must promise to take a lot of pictures."

There was no need to explain to one another how we felt at that moment. How they would sit quietly at home on the night of my big piano triumph, or how, in the few seconds of applause, I would look from the Carnegie stage to see just an empty hall, a world in which I knew and loved no one.

In all the years of hard work, of me practicing endlessly and both my parents taking extra shifts to pay for piano lessons and music camps and recording studios and contest fees, none of us had seen this coming. That one day I would live in America. That the flight from home and a week's hotel stay in New York would cost more than their annual salary. More than I could earn in the dining hall the entire freshman year.

I hung up the phone feeling so sad I almost went back to Colonial. But that would have accomplished nothing (except maybe elicit more worried looks from my friends), so I headed to Forbes instead—down bleak alleys, through courtyards stirred only now and then by an insect crashing into a wall lantern or the blink of a window turning black. The campus had sunk into the languor of an early-October night, a crease between seasons when the dense heat of summer still smolders inside stone and bark, but less so with each day, weakened by shivers from the approaching fall.

Finally, Forbes glimmered in the distance. On a Thursday night, when everyone went partying, the dorm had the vibe of a sinking ship: abandoned yet still brightly lit, dragged down by its own silence. I walked along the empty corridors to my room, took my key out, and slipped it in the lock—

"I was worried you might not be coming back alone." A hand reached and pushed the door open for me.

"Rhys? I don't appreciate the scare . . ." Only a second ago, I could have sworn the hallway was deserted. "Who told you where I live?"

"Serial killers have tricks. Blackmail. Bribery." He saw that his old joke was creeping me out again. "Or, in this case, extortion of Forbes staff. Which was a challenge, given that I still don't know almost anything about you."

"And so what if you don't? You said you didn't need to know me, right?"

"I didn't mean it that way."

"What other way is there?"

"Just . . . wanting someone. Without the kind of background checks you ran on me earlier—who I am, what I do, where I live."

"Well, yes, but I can't go out with a guy unless I know whether he—"

"Whether he'll admit he screwed up? I acted like an ass back there. But it won't happen again, I promise."

"What, you needing to 'have me'?"

"No. Me leaving you by yourself."

Something about his promise scared me. I realized how quickly I was starting to rely on another promise, one he hadn't even implied: that he would continue to be in my life.

"By the way, speaking of background checks—what was that girl telling you about me?"

"Which girl?"

"Your girlfriend at the club tonight. She was checking me out and clearly giving you some savvy advice. To stay away from me, I'm guessing?"

"Why? Is this what I should do?"

"You should do only what you want, not what anyone else says. Including me." Somehow, his smile continued to imply the opposite. "So the question is: Do you want to stay away from me or not?"

"I don't. But I also don't understand why you left Colonial as if we didn't know each other."

"I hate public displays. Besides, it looked like you had a date."

"You mean my friend Ben?"

"He seemed a bit too smitten for a friend. I hope you're not planning on going out with him again."

"I wasn't 'out with him.' He lives here in Forbes and we—"

"There is no 'we,' Thea. I'm not going to share you."

"Share me? Rhys, what are you even saying?"

"That I want you as my girl. And I absolutely mean it." He kissed me, blocking any attempt to argue. "Now, if you still have energy left, I'd very much like to take you somewhere."

His girl. I tried to think clearly—about Rita's warning, and the better question of why I would leave with him, in the middle of the night, to go to one more party or whatever else he had in mind—but he leaned over my ear and whispered:

"I'll behave this time. Come with me."

THE GOLF COURSE LOOKED AS it always had—dark, vast, and solemn. I had already walked out there at night, when I went to play in Procter Hall. But it wasn't until we vanished deep into its hills that I sensed the difference: there was no moon this time. The grass rose and fell in invisible curves under our feet. The sounds of creatures had multiplied from all sides. And each tree appeared distant, then suddenly turned up next to us—a deformed giant, locked against the unending black of sky.

I had no idea where he was taking me, but I knew what would happen once we arrived there. Awkward scenarios ran through my mind, about whether—or how and when—to tell him that I hadn't had sex before. Turning it down in high school had been easy, especially after seeing a few of my girlfriends get their hearts broken when they wouldn't wait for the right guy. Now I wished I had just done it, with one of the nervous boys who swore their eternal love to me back then. It would have made things with Rhys much easier. No strained moments. No need for explanations.

Mercer Street was fully dark. There were no streetlamps, only houses whose dim light faded long before it reached the sidewalk. He led me in silence, absorbed in his own thoughts.

I was a mess. How did other girls do it? I had been to a few parties at Princeton, enough to know that in college sex wasn't a big deal—after a few beers, there was hardly anything people didn't do in front of everyone. It happened casually, with rehearsed nonchalance, as if a single glance and a quick *cheers!* was all it took to agree on the rest. And "the rest" was an even bigger mystery. Somehow, you were supposed to not care. To detach your body from any source of complications (the mind, the heart), and walk away afterward as if nothing had happened.

We reached a cluster of trees—the same trees under which he had left me the last time—and came out on the lawn. There was no light in the mansion. No trace of moon or stars; clouds had wiped out the entire sky. I could barely see his face but I felt his breath, the question in it.

"Will you come where I want to take you?"

The night had hushed around us, not a trace of wind left.

"Yes."

He headed straight for the mansion. Several stairs separated the lawn from the French doors that looked out over it. Before we had even reached the top stair, before his hand had found the unlocked handle—perfectly sure of its location in the dark—and opened the glass frame to let me in, I already knew. I knew where he was taking me now, where he had wanted to take me before, and why my stubborn refusal to walk through the lawn had amused him earlier.

This was his house.

.

"YOU SAID YOU WANTED TO know where I live. So here you are, in the den of your lynx."

I had said it, yes. But now the "den" made me feel out of place—Cinderella at the ball, arrived way past midnight.

He flipped a switch. Several lights shimmered along the wall, creating an illusion that candles were being lit all around us. I heard a noise and instinctively squeezed his hand: a figure had appeared under the arched entryway. Dark, well-fitted jacket. The shirt strikingly white, as if a black light had been turned on somewhere.

"Ferry! Why are you up this late, my friend?" Rhys took a few steps in the man's direction, without letting go of my hand.

"I was under the impression that the master had returned to New York and would not be expected back in Pebbles for a while."

"Well, I've decided not to leave—now or anytime soon." He looked at me and smiled. "Thea, meet Ferguson, the man behind the scenes who runs this household. Ferry is practically family, but he insists on calling himself our 'butler.' Brings back Europe for him, I guess. So we indulge his fetish for old traditions."

"Pleased to meet you, sir." I had no idea how to address a butler, especially one in his seventies who looked and spoke as if he belonged in a Victorian novel.

"Likewise, miss." His eyes lingered on my face—a subtle curiosity, or an attempt to assess how long the attention of a guy like Rhys could stay focused on someone like me. "Will the master be requiring anything?"

"No, not tonight. Thea?"

I looked at Rhys, unsure what he was asking. "I don't need anything, thank you."

"We're all set then, Ferry. Go get some rest."

When the man left, I finally looked around. There wasn't a hint of the heavy dark wood that filled such mansions in movies and magazines. A white marble floor made everything appear weightless, floating on air, all the way to a fireplace carved from the same stone (or maybe the floor had risen in a wave and splashed against the wall). In the corners facing it, lush palm leaves balanced their fans over Chinese ceramic pots, while in the middle an Oriental carpet burst its geometric patterns of red, green, black, blue. A sofa and two armchairs completed the setup, all in a leather whose white rivaled that of the walls. But by far the most striking objects in the room were two black grand pianos, placed opposite each other across from the windows.

"Who plays on the second one?"

"The devil himself. We often hold competitions." He smiled, not realizing how believable that sounded. "Play something for me."

"No, you play for me this time." He had already heard me once, it was my turn to listen. "We'll consider it payback."

"You mean *advance*?"

That wasn't at all what I meant, but maybe Alexander Hall mattered less to him than it did to me.

"All right, give me your favorite." He walked over to the piano on the left and sat down, waiting for me to choose, as if he could play anything on the spot, without scores.

"I think you know my taste."

"Your taste . . . the moody Pole? Come on, does it have to be him?"

"Why not?"

"He's too saccharine." A few measures from a polonaise trickled from the keyboard. "So intent on melting you. It can get unbearable."

I remembered him making a similar comment that night at Louisa's, and it unsettled me. Had I been wrong about him? My quick assumption that he understood Chopin's music (and, by extension, everything else) the same way I did now seemed just a trick of my homesick imagination.

"This one's better—" He started a mazurka, only to cut it off abruptly. "Except it gets so sugary, I just have to stop right there." One look at my face, though, and he knew he had gone too far. "Fine, the moody Pole it is!"

This time he really began playing. Sounds filled the room—flawless, merciless in their beauty: the Fantaisie-Impromptu in C-sharp Minor, one of Chopin's most virtuosic works. Incredibly fast at times. Heartbreakingly lyrical at others. Rhys had called this music saccharine, yet for a moment even he seemed swept by it. There was nothing sweet, or condescending, in the way he played. The piece poured out of him as if he was improvising on the spot, charging each note with as much intensity as it could possibly carry.

I do play. And your Chopin is stunning. It had sounded so casual when he said it; as if, compared to me, he could barely hold a tune. Now he was turning out to be the far more accomplished pianist. We were a few years apart, granted. But age probably had nothing to do with it. He appeared to have a rare natural talent. An utter ease with the instrument that I had never heard, not even on recordings.

Once again, the questions raided my mind. Who was he? Old Princeton money, of the kind Americans considered aristocracy? A musical prodigy? Both? Or just a young, rich, eccentric genius who had decided to withdraw from the world, on the outskirts of this famously secluded campus?

Intimidated and shaken by all this, I absorbed each sound while he played. Yet in every single one, I also felt a sting from how, only moments earlier, he had dismissed this very music—the music that had brought me to him.

Finally, his fingers ended their self-indulgent stroll above the keys. The last notes fell over the piano and dissipated, lost in the space between me and this guy whose presence, for the first time, felt irreversibly foreign. I still didn't know if he was a student at Princeton, had been in the past, or had found some other access to the only local party scene—the eating clubs. Either way, I was getting my first taste of the Ivy crowd: impudent, at times arrogant, too good even for its own privileged surroundings. It was a world I hadn't expected to ever be allowed into, let alone this quickly. And part of it already enticed me. The ease with which Rhys did everything. His confidence. Even the way he mocked Chopin, so different from the way people mocked things they didn't understand. He knew Chopin's music intimately and played it better than anyone, including me. What more could I possibly want?

I tried to smile. To thank him politely. But my voice came to me through the silence—distant, as if belonging to someone else—telling him that his Chopin was stunning, then asking him to take me home.

THE NEXT DAY I RECEIVED both things the Dean's Office had promised me. First: a copy of Elza's transcript. Greek Art. A seminar on Pompeii. Advanced Composition. Methods of Modern Music. Not exactly a surprise, with her two passions being music and archaeology.

The second thing was a call from the counseling center, offering me an appointment that same afternoon.

"I am really glad you decided to come in, Thea." A warm handshake, brief and professional. "Jane Pratt. Sorry, McCosh is a bit of a mess these days. Was it easy to find us?"

I figured she was referring to the elevators, temporarily shut down for maintenance. "The receptionist was very helpful, even gave me a map."

"Right, right . . . Please, take a seat." She pointed to an armchair in the middle of the room, choosing for herself the couch across from it. "This is your first time, I take it?"

"Luckily I haven't been sick at Princeton yet, so no reason for health center visits."

"I didn't mean McCosh. I meant whether you've been in"—her eyes narrowed in a sudden web of lines, adding at least a decade to a face whose deli-cate, densely freckled skin had made her look no more than thirty, barely out of medical school—"in therapy before."

"Me? No, I haven't."

We observed each other in silence. I wasn't trying to come across as hostile, but the calculated tact with which she had said the word *therapy*, and even the word itself, irritated me.

"Dr. Pratt, the Dean's Office asked me to see you for an informal hand-shake, whatever that means. So, to be honest, I didn't realize this would be a therapy session. Or that I needed one."

"No one is saying you need therapy. Needing it and being able to benefit from it are very different things. We can all benefit from therapy, if it's done correctly."

Sure, whatever. This was probably the usual spiel, to put my mind at ease while she "diagnosed" a long list of things I never knew were wrong with me.

"It won't take more than an hour. Just give it a try."

"Try what exactly? Psychiatric tests?"

"No, no." She shook her head, a notch too eagerly. "We'll talk about what happened in the past and how it might—or whether it even should—impact your life here."

"I assume by 'it' you mean my sister's death?"

Of course she did. Like my Greek Art professor (and probably many other people I would meet at school), she had a hard time perceiving me as a separate person, outside the Elza context. Somehow, my behavior was expected to bear the mark of a tragedy that had taken place while I was still an infant. And for the first time, I caught myself thinking that maybe my parents were right. Maybe coming to Princeton had been a mistake.

"Thea, we seem to have started off on the wrong foot. Why all this resis-tance?"

"Where I'm from, nobody goes to a therapist. People are offended by the idea of having to hire a stranger to listen to their problems. That's what family and friends are for."

"Except there is a science to how we feel, a complex chain of cause and effect that your friends and family might be unaware of."

"They know the most important thing: how my mind and heart work."

"I wouldn't mind knowing that, too." She smiled, sensing the first crack in the ice. "So, can I try? Just five minutes. And then if you still want to leave, I won't insist, I promise."

She clasped her hands over her knees—bony hands, freckled, no rings. No other jewelry or makeup either. Gray pantsuit, a size too big. And sleek ash-blond hair, cut safely to just above shoulder length. It was as if she had wanted to be invisible. To merge with the room whose neutral, almost insultingly run-of-the-mill decor was probably a therapy device in itself.

"All right. Let's start with your home."

"What about it?"

"How many windows does it have?"

I did a mental run through our house in Sofia. "Seven."

"Are you sure?"

I pretended to do another count. On the wall behind her, a framed print in the neurotic color blotches of Cézanne showed a still life with five pieces of fruit: three apples, a lemon, and a quince. "Yes, I'm sure. Seven windows."

"And when you counted them just now, were you inside or outside the house?"

"Inside . . . Why?"

"Good, that's all I needed to know. Now let's see if I'll be way off on the backstory." She unclasped her hands and leaned forward, as if to reassure not so much me as herself. "You grew up as an only child, yes? Your parents never told you about Elza. Kept her belongings locked away in the house, perhaps in a room to which you gained access by accident—you were what, five or six years old?—and that's where you found her piano. It wasn't until much later, probably around the time you decided to come to America, that the family secret finally surfaced. And she began to haunt you. Strange episodes. Creepy, even. At times you could almost feel her physical presence like a ghost. Which made Princeton the natural choice for you. The *only* choice, really, if you were to ever be free of her. By the way, how am I doing so far?"

I was stunned. For a moment, even the apples of Cézanne seemed to shudder in shock, about to roll out of the frame and topple to the floor.

"I take your silence as a sign that I was right, at least about some of it?"

"Yes. About all of it, actually, but . . . how did you figure these things out?"

"That's my job, Thea. The technical term is 'replacement child syndrome.' It gives a very accurate prediction of how a child's behavior patterns will change following an older sibling's death. Even Sigmund Freud himself—although not strictly a replacement child, since he was the firstborn—suffered from similar symptoms after the death of his younger brother Julius."

"Suffered from what exactly?"

"From the burden of being viewed as a replacement child: the one who would fill the unfillable void, erase the loss, act as panacea. It's obviously an impossible task, because children aren't fungible and the agony of losing a child can never be healed simply by having another. Instead, parents should acknowledge the loss, allow the dead child a place in the family, and let the mourning process run its course. Failure to do so would project their trauma onto the surviving children, triggering the syndrome."

"What makes you think my parents failed?"

"Most people assume that the best way to heal is by suppressing the pain or blocking it out altogether—even if this means permanently erasing the dead child from the family history, locking up the physical reminders out of reach, and so on. This is especially true of parents who never had a chance to grieve properly. For example . . ." She looked away, as if no longer sure that giving an example was a good idea. "Historically, women whose babies had died at birth weren't allowed to hold or even see them—it was considered harmful to the mother. Clinical studies have now shown that such denial only leaves the grief unresolved. And the wound, so to speak, forever open."

I finally realized where she was going with this. The disappearance of Elza's body had left my parents' grief as unresolved as grief could be.

"In such cases, people either withdraw and neglect their other children, or become overprotective, doting on the children too much. You counted the windows from the inside, which meant you must have been a happy child raised in an inclusive, loving home. I know many who aren't as lucky."

"They count the windows from the outside?"

"Almost invariably. Alienated children are outsiders. Some report feeling literally invisible in the family."

"Yet counting from the inside doesn't necessarily mean a loving home. It could be just the opposite: a home perceived as a prison."

"You're absolutely right." She smiled again, but so confidently that it probably meant I wasn't. "Except a prisoner would know the windows right off the bat, no? There would hardly be a need to count them for me. And certainly not a second time, as you did."

This bothered me more than anything else she had said so far—because I hadn't counted them a second time. Then . . . could it be true? Over the years, piano practice had often made me feel trapped. And my parents were overprotective, sure. But I had never thought of my home as a prison. Or had I? After all, here I was. In a foreign world. By myself.

"Are you thinking jails and shackles?"

The choice of words startled me—a joke, clearly, but by now I knew better. If the human mind were a musical instrument, this woman would be no less of a virtuoso than Rhys had been the night before.

"I'm just . . . I still don't see how you guessed all those other things about my life."

"To be honest, it was a bit of a conundrum. Here you are, at Princeton. And a celebrated pianist, no less. In short: doing everything exactly like your sister. But why would your parents allow it?"

"Maybe so I could become the ultimate replacement child?"

"No, it doesn't work that way. The overprotective pattern is to keep the replacement child—and I hope you don't mind the term, I use it only descriptively—as close as possible. Not send her to another continent. And definitely not to the same school where the first child died. In other words, all those decisions must have been yours. The piano, for example. To achieve such a level of success, you'd need to start at a very early age. But a six-year-old doesn't just wake up one day craving to play classical music, right? The parents must push for it. Yours, of course, would never do such a thing, as it was the piano that won Elza the accolades required for admission to Princeton. So there had to be some other trigger. Some event that, to a child, must have felt mysterious, and captivating, and enticed you to play despite Mom and Dad's objections. Such as, let's say, discovering a world that had been locked away. And in it—a piano waiting. Except your parents made a big mistake right there."

"By allowing me to play?"

"No, by not telling you about your sister. Think about it—much of your childhood was still at their disposal. Plenty of time to ease you into the truth, shape your reaction, and ensure what they probably wanted most of all: to steer you away from the American bug that so many young people in Eastern Europe seem to catch just from breathing the post-Communist air. But instead they waited. And once you had a mind of your own, it was too late."

"Not entirely. When I found out what they had gone through, I offered to stay in Bulgaria."

"Their happiness in exchange for yours. What parent would accept such a bargain?"

"I wasn't bargaining. I really meant it."

"Of course you did. Empathy. Self-sacrifice. Early understanding of grief and loss. These are all typical, because a replacement child doesn't expect to be the center of the universe. Huge difference there, between you and Elza."

The difference wasn't quite as huge, given how I had chosen Princeton knowing it would devastate my parents. Yet there was something else, in that last statement of hers. It sounded personal. Not so much a deduction—a specific observation.

"Dr. Pratt, how long have you been at Princeton?"

She rose from the couch, walked over to a desk in the far corner of the room, and took a bottle of water from a stack next to it. "Would you like one?"

"No, thanks." A diploma in Latin above the desk had her name, that of Johns Hopkins University, and the year 1990. "You were here in '92, weren't you?"

She unscrewed the cap and stared inside, as if the clear liquid held molecules of the past itself.

"Did my sister come in for therapy too?"

"Not voluntarily."

"You mean she needed . . . psychiatric help?" I almost choked on the words, wishing I had taken that water bottle.

"I didn't think so, at the time. But the school disagreed. Have you heard of the Nude Olympics?"

It sounded like a Dionysian version of the Olympic Games. "Does that have anything to do with ancient Greece?"

"Unfortunately, no." The suggestion amused her. "It's a Princeton tradition. Used to be, until 1999, when the Board of Trustees banned it. Every winter, on the night of the first snowfall, sophomores would run naked in the Holder Courtyard over at Rocky College, and from there—out on the town, bolting into local stores and restaurants. Depending on the level of inebriation, there could be sex and vandalism too, leading to arrests, criminal charges, and even hospitalization."

"But my sister was never a sophomore."

"Right, she wasn't. Which was part of the problem. That year, the first snow fell on December thirteenth—"

"The same weekend her body disappeared from the funeral home?"

"Yes, although I don't think there's a connection. The point is, in the winter of 1992—and, to my knowledge, for the first and only time in the school's history—the Nude Olympics seemed to have happened twice. On December thirteenth, the night of the first snowfall. But also a month earlier, on November tenth, with a group of students starting at Holder and ending up in the woods south of campus. There was only one nonsophomore involved: your sister. Incidentally, she was also the only woman."

I felt my cheeks flush. Apparently, Elza had been much wilder than I had suspected. "Did anyone get arrested?"

"Unfortunately, yes. Borough Police officers were dispatched after reports of the initial ruckus. The students, I believe there were six of them, faced disciplinary charges. It came down to just mandatory counseling, but at first there had been talks about suspension for the entire spring semester."

"Suspension? For running around naked?"

"Well . . . there had been much more to it than running. I'm sure you can imagine."

I couldn't quite. My sister. Naked. With five men in the forest. In the middle of the night. "I still don't understand, though. Why would they do this a month early, instead of waiting for the first snow with the others?"

"*Because we don't do what the others do.* These were her exact words, when I asked her the same question. *And besides,* she said, *it was first frost—doesn't that sound more like freedom?*"

It didn't sound like freedom, not to me. But I wished I had known that girl. Wished I could be like her: defiant, brave, a rebel.

"Dr. Pratt, do you think that this is how she . . . that this incident is linked to the way she died?"

"It doesn't matter what I think, Thea. We will never find out. And even if we did, you can't reverse what's already happened. The only thing you can do is keep your life free of ghosts."

The word gave me a shudder, before I realized she didn't mean it literally. "I'm not sure I can. Elza is a part of me—a part I'm only now beginning to know."

She shook her head. "What's part of you is the anxiety and grief you've been picking up from your parents, subconsciously, over the years. When a secret festers for so long, learning the truth can bring nightmares. Some people internalize the trauma so much they start to see their dead sibling's ghost. An apparition by the window at night, that sort of thing."

"And it's just . . . hallucination?" For the first time since Tsarevo, I felt relief about the white figure I had seen there.

"You can call it that. Scientifically speaking, it's a cognitive distortion: your brain's effort to make her seem real, in order to minimize the loss. But don't fall into the trap of identifying with her."

"Why not? I often wonder if the two of us are alike."

"You aren't. And trust me when I say this, as I met the girl. She harbored a certain aggravation with the world, a latent anger at nobody and nothing in particular. You don't seem to have any of that in you." Then a pause, to weigh the next words: "Which is a good thing."

THE ALLEY HAD ENDED; I would have known even with eyes closed. My steps, only a moment ago muted by a myriad of sounds on a busy campus, now clicked distinctly on the pavement, lifted in ripples through the vaulted stone like the voice of a worshipper entering a church.

It was always Princeton's arches that took the breath away. A world of fuss left behind. Ahead—distant lattice windows, a tree, perhaps a patch of sky. But in between, you felt on the cusp of miracles. The low ceiling would close overhead, ready to keep your secrets. Feeble light would stretch your shadow across the walls. Amplified, your steps would turn into music. And for a few seconds, as you made your way down the eerie passageway, there would be only you and the stone. Nothing else.

On the other side of this particular arch was the Holder quadrangle of Rockefeller College (or "Rocky," as it was affectionately known). I should have figured it out long ago, way before I heard mention of Rocky in a psychiatrist's office: This was Elza's dorm. Had to be. Years back, I had witnessed an incident. An odd lapse of poise that, like all seemingly insignificant memories when one is trying to piece together the past, took on a new meaning in hindsight:

"Hell, I don't know. Do you think these Americans are onto something? Because in the old days, we used to call it child exploitation."

The man was my father's boss: head of a forensic lab, and one of several guests my parents had invited over for dinner. Apparently, he was also adamant that nobody under the age of eighteen should work—a topic spurred by a program on TV while everyone at the table waited to find out whether or not the Bulgarian soccer team had qualified for the World Cup.

"Pavko, come on." His wife frowned, a few seats over. "How can you say this, when the Communists used to make us spend most of the summer vacation doing mandatory labor? I still remember the student brigades: sweating to death from the heat, either out in the field or at the canned food factory. And all this in the name of 'communal well-being'? At least in America those kids are getting paid!"

"I'm not defending the Communists. The way I see it, these brigades were just something we had to go through as part of growing up. It's one thing for the state to say everyone has to contribute. But to have parents send their children out to make money? I don't know, seems messed up to me."

"I agree." Our youngest guest, a lab assistant, nodded across the table. "If you can't afford to pay for your children, you probably shouldn't be having them in the first place."

"It's not about *affording*." Pavko's wife raised her voice over that of the TV host, who had just remarked how idleness was toxic for adolescents. "This is America we're talking about. I'm sure people can afford a lot, compared to us and to the rest of the world. They are only trying to teach their kids values early on."

"Really? Like what?" My mother could no longer contain herself. "That the best thing they can do with their time is to wait tables six days a week?"

"Point taken! Who are we to argue about raising children with someone who has raised *this*?" Pavko laughed, pointing to my piano awards framed on the wall. "The parents' job is to make money, while the kid's job is to become a genius, right? Slavin, what do you think?"

"What I think is that . . ." My father paused, glancing at Mom to make sure she agreed with what he was about to say. "I think that if you wait to teach your children values only after they are old enough to work, by then it's too late."

There was silence at the table. On-screen, a woman in a fiery red suit who claimed to be a "family wealth consultant" began to talk about the Rockefellers, and how the grandson used to earn his twenty-five-cent allowance by raking leaves eight hours a week.

"Which is why the Rockefeller children never became world-famous pianists!" Pavko winked at me, but nobody else was laughing.

My parents stared at each other. Then my usually composed-to-a-fault mother stood up, changed the TV channel and, without a word to anyone, left the room.

Now, years later, I looked around at Rocky—the opulent Gothic dorm that the fortune of the leaf rakers had bestowed upon the school. One of those cloistered rooms had belonged to my sister. Through its window, she had watched life unfold in the Holder Courtyard. Buzz of early mornings. Drop of fall leaves. Students going in and out of arched entryways. Dusks. Rains. And that infamous first frost which, as Pratt just told me, had spiraled into the first sign of trouble.

We don't do what the others do . . .

Then it struck me: What if my parents knew about the Nude Olympics? If my mother's reaction had nothing to do with Elza's dorm, but with having been told that her daughter had run naked, one November night, with a group of men outside Rockefeller College?

And so—I was back to square one. Elza may or may not have lived here. She may or may not have walked down these alleys, under these trees, through these arches . . . But did it make a difference either way?

I realized the futility of it. Of my quest for clues that seemed to point in a certain direction until, inevitably, they began to point in another. And as I headed back to Forbes, I decided to try what everyone seemed to think would be best for me: leave the ghosts to the past and live my own life.

"VEGETARIAN MEDLEY OR MEAT CASSEROLE?"

Medley—casserole . . . Medley—casserole . . . I didn't know what either word meant, and taking a look at the dishes didn't help either. Usually closed on Saturdays, Procter Hall had a special event featuring food from local restaurants, and my job for the evening was to give each graduate student a choice: two dubious food concoctions, one of which sounded like a drunken party and the other—like a fancy horse carriage. Worst of all, we were required to wear chef jackets and tall paper hats.

"Would it be such a disaster if we skipped the hats?"

The dining hall manager gave me an offended look. "Skip them?"

"I was thinking what happens if this thing falls off."

"Well, just make sure it doesn't."

Clearly, asking management to reconsider the protocol was equivalent to telling a cop he should rob a bank with me. So I just went through the shift, hoping to be done before Rhys would walk in to see me armed with a spatula and crowned with a paper cylinder.

"When and where am I picking you up tomorrow?" he had asked me the night before.

"At nine, from work."

"Work?"

"Graduate College dining hall. It's part of my financial aid." I waited for a reaction but there was none. "You aren't saying anything. Is there a problem?"

"Not yet, no."

Yet. A tactful way of saying that dating the dishroom girl was fine, so long as no one had seen him with her (except perhaps his butler).

"Rhys, I am not rich. If that bothers you, I'd rather know it now."

"Why would it bother me?"

Because I've heard about the friends you hang out with. And I've seen the car you drive. And the house you live in.

When I didn't answer, he hurried to explain: "I just don't want a job to take too much of your time away from me. Especially on weekends."

Luckily, by the end of the shift there was no sign of him. Since everyone else was in a rush to hit the Street, I volunteered to shut down the place and started the usual checklist:

Power off the dishwasher.

Lock the freezers.

Turn off the lights (kitchen, pantry, serving area).

Then the final stop: Procter Hall.

On the other side of the stained glass, night had already fallen. The windows had lost their color, so now the only light came from the hesitant bulbs of the chandeliers. I turned around, to check if the vestibule door was still open—

And I found myself face-to-face with someone who had been waiting in silence, leaning against the closest table.

"Hi, Thea."

I recognized him intuitively—his voice, the way he said my name. Then I saw the silhouette. The white flower in his hand. But also something else: unmistakably different body, unfamiliar face. For one last instant, my brain refused to accept it. Then I was hit with the obvious truth:

This had to be the guy from my concert. And it wasn't Rhys.

Before I could react, he smiled and came up to me. The slow, cautious moves again, stopping just as his body was about to touch mine.

"Who . . . who are you?"

"I think you know." He reached for my hand. Slipped the flower in it. "I had to go away for a while. But I thought of you and your Chopin every single minute."

The air began to spin from his quiet voice.

"How did you . . ." My throat was dry; the words stayed trapped in it.

"How did I what?"

" . . . know I was here."

"I promised to find you. And I did."

I took a step back. How could I have mistaken Rhys for him? They looked alike, but only from a distance. Up close, everything was different: the body (equally strong but leaner, less assertively built up); the face (just as stunning but more chiseled); and the eyes (a darker blue but also warmer, unimaginably warm)—

Steps echoed through the hall.

"I see the two of you already met?" Rhys hurried over to us, leaving no time for a response. "Ferry mentioned you might be coming home tonight, but I didn't think he'd tip you off to look for me here."

The guy shrugged mechanically, the lie made easy for him.

Rhys put his arm around me. "My brother is mad at you because you ruined his plan."

Brothers? I stared at him, horrified. "What plan did I ruin?"

"For years, I've been sick of this campus and trying to convince Jake to move with me to Manhattan. But he loves it out here—the peace, the quiet. Beats me, frankly. So we struck a compromise: stay for another year and be done with it. Then two weeks ago, out of the blue, he agrees to move. Even finds us a place in SoHo, gets me to pack and drive out of here. Except . . . you know the rest. I came back for one night and, unbeknownst to him, I ended up meeting you—which, to my dear brother's chagrin, has put my move to New York on indefinite hold. Unfortunate timing, isn't it, Jake?"

There was no reaction, not even a nod this time.

"Funny how Princeton always manages to keep me on a tight leash. First my brother, now you." Rhys took my hand, finally noticing the flower in it. "And this is from . . . ?"

It was the moment I would always remember. That split second in time when, against all odds, the universe pauses to catch its breath, fate looks the other way, and you are allowed, just this once, to have what you want if only you can name it, but you must speak up or else it would become too late, and once it is too late it remains too late forever.

The flower is from . . . ?

I felt their eyes on me, expecting my answer. But what was I supposed to say? That I was dating Rhys because I had mistaken him for his brother? Jake was the one who owed Rhys the truth. This was his mess, not mine. And the rest was something the two of them had to hash out between themselves.

I walked up to one of the centerpieces still left on the tables—all kinds of white blooms, including roses—and slipped the stem among the others, as if it had been there all along.

"Guess I'm off the hook, then." Rhys smiled—his usual nonchalance. "For a moment there I thought I'd have to challenge my own brother to a duel!"

Jake looked away. *Coward*, I thought. *You are such a coward.*

"I'll see you at home." He walked past Rhys, without acknowledging my presence, and before the air found its way back into my lungs, he was gone.

CHAPTER 7

Seven Letters

THE RAIN HADN'T stopped all day. I kept hearing its tap against the window: . . . *now what? what? . . . what?*

Then, around six o'clock, it got tired of being worried—and gave up.

I wished I could do the same. Or at least not see anyone. But I was due at the Mercer Street residence by seven, for dinner with Rhys and his brother.

My attempt to find a way out of it hadn't gone very far. Rhys thought the occasion (my meeting Jake) called for a special celebration. And, as usual, he had to have things his way. I was sure that the dinner wouldn't happen, that he would call and cancel as soon as Jake told him the two of us had already met—twice—and almost kissed in a museum basement. But Sunday afternoon rolled into evening, and that phone call never came.

I couldn't stop thinking about our Procter Hall episode. What should I have done differently? Had my real connection been with Jake all along? Or was Rhys the guy for me? And who was this mysterious brother of his anyway—this subdued, elusive, unfathomable Jake, who affected me so much I was barely able to finish a sentence in his presence?

Rhys hadn't revealed much about him the night before and I hadn't asked much either, afraid that my curiosity would seem suspicious. No, they were not twins. Jake was his little brother—"little" meaning twenty-seven, but as for himself Rhys would only tell me they were close in age. They were also close, period. Although he feared this might change, with Jake now living in New York.

It took me half an hour to figure out what to wear: black leather pants and a black wraparound sweater, hopefully sexy enough without trying to provoke anyone. Now the real nightmare was about to start. Me, with the two of them. Stuck for hours—doing what? saying what?—in the same room.

When I reached the familiar trees, the wind woke their branches with its melancholic hum, shaking down a few drops of leftover rain. A figure rushed out of the house. *Rhys or Jake?* This was just the beginning. I had to get used to it: the intuitive question, the attempt to distinguish one silhouette from the other. And the need to prepare my heart either way.

It was Rhys, of course. He had offered to pick me up from Forbes but I insisted on walking; I needed it. Now he ran over and lifted me in his arms.

"Rhys, what are you doing?"

"The ground is all wet. You'll ruin your shoes." He carried me across the entire lawn, didn't even seem out of breath. "Remind me to show you the main entrance next time. The driveway is the reason we call the house Pebbles— looks like gravel, but it's actually made of marble pieces supposed to evoke some sort of riverbed. The guy who built it imported them from Italy."

So—Jake hadn't said a thing. I gave myself too much credit, thinking that he might. That he would try to win me back, fight with Rhys if he had to. Instead, he was going to sit back and watch his brother be with me.

We came into the living room. Jake was facing away from the windows, in one of the armchairs, and for a moment the only visible part of him was his hand—his long, sculpted fingers, hanging down from the armrest. Under them, on the floor, was an empty glass.

He must have heard our steps but remained still—so still it could pass for sleep. Our voices didn't startle him either, and the deliberate calm with which his body unfolded from the chair made it clear that he had sat in silence, waiting.

"Hi, Thea."

My name out of his lips again. I remembered being with him in another room, just the two of us, when he had said it for the first time.

"Now you know who plays on the second piano." Rhys patted his brother's back. "The undisputed talent in the family. I'm his envious sidekick."

Jake looked more still than the piano itself.

We often hold competitions. I imagined the two of them playing. If my sister had been alive, she and I would probably be doing the same.

"That's my brother for you: not a single word." Rhys shrugged, sensing the odd vibe and having no idea what was causing it. "Thank God dinner is ready; otherwise it might take us hours to break the ice."

A table was set right there, in the living room—most likely for added intimacy, as the house was certainly big enough to have a separate dining area. Three candles quivered in the middle, refracting shadows from the potted plants over the walls and ceiling, transforming the room into a monochrome jungle very much alive. There were three wineglasses, already filled. Three place settings. I recognized the porcelain set Rhys had brought to the willow field and it reminded me that he and I had secrets too, moments Jake was not a part of.

We sat down. Rhys made a toast—to my first dinner at Pebbles—but the sip of red wine choked my throat. I tried to picture dating him from now on. Coming to the house. Running into Jake. Having casual chats with him, pretending not to care. And more dinners. Music evenings. Maybe even double dates . . .

I had to force myself to begin eating. My mind glided through the food without registering any taste, until it occurred to me that the dishes were strangely familiar: cold cucumber soup, feta cheese pie, stuffed peppers.

"Where did you find Bulgarian food?"

Rhys laughed. "I was starting to think that you wouldn't notice."

"Sorry, everything is a bit overwhelming."

"I can imagine!" He pointed at my plate. "Is it any good? I asked Ferry to work his magic on the chef."

"Yes, it's perfect. But you didn't have to."

"Of course I did. You are too far from home, that's the least I could do."

Jake looked up from his own plate. "I hear Bulgaria is beautiful. Haven't been there myself, but my brother has."

I stared at Rhys in disbelief. "Why didn't you tell me?"

"You didn't?" Jake pretended not to notice the frown on his brother's face.

Rhys put his fork down—carefully, as if aligning it perfectly along the plate could change the outcome of the entire evening. "I don't believe I've mentioned it to Thea, no. Why? Is that a problem?"

They locked eyes across the table. I sat there, speechless. Something was charging up between them, and from the sound of it, their animosity had nothing to do with me.

"Right, didn't think so." Rhys softened back into a smile and turned to me: "I traveled to Bulgaria years ago. A gem of a country."

"When were you there?"

"When it would have been still too early to meet you." He lifted my hand and kissed it, the way he had done by the willow. "More wine?"

Obviously, the subject of Bulgaria was closed for now. He filled my glass. "Looks like we have an important decision to make."

My body stiffened up. "What decision?"

"Whether to have you play before dessert, or after."

I warned him that it would be neither.

"I'm afraid 'neither' is not on the menu tonight. I am dying to hear you play. And so is Jake."

How could I tell him? I knew I should have. But it wasn't the kind of thing you threw in someone's face, out of nowhere:

Actually, your brother has already heard me play. He just doesn't have the courage to say it, so both he and I have been lying to you the entire time.

"I am not playing tonight, Rhys."

"Why not? Just one piece, even if it has to be Chopin! Besides, you owe me for the other night, remember?"

He tried to kiss me but I pulled away just in time. Jake's face had turned whiter than the porcelain.

"I must head out." Nothing in his voice gave away an emotion, but his eyes avoided both of us.

"Head out? Ferry told me you'd be here for the week!"

"Not really." He stood up as he said this. "I promised to be back in New York tonight."

"Promised . . . to whom? Anyone I don't yet know about?"

The question was ignored.

"Jake, come on. At least stay the night!"

"It will have to be some other time."

Now Rhys looked baffled. "He's killing me, Thea! I swear, this is so unlike my brother . . ."

Jake walked around the table to give Rhys a hug, then turned to me. I froze, terrified that he was about to hug me too. That for one impossibly short instant, I would finally be in his arms. But he reached out only with his hand. Waited for mine. Took it carefully, as if touching an object made of glass, and just held it, briefly, while his eyes held mine.

"It was nice to meet you, Thea Slavin."

The rest happened quickly. Rhys must have detected something in Jake's voice, or on Jake's face, or in the nervous posture of Jake's body on the way out, and the casual "nice to meet you" didn't fool him. Looking infuriated, he ran after his brother. When he came back, he didn't say a word about what had happened outside. But it wasn't hard to guess: he had probably confronted Jake and found out the truth.

In a final nod to his good manners, he drove me back to Forbes—in silence. Dropped me off in silence. Wouldn't even say good night.

"Rhys, I am so sorry . . ."

"Sorry for what? You have nothing to apologize for."

The last sound I heard was that of screeching tires, as his car turned the corner and disappeared.

"I DON'T UNDERSTAND, THEA." DONNELLY'S face gathered up its storm in the familiar frown, except this time the catalyst wasn't my choice of majors.

In more than a week, I had learned only half of the Albéniz. And that, to her, was a personal insult. "You know what Carnegie means for a musician's career, right?"

Of course I did: the ultimate jackpot. But I had other things on my mind too. My entire weekend had felt surreal. The guy I was seeing had split into two different people, then I had lost both of them.

"We are walking a very tight rope and I can't let you waste any more time. What's distracting you? Is it school?"

"Partially."

"And the other part?"

I used the campus job as an excuse, yet the frown stayed.

"As I told you, the Financial Aid Office insists on this work nonsense. The earliest I can get you out is January."

Getting me out of Procter Hall wasn't the point. I needed Donnelly to get me *in* it.

"They keep a piano there that no one seems to be playing. If I could practice on it after work . . ."

"Why can't you?"

"The place is locked at night."

She reached for her phone. "When are you working next?"

"This evening."

"Excellent. Give me a minute."

A minute was all it took. She dialed a number, exchanged a few words, then hung up looking triumphant. "Someone will bring you a key by the end of the shift."

And so finally I had it—my own piano, in a space so beautiful it infused the mind with music!

While thanking her, I wondered whether this "someone" might turn out to be the janitor (or, as he had called himself, *keykeeper*) who had once unlocked Procter Hall for me. I found him oddly fascinating and hoped to run into him again. Chat him up some more. Figure out why he talked so poetically about music. And, above all, get him to open up about those Princeton suicides he had mentioned the last time. Not that I could picture my sister jumping from Cleveland Tower. But maybe he had heard of other incidents too? A dead girl found by a hiking trail, for example. Or a funeral home scandal involving the most morbid of thefts.

Unfortunately, no one brought the key. It waited in an envelope when I went to work, and once everyone had left after the shift, I resumed my struggle with Albéniz.

The beginning was deceptively simple, with the right index finger pecking the tempo on a single key while the left hand circled around it in staccato patterns. It was a joke, a child could play it. Until the music erupted. Octaves, slammed at the opposite ends of the piano as if, all of a sudden, you were expected to grow a third hand, then a fourth, and cover the entire keyboard without any disruption to the melody.

I was going to need weeks just to get the notes right. Wylie had called this "a basic read," while my piano instructor, years back, had referred to it as "teaching instinct to your fingers." Either way, I hated grappling with new music. Feeling crippled. Hitting wrong keys. Dissecting the piece down to its bare bones and cramming it into so many mechanical repetitions that, yes, the fingers did go on autopilot. But so did the brain. While the ear, washed out from hearing the same sounds over and over, simply stopped registering them.

I forced myself to play it to the end once, then turned off the lights and became absorbed in different music—music I knew by heart. The last time I had played it on this same piano, I had imagined someone listening. Hidden, invisible in the dark.

I thought of you and your Chopin every single minute—

A hinge squeaked and made me jump from the bench. I could have sworn I shut the door. Fully shut, so that no one would hear. *Sounds don't escape walls like these.* Maybe Silen had lied?

The bright triangle began to stretch across the floor: a hand was pulling on the doorknob, this time all the way.

"Hi. Sorry if I interrupted your music."

I recognized the voice even before my eyes had adjusted to the backlight framing him. "Jake . . . what are you doing here?"

"Looking for you."

"I see that. But how did you . . ."

"Know where you'd be?" He smiled—I still hadn't figured out that when he wanted to find me, he knew where and how. "Tracking you down isn't a problem. The problem is that I seem to get there only when it's too late."

His eyes were turned to the closed scores, but we both knew he meant something else.

"You didn't go back to New York last night." It wasn't a question. The real question was why.

"I had to see you and apologize."

"For what?"

"For the way things happened."

"What happened was simple. You promised to find me, but instead the one who found me was your brother."

"Why did you pick him, Thea?"

It struck me for the first time: He didn't know. He thought I had chosen Rhys over him on purpose.

"I'd seen you only in the dark. When I ran into Rhys, I assumed it was you."

"You did? We don't even look that much alike."

"Apparently you do. Or . . . maybe I just wished it was you, until I actually believed it."

"It should have been me." He said it so quietly I could barely distinguish the words.

"Then why did you disappear?"

He hesitated.

"Why, Jake?"

"I had my reasons."

"That's all? You had *reasons*?"

We were only steps away from each other. I looked at him. Waited.

"I didn't disappear. I had to get Rhys to move to New York first."

"Why?"

"Because being with you wasn't an option. Not with him still around."

"What does Rhys have to do with anything?"

While he agonized over the answer, I tried to follow this new twist: Jake's sudden decision to move to Manhattan only days after my concert, then the two of them ending up there.

"Are you saying that you can't date a girl who lives in the same town as your brother?" The words made it sound plausible but I refused to believe it. Jake—threatened by Rhys. Weak and insecure. "Sorry, that's ridiculous."

"You don't know my brother."

"Yes, I do."

"You don't. You don't know the full impact he has on women." As soon as he said it, he must have realized that Rhys's impact on women was exactly the part I already knew.

"Do you ever think about the full impact *you* have on women?"

"I don't care about other women."

"I am not talking about other women, Jake. Why did you . . ." Now I was the one afraid to finish a sentence. "Why do you always leave?"

"You don't understand. I have to force myself to stay away from you." He lifted his fingers to my face but ran them down a safe distance from it, brushing my hair with the back of his hand only briefly, by accident. "I have to force myself to not touch you."

"Why?"

"Because I love my brother."

What could I say to this? I turned to walk away but he caught my elbow. "Wait . . ."

"What, Jake?" I tried not to look up at him, at whatever it was about this guy that made me forget my anger. "What else do you want?"

"I can't have you upset with me."

All I heard was *I can't have you.* "Why not?"

For a moment he looked confused.

"No, I mean it. What difference does it make?"

"I'll be running into you on campus, that's for sure."

"You will?"

"I go to school here, Thea."

The thought hadn't crossed my mind. After Rhys said his brother was twenty-seven, I assumed they were both done with studying and only lived in Princeton because it was their home.

"You seem surprised."

"I just . . . I didn't think you were a student. Are you in graduate school?"

"No, I'm a senior. Took time off and now have to finish."

"But then how can you live in New York?"

"I have class only three days a week. The commute is less than an hour."

It made sense—I had heard that in America commutes were the norm, not the exception. What didn't make sense were his next words: "You won't have to worry about seeing me around the house. I took a dorm room, so I'll have a place to crash when I come to school."

"The house . . . *your* house?" This time the logic escaped me. Given how things had ended the night before, why was Jake so certain I would be at their house again? Then it finally dawned on me: "You never told Rhys, did you?"

He shook his head.

"Why not?"

"Because I wanted the choice to be yours."

"Jake, he is *your* brother, not mine. You should be the one to tell him."

"Tell him what? That we made a fool of him last night, lying to him through the entire dinner?"

He was right: telling Rhys now would have been incredibly selfish. Yet selfish was exactly what I needed him to be, as it seemed the only way he could be with me.

"So then . . . that's it? You really came here only to apologize?"

"Rhys cares about you too much. I can't step in the middle."

"And how I feel doesn't matter?"

"Of course it does. But can you honestly tell me that being with him was a mistake? That you feel nothing for him? Absolutely nothing?"

I knew what answer he wanted to hear, but it would have been a lie. So, while he held the door open for me, I wished him a safe trip back to the city, said good night, and left.

BEFORE I COULD FIGURE OUT if Rhys really cared about me or not, Forbes announced its Fall Dance.

"I bet you anything that Ben will swoop in first," Rita chirped over cereal. "Have mercy on the guy, Tesh. It isn't his fault he failed Stalking 101 so miserably."

"Mercy" probably meant agreeing to be his date, but when he asked, all I could do was soften the blow by telling him that I had half promised another guy already (which was a lie) and that I most likely wouldn't even go (which wasn't).

"Actually, skipping the dance won't make me inconsolable either." He gave me one of his endearing, childish smiles. "But having you turn down my other offer might."

"What other offer?"

"Scrabble Challenge. Starts at five, earlier that same day. You've played it, right?"

"No. What is it?"

"A board game. All-time American favorite. I thought it was also big in Europe, but maybe not so much?"

"It probably is. I'm just a music nerd, remember?"

"Then you'll love Scrabble, it's nerd heaven! Basically, you score points by forming words on a crossword grid. A bunch of us team up for a slam once a month."

I smiled to myself. If Donnelly saw me trade off the keyboard for a game board, she was going to be a wreck. *I don't understand this waste of time, Thea. It is equivalent to suicide, for someone with your ambition.* Yet I didn't want to disappoint my friend (and how would Donnelly find out anyway?), so I said that a detour through nerd heaven the following Saturday would be lovely.

I was asked to the dance twice more that day. People were rushing to find dates, but I couldn't imagine going with someone other than Rhys or Jake. Not that I should have wanted to go with one of them, either. By now, Jake was probably back in New York, staying dutifully out of his brother's way (and mine). As for Rhys, I had no idea whether I would hear from him again.

To my surprise, he called that same weekend.

"Aren't you sick of this campus? Let's escape the damn place for a few hours!"

"Rhys, don't act like nothing happened."

"What do you mean?"

"Your strange mood the other day, after the dinner at your place."

"Sorry, I was just . . . Jake had given me some bad news and it threw me off. That's not an excuse, I know. So let me make it up to you."

"Make it up how?"

By taking me to the ocean, as it turned out. The town, Cape May, was a historic landmark at the southern edge of a peninsula off the New Jersey shore, a two-hour drive from Princeton. According to Rhys, this was the oldest seaside resort in the country, named after a seventeenth-century Dutch captain who charted the area. Now its main tourist attraction was the dazzling display of Victorian houses, decked out with white wooden balconies and bright-colored turrets.

It was already mid-October and too cold for the beach, so we just walked along the sand, jeans rolled up to our knees.

"What are you doing next Saturday?" Since he was always the one asking to see me, I decided to break the pattern, for once.

He smiled. "Sounds like I'm about to find out."

"We have a dance at Forbes. Will you be my date?"

The seconds of silence began to accumulate.

"Look . . . if you don't want to, just tell me. Nobody will die."

"What I want is to spend next weekend with you. But I don't think a dance at Forbes is a good idea."

"Why not?"

He continued walking, eyes fixed on the foam that broke and formed again at our feet. "It's better to keep me out of your social life at school. At least for now."

"I didn't realize being with you was strictly an off-campus offer."

"Don't worry. Nothing with me will ever be strictly an off-campus offer."

I had no idea what he was talking about. When he finally looked up, I sensed a new resolve in him.

"I can't be what you want me to be, Thea."

"How do you know what I want?"

"Believe me, I do. And you have every right to want it. But it's something I cannot be."

"Then why are we here?" Rita had been right: good luck with someone from the Ivy crowd.

"Because there has to be a compromise. What you want is a boyfriend, isn't it?"

Boyfriend. The label of ultimate curse. To me it was a given—in Bulgaria people were either together or not, there was nothing in between (at least not among my friends). Here, you graduated into someone's heart in stages: hanging out, hooking up, seeing each other, dating, going out, being exclusive . . . Just to keep the nuances straight was a science. Now I wondered where on that continuum Rhys had decided to place me.

"I'll come to the dance if it means so much to you, but that won't change anything."

"What do you think I am trying to change?"

"I don't know. Me, I guess? I'm not exactly"—he took a deep breath, looked away and exhaled—"what they call a one-woman guy."

There was no need to ask what he meant.

"Not that I want to be with anyone else—I don't. I am absolutely, desperately infatuated with you. You know this, right?"

"But?"

"But . . . I can't make promises that I will not keep."

Will, not *may.*

"The decision is yours, Thea."

I tried to convince myself that staying with him was safe. That I could have this fantastic adventure and not fall in love, especially with someone who had made it clear he would never fall in love with me.

"So?" His lips touched my cheek. "We continue or not?"

"What if I said no?"

"Then I'd keep asking until you gave me the answer I want."

I knew he meant it. I also knew there were many reasons to walk away. But one thing I loved about him: he wasn't a coward. Unlike Jake, he was not the type to give up and disappear when he wanted someone.

THE WEEK SLIPPED BY QUICKLY. With midterms coming up, I couldn't focus on anything except piano and school. Rhys, on the other hand, had endless time at his disposal. He didn't seem to have a job (or to need one). There was no mention of parents. And he lived in that enormous house by himself, now that his brother had decamped for Manhattan.

Neither one of us mentioned the dance again, nor anything else we had said on the shore that day—it was easier to pretend the conversation had never taken place. But it had, of course. And if he insisted on staying out of my social life, then I was going to allow others back into it.

So when Ben came to pick me up for the promised Scrabble break on Saturday, I didn't think twice:

"Did you find a date for tonight?"

He shook his head. "I'm boycotting the event."

"Not anymore."

"No?" A smile caught his dimples as he began to realize what I was saying. "I thought I was."

"You were. But this is college, right? We have to stay part of the pack."

The "nerd heaven" he had promised me felt more like purgatory: an overheated game room; empty crossword grids on every surface, including the floor; and pepperoni pizza, to keep you occupied until it was your turn to play.

Ben explained the rules to me before he and I teamed up against two of his friends while everyone else watched. At first, it all went great. Then someone had the idea that I should play the next round without a teammate. Scrabble Challenge proper: the non–native speaker against some self-proclaimed thesaurus wiz.

Having become the center of the spectacle, I pulled seven wooden blocks and started shuffling them. The four-letter words were easy: *MIND*, *MOAN*, *MAIN*. Then I did five: *MANIA*.

"You can do better than this." Ben was staring at the blocks, no longer allowed to help me.

There had to be a six-letter word. And when I found it, I wished I had never walked into that game room. Or agreed to play. Or even heard of Scrabble.

Ⓜ Ⓐ Ⓘ Ⓝ Ⓐ Ⓓ

I placed the letters on the board, hoping that no one would notice my shaking fingers. The *O* remained by itself.

"Challenge!" My opponent, a senior majoring in Classics, didn't waste a second. "It's MAE, not MAI."

For once, my high school Latin was about to come in handy: I reminded the guy that "ai" and "ae" were both Latin equivalents of the Greek "αι." When transcribing a Greek word into English, you could spell it either way.

Not according to Scrabble rules—the official dictionary rejected my spelling. While Ben was checking on his phone and showing everyone that *mainad* did exist as a recognized word, I couldn't take my eyes off the board. How had I picked these letters? This time it wasn't a vase or a paper topic assigned to me. I had simply dipped my hand into a pile of wooden blocks and, without thinking, pulled out exactly those seven.

" . . . which is technically against the rules, but you can go ahead anyway."

Ben seemed to be talking to me, so I forced myself to pay attention. "Sorry, go ahead with what?"

"Take another turn. With the same letters."

I reshuffled the blocks. With all eyes on me, the last thing I wanted was to argue my way out of this.

"Too bad you're missing an extra *D* for the girl's best friend," someone joked behind me, having stolen a peek.

And this joke made me see the new word instantly, but it had nothing to do with diamonds. It had to do with a pair of creatures from an old legend, alleged to be only a myth:

🄳 🄰 🄸 🄼 🄾 🄽

This time, the letter on the side was *A*.

I felt the room close in on me. *Maenad . . . Daemon*. They were the same word. Almost the same, except for those interchanging *A* and *O*.

Alpha and Omega. The beginning and the end.

That was it, the pun Giles hadn't solved! But how had my sister come up with it? Maybe this was the way ancient riddles revealed themselves—in stuffy game rooms, on perfectly normal college nights, in front of a crowd of pizza-eating students?

As it happened, the dictionary blessed the word (we all carried demons inside, so the second Latin spelling had managed to sneak itself in).

"*DOMAIN* would have been much less risky," Ben pointed out while I was getting up to leave. "Are you sure you don't want to finish the game?"

I was certain.

On the way to my room, I saw festive lights. Entire garlands of them, lit throughout the hallways. But who cared about a party at this point? I had finally found a clue left behind by my sister. All those years ago, Giles had dismissed her talk of daemons and maenads as crazy, but could she have been onto something? What if it turned out that the key to the Dionysian mysteries—the greatest enigma of the ancient world—lay buried in an old student paper at Princeton?

I needed a plan. Even an unrealistic one. Anything that would bring me closer to the answers I had hoped to find on this campus. Maybe befriend Giles? Assuming, of course, that someone who called me "Miss Slavin" would allow himself to be befriended. He was the perfect co-conspirator: haunted by the past, eager to decrypt the rituals. And best of all, he was discreet. Scandal could tarnish his academic reputation, so he was probably going to think twice before picking up the phone—to call the police, or my parents, or send me to a shrink, or declare anyone a stalker—if things went out of hand. Unless they already had?

I slipped two of my free tickets to Carnegie inside a note ("I hope you would enjoy this concert as much as you enjoyed my first one") and signed my name in Greek: Θεία. Just as I was sealing the envelope, a blast of music shook the building—someone was testing speakers in the main wing of Forbes. I could already hear the first signs of commotion through the corridors. Doors slammed in a hurry. Phones starting to ring.

In less than two hours, the Fall Dance was supposed to begin.

CHAPTER 8

The Theia Hypothesis

FOR ONE NIGHT only, the Forbes dining hall had decided to impersonate a carnival stage: tables were lined up along walls, color projectors blinked nervously, helium-pumped balloons bounced off the ceiling in a risky attempt to spice up the mood, and a disco ball swirled its shiny cheeks in the middle.

My last-minute whim to show up at the dance—with another guy and in the most revealing dress I owned—was just an impulsive attempt to get back at Rhys. But the plan backfired from the start, when Ben showed up at my door holding an orchid.

"Wow, Thea . . . you look amazing!"

I probably did, as the strapless red dress was so short it could pass for a tunic. Mistake number one: dressing up for someone who wasn't going to be there. Ben, of course, assumed I had done it for him.

"Thanks. You didn't have to bring me a flower."

"Custom says you should wear it on your wrist." A thin elastic band was attached to the stem.

"What if we broke custom and let the flower live a bit longer?"

He watched as I dropped the orchid in a glass of water. It felt awful to do this to him. But "custom" applied when one had a date, and this was definitely not our case.

As we were leaving, my phone rang somewhere in the room—most likely Rita, who had called twice already to convince me not to skip the dance. We ran into her soon enough, and the relief to see me oozed through the air.

"Thank God, Tesh! I was starting to think you were in eternal mourning." I didn't see how showing up with a friend proved that I wasn't. "Come, I want you guys to meet Dev."

Dev was a sophomore from Forbes who had scored the hottest date for the night and knew it. Originally from India, he epitomized the perfect human specimen: tall, muscular, with hair down to the shoulders and the dignified features of an ancient god. But my favorite thing about the guy was that he looked completely besotted.

Watching the two of them reminded me that I had wanted to be there with Rhys. That I had asked him and he had said no. Now no matter what Ben and I did, I wondered how it might have felt with Rhys. To walk in as his date. To dance with him. The entire evening transformed, exciting, magical. It was as if my life had split in two: the reality of what was actually happening, and then in parallel, played out only in my head but just as vivid—the reality I wished for, of things that could have been.

Even Ben's adorable sweetness didn't help for very long. When my mood dropped visibly, he suggested taking a break from the crowd and we sneaked out through the fence separating Forbes from the golf course. As soon as our feet reached the much thicker grass outside, the air became cooler. Shivery. Scarred by a deranged wind roaming the open hills.

"Thea, what's wrong?"

"Nothing." The pond lay quietly, staring back at the sky with the silver eye lent to it by the reflected moon. "Why would anything be wrong?"

"I can tell. And sometimes . . ." He stopped and looked at me. "Sometimes talking about it helps."

Of course it did. It relieved the talker at the expense of the one who listened. "I'm just . . ."

. . . tired.

. . . overwhelmed.

. . . homesick.

It was all on the tip of my tongue, but I didn't want any more lies.

"I'm sad about something, that's all."

"A guy?"

I looked away, trying not to answer.

"Is this why you wanted to skip the dance? The almost-promise you told me about?"

"I guess so, yes."

He didn't say anything, just gave me a hug—the warm and careful hug of a friend—then pulled back quickly. Somebody was coming. A girl. In a rush.

"Tesh, can I talk to you?"

"Right now?"

"Yes. Sorry, but it's urgent."

In his usual tactful way, Ben said he would wait inside and left us.

"What's the matter? Are things with Dev all right?"

"Dev is fine. Your stalker, on the other hand, clearly isn't."

"What are you talking about?"

"Come on, don't play dumb. The guy who was staring at you that night in Colonial. You didn't tell me the two of you were an item!"

"We're not an item."

"Then why was he at the dance looking for you? And not only that—when I mentioned you had a date, he seemed ready to kill someone. Didn't say a word, just stormed out."

"Sounds like him. He tends to storm out a lot, but that's his problem."

"Judging by that big smile on your face, the problem is yours too. I used to joke about the whole stalker thing, but now I'm getting a really weird vibe from this guy, Tesh. He acts as if he has a claim on you and, frankly, I can't believe you are okay with it."

As my RCA, she loved worrying about me. Still, there were worse things than being "stalked" or "claimed" by a guy like Rhys. And what was this American obsession with stalking anyway? We had no such word in

Bulgarian—people expressed their emotions in all kinds of ways, and to pursue a woman was expected of men; it didn't automatically mean crossing criminal lines. Yet now was not the time for existential arguments with Rita, so I thanked her and headed to my room to call him.

I had barely walked in when someone pulled me inside, shut the door, and pushed me against the wall.

"Why are you playing games with me, Thea?"

I tried to move away but couldn't. "I'm not the one playing games."

"No? Except for blowing off my calls so you can go out with that guy again."

I remembered the phone ring I hadn't answered earlier. "As I recall, you weren't supposed to be part of my social life."

"I said I'd come tonight if it's such a big deal to you."

"Then where were you?"

"At your door! But too late, apparently. I wanted it to be a surprise. And it certainly was one—for me!" He lifted my hands against the rough edges of the cinder blocks. "I decided to be honest with you. And you take that as a license to go behind my back?"

"I told you, Ben is just a friend."

"Not according to your girlfriend. Who, by the way, seems to know more about your dating life than I do."

"There isn't anything to know. You're imagining things."

"Am I? How about you in his arms a few minutes ago—am I imagining that, too?"

There was something intoxicating in his jealousy, even in his rage. It left him vulnerable and gave me a strange sense of power.

"Rhys, you are crushing me. I can't even breathe . . ."

He pulled back just enough to let me catch my breath, but his grip around my wrists tightened. "I said that I'm not going to share you. Which part didn't you understand?"

"I thought we agreed on the sharing when you told me you were not a one-woman guy."

This must have confirmed his suspicions about me and Ben, and it drove him absolutely crazy. He hit the wall with his fist, sending a tremor up my spine.

"I made it clear there's no other woman I want to be with. So you could have had the decency to stay away from that guy, couldn't you? But no, you had to get it on with him in my face! And I should have known—no better place than the Princeton fucking golf course!"

"Better place for what? Stop acting this way . . ."

"I'm not the one who's been doing the acting. Dying to make love to you all this time and fooled by that clever shyness of yours—" His leg pushed between mine. The wall blocked it but he pushed again, sliding his hand up my thighs while his knee kept them open. "Is this what you wanted out there? Because if it is, I can give it to you better than anyone. Better than you ever imagined . . ."

He knew exactly where to touch me and how—insistent, erasing my anger, leaving me ready for him. Embarrassingly ready. Warm, wet, swollen. Yet I was still terrified of having sex with him. Of everything that could, and probably always did, go wrong the first time.

"Rhys, we should stop."

He wasn't listening. We were both turned on and the rest didn't seem to matter to him.

"I can't do this now . . . Rhys, I need more time." My body was turning stiff with panic. "I haven't had sex before. Please stop!"

His breath vanished. His hands fell, the rest of him still in shock from what he had heard.

"You really mean . . . never?" As if my words could have meant anything else. "Why didn't you tell me?"

"I just did."

"No, earlier. In the field, when I tried to . . . My God, I wish I'd known!" He rubbed his forehead, deep into some invisible knot of guilt. "I'm so sorry, Thea. I had no idea."

"Now you do. But, either way, I think you should leave."

"I tried. I can't be away from you."

"I meant my room, right now. And this isn't me being shy or clever. I really mean it."

"I can't be away from you. Do you understand that? I've never been someone's . . ." Then he corrected himself, to avoid the taboo word: "I've never been serious with anyone. But I'm trying. I want to try."

"Try what exactly?"

"To be with you and not see you get hurt. You just have to be patient with me."

"I don't have to be anything."

"Of course you don't. That's not how I meant it." His eyes always hypnotized, but until now I had never seen them pleading. "Come home with me; the car is outside."

"I need to rest. In my own bed."

"Then let me stay here. We'll just go to sleep, I promise."

My phone rang and the sound was so jarring I realized he had been whispering. It was Ben. I apologized to him, asked if he would mind finishing the party without me, and promised to make it up to him soon. He was nice about it, as always.

Rhys observed, waiting for me to hang up. "I love how sweet you are with everyone."

"Sweet? I was rude to my friend just now because of you. It can't happen again."

"I'm sorry, Thea. I really am." His fingers ran down my cheek, fast but barely touching it, as if afraid to harm the surface of a butterfly wing. "Let me stay here tonight. Please."

"Stay how? My bed is barely big enough for one person."

He kissed me quickly. Turned. Grabbed the end of the covers and pulled them off in a single sweep, throwing everything on the floor—blanket, sheets, pillow. Before I could say a word, my shoes had been taken off, my dress was slipping down and my feet were being placed on cotton fabric that was incredibly soft, much softer than I would have imagined my linens against the rough carpet. Then he folded everything in two and tucked us both inside, kissing my face for a long time . . .

And so, the two realities had converged again. At least on the outside, my evening was ending exactly as I had wished—with me in his arms.

I DREAMED THAT I WAS with Rhys. In a field. A field that spread its astonishing grass under us—red, devastatingly red, as if the ground had bled its entire sadness out at the tar-black sky. Begging it. Exhausted from waiting.

All around, paled to the white of winter birds, frail skeletons of trees wove their secrets into a dense web of silence. And within it the air pulsed, ready.

He went in first—sinking us deep into the forest, into its lifeless labyrinths. I followed his steps with the softness of a shadow. Moving with him. Breathing him. Existing only in him, as if I had belonged to him always.

While we walked, he spoke to me about darkness. About his perpetual darkness and how he wanted to take me, the way a heavy night sweeps the earth: storming it, bursting through each of its crevices and hard, hard as a root from which we would both fall toward each other, madly, irreversibly, without even knowing it—

· then he turned.

I felt his eyes. Their guilt. His voice, fading as I slipped away:

far from lost   *if you don't open your eyes, I will*

alone   famished

impossible to bring you back

from the abyss of

He didn't see it, but I did: a white figure approaching through the forest. Skipping steps. Smiling. Twirling like a child, while a dress poured silver around her tiny body. She reached him. Kissed his face. Drowned it with her golden hair: a lost sun looking for its moon—

"The sun? No, the sun is far from lost. It's out already, and if you don't open your eyes . . ." The familiar laughter spilled in my ear. "If you don't open your eyes, I will be forced to have breakfast without you. Don't tell me you want to wake up here alone and famished."

I looked around and found myself curled up on the floor in my room. Rhys had bent over me, smiling.

"Good morning. It's impossible to bring you back!"

"Back where?"

"Here, from the abyss of sleep."

He had already gone to the dining hall and brought a tray with food: warm toast, two omelets, coffee, and a plate of fruit. Once again, though, he seemed more interested in watching me eat than in the food itself.

"Aren't you hungry?"

He shrugged, biting into a piece of toast. "Crowds drain my appetite. I'd forgotten that Forbes is a zoo in the morning."

My fork stopped in midair. *Forgotten?* I could see the bread force its way down his throat, as he realized that the slip hadn't escaped me.

"When were you a morning person in Forbes before?"

Just two words, carefully chosen:

"Way back."

Then two more:

"Sophomore year."

I had finally managed to bait it out of him: he had once attended Princeton. "Why didn't you tell me you used to live in Forbes?"

"Because I didn't. Live in Forbes, I mean."

He sounded resigned to my questions, but I stopped them right there. Why bother? Only one thing could have kept him away from his dorm overnight, back then: the same thing keeping him away from his house now. As it were, for the moment that "thing" happened to be me.

I stirred the sugar in my coffee. "By the way, I probably won't be able to see you until Friday."

"Why not?"

"Midterms are starting tomorrow. I have to take the book vow."

"There's something else, Thea." There always seemed to be something else. "Friday won't work. I'll be gone for a while."

"How long?"

"Just a few days, I'll be back by Saturday. But until then, I need to be on my own."

Need to be. At least, unlike Jake, he was letting me know in advance.

"Then I'll see you over the weekend. It's not a big deal."

But it *was* a big deal. I could tell it was, even more for him than for me. An inexplicable guilt had sneaked into his eyes and remained there.

Crazy scenarios began to swarm in my head. What if he was secretly married? Had a child? Or where did all his money come from? Corporate scams? Mafia schemes? Then I forced my thoughts back to reality: Rhys had plans and those plans didn't include me. I had no right to be upset about it, nor did he owe me explanations.

Before he left, he helped me make the bed again. And in daylight, the dreamy cloud of cotton went back to what it had always been:

Ordinary linens.

"SO, WHO IS HE?" RITA had tracked me down at dinner. Her tray landed across from mine and the coffee mug almost tipped over—an exaggerated bang, to show me she was still ticked off that I had kept the stalker saga a secret. "Tesh?"

"Do we really have to talk about him?" It was the night before midterms and all I wanted was a quick meal.

"I'm just trying to protect you. So yes, I guess we do."

"Protect me from what?" I took a sip from the orange juice. "He isn't my boyfriend, if that's what you mean."

So much, at least, he had made clear.

"Then what is he?"

My fingers played with the glass, rotating it in place.

"Tesh, I'm not blind. What is he?"

"I've seen him a few times. It's complicated."

She reached across the table, sliding her hand over mine. "That's exactly why I'm worried. The guy seems cut out for the eating club scene—which I'm not sure is a good thing to begin with—but he's also older, right?"

"Not that much older."

"Okay, Miss Vague, give me the actual number."

"I don't know, late twenties. Who cares?"

"What do you mean *who cares*! Wouldn't you rather be with someone your age? Or is falling for older men a Bulgarian thing?"

"Not everything has to be a Bulgarian thing. How different do you think people are over there?"

She acted like I had landed from Mars. And she wasn't the only one. Whenever I did anything out of the norm—wear heels to class, leave a party sober, or (gasp!) prefer a moody and obsessive man to the nauseating Princeton boys whose idea of "cool" was to chug beer from a hose and compete over who would get laid the most—people assumed it was a culture clash.

"Listen, there's nothing to worry about. I can look after myself."

"Of course you can. But this isn't about you. It's about Rhys."

Rhys? I didn't recall mentioning his name to her. "So . . . you know him?"

"Me? Yeah, right." She rolled her eyes. "Like they'd let me into Ivy. Dev knows him, though. I mean . . . 'know' might be a stretch, but he's certainly seen him around a few times."

"What does Dev have to do with the eating clubs? Isn't he just a sophomore?"

"Yes, but he's also on the crew team. And they hang out at Ivy. A lot. As do the swimmers—which is how your guy enters the picture."

"Rhys is not 'my guy.' And he isn't a student either, so he can't be on any teams. I think the picture is safe."

"I didn't say he's on the team. At least not anymore. But, apparently, the swimmers don't go anywhere without him. Dev called him their mastermind. I have no idea what that even means!"

Neither did I.

"All I know is that he seemed a bit out of control last night, Tesh. And that sort of thing gives me the creeps." She looked around and lowered her voice. "From what I understand, a ton of strange stuff has been going on."

"What stuff?" I thought the strangest "stuff" at Princeton took place during bicker week.

"Supposedly, once a month the swimmers have these wild parties. Not at the club. They start at Ivy and then go somewhere for the real thing. It's super hush-hush, the whole shebang. But the rowers get invited from time to time—to up the ante, I guess. Dev has gone a few times and says he can't begin to describe what takes place there."

"Drinking? Sex?" I tried to sound casual.

"Both. Although I think this is only . . . warm-up, you know? Dev wouldn't talk about it, but let it slip how once he had to leave because he couldn't take it. And Dev is not a guy with inhibitions, that's for sure."

I wondered whether to believe her or not. The story certainly fit in with Rhys's guilt-ridden secrecy. His sudden need to be on his own.

Then an idea crossed my mind.

"Can I ask you a favor? Suppose the swimmers had something coming up this Friday. And suppose Dev knew about it. Do you think he might be persuaded to tell you?"

AFTER RITA LEFT, I WENT back to my room. But instead of studying, I turned on the computer and found the webpage of Princeton's swim team.

Ten years of photo archives—and not one face remotely familiar. Poor Dev must have been desperate to impress his date. Conjuring up stories of evil masterminds, nocturnal ventures, clandestine sex . . . and claiming he was part of it! Rhys had never been on that team. So, even if a monthly "shebang" did happen hush-hush, why would the swimmers bring an outsider into it?

I closed the browser and reached for my book. Yet something didn't feel right. While I had been out at dinner, something between those four walls had changed. And it took me a moment to realize what that was:

Ben's orchid was gone. In its place, a vibrant poppy burst its red at the rest of the room.

GILES KEPT HIS INDIFFERENT STARE on the clock while we scribbled the sentence on the covers of our exam books: *I pledge my honor that I have not violated the Honor Code during this examination*. Then he wished everyone good luck and left.

My first midterm at Princeton. I rushed through the questions, lifting my eyes now and then to glance at the auditorium, at the rows of lowered heads. It was remarkable to see the famous Honor Code in action. The premise was simple: you didn't cheat and you reported anyone who did. In exchange, the school gave exams without supervision. People would drop off their answers and walk out, even when the pages were mostly empty. If you hadn't studied enough, the grade was going to be bad and that was it. No one cheated.

Midterm week itself was brutal. Physical misery. Mental exhaustion. Feeling as if I had been run over by a bulldozer. After my last exam on Friday all I wanted was a nap, but a voice mail from Ben reminded me that we had plans—dinner with friends at the Jewish Center. My first foray into the intricacies of kosher food.

Meanwhile, a question had been nagging me all week: What happened to Rhys? He never called to ask how my exams went. Not even a text message. And I had no idea where he was. Where, and with whom.

"So, did you change your mind about Boston?"

Ben's voice brought me back to the table chatter and the only topic anyone seemed interested in: fall break. He had invited me to his house in Boston with a few other friends from Forbes. His parents were in Europe for the week, and we would have the place to ourselves.

I repeated the answer I had given him earlier: Carnegie was in less than a month; I was supposed to stay at school and practice.

"You realize the campus will be a ghost town, right?"

"I think that's the point."

"Except this is college, not the army! You're allowed to have fun at least some of the time. Plus, we have a piano at home."

"It would never work, Ben. Too many distractions."

I was running out of excuses. Practice was practice, but the real reason I wanted to stay, of course, was Rhys. That, and my Elza quest. I couldn't stop thinking about her paper. Was there more to it than girlish fantasies? I had to find out, with help from Giles or not. Add some luck, and I might even stumble onto something by accident. If those first two months were any indication, clues revealed themselves when I least expected. Who knew what else might turn up, once I actually started looking?

"Fine, I get it. True art demands sacrifice." Ben spread his arms, enacting a crucifix. "But can we at least go out tonight?"

"Sure. What's the plan?"

"Nebulous so far. I know of a party in one of the dorms. And there's always the Street."

"I thought the Street was dead on Fridays."

"Not tonight. It's fall break; everyone goes wild out there."

Wild. A detail I wished I didn't know.

When we left, I heard music from the eating clubs only a block away. The postexam partying had started.

Whatever, don't think about it. Just follow Ben. Cross the street.

But even the street sign mocked me: IVY LANE. Everything that night was conspiring to remind me of Rhys.

"Come take a look at this, it's incredible. Frank Gehry's newest creation." Ben pointed to a large construction site on the corner of Ivy Lane and Washington Road. "Lewis Library. Biology, chemistry, math, and astrophysics."

Even a fence couldn't hide the mad genius of what was trapped inside. A giant silver lizard had tried to swallow a brick tower, but the bite had ripped his throat and the creature had collapsed around it, choked up in heaps of permanent defeat. Crumpled metal ribs had become roof shapes; slabs of steel razored up into the air on one side—atrophied wings cursed to always dream of flying; and below, sliced open like folds of extremely fragile skin, glass windows carried proof that somewhere, underneath, the animal still breathed.

"Have you been inside a Gehry building?" Ben continued to play tour guide, encouraged by my admiration.

"No, I've only seen pictures."

"The experience is beyond this world. It's as if all three dimensions collide and you are at the very center."

Being at the epicenter of a collapsing world. I had come close a few times, although it had nothing to do with architecture: Playing onstage, with Jake walking in. The two of us in the dark museum. My hand in his at the end of dinner, while his brother watched . . .

"There used to be an opening, but they must have closed it." Ben inspected the fence as we walked down Ivy Lane. "Amazing, isn't it? A science library that looks like an art building. I guess the eye needs a break from science, at least mine does. Slam the brain with too many numbers, and it starts to crave art desperately . . ."

His voice still reached me but I was no longer listening. Someone had come out of the building next door—a miniature compared to Gehry's indulgence, with slim windows chasing their identical arches down receding walls—and I recognized the figure instantly.

The dimensions had collided again. Caught at the epicenter, I wondered how to tell Ben that I wouldn't be returning to Forbes with him.

"HI, THEA." HE SAID MY name almost in a whisper, as if it held a secret. The way he always said it. And the way his brother never did. In fact, Rhys hardly said my name at all—except to warn me or apologize. "What brings you to Ivy Lane?"

"My first kosher meal. You?"

"This is my department." His eyes glided along the arches. "Astronomy."

I imagined him looking at the sky, at the cold darkness of its universe. "And what did the stars tell you today?"

"The stars have been silent for a long time." He must have regretted the weakness instantly, because his voice became formal again—formality I couldn't stand. "What else have you been up to?"

"Keeping your brother entertained. Wasn't this my mandate?"

"You are much more than entertainment to Rhys."

"Let's hope so. But you and I both know I can be wrong about what I mean to someone."

He remained silent. It felt good to provoke him. To accuse him of what it was already too late for him to fix.

"Do you always look out for your brother like that? Stepping aside, so things will align for him. It's very altruistic of you."

"He deserves to be happy, Thea. More than anyone else I know. Certainly more than me."

"Yes, he seems to think so too."

I expected that he might argue, try to justify himself or defend Rhys. But he only shook his head. "Come. I want to show you something."

I followed him into the building, up a staircase and into a room that looked ordinary, gray—until he pushed the lever of a shutter and the sky poured in, released over us through the glass of a magnificent domed ceiling. Under it, negligible against the vastness it would soon carry to our eyes, waited a teal-blue telescope.

He typed something into the control panel, and the words [STAR object:___] popped on-screen. Next to the keyboard, an instruction sheet listed several codes.

"What do you want to see first, a planet or a star?"

"Neither." I reached out and pressed three digits, 9-0-3: the moon.

As if woken by a spell, the telescope began to align itself until the lens chose an angle and froze in it. I lowered my face to the eyepiece—

Deep black. A scattered mosaic of distant stars. And within it—a silver orb. Strangely pale, desolate. Lost in the folds of a bottomless sky.

"It's a full moon, isn't it?"

He didn't answer, but the perfect circle was unmistakable. "Do you like the moon?"

"I always have."

"Of course. You created it." A smile brushed the corners of his lips. "Ever heard of Theia?"

Not exactly my name, but almost. Someone else had pronounced it that way, on a full-moon night like this. A night that had demanded its music.

"It's a planet. A mystery one. The chase after what's left of it still keeps NASA awake at night."

He drew the sun on a sheet of paper. A smaller Earth next to it. And a circle around the sun—the Earth's orbit. Then he marked five dots: three along the circle, one inside it, and another one outside, next to the Earth.

"These are the five Lagrange points in the sun-Earth system. They are regions in space where the pull between us and the sun creates a gravitational static, collecting floating wreckage from the cosmos much like water gathers at the bottom of a well. Anything caught inside that well will rotate with the Earth and the sun indefinitely, unless another pull of gravity interferes from outside. Here, in L4 or L5"—a small *x* appeared over two of the dots along the circle—"is where Theia is rumored to be floating still, after five billion years, in the form of leftover asteroids."

I tried to picture my mystery namesake and not get lost in Jake—in his voice, whose stories I could listen to endlessly; in his fingers that held the drawing of gravitational wells and cosmic secrets. "And this planet created the moon?"

"So they say. Disturbed out of its equilibrium, Theia collided with Earth, then the debris from both coalesced into the moon. It's known as the Theia hypothesis, and the part about the origin of Theia began right here."

"At Princeton?"

"Yes. Belbruno and Gott. Gott is my thesis adviser."

"You are writing about all this?"

"I wish I were!" The laughter cleared his eyes to a softer, almost transparent blue. "It would have made a fantastic thesis: *Astronomy and the Greek Myths*."

I thought he was making things up to provoke me, alluding to our chat by the Greek vases. "Jake, this isn't funny."

"I'm not joking. Sort of eerie how everything is linked, right? Theia is the Greek Titan who gave birth to the moon goddess Selene—which is why your name is by far the best choice for the colliding planet. Every once in a while, though, an alternate name is thrown around: Orpheus." He gave me a moment to absorb that last detail. "And it doesn't make sense, because Orpheus has no connection to the moon. None whatsoever."

Maybe not to the moon, but he had a connection to me. So much, in fact, that hearing the name no longer shocked me. Orpheus—and through him, Elza—had permeated my entire life at school. Why would they miss my few moments with Jake under the dome of stars?

"This reminds me what I wanted to show you." He typed new digits into the panel, erasing the moon from it. The telescope went back into motion. Searched the sky. Stopped. "Constellation Lyra. The lyre of Orpheus. Not exactly the one from your vase, but still—"

"Jake, would you mind if we . . . can we look at something else?"

My request startled him but he didn't ask anything, just changed the digits again. "Okay, how about my favorite piece of the sky? Here . . . take a look."

It was as if his eyes had left behind the stunning residue of their color: a cluster of stars imbued the night with a pale sapphire glow.

"That's the most luminous constellation in our hemisphere. And one of the closest to Earth."

"How close is 'close'?"

"Four hundred light-years." He waited until I looked back at him. "Amazing, aren't they?"

"I never knew stars could be this color." *Nor eyes. Your eyes, the blue universe of their silence.*

"These are the Pleiades. They owe their color to a very fine interstellar dust through which they happen to be passing. It reflects blue light from all the younger stars."

"How old are the Pleiades?"

"A hundred million years. About twice as much left to go."

"And then what?"

"Then the gravity of the universe will take its toll, forcing the sisters to go their separate ways."

"Sisters?" Something about the way he had said that word gave me chills.

"The Pleiades are seven sisters. Orion tried to woo them, but they fled from him until Zeus turned them into stars." He looked through the telescope and adjusted the lens. "They should be easier to spot now. Do you see them, all seven?"

This time the shapes emerged distinctly in the sky. A four-cornered diamond and a small triangle next to it, encrypted into dots that even a child could have connected within seconds.

I asked him why one of the stars was less bright, the one at the very bottom.

"That's Merope, the youngest Pleiad. She barely shines because she is eternally shamed."

"For what?"

"For falling in love with a mortal man."

His voice had become so quiet that I lifted my face from the eyepiece. "How can falling in love be shameful?"

"Apparently it could be, to the Greeks." He put the cap back on the lens. "Let's go, I'll take you to Forbes."

I would have loved to be with him longer. To walk in the moonshade of trees and buildings, all the way across campus, back to my room. But this was Jake. There could be no "back to my room" with him.

While he was shutting down the telescope, I checked my phone and found a text from Rita: *Dev did get persuaded. The answer to your question is yes.*

"Ready?" Jake was at the door, waiting to turn off the lights.

"Thanks for showing me all this. But don't worry about coming to Forbes. I've taken up enough of your time, and given that it's Friday night—"

"My time is yours whenever you need it."

Mine? Since when?! This was the guy who had wanted a dorm room just so he wouldn't run into me at his own house. Now, all of a sudden, he was giving me astronomy tours and offering to walk back with me? Unless he had done it out of pity. Some vicarious guilt for what his brother—that same brother of his who so deserved happiness—was doing right now on the Street, behind my back.

"Good night, Jake."

The staircase flew under my feet, the door of the building flung open for me, and the quiet Princeton night took me in, rushing my steps while I made up my mind—about Rita's text, about Jake's role in all of this, and about what those mocking stars must have known all along was going to happen next.

"GOOD EVENING, MISS THEA. IS Master Rhys expecting you?"

This had been a bad idea, I knew it the moment I saw the butler's sullen face. He didn't invite me in, didn't move an inch from the door. Only glanced at the bike I had borrowed from Rita—it waited by the wall, ready to take me back.

"I don't believe Rhys is expecting me, no. This was a . . . spur-of-the-moment visit. Would you mind telling him I'm here?"

He minded. It exuded from every pore of his being. But a voice echoed down the hallway:

"Tell them I'll be a minute, Ferry. I just need to find the damn—" Then he saw me and froze. "You?"

The old man stepped aside, making way for Rhys to come out and close the door.

"What are you doing here?"

Good question. Clearly, I was no longer even allowed in his house. "I wanted to talk to you."

"About what?"

"About everything you haven't told me."

He tensed up—the instinct of an animal preparing for an ambush. "And what do you think that is?"

"You know very well."

"I don't. And I also don't have much time. So whatever it is you came to talk about—say it."

His voice was calm but he left no doubt about the icy distance in it. I felt humiliated. Lower than those precious pebbles under his feet.

"Thea, will you please tell me why you're here?"

"I can ask you the same thing."

"Me? This is my house!"

"I thought you said you'd be gone."

"Plans change."

"Party plans?"

He might have answered, but a rumbling noise stormed up the driveway and we were drenched in the glare of two giant headlights. An open jeep full of guys, louder than both the engine and the blasting music.

One of them jumped out, only inches from me. "Nice! Who is she?"

Rhys was already standing between us. "Get back in the car, Evan."

"Chill, man. I was just checking her out. She's coming, isn't she?"

Rhys pushed him back. "Get in the car and shut up!"

The others were laughing, shouting things I tried not to listen to.

"What's your problem?" It was Evan who pushed Rhys this time. "I thought the rule was we don't bring our own snacks to the picnic."

"*I said shut up!*" Rhys's voice drowned the music, the engine, and any other sound still coming from the jeep. "Since when are *you* telling *me* what the rules are?"

He grabbed Evan and hurled him back with such rage that the guy hit the front tire and collapsed on the gravel. The others watched. Rhys grabbed him again, pulled him up, and shoved him in the front seat.

"You don't make the rules, you fucking asshole!"

Someone had stopped the music. The engine was now the only sound left.

"Get the hell out of my house! *Out!*"

They didn't wait to hear it a second time. And neither did I. The moment that jeep drove off, I reached for the bike.

"Hey—" He turned me around. The bike fell to the ground, tires spinning. "Sorry about all this. Let's pretend it never happened."

"Pretend? As in get amnesia?" I pulled myself out of his arms. "It doesn't work that way, Rhys."

He lifted the bike and leaned it back against the wall. "I already said I'm sorry. What more do you expect me to do?"

"At this point—nothing."

"Come on, I don't want to fight." His voice was receding back to its disarming velvet. "Let's finish this inside. Then I'll drive you to Forbes."

And drop me off and be free? All according to plan.

"I think the snack is leaving, Rhys. Have fun at your picnic."

Then I got on the bike and left. He shouted something after me—it sounded like a question, but I had no more answers for him.

BEN OPENED THE DOOR AND his face flushed with relief. "Finally! I've been calling you all evening. Did Ivy Lane swallow you whole?"

I skipped the explanations. "Is the invite to Boston still open?"

"Of course it is."

"When are you driving there?"

"Tomorrow, with the others. Why, what's wrong?"

"Would you mind if you and I left tonight instead?"

"Tonight?" His eyes searched mine, cautiously. "I thought we were going to a party later."

"We were. I just . . . I really need to get out of this place, Ben."

It was obvious that my change of mind had nothing to do with him, but he didn't hesitate. "Come, I'll help you pack."

Then, without asking anything else, he headed down the hallway.

CHAPTER 9

Noche de Brujas

BEN'S HOUSE WAS a historic brownstone in the heart of Boston's Beacon Hill. It had belonged to several generations of his family—and still did, except now they had taken the form of hallway pictures, mostly faded.

We arrived late. I had dreaded spending the night in someone's home, by myself, upset at Rhys and his games. But I fell asleep as soon as my cheek touched pillow, and when I woke up, Ben was already downstairs, reading.

"There she is!" He closed the book, looking refreshed and cheerful. "You must be starving. Ready to go explore the local flavors?"

As we grabbed our coats, he asked which part of Boston I wanted to see first. I didn't know much about the city. Mostly Harvard, and only from the Internet.

"Harvard is not a bad idea, actually. We should check it out, so you know what you've been missing." His hand traced an imaginary band of subtitles through the air: "*A day in the life of Thea, had she gone to a certain other school.*"

Going to that "certain other school" might have been a safer bet, away from ritual-obsessed art professors, mysteriously vanished relatives, and elusive guys who came in doubles and lived in butler-run mansions. But I kept all this to myself, telling Ben I was ready for whatever part of Harvard he thought would cause me the most envy.

That part turned out to be Harvard Square. Frantically alive, contagious, a cauldron of energy—nothing like its tame Princeton equivalent, Palmer. Three streets converged in the middle, cars dashing through: a giant star about to collapse in on itself. And wherever you looked, spilling from the campus gates, a dizzying kaleidoscope of people reconfigured its shape constantly.

We bought sandwiches at a local deli and my tour began. Ben was an encyclopedia. School history. Names of buildings. Trivia that would have earned even a professional guide extra credit. But despite his vivid stories, the campus left me cold. There was none of the white-stone mystery; no cloisters, arches, or secret corners. Only redbrick structures, crowned with Harvard's famous white bell towers.

When I couldn't take any more sightseeing, we went to Ben's favorite café, Tealuxe, whose menu boasted more than a hundred types of tea. He found us seats by the window, next to an old typewriter and a display of tea sets.

"This reminds me of Lewis Carroll." I lifted one of the teapots: mint-green belly, curved like an inflated meadow over a chess-checkered base.

"You'd make a fantastic Alice—if only you could learn to whine a bit! That girl does it all the time, and I don't think I've ever heard you complain about anything."

"It would be weird if I did."

"Why? It's not like everything here is perfect."

"Maybe it isn't. But I can't go around complaining just because I'm in a new country that confuses the hell out of me. Better try to figure it out first, right? I mean . . . there must be a reason things work the way they do."

"Not sure how much there is to figure out. You can always look for hidden subtext, but with us Americans what you see is usually what you get."

"Yeah, if only!" I laughed and took the teabag out of my cup. A smell of roses, pine, and berries filled the air. "So if I'm Alice, does that make you the Mad Hatter?"

"I'm more of a Cheshire cat." He flashed an exaggerated grin at me. "Except I suck at the vanishing act."

And thank God he did. Too many people in my life excelled at it lately.

"Thea, does being in America really feel like Wonderland?"

"Exactly like it. One wrong move, and they'll chop my head off."

"No, seriously. That thing you said, about being confused—I can see why. New place, new crowd. Besides, Princeton is definitely not middle-of-the-road. It was a bit of an adjustment even for me, and I've lived in the U.S. all my life."

"You don't seem confused by Princeton."

"I don't?"

"Not at all. Which is sort of like Wonderland. Everyone here seems so . . . sure of everything, as if they've never made a mistake and never will. Don't you think that's madness?"

"Confidence isn't a bad thing, just a survival tactic."

"Still . . . I like people who can be fallible now and then. We're all human, you know? Might as well be humble about it."

While he looked for a response to this, his phone rang. He muted it, but saw who it was and decided to take the call. Said almost nothing for a while. Then hung up and gave me a long, guarded look.

"That was Rita. I had several missed calls from her."

"Is everything okay? I didn't get a chance to say good-bye."

He put the phone down—slowly, as if to minimize the sound it would make against the copper tabletop. "Who is Rhys?"

I almost choked on the last sip of tea. "Why?"

"Some guy named Rhys has been looking for you."

"Looking for me . . . where?"

"Apparently, he couldn't find you in your room and your cell kept going straight to voice mail. So he tracked down Rita and she told him you were in Boston."

"How does she know I'm here?"

"I e-mailed her this morning. Maybe I shouldn't have." He rose from the chair. "Whoever that guy is, he wants you to call him. I'll wait outside."

"Ben, stay. I don't have my phone anyway; I left it at your house. But even if I hadn't—"

"Here. Use mine." He pushed it closer to me and wrote something on a napkin. "This is our address. He'll probably ask for it."

"What are you talking about? Why would Rhys want your address?"

"Rita said he left for Boston earlier today—something about an apology he owes you. By now he must be already in town. Come get me when you finish, I'll be at the newsstand across the street."

I watched him walk away. And with that, my last chance of a peaceful fall break dissolved under the flash of the streetlights.

BEN WAS RIGHT: RHYS DID ask for the address. And by the time we arrived at the house he was already there, waiting.

The two of them exchanged curt greetings. Rhys had managed to suppress his dislike of my friend, although not enough to accept an invitation to come in.

"Thanks. I mean it. But let's not drag this out—I'll wait here while Thea is getting her things."

"Why do you assume I'll be getting anything?"

"Because I'm not leaving without you."

To avoid an argument in front of Ben, I said nothing, just waited for him to go inside.

Rhys checked his watch. "We've got fifteen minutes. Can you make it?"

"Fifteen minutes until what?"

"Until we have to be on the road."

"Rhys, I am not going anywhere."

He smiled and tried to put his arm around me. "Fine, I'll take extra punishment if you want. Although, by most standards, the way you vanished on me today would have been sufficient."

"I wasn't trying to punish anyone."

"No? Strange, then, that I should wake up this morning to find out my captive had become a fugitive. Why did you run away from me?"

"From you? Does it cross your mind that not everything I do revolves around you?"

"It does, it crosses my mind quite a bit. But does it cross *your* mind that everything I do revolves around *you*?"

"Including last night?"

"I'm sorry about last night." The smile disappeared. "There are things I can't change, Thea. Even for you."

"What things? The guys in the jeep?"

"The guys in the jeep are just habit. I won't let them near you again."

"Do you have other habits too? Snack picnics, maybe?"

A sigh. I hadn't heard him sigh, didn't know he was capable of sighing. "That's more than a habit. It's part of who I am."

"So you expect me to pretend it doesn't bother me? To just step aside when you need your breaks from me, no questions asked?"

His eyes rushed up the street. Chased possible answers. Then came back with the one that served him best:

"Just *be* with me. Is that so difficult? I don't need breaks from you, quite the opposite. And I'll do my best to bring things closer to where you want them to be. But I can't go into explanations now."

"Why not?"

"Because we have to leave."

"Maybe you do. I don't."

"All right, here's the scoop." He poured "the scoop" right into my ear: "First, we have a ferry to catch. It's the only way to get where I want to take you. And don't ask me where that is—you know I don't like my surprises ruined. Second, I'm new to this whole dating thing, so apparently I screw up all the time. But it won't always be the case, I promise."

"I thought you didn't make promises you couldn't keep."

"I don't. And third, we have to stop fighting. I am wrapped around those beautiful fingers of yours. If you don't want me there, say it and I'll leave."

There was nothing to say. I was still upset about Friday night. And yes, I had run away from him. But now that he had chased me all the way to Boston to apologize, my anger was evaporating and he knew it.

"Go get your things. And hurry."

When I walked in, Ben was sitting on the couch, holding a magazine. He didn't ask anything, just lifted his eyes and waited for me to speak first.

"Ben, he . . . he wants me to go with him."

"Of course he does. I understand."

"But I feel terrible, especially after making you drive so late yesterday."

"Don't worry about me. The others arrive tonight, this place will be a madhouse. I'm just glad you and I got to spend the day by ourselves."

"Yes, me too, but—" I stopped myself. What right did I have to talk to him this way, as if he were a rejected victim?

"Thea, don't feel guilty. You like this guy, right?"

I nodded, hoping that I was only confirming what he already knew.

"And the guy obviously likes you, or he wouldn't have driven halfway up the East Coast to look for you. So there you go. Not much room for debate."

"Okay then, I won't debate it." *Don't look for subtext. What you see is what you get.* "Yet you are my friend and the last thing I want is to upset you."

"Friends should never get upset when you follow your heart." Then the shy smile I loved so much about him came back. "And even if they do, you should follow it anyway. I would."

ONCE WE WERE ON THE road, Rhys called someone and asked if the cottage was ready.

"It needs to be, when I get there." He hung up, looking peeved. "Jake left this afternoon. I don't understand what's taking them so long."

So this was the surprise, one he didn't realize he had for me: a secret getaway that would remind me of his brother. I could only imagine what waited for me in this mysterious cottage. Things that belonged to Jake? Pictures of Jake all over?

I didn't say much for the rest of the ride; Rhys probably thought I was tired. After the ferry we drove through winding roads for a while, until finally the car stopped. The headlights went out. In their place, an automated lightbulb signaled through the otherwise undisturbed darkness.

"Don't look so terrified; the cottage isn't haunted." He opened the passenger door for me. "Although a ghost or two certainly would be nice. Gets too quiet at night around here."

The "cottage" turned out to be a stunning modern villa, sprawled decadently high above the ocean. Its front was a plain wall (a cover-up, for maximum privacy), but the back more than made up for it. First came a lavish expanse of floor-to-ceiling windows. Then a stone patio. An infinity pool. And beyond them—treetops and water, now invisible until dawn.

Those anonymous hands that had prepared the house for Rhys had left the lights on, and a soft yellow illuminated the first few steps outside where a table was set for dinner, with candles and a bottle of wine.

"Martha's Vineyard." He wrapped his arms around me and pointed to the darkness in front of us. "It's an island to the south of Cape Cod. We've been coming here for many years."

That "we" sounded as if the other person, still missing, could walk out on the patio any moment.

"You have no idea what you did to me when you left so suddenly. Or maybe you do?" He bent over to kiss my neck but felt me shiver. "My God, you're freezing! Let's get you warmer clothes. And some food."

While he inspected the fridge to see what had been left for dinner, I retrieved my jacket from the hallway. When I came back into the living room, he was already headed out, carrying two full plates and a baguette.

"Can I help?"

"No, just give me another minute. By the way, look what I have for you—"

He pointed to the back of the room and I noticed it only now: a grand piano, taking up the corner by the fireplace. Music scores were stacked on top of it, with one still open on the stand. I came closer, close enough—

In the back of my mind, I was still aware of Rhys walking by: a gust of air from an open door; his steps outside; clink of dishes landing on a table. But the room, and everything else in it, had become haze. All I could see were the notes on these pages, notes that I loved: Chopin's Nouvelle Étude in F Minor.

It was the single trace of Jake's presence missed by those who had cleaned the house after him. They had erased him from the keyboard, from the door-knobs, from the plates and glasses and every piece of furniture. But the music had managed to blend in, enough to not be put away. Maybe he had left the pages there on purpose, a coded welcome only I would understand. Or, in a rush to leave, he might have simply forgotten to close them. Either way—he had played my étude in this room.

"It's the piano or me. But choose quickly." Rhys was waiting by the door, holding it open.

I had an urge to tell him the truth. Then I remembered the last twenty-four hours: our scene at Pebbles, his still unexplained absence. We were now even. A secret for a secret.

During dinner, I couldn't stop picturing Jake in this house. What if, like his brother, he was in the habit of bringing girls to his posh cottage off the coast of Cape Cod? Taking them around the island. Pouring wine for them in the darkness outside. Guiding their stunned eyes through constellations. Playing piano for them.

"Why was he here? I mean . . . Jake." The air held his name for one last second. "To spend fall break on the island?"

"As always. And I was going to take you on a surprise trip south. But when I found out you were in Boston, the plan changed."

It had, although not as much as Rhys suspected. Like those ghosts he wished for, I had entered this house long before he brought me there. I had moved in it, laughed in it, existed in it for an entire night and into the next afternoon—because someone else had imagined me there, through the most beautiful music I had ever heard.

"What are you thinking about?"

"Me?" For the first time, I realized that the truth could also be a lie. "About your brother getting thrown out of here today because of me."

"That's one way of putting it."

There was only one way of putting it, really: Jake hadn't given me up. Not if he still played that étude.

"Needless to say, I am now very, very indebted to my accommodating brother." Rhys took my hand and I followed him through the living room, a corridor, and into the bedroom. "But enough about Jake. Or anybody else."

My clothes slipped to the floor and my body let itself be pulled under his on the bed—unresisting, resigned to him, waiting.

"Don't be afraid of me." His fingers pressed my hipbone, ready to move down from it. "I'll stop as soon as you tell me, I promise."

I felt that Jake was there. With us, in the room. *Is this how you imagined it, me belonging to your brother? Is this what you wanted?*

A hand pinned both of mine above the pillow, while another one separated my knees.

"Rhys, let go of my wrists. I won't stop you this time."

"Shhh . . ." His breath filled my ear. "That's not what I'm about to do."

"Do what?"

"What you've been panicking about, ever since I laid you on this bed. You've never trembled in my arms like this!" His hand continued to move up my legs. "I had no idea it would be your first time. So I won't go there for now. Not if I can help it."

"Why?"

"Because—" He ran his nails along my thigh until I began to ache for him, all the way to my stomach. "Because . . . you fucking gorgeous thing . . . I want to do everything else to you first—"

His mouth found my neck and I felt my whole body erupt from it. He pressed hard at first, sinking his tongue into the inch of skin still wet from his lips, then everything softened, until all I could feel was his breath. He waited and did the same thing again—this time much harder, going at my neck as if he had long been hungry for it—only to pull away once more, everything in me left begging to feel more of that kiss, the fury of its touch. When I finally did, I also felt his fingers open my thighs and slowly push inside me, reaching in as far as they could without hurting me. Then, suddenly, they pressed farther just when his mouth was closing over mine, taking the voice from it as I came in his arms.

"SORRY, WHAT?!" RHYS CHOKED, SPITTING the coffee back into his cup. "Carnegie . . . you mean the one in New York?"

"Yes, that one."

He stared at me as if I had just told him I was quitting college to take up stripping. "And what did they ask you to play?"

I told him. He burst out laughing. Walked up to one of the windows and stood there, looking at the clear morning sky outside. When he turned around, there wasn't a hint of laughter left.

"I had no idea you were this good. But Albéniz is a hellride, and four weeks is nothing. I just hope that coming here wasn't a mistake."

"Rhys, I'll be fine." My voice sounded much more convinced than I felt. "I need to practice a lot, that's all."

"A lot? What you need to do is shoot each damn note up your veins like it's heroin!"

"So I'd be high on both of you?" I smiled but he didn't. "Okay, stop freaking me out. Four weeks is a long time. And for now, I thought you wanted to show me the island?"

"The island can wait. We'll see it in bits and pieces, whenever you need a break from prison."

For the next two days, I had the "prison" mostly to myself. He understood that piano practice required solitude, and errands lined themselves up every time I was about to start playing.

At first, the thought of Jake still bothered me. Being in the same rooms, touching the same things. It was impossible to tell what belonged to him and what—to Rhys. The toiletries in the shower. The clothes behind the sliding closet doors (neatly hung shirts, folded sweaters, piled-up jeans), none of which Rhys had brought with him. Maybe the brothers wore the same clothes when one of them happened to be on the island? And then there were things that were clearly Jake's. The open Chopin score. Or the *Celestial Star Atlas*, left on top of the coffee table.

Inevitably, though, these reminders began to fade the longer Rhys and I stayed at the house. As for the island's "bits and pieces," he had a lot to show me: historic towns, harbors, beaches, even a carousel from 1876 claiming to be the oldest in America. But the place that stole my heart happened to be a lighthouse, perched in isolation over a cluster of multihued cliffs.

We had climbed the spiral staircase and were standing on what Rhys called a "gallery"—the narrow railed terrace that encircled the tower. Down below zigzagged the western shore, wrapped in vast stretches of dry grass that made the cliffs look furry, like the back of a giant golden hound.

"The Indians used to call this place Aquinnah." He slipped his arm around me and let the wind run its rage through us. "It means 'end of the island.' But it's an end in flux. See those cliffs?" He pointed at the undulating patches of red, brown, and ochre where the waves crashed, over a hundred feet below. "As the water washes them away, the end of the island continues to creep back in. The lighthouse was already moved once, to keep it safe from the collapsing clay."

"Clay?"

"The cliffs are all clay, formed by glaciers more than a hundred million years ago."

"A hundred . . . *million*?" All of a sudden, the "baked clays" of the ancient Greeks seemed anything but ancient. "Too bad the water is finally winning."

"Erosion always wins," he said quietly. "Nothing can be kept safe from it forever."

I felt I was being warned. But of what? An entire island eroded under our feet, invisibly, even as we spoke. And I, was I safe on that island? Or had I come here with someone who, just like those waves, always won in the end?

We didn't return to the house until after dark. Rhys wanted to have dinner on the floor, in front of the lit fireplace, among cushions and candles whose flickers bellydanced their magnified panic on the ceiling whenever a hidden draught sneaked into the room.

"Ready?" We were done eating, so he pulled me up from the floor.

"Ready . . . for what?"

He walked over to the piano, opened the pages with Albéniz, and propped them on the stand.

"I don't think so, Rhys."

"Why not? My payback is way overdue. Besides, you can't be coy and play this kind of music. So—let's hear it."

He came behind me and sank back among the cushions, to give me the illusion of being alone in the room. But nothing worked, I was still aware of him. Of him looking at me, ready to listen. And absorb. And judge.

Sounds hurried out: glass beads spilling down a cobbled Spanish street as a necklace broke over a girl's shoulders. Yet beads were not enough. What had to flood that street was a summer thunderstorm, crashing, rolling down the cobblestones until they shattered into dust.

By the time I reached its slower middle part, the piece had fallen flat. Drained of its beauty. Lifeless.

"I told you . . ." My hands dropped down. I couldn't even look at him. Then—

Lips. Brushing against my shoulder blade. And the rest of him, slipping down on the bench next to me.

"See?" He lifted my hand and placed it over the zipper of his jeans. Everything inside was bursting, hard with pulse, as if the music still shot waves through him. "That's what watching you at the piano does to me." Then he let my hand slip off. "Now you need the madness of Albéniz. You've got the technique down. But you don't have Spain yet."

"I'll never have it. I haven't even been to Spain."

"That's where I was just about to take you."

The pages flipped back to the beginning and his voice turned plush, solemn, as if coming from centuries ago:

"Albéniz named it *Asturias,* but the music has nothing to do with northern Spain. Its heart is from the south, from the flamenco of Andalucía. Imagine fire. In Spanish, *flama* means 'flame.' "

"I don't hear fire in it."

"Because everyone gallops through the piece, trying to show off. And the result is Albéniz turned into a Bach fugue! The flamenco is different. It isn't about speed or loud torrents of sound. It's about contrast. The fast against the slow. The loud against the quiet. So start with a whisper. And keep it benign, like this—"

Shy notes bubbled up under his fingers. Hesitant, lifting their heads only for a peek.

"Then there's the whole legend thing, right?" He smoothed out the cover page where the title—*Asturias (Leyenda)*—was printed in bold cursive at the top. "Remember: nothing is ever safe in legends."

"What legends?"

"In this case, those of the Andalucían gypsies, whose hot blood fueled the flamenco rhythms. They used to die for love like nobody else, so can you imagine how much passion went into their music? A man like that might fall for you, worship you, lay his life and his future at your feet. But once you trigger his jealousy, all bets are off."

He played the next phrase, delaying the last octave for just a fraction of a second, then slammed it at both ends of the piano.

"Make every sound a threat as you play. Pause. Aim that revenge. Then strike. Don't think, just hit. Rip it open—"

He kept playing, hammering the octaves. And with each, the initial grain of silence was breathtaking. It affected you with sounds you hadn't even heard yet. Because in a flash, while time stood still, you anticipated the music that was about to follow.

"What's the verdict?" He was looking at me, smiling. "You haven't said a thing."

What could I say? This was no longer the guy who mocked music. Now he spoke of Andalucían nights, gypsies, flamenco, and a certain madness they could all bring into me. By the time he had stopped playing, I felt infected by that madness already.

"Play the rest for me. Please."

He rose from the bench. "For the rest, we need something else."

A CD slid into the player. A guitar. Delicate, almost as frail as the sound of water glasses at Louisa's. It was the same Albéniz piece but utterly transformed, carrying a humility one could never draw from a piano. Music that flowed, almost unnoticed, with the subdued power of air flowing through a room.

He pulled me to the floor and we undressed each other—quietly but quickly, under the waves of that guitar. His face moved down my skin. If he had stopped, I would have begged him not to, but his lips rushed up my thighs as he pushed them apart and dived his tongue inside me, driving me wild, wild to get more of his mouth, all of it, and to dissolve in it, to obey its every whim. He went at me without letting me say yes or no, breathing into me, kissing up a storm through places I didn't know I had inside, opening me, wetting me, pressing into me with those fantastic lips that could be so incredibly soft and at the same time absolutely ruthless—until he decided to make me come and I felt him take it all in, with his mouth and his tongue, every last drop of me. When he pulled himself up and touched his cheek to mine, it was still wet. Then he buried his face in my hair and whispered:

"I had done this in my head a thousand times, but you taste so much better than I could have imagined."

The words flooded my body. There wasn't an inch of me left that didn't crave to be his, completely his, or that could be at peace unless it felt him. I wanted to keep kissing him, to do anything for him—to him—that would turn him on and make him come, but he was moving away already.

I pulled him back. "Take me. Take me any other way you want."

He struggled with his decision for a second, then stood up to pour himself a drink. As the empty glass was landing on the table, I began to kiss him—neck, shoulders, chest—but as soon as I reached his stomach, he stopped me. I held his hands down, until they closed around the edge of the table and stayed there. Then I kissed him one last time:

"Now it's my turn. Let me."

LATER THAT NIGHT, WHILE FALLING asleep in his arms, I wished for the first time that he would never find out about me and Jake.

THE WHISPER IN MY EAR woke me up, but I couldn't figure out the words. Something about a trick.

"So which *T* is it?" Rhys was lying next to me, already dressed. "Just pick one."

"Trick or what?"

"Cute. It's your first Halloween, isn't it?"

I nodded, eyes half shut with sleep.

"Or treat. Meaning you'd have to feed me candy. Except I don't see any lying around."

"And the trick?"

"I'd steer clear of the trick, if I were you. Where we come from, tricks are a serious business."

"We?"

"My family. I'm Irish."

We had met more than a month ago, and there was still so much I didn't know about him. Part of it was my fault. I had seen other girls spy on their boyfriends—searching the Internet, checking the guy's phone, reading his e-mails, everything Rhys had called "background checks" and more—so I had sworn never to be obsessively curious. But with him, even healthy curiosity wasn't an option. Or was it?

I rolled over on the bed, closer to him. "When did you leave Ireland?"

"I didn't. I've never lived there. Always wanted to, but never did."

"Why not?"

"Because not everything is up to me, Thea."

It was hard to picture him wanting something and not being able to get it. "You sound as if you're grounded in New Jersey."

"Maybe I am . . . grounded. But let's leave my wish list alone. The point is, that's where trick-or-treating began."

"In Ireland?"

"Of all places. They didn't call it trick-or-treating, of course. The Irish word is *souling*."

"As in baring one's soul?"

"Ha, never thought of it that way. But no, as in praying to the souls of the deceased. The Celts believed that on the night of October 31, the boundary between the living and the dead disappeared. So if the poor knocked on your door that night, you gave them food and in exchange they prayed to the dead souls for you."

I tried to imagine the dead listening, on an October night in Ireland.

Gaunt. Wide-eyed. Haunting the rainy Dublin streets. "And if you didn't give them food?"

"Then you got very, very badly tricked." He sneaked under the sheets and began kissing me all over.

"Rhys, wait. It's my turn."

"What turn?"

"To *soul* you."

"Me?" His head popped out: hair a mess, cheeks flushed. "I don't think so."

"Because you aren't a soul-baring kind of guy?"

"That too. But even if I were, you don't get to trick me if the treat's on me anyway. I'm going to fix us breakfast."

Breakfast wasn't exactly what he could fix, given that it was already one o'clock. While the smell of fried eggs and some sort of meat crept throughout the house, I waited for him in the living room. The place was impeccably furnished. Steel. Glass. Leather. Flowing into one another in clean, minimalist shapes. The fireplace itself was a line of river stones stacked under a hanging wall—one touch to a remote control, and flames sprouted up directly from the stones. There was no other decoration; the walls were completely bare. Except one of them afforded a brief indulgence. A sign that, somewhere, the house nonetheless had a heart—

Books.

About twenty of them, on a single shelf. It looked like someone had enlarged a cardiogram, mimicked its curve out of steel, then nailed the resulting shape to the wall, slipping into each inverted peak as many books as would fit there. Shiny little volumes, nestling perfectly inside their slots. Only at the very end, where the heartbeat had dropped one last time, a book with a cracked spine and worn corners leaned at an angle, all by itself.

I picked it up. Rainer Maria Rilke. The two words on the cover, *New Poems*, were so generic that I wasn't sure they were even a title. But another title was waiting, a few pages in, made up of three names: *Orpheus. Eurydice. Hermes.*

The poem was long and I didn't get to read it, because at the bottom, under the printed text, was a splash of red. Two more lines, added by hand, the letters tiny but still legible, beautifully beaded over long slanted loops:

*I will know you
even in my death*

What kind of a promise—or threat—was this? And who in their right mind would make it? Maybe one of the inexplicably missing parents had written a love note to the other, years back. Or what if the handwriting was Jake's? This was his house too. His books. He had probably figured that I might browse through them, once Rhys brought me here. And so, just like that open Chopin score on the piano, the Rilke volume had ended up strategically at the end of the shelf, where I was most likely to find it.

"Food is served." Rhys pulled the book from me and slipped it back among the others. "You must be starved to death."

"Death seems to be the theme today. I just read about—"

"I know what you were reading."

"Even the handwritten note?"

He shrugged. "Books go through many hands. People scribble."

"It was more than just a scribble."

"We collect old editions, Thea. And old editions come with baggage." Everything about him seemed to come with baggage. He kept dodging my questions, even now. "By the way, I didn't know you liked poetry."

"Some of it."

"Who are your favorites?"

"Neruda, Rumi, E.E. Cummings."

"You've read my namesake? Cummings would have been pleased to know he's big in Bulgaria."

"That's your last name?"

"Rhys Cummings? No, God no! It's Estlin."

I recalled the second *E* in E.E. Cummings: *Estlin*. Brief and stunning, like the sound of icicles clashed together by a wind.

"How about *your* favorites?"

"We'll save those for dessert. Now let's eat."

Eating wasn't in the stars that day. We had barely started when the doorbell rang.

"Carmela is here! Come, she's been dying to meet you."

Everything about the woman radiated cheer: the flowing clothes, wrapped in blocks of color around her bursting figure; the wrinkles projecting laughter away from the quick black eyes; and more than anything—the bubbly exuberance of an accent that carried her voice to every corner of the house.

"*¡Hola!* How are you, Señor Rhys?"

"Very well, thank you, Carmelita." He plunged into her arms for the longest hug I had seen him accept from someone, then turned to me: "Carmela is a very dear friend of the family. She was born on the Costa del Sol, but now lives here on the island. Keeps an eye on the house for us, which we greatly appreciate."

"Then stop chasing the pretty college girls and come to see us more often!" Her smile grew into a wide crescent as she looked me up and down. "Ay, Señor Rhys, she is so beautiful, your girlfriend!"

Girlfriend?

He didn't correct her, just put his arm around me. "Yes, isn't she? But now it's up to you, Carmelita, to make her look devastatingly Spanish for me tonight."

"*Claro,* she'll make a perfect *bruja.*"

"And that," Rhys snapped, as if she had committed a sin known only to the two of them, "is exactly what I don't want."

"I'll make a perfect what?"

"A perfect you." He kissed my cheek. "Now go get ready. I'll be back at six."

THE MAKEOVER FROM "SO BEAUTIFUL" to "devastatingly Spanish" was a challenge. It involved not only matching all the requisite visuals, but also feeding Carmela's curiosity.

"What is your name, *niña?*"

"Thea."

"*¡Muy bonito!* Thea . . . like breeze over the Mediterranean."

She filled up the bathtub and lifted the soap to her nose for a quick sniff before handing it to me:

"Pure *castile,* made from olive oil—the green gold of Andalucía. When you are finished, your skin will carry the aroma of olives."

"How come Rhys has original Spanish soap here?"

"Because he sometimes listens to what I tell him!" Having given Rhys advice on soap seemed to make her genuinely proud. "I've been his housekeeper for many years; he knows he can trust me with anything . . . But now hurry, take your bath! I'll go get a glass of wine and then we can do your makeup."

The glass must have included refills, because she came back with a bottle already half empty.

"So tell me, how did you meet Señor Rhys?"

"At school."

"You met at school and fell in love?" She watched while I twisted my hair to squeeze the water off. "Don't be shy, you can tell Carmela everything. It was love at first sight, no?"

"For me at least." Technically, it wasn't true. Not unless "first sight" included Jake.

"Only for you? Ay, *pero, niña,* it's written on his face! The boy is finally in love. It's been a long time since—" She sat me down in front of the bathroom mirror and stood behind me, holding a comb, hesitating.

"Long time since what, Carmela?"

"Since I gave my big mouth a siesta!" The comb finally risked its way through my hair. "Old people, we dwell inside the past; it dulls the sound of death approaching. But things that are far gone shouldn't worry a young girl like you."

I had heard this speech before—from my parents, from Giles, from everyone who dwelled inside the past but didn't want me to be curious about it. Yet if those "things far gone" were so harmless, why was I constantly shielded from them?

"Have you known him long?"

"Who, Señor Rhys?" She brought her hands together, palms almost touching. "Since the day he was this small! I was his *niñera*. How do you call it . . . *nursemaid*."

"So you also know his parents?"

"Of course."

"What are they like?"

For a moment she looked stumped, as if my question was a trick one.

"I mean, is he at all like them?"

"Those we come from, *niña*, are always who we are. And that boy was born from love like no other I have seen in this world." She poured herself another glass of wine, pulled up a chair, and sat down next to me. "His father, Archer, was the devil. Old noble blood, rich as a king. And handsome. Ay, *Dios mío,* was he handsome! Women fell at his feet and he laughed at them. Only one thing existed for him: cars."

"He collected them?"

"No, he was a racer. Those car races were his one true love, and he had won all of them."

This explained why Rhys was so confident at the wheel, even when driving way too fast.

"Then he met my Isabel. Went crazy. *¡Abso-luta-mente loco!* Chased her all around the world. Every capital, every concert."

"What kind of concerts?" I was already beginning to guess. "Piano?"

"The piano obeyed her the way those cars obeyed him. After the wedding, she still played. But he never did another race."

"Why not?"

"No longer had it in him. *On the racetrack you must be ready to go to hell,* he used to say, *and how can I settle for hell once I've been to heaven?* It made her laugh. She begged him to put her in one of those cars, at least once, so she could feel like the two of them were flying. But he wouldn't hear of it, that's how terrified he was of losing her. As if, in this life, you can ever cheat fate . . ."

"Why, what happened?"

Her eyes vanished from the mirror: a sudden wind had robbed the last two olives from a tree, leaving it barren.

"What did fate do to them, Carmela?"

"One day, Isabel stopped sleeping."

"Just stopped?" It sounded simple, like someone deciding not to wear a certain color. "How can a person stop sleeping?"

"The same way a person stops laughing, or hoping, or dreaming. It just happens. And changes everything."

But it hadn't just happened, it had been happening for generations. I listened in dismay as her tale went back, all the way to a man in eighteenth-century Venice who stopped sleeping and, a few months later, was dead. After him, records began to list deaths in that family as epilepsy, meningitis, schizophrenia, dementia. When, in fact, it would turn out to be something far worse.

"At first, she was just exhausted. Then it became agony. Pain, every part of her body aching. And deliriums. Like having nightmares while you're still awake."

"What about sleeping pills?"

"It was all useless. An uncle had died from the same thing, not long after little Jake was born. The doctors said when they opened his brain, part of it looked like this—" She pointed to a powder sponge in her makeup kit. "The part that lets you fall asleep. That's when they started talking about a cursed gene, a disease that runs in families."

Her hands began to shake and she slipped them between her knees, locking them still.

"Every doctor told her the same thing: once it starts, you die very soon. The body shuts down, you can't even speak, but the mind knows—all the way to the end. A brave girl she was, my Isabel. Kept asking little Jake to play the piano, couldn't get enough of it. *I love my boys so much, Meli*—Meli, she used to call me. *If music can reach to the other side of those clouds, I will be able to hear them from up there, won't I? Won't I, Meli?*

"The last doctor they saw was in San Francisco. From there, a road winds like a serpent down the coast, high above the ocean cliffs. Archer laid his wife next to him in one of those racing cars. And they flew, just as she had always wanted—all the way across the clouds . . ."

I wished I could say something. Anything, to comfort her. But nothing felt right after what she had told me. At that moment, all I wanted was to see Rhys. To be able to touch him and know he was well and breathing.

"Let's finish you up. I almost forgot why I'm here!" She jumped from the chair, the sadness now folded back in, deep into the locked drawers of her heart. "We will need more black around the eyes. And the hair . . . what shall we do with the hair?"

She rolled it up and pinned it in a simple low chignon. Sprayed a few drops of lavender over my shoulders. Took my chin and turned it—left, then right—pleased with her own creation.

"*¡Qué linda!* Do you like it?"

I told her I did, but I wasn't so sure. The makeup was too much (thank God it was Halloween), and the glamorous, sexy gypsy I expected to see in the mirror looked more like a tired ballerina under the glare of the bathroom lights.

While I was trying to get used to my Spanish face, she asked me to wait in the living room and promptly joined me, bringing a big red box.

"A present, from Señor Rhys. Go on, open it!"

Inside was a dress—an exquisitely layered white silk dress. In a heap next to it, a fringed black shawl exploded with flowers, all of them red poppies.

"This is your costume. A flamenco dress carries power. The fire of the gypsy blood, of Andalucían *brujas*."

"What is a *bruja*?"

"Witch. One flip of the skirt"—she kicked back with her foot, pretending to catch a load of fabric in the air—"and you can do anything to a man."

I slipped the dress on and the silk poured down to the floor: a one-shoulder gown, tracing the body to just above the knee, from where it spilled into a wild cascade of ruffles.

"My country has its own *brujas*, whose power lies in the dress too. Long white dress, a bit like this one."

It was my favorite part of the *samodivi* tale (or "wildalones," as Giles would have called them). The lovestruck shepherd sneaks up to the lake for a closer look at Vylla. She hears steps. Turns. And the treacherous moon reveals the young man to her. But it also reveals what he has already found on the shore and taken: a dress made of pure silver, woven with moonthreads. The dress that keeps all of Vylla's power.

"*Claro, sí.*" Carmela listened and nodded, as if everything in that story was turning out the way she expected. "The man steals the dress and wins his *bruja* forever, no?"

"Well, *forever* is not exactly how it ends—our fairy tales don't always have happy endings. But yes, he does steal the dress and they are married for some time."

"Something is telling me your man will steal *your* dress tonight!" She winked at me before glancing at the clock. "We have just enough time for one more drink, and then I can leave you to your Halloween night. *Noche de Brujas,* as we call it in España."

We went outside, on the patio. She poured wine for both of us, lit two candles on the table, and handed me a few floating ones. "Here, take these to the pool."

I dropped them in, one by one.

"Ay, *niña,* nothing like real fire when you need to warm the heart . . ."

"You said something about Rhys in there, about it being long since his heart got warmed."

She remained quiet. A wind ran through the water and the entire pool started shivering in a web of light.

"Carmela, I need to know. Was he really in love?"

"Almost."

"How can someone be almost in love?"

"Like that, like any one of these—" She kneeled down and reached for the nearest candle. "Such a small flame, not a fire yet. Push it even a little"— her thumb pressed, just enough to let the water seep in—"and it will drown. Leaving behind only smoke. Brief but poisonous smoke. Yet I told him—"

The past stole her again and took her far, through the darkness of the ocean in front of us.

"What did you tell him?"

I was worried that my questions might open the drawers of sadness again. But she turned to me and smiled:

"I told my boy that love will come to him one day. Beautiful, complete—just like the sun. And pure like the sun. That it will ask for nothing. Expect nothing. It will simply *exist* for him. I think he believes me now."

I wanted to believe her too—that Rhys was in love and not just chasing the next college girl. But hearing it from her wasn't the same as hearing it from him. Not by a stretch.

When she left, it was already a quarter to six. I went back to blow out the candles, but didn't get to any of them. One glance at the pool, and I thought I was hallucinating. Too much wine. Too many witch stories. Unless, in an attempt to play a trick on me, water and sky had decided to switch places?

There was no sapphire blue this time. Only yellow—the fevered yellow of the burning flickers. I had lit them without keeping count, yet they had ended up exactly seven. And now, far from reach in the middle of the pool, was a figure I had last seen through a telescope: a triangle over a diamond, the seventh candle strangely mute (the one extinguished by Carmela), just as the youngest Pleiad had been barely shining, shamed for falling in love with a mortal man.

I ran back inside. Was I losing my mind? After all, anything was possible on the Night of Witches. Maybe the house was really haunted, with Carmela being one of its many ghosts?

Then I remembered the book I hadn't dared to open all week—the *Star Atlas*—and its index led me to the Pleiades in seconds:

The brightest stars in the cluster were named after the seven sisters who had nursed the infant Dionysus. Known also to the Celts, these stars were linked to funerals and mourning and remembrance of the dead. Because, as the border between the two worlds thinned on Samhain (the Irish word for Halloween or All Souls Day), the Seven Sisters rose in the northern sky, aligning themselves exactly overhead by midnight.

A car came to a stop outside. The *Atlas* slid back under the coffee table. The shawl of poppies swirled its fringes around my shoulders, and down.

Then I noticed a small envelope at the bottom of the dress box. Not a letter, something else. In a distinctive, exquisitely controlled handwriting:

like concentric rings
on the water,
your words
in my heart.

like a bird that collides
with the wind,
your kiss
on my lips.

like fountains unleashed
on the night,
my eyes
on your skin.

"Federico García Lorca, the voice and heart of Andalucía." Rhys had walked in, dressed in black, with a red bandanna around his neck. "You wanted to know my favorites."

"Yes, but that was literally right before you left. How did you—"

"Shhh . . ." He pressed a finger to my lips. "I could tell you how. But what would be the magic in that?"

With his other hand, he was already pinning a poppy in my hair.

GETTING TO NEWBURY STREET ON Halloween meant driving through half of Boston and then walking straight into the epicenter of madness—a pandemonium of creatures come back to life. Fluorescent skeletons. Coiffed zombies. Promiscuous corpse brides and debonair vampires. Even a mummy, flying on a skateboard past everybody else. By the time we arrived at the restaurant, my own head was ready to roll off on wheels.

"Welcome to Tapeo! Sorry, we are fully booked tonight."

A ravishing buccaneer-hostess recited the greeting without lifting her eyes from the computer, but as soon as the name Estlin rippled through the air, she looked up, blushing. In an even higher falsetto, she apologized to Rhys for not recognizing him right away and instructed a nearby pirate to take us to our table.

The ground floor was a mishmash of costumes, noise, and food vapors. People had come for the carnival spirit as much as to eat or drink, and many of them had abandoned their tables, crammed in the tightly packed space— singing, shouting, sweating, yet somehow managing to balance a tapas plate or a wineglass or both.

We made our way through, and up a staircase.

"Welcome, Señor Estlin. Señorita." The pirate took off his hat and bowed. "I hope everything is to your liking?"

By "your" he probably meant Rhys's, because I realized that the adventure had been planned in advance: the restaurant was fully booked, yet we were the only ones upstairs. Tables were lined up along the walls, already set for dinner but with no one sitting at them. In the middle waited a table for two.

"Why did you book the entire place?"

A kiss on my shoulder, the one not covered by the dress. "You'll see."

We sat down. A waitress in matching pirate costume brought a tray with food and a large pitcher. Rhys explained each dish to me while pouring our drinks.

"Their sangria is out of this world. Can you taste the pomegranate? They throw it in fresh and crush it, to bring out the wine."

The buzz was just getting to my head when voices rolled up the staircase. At first I thought people from downstairs had assumed the second floor was open. But Rhys greeted the newcomers—hugs, handshakes. It was a fascinating bunch. A guitarist. A younger man wearing a black velvet suit. And two women. One still a girl, in a red ruffled dress. The other so old she could pass for everyone's grandmother.

"They are gypsies, from Granada." He sat back down next to me. "I wanted you to experience flamenco at its best: authentic and in private."

The old woman approached our table. I noticed only now the clusters of jewelry, the heavy black eyeliner, the beaded pins trying to tame her thick white hair. She sank to the floor, spreading her skirt over the tiles in front of me, and lifted her hand—palm up, as if expecting money.

"Go ahead." Rhys pointed with his glass. "She is the most trusted palm reader one can get these days in all of Spain."

Everyone was looking at me, and I realized he wasn't joking. "I don't think that's a good idea, Rhys."

The woman flashed a gold-toothed smile at me. "I can tell you things. Things you have been dying to find out."

I didn't want a stranger poking around my life, pretending to know anything about the future. But there was no polite way to refuse, so I went along with it.

"Which hand do I give you?"

"The dominant one always reveals more." She took my hands, flipped them up, and stared. "Strange . . . They both dominate with you."

Of course they did, otherwise how would I play the piano? I wondered what else Rhys had told her.

"The line of your heart is deep . . ." Her nail traced a horizontal trajectory that curved up toward the index finger. "But you tread a path not entirely your own. An old path. More than a decade."

I pulled my hand back. How could she possibly know this? Even Rhys had no idea about my family, or the "old path" that had led me to Princeton.

"You make your own fate, child, so don't be afraid of it." She reached for my hand again. Big metal rings clasped each of her fingers. "I see you with him, in front of a mirror—vast, dark mirror, like a sea of night. But only one reflection in it: his. The man is double, the girl is only one. And the two are looking at you. Same face, same heart."

She lifted her eyes, waiting for me to say something. *Palm reading is a scam,* I reminded myself. *She can't be "seeing" things, least of all about Jake or Elza.* Still, I felt anxious. There had to be a logical explanation. The woman obviously knew Rhys, and that he had a brother. The rest was just bluffing, a job she had been paid for: to throw "clairvoyant" guesses at me and take clues from my reaction.

"This has been very . . . interesting. Thank you." I tried to pull my hand out again, but she wouldn't let me.

"You wanted to ask me something. About the choice waiting for you down that path."

"Actually, it sounds like I've made my choice already." I looked at Rhys and smiled. "Two identical men—that's just another way of saying I'm dealing with one very complicated guy. A guy with a dual nature."

"Not so fast, child; don't dismiss my words so fast." Her finger touched the middle of my hand, drawing two lines away from it in opposite directions. "I see a white path spilling one way, while a red path spills another. Love will walk away from you, unless you make a choice. The hardest choice of all. It may require—"

"I think Thea is right, that's enough future revealed for now." Rhys jumped in, probably sensing my unease, and helped the woman off the floor. "If there's more, we can find out by living it."

He gave the guitarist a nod and the music began. A few quick chords. Heavy silences in between, each wave of sound broken by syncopated handclaps. The woman who had read my fortune opened her mouth to sing. Sudden, desolate agony crept out of her throat and through the room. It ignited everything. I had never heard a woman's voice so deep, deeper than the howl of a man after years of drinking and sorrow. Angry, her heart thundered up and sobbed—words that could open wounds just with their wail, magnified by the guitar's anguish.

The man in the velvet suit stepped forward. His heels slammed the floor. He glided in a semicircle, facing us—slowly, as if taking his time before a bullfight. His arms flashed through the air. His body froze, arched like the sinew of a bow. Then the guitar brought him back to life: fingers first, then wrists, then arms—chest—hips—until the music swept him and he stormed across the floor, stomping the beat with fury.

When the girl in red took her first steps toward him, everything turned quiet. The guitar was just a humming. The old woman's throat sang with barely more than knots of breath.

Rhys leaned over and began to whisper the words to me:

> *If one day I called you*
> *and you didn't come,*
> *bitter death could descend on me*
> *and I wouldn't feel it.*

The girl hit the floor with her heel, only once, then leaned backward—shoulders sinking, still high above the floor, baring her neck for the guitar to crawl over it. Her right foot flashed to the side (a single warning), throwing the train of her dress back in place. Her arms broke and unbroke their exquisite spirals: enchanted snakes, drawing the man in. Then the two of them stepped into each other—filled with grief, as if the world had long ago come crashing down around them—and fell in love inside the music, through it, even though for the entire dance their bodies never touched, not once.

When we walked out of Tapeo, the chaos on the streets continued. Rhys checked the time.

"Are you ready for the rest of Halloween?"

"How much more is there?"

"The best part. It's not even midnight yet."

Midnight. My eyes searched the sky, I couldn't help it. Somewhere up there, four hundred light-years away, a cluster of stars was already rising . . .

THE "BEST PART" TURNED OUT to be a posh party—masquerade ball—in a loft overlooking the Boston harbor. Everyone had to put on a mask at the door and was then ushered through a pair of heavy black curtains.

"May I have the password?" A male Grim Reaper nodded at us ominously from behind a velvet rope.

I glanced at Rhys, half expecting the magic word to be, once again, Estlin. But he smiled, lifted the rope, and let me go in first.

"Don't worry, the guy is just kidding. They should have opted for a Kubrick theme but didn't."

"They" were probably the undisclosed hosts who owned the venue. It was enormous. A massive cube of windows with an internal suspended bridge, giving you the illusion that a gondola was about to glide across the floor and whisk you on a tour of a steel-and-glass version of Venice.

We took drinks from the bar and walked over to the nearest window. Rhys had wanted to show me the harbor, but something behind me distracted him.

"What is it?"

"Nothing, false alarm. For a moment, I thought I saw Jake."

My hand became unsteady and I swished my glass, to hide the real reason for the sound of ice clinking. "What would Jake be doing here?"

"He's involved with the charity organizing this. Comes every year, yet this time backed out at the last minute."

"Why?"

"No idea. Something happened to him in New York. But whenever I ask, he blanks out like a dead man."

I suspected the reason for Jake's absence: he had probably found out that Rhys and I were coming.

"It has to be a woman, Thea. Just has to be. Although I can't imagine why anyone would break Jake's heart. How the hell does it get any better than my brother?"

I took a sip from my vodka tonic. Jake's heart—broken. I no longer had to guess, from hints or errant words or piano scores he happened to leave behind. Still, knowing only made me feel worse. What if I had made the biggest mistake of my life? Losing the guy who could have been my soul mate, while I let his brother parade me in front of him like a trophy doll. Dinners at their house. Vacations on the Vineyard. Even here, in Boston. At Jake's own party.

When a group of people accosted Rhys to hear his take on some recent scandal involving the charity, I went to get another drink. The bar was crowded. Noise. Dense heat of bodies. Bottles and glasses flying about, from the hands of bartenders who rushed as if a fast-forward button had been jammed to a permanent "on."

Suddenly, a hand placed an empty glass next to me.

I recognized the long fingers instantly—their shape, the slow shift through the air as they made their way from the glass, down to the edge of the bar, and rested on the marble. I was afraid to move. *Jake.* Standing behind me, so close I could probably feel his chest if I leaned back an inch—

Then he was gone. I turned around but there was no one, only a costumed crowd of strangers.

Later that night, I saw him once more. Like everybody else, he wore a mask. Yet I knew it was him, the way he leaned against the wall—lost in shadow, arms folded over his chest, head tilted back, observing. I felt his eyes across the room. This time they watched his brother dance with me, claim me in the music as he did in everything else: with his hands, with his lips, with every part of his unrelenting body. From their distant place in the dark, they looked on as Rhys bent me back and kissed me—long and hard, as if nothing was to be left of me after that kiss—and they took it all in, quietly, like poison they had come to seek on purpose.

I wanted to run over to him. Tell him that I knew everything, how he felt. That I felt the same way and at this point the only solution would be to talk it over, the three of us, and decide who stays and who leaves. But once again, he decided on his own. Took off his mask, then turned around and left.

Rhys, of course, saw nothing. It was always going to be like this. Jake might be sitting at a table with the two of us. Or watching us from a distance. Or even not be there at all—some subtle sign of his presence could simply emerge in the room, and everything would be ruined.

Unless—

"Take me somewhere and make love to me."

Rhys froze. "What?!"

"Anywhere, it doesn't matter."

"I thought we agreed to wait?"

"We didn't." Only one thing could free me of Jake, and I needed it to happen right away. "Make love to me."

"Don't ask me again, Thea. I won't be able to say no."

"Don't say no."

He grabbed my hand and dashed out—running down the staircase, storming through the front door, and crossing the street so fast I could barely follow. Another door flew open and I realized we had entered a hotel. He went straight to the reception desk, throwing an ID and a credit card on the granite.

"I want your best one. Hurry."

His hand reached out just as a keycard was landing in it, and he rushed into the elevator, leaving his ID and credit card behind. The doors hadn't even closed when he started kissing me, pulling the dress off my shoulder.

"Rhys, what are you doing?"

"Giving you what you want. Quick and anonymous, right? I didn't think you'd be into this."

"Into what?" As I said it, I realized we were still wearing our masks and pulled mine off. "If you mean anonymous sex, that's not what I want."

"No? Then what's with the sudden rush?" He pressed me against the mirror and its cold surface singed my back. "I'm guessing there are many things you think you don't want. But we'll have to change that."

I had no idea what he was talking about, whether to be excited or scared. The elevator stopped. He headed for the nearest door across the hall, while I told myself that I needed to relax. That it was too late to change my mind. That even if I did, Jake was never going to change his.

We walked into the dark room. Someone had left the heat up and the air was hot. Unbearably hot. His mask landed on the floor; getting us both naked took him only seconds. Unstoppable, an avalanche, his body crashed over mine, sweeping me back, then down on the bed, bursting with impatience from what he had wanted for so long. I stiffened up, drowned in his heavy breathing. His weight. His sweat. All I could do was close my eyes and imagine it being different. Completely different. The way it could have been with Jake.

"What's wrong? Hey . . . are you crying?" He turned on the light. "Why are you so upset?"

I wasn't just upset. I was embarrassed. Confused. Sad. He wiped my cheeks and pushed my chin up, until I was looking him in the eyes.

"Please get this in your head: I want you. Like a mad fool. The way I never knew someone could be wanted. But your first time shouldn't be like this."

"Like what?"

"With you in tears and terrified of everything I do."

"Then make it be the way it should be."

"It isn't only up to me, Thea. You need to be ready."

"Maybe I am . . . "

"That's not the kind of ready I want." He rolled back against the pillows and pulled me next to him. "There are things about me that you don't know yet. They're the reason I don't date, or fall in love, or get close to anyone. At least I try not to."

"What things?"

He shook his head. "Now is not the right time."

"It will never be the right time. Please tell me what they are."

The list was already running through my mind: His love of freedom. His contempt for boyfriend labels. The swim team's parties, or whatever else he did when he wasn't with me. And worst of all—a genetic disease without a cure. *Fatal familial insomnia.* According to Carmela, the odds of a person developing it were one in thirty million. If the gene ran in the family, the odds became one in two.

"Rhys, I need to know."

"Of course you do. But trust me, now is not the time. We've had a fantastic evening. Would be a shame to ruin it."

I WOKE UP IN THE middle of the night. Darkness. The half of the bed next to me—empty.

Where is he?

My chest began to throb, as if I had been stabbed in my sleep. Rhys had sneaked out, leaving me in a hotel room. Not even a good-bye.

Then I noticed the cigarette light. A red laser dot, doodling its silent trajectories over the balcony, on the other side of the drawn curtains.

I jumped from bed and rushed out—sliding my arms around him in the cold air before he had a chance to turn, glued to his back, tight, as if we were the only two creatures alive, suspended on a tiny concrete island halfway between sky and earth.

"How long have you been out here? Why—"

I couldn't say the rest. Up until now, this would have been the most natural question in the world.

He leaned back, into me. "Why what?"

"Why aren't you sleeping?"

"You're all the sleep I need."

The red dot hissed bright, then took a plunge: twenty stories down, toward the ground.

Part II

CHAPTER 10

The Moon Countdown

MY UNEXPECTED TAKE on Albéniz catapulted Donnelly into a nervous breakdown. She had assumed I would come back from fall break with a dazzling technique, but now all she could hear was a moody collage of ruptured sounds.

"I really hope this is some kind of joke, Thea. Because if it isn't, I wouldn't even know where to start."

I tried to tell her about the flamenco and the Andalucían gypsies and the magic of the *brujas*—how they lived inside the music, waiting to come out, but could be lost in the chase for tempo.

"And that's all fine"—she rolled her eyes, making clear it wasn't fine at all—"if you are entertaining guests at a home soiree. But you'll be playing for some of the most discriminating ears in this country. Do you realize what that means? No one cares about tricks or special effects. What they demand is absolute, blemish-free perfection."

I wanted to say that perfection was relative. Yet this woman had four decades of music on me. Who was I to argue?

My last hope was Wylie, and I suggested that perhaps we should let him hear my version of the piece before writing it off completely.

She sighed and caressed my shoulder, almost motherly. "I think you ought to see a counselor, dear. The pressure of Carnegie always takes its toll, but in your case I'm afraid it has gone too far. You are in complete denial."

In denial or not, I didn't need another therapy session at McCosh. Instead, I decided to take the rest of Friday off and have dinner with my RCA group. But when I walked into the dining hall, Rita was suspiciously thrilled to see me. And suspiciously alone.

"Where is everyone?"

"Two people canceled, so we had to reschedule. It worked out great, actually, because I've been dying to talk to you."

"About what?"

"All the juicy details from fall break. I think I deserve them."

This time she didn't sound worried, only curious. Which meant that in his second encounter with her, Rhys had managed to be pleasant.

"We went to Martha's Vineyard. He has a house there." I wasn't sure if this qualified as juicy, but judging by her smirk—it did.

"And?"

"We had a nice time; I saw most of the island. The rest was piano practice."

"Tesh, do I have to fish every word out of your mouth? What is he like?"

"You've seen him. Mysterious. Charming. And a bit of a control freak."

"A bit?" Her laughter echoed through the dining hall and a few heads turned. She lowered her voice: "You haven't had any issues with his temper, have you?"

"No, quite the opposite. He can be surprisingly . . . soulful, once you get to know him."

"Being soulful doesn't mean he won't act out of line. So I'd feel much better if I knew his vital stats."

"Vital what?"

"Statistics. Not literally—just who he is, what he does."

"I don't think he has a job. Family money."

"Yeah, I figured." That last detail didn't seem to be the kind of vital stats she liked. "It certainly explains a lot. Although I don't see you as the timid little girlfriend."

I didn't see myself as the timid little girlfriend either. Yet Rhys stood for everything that intimidated me about Princeton: the elitist traditions, the sense of entitlement, the wealth. To earn my place in his world, I felt compelled to agree with him (or at least to pretend I did). But Rita was right—why would I want to enter that world if the price of admission was my tacit obedience?

Later that night he came to my room and just stood at the door, waiting.

"Rhys, what's the matter? Why won't you come in?"

"Because we're not staying here. I want to take you home with me this weekend."

He had thought of everything: I could do my schoolwork at his house, practice on either of the two pianos, or better yet—do nothing, if I felt like it. All I needed was a change of clothes.

While packing, I showed him a book I had checked out of the library earlier. Finding it had been a challenge, with the poetry stacks two levels belowground, in an obscure corner of the building. From among several shelves dedicated to Lorca, one title—*Gypsy Ballads*—had promised exactly what I wanted: a glimpse into the man Rhys had called "the voice and heart of Andalucía."

He gave it a cursory look. "You picked one of his best, the flamenco is all over it. By the way, that's exactly your type of guy."

"I have a type?"

"Before he started writing poetry, Lorca was a pianist. Absolute Chopin addict. Wrote essays about the nocturnes and waltzes."

My type of guy. The thought of Jake began to creep up from the back of my mind where I had managed to bury it.

"If this is my type, then I'm out of luck. Last time I checked, you thought Chopin was all sugar."

"Then let's prove me wrong! Bring your scores and play for me tonight."

"You don't have Chopin at your house?"

"We did, but Jake took every last one to New York with him."

The blood rushed to my face. What was I thinking? As if I could play Chopin for Rhys and not imagine his brother . . . But since I didn't have an excuse on the spot, I pulled the stack of music sheets out of the suitcase and threw them in my bag.

When we arrived at the house, its heavy door opened and this time Ferry's inscrutable smile readily invited me in.

"You look tired all of a sudden." Rhys touched his lips to my forehead, as if checking for fever. "Would you rather go to bed?"

To bed. With him. In one more house that Jake had been forced to leave because of me.

I dropped the scores on one of the pianos. "Play for me first."

He turned off the light, grabbed a pillow, and had me lie down on the sofa. "Any requests?"

"Up to you. Whatever you'd play if you were alone."

I assumed he would show off with something difficult. But I realized how little I knew him—in this as in everything else. The sounds were breathtakingly simple: Liszt's third *Consolation*. It was astonishing music, music whose texture dissipated almost instantly, as if a shy moon had spilled its sporadic web of secrets from the ceiling.

"Now it's really time for sleep."

I hadn't heard him get up. My mind was still absorbed in the last notes, and in something I had been meaning to ask him for a long time: "Rhys, I want you to come to Carnegie with me."

He pulled me up from the sofa. "Glad you finally asked, I was starting to wonder. And the magic date is when?"

"Two weeks from today."

I felt his breath stop. His head fell back, dragged down by an invisible weight behind his shoulders. Then he forced himself to look up again.

"Let's go to bed."

Before I could process what had just happened, he took my hand and headed upstairs.

IT HAD TO BE HIS room, but he didn't turn on the light. As we undressed, I felt the cold floor. A low bed. Sheets, softer than any I had ever touched. He pressed a switch and faint ochre glimmers peeked down on us through the openings of a carved headboard—lavish wooden patterns, an intricate lace of foliage—but he was already kissing me and I forgot about the bed and the room and everything else . . .

When he finally pulled the covers over us, they felt soothing—snow that cooled the skin without melting from its heat.

"It's nice being here, Rhys."

He made sure I was fully tucked in, and into him. "Get used to being here."

One more press on the switch—and the ochre glimmers disappeared.

I WOKE UP NOT KNOWING what time it was. A ray of sun had sneaked through a cleft between the closed curtains, and in its diffuse light I saw his room for the first time.

White marble floor, absolutely bare. Dark mahogany bed. No nightstands. On each side, a trio of cast-iron lanterns hung from the ceiling, cascading down a metal chain until the last globe dropped almost to knee level. A floor mirror leaned against the opposite wall, in the same carved mahogany as the headboard. But it was something else—a painting—that infused a spell into the room.

Wild, ravening flowers burst against the sharp burgundy of a late sunset. Lush blooms, caught in thick patches of paint whose edges cut against one another like shards of glass broken by a careless hand and left in chaos. At the center, alone in this explosion of color, was a devastatingly beautiful man. He sat in the falling darkness—knees drawn to his chest, arms hung over the rich blue of the pants, chiseled, every muscle set aglow by the slipping sun. His neck was strained forward, as if he still couldn't let go of something or someone vanishing away, and a black mane of curls spilled from the touch of an invisible wind. Under those curls, lost in impenetrable desolation, was his face: Rhys's eyes, Rhys's cheeks, Rhys's lips . . . and their silence.

I went downstairs. The house seemed abandoned. Not a sound, just the unnerving echo of my steps. Next to the living room was a library from which I walked out on a terrace overlooking a meticulously landscaped garden.

Rhys was sitting on the steps with his back to me, and I couldn't tell if he had heard me or not.

"I like you with very long hair."

He turned abruptly. "What are you talking about?"

"The painting in your room."

"Ah, that . . ." The alarm began to clear from his eyes, restoring them to their deep aquamarine. "You think we look alike?"

"Very much."

"I'll take the compliment. But it isn't a portrait, certainly not of me. Have you heard of Vrubel?"

I hadn't.

"A Russian painter. Siberian, actually. They keep the canvas at the Tretyakov." He said it with regret, as if the canvas belonged elsewhere.

"I had no idea this was a copy."

"Strictly speaking, it's not. It's much better than the original."

"How can a copy be better than the original?"

"Trust me, it is." He rose from the steps, smiling for the first time since I had come down. "Did you sleep well, by the way? Breakfast has been getting cold."

What turned cold, right at that moment, was the blood in my veins. A table was set for three, in the far corner of the terrace.

"Are you expecting someone?"

"My brother. He should have been here by now, but maybe traffic is bad."

I tried to stay calm. If traffic had been good, I would have found both of them waiting to have breakfast with me.

"Don't look so disappointed. You'll love Jake, once you get to know him better."

It's exactly what I'm afraid of. "I thought you and I would be alone."

"That was the plan."

"What changed it?"

He wouldn't tell me. Whatever it was, it had happened overnight.

"What changed the plan, Rhys? Your brother just . . . decided to come join us?"

"It wasn't his idea. I asked him to come, so he could spend the weekend with us."

The answer surprised me, but it shouldn't have. Naturally, Rhys wanted the three of us to get along.

"Come on, what's the big deal? We'll hang out with Jake for a day or two. I don't see the problem."

"The problem is that you simply inform me of these things, and it doesn't occur to you that I should have a say in them."

"I didn't think you'd mind."

"And what if I do? Unlike you, I can't spend my weekends just having fun and being social. So when you set aside some time for just the two of us, I'll do the same."

"It's not about being social, Thea. The thing is . . ." His hand slipped around my waist and wavered. "I can't be at the concert. Jake has to go in my place."

"You mean . . . you aren't coming?"

"Believe me, I wish I could. But there is nothing I can do. Not that weekend."

"No, of course not." I had been such a fool. Inviting him, imagining him there. "And what's the occasion this time?"

"Occasion?"

"It must be something—or someone—very special, if you are ready to leave me on one of the most important nights of my life."

A vein went mad inside his cheek. Still—no answer.

"Rhys, I can't be with you unless you tell me the truth."

Silence. It was ripping out my heart. The way he looked at me, saying nothing.

"You know what, then? Have a nice time with your brother. And please tell him that he's welcome to come to Carnegie. Having at least one Estlin in the audience would certainly be lovely."

While he stood on the terrace, shocked from the turn of events that had ruined his beautifully mapped out weekend, I ran back through the library, grabbed the bag I had dropped in the hallway the night before, and left.

IT WAS A PERFECT NOVEMBER morning. Gold leaves everywhere—a saturated, red-flushed yellow as if the sun had decided to show me there was still a world out there, a beautiful world, regardless of whether Rhys showed up at Carnegie or not.

"Whoever saddens a nymph has cut a flower and planted it in the desert."

I looked in the direction of the voice and saw the janitor who had once unlocked Procter Hall for me. The ground at his feet was covered with twigs. He had been snipping away at one of the pine trees by Cleveland Tower, a pair of shears still ready in his hand.

"Silen . . . how have you been?"

"In harmony with the universe, thank you." He seemed pleased that I remembered his name. "And you? Is college life all you expected it to be?"

"Mostly. Although sometimes it does feel like a desert."

"Then may I offer to be water?" He pulled the same dining hall key out of his pocket.

"Thank you, but I don't need it today."

"No?" His eyebrows furrowed. "Be careful. The desert might become worse if you turn your back on music."

I wasn't turning my back on anything—now I had my own key to Procter Hall. Strange that the keykeeper wouldn't know about it.

"I will play again, for sure. When the night demands its music."

He smiled, recognizing his own words.

"By the way, why do you keep calling me a nymph?"

"Because nymphs have an ethereal beauty. Yours reminds me of a . . ."

"Dandelion?" It just slipped out. The man in Tsarevo had described my sister that way.

"Dandelion—possibly, yes. The flower of dreams that may or may not come true. But tell me, who saddened you?"

"Someone I should forget."

"That bad?" He shook his head. "Those who sadden you this much are rarely worth your sadness."

I had been telling myself the same thing. The trick, though, was to start believing it.

"So what did this someone do?"

"He keeps secrets from me."

"Ah, secrets. One is always besieged by secrets. And you think forgetting him is easier than living in a secret's shadow?"

I imagined the dandelion seeds—blown off on their tiny parachutes, one by one: *Maybe. Maybe not.*

"How do I decide if I should forget him, Silen?"

I was hoping for something simple, advice I could follow safely. But he gave me the most indefinite answer of all: "That depends."

"On what?"

"On whether the reason he keeps secrets is not him, but you."

"Me? Why would it be me?"

The frown had now merged his eyebrows into one big, unruly mess. "You want the truth? Of course you do. And truth is always a beautiful thing, always. But before you demand the truth, you must be ready for it."

The shears resumed work on the pine tree. Metal flashed through the branches; dead ends snapped and fell to the ground. It was clear he had nothing more to say to me. Or maybe he did, but like everyone else preferred the easy way out—because I wasn't, you know, *ready*.

All of a sudden, he stopped and turned around.

"Don't let my inopportune rant upset you; there are more important things to worry about. Carnegie, I hear?"

"Yes. The concert is in two weeks and I'm terrified. No matter how much I practice, it's never enough."

"Music isn't an Olympic discipline, Theia. Inner peace matters more than practice."

"I wish you could say this to my two advisers." *And also to the guy who just destroyed whatever inner peace I had left.* Then it occurred to me that I hadn't mentioned the reason for my fight with Rhys. "But how did you hear about Carnegie?"

"Through the proverbial grapevine, I guess. News of this kind certainly gets around. Now, if you want my advice—take the day off. Try to rest, and have a good time at the chapel this evening."

"The chapel?"

"Yes, the one on campus. Nothing beats the story of a phantom on a moonless night. And the organ is spectacular." Then a suspicion crossed his mind: "You are going, aren't you?"

"If it's an organ concert, I doubt I'll go. My friends aren't really into organ music."

"Friends, acquaintances—one always needs a retinue. But tell me, if some day your heart must sink into its labyrinths, where would your friends be then? Would they descend with you or would you venture in alone?"

He said it with such pathos that I almost laughed. "I don't think my heart has many labyrinths, Silen."

"Not yet. But wait until it has to make a choice. The safe promise of a man or the dark promise of a phantom."

For the first time, something about the way he talked scared me. "I'm not sure what you mean."

"Only that you should go tonight, that's all." He smiled and the eyebrows floated back to their separate corners. "I wouldn't miss it for the underworld!"

Just as I was about to leave, he started frisking the many pockets of his overalls.

"First, I must give you this—" He finally found it: a small wooden tube, too thick and short to be a flute. "The key to the chapel's windows. They won't speak to you without it."

"You are the keykeeper to the chapel also?"

"Possibly." He gave me a mysterious wink. "Keykeeper to anything that has been locked away for too long."

On my way to Forbes, I looked more closely at the tube. And, of course, it wasn't a key at all. What I was holding in my hand happened to be just a tiny spyglass.

THE NIGHT HAD SUBSUMED THE chapel in impenetrable darkness, transforming it into a fairy tale of stone and color. Deep, famished black had crept along the walls. It had gorged on them, swallowing their contours completely. And now the only things left were windows. Lace patches of red and blue. Suspended in solitude. Floating in a mute, merciless sky.

"Good evening, miss. Are you here for the screening? We will be starting soon."

I passed by the usher. Climbed the few stairs. But it wasn't until I stepped inside that my eyes were swept by the raw magic of the place. By its absolute, unabashed splendor.

Earth and sky, man and god, life and death—everything was fused in a vast expanse of line, light, and air. Endless arches rose all around, shooting high through a distant vaulted ceiling like giant capillaries of stone. And the windows, their colors now maimed to the monochrome of night, balanced their fragile skeletons against this massive span of walls, held in place by an elusive geometrical enigma. In comparison, Procter Hall seemed a dollhouse. Intimate, a jewel in its own right, but trapped in the confines of sensible proportions. This chapel was oblivious to scale. It reached for the sky, knowing that even a dome of stars could not contain it.

I walked along the nave. Sat down. Everything around me was breathing and alive: frayed floors, expectant pews, flickers of chandeliers gone mad inside the iron cages. People scurried, choosing their seats. Far ahead, a crimson rope separated the wood-carved altar where an organ—spectacular, as Silen had called it—lined its pipes along the walls, solemn like guardian knights on both sides.

"Take a look at the wood surrounding us. It comes from Sherwood Forest. *The* Sherwood Forest. And some of it may even date back to the time of Robin Hood."

A girl's voice had risen over a group of tourists who blocked the view (probably the last tour of the day), and I half listened while she explained how the carvings had taken one hundred craftsmen an entire year to complete. Then I heard a mention of music: " . . . for there is a rhythm to these carvings, as to everything else in this chapel. You can see the figures: Ptolemy, Pythagoras, Orpheus . . ."

The name took a moment to sink in. Orpheus again. This time in an American college chapel, whose interior wasn't supposed to have any link to Bulgarian legends or Greek myths.

The tour group was already moving on to the next point of interest.

" . . . where you can see a quote from John: *And you shall know the truth and the truth shall make you free.* Truth is the theme of this entire transept. Now, if you could please follow me back to the exit . . ."

I caught up with them just in time. "Excuse me, I overheard you mentioning Orpheus."

"Oh yes, he's right there." She pointed to a few wooden figures carved on top of the altar benches. Orpheus was first, facing the entire chapel. "Beautiful, isn't he?"

Even from a distance, the tiny statuette projected the bleak silence of its despair: the wood had given shape to his lyre, but could never give it voice.

"How come they have Orpheus here?"

"Because of music. These benches—this is where the choir would sit." The lights went out and a large white screen loomed next to us. "You must take your seat; they'll be starting any minute."

The moonless night story that Silen had made me promise not to miss turned out to be *Phantom of the Opera* from 1925, screened to the accompaniment of the chapel's eight-thousand-pipe organ. Smudged credits popped on-screen. The long-dead high society of Paris ascended the grand staircase of the opera house, caught up in glamour, in worldly gossip, hungry for the prospect of being seen but deaf to the warnings of dread sent by a creature from the catacombs. A phantom. A music genius who fell in love with a young opera singer and became her teacher—her "spirit of music"— determined to make her a star by showing her that the heart, not the mind, was where music should come from.

The scenes flashed on. I began to feel suffocated, observed, as if a hidden stare was fixed on me under the glare of that screen. *You shall know the truth and it shall make you free.* The words were probably inscribed somewhere, in the maze of the transept's window. What truth exactly would I know? That Rhys was my phantom? My "spirit of music"? That in two weeks, when I would play on the Carnegie stage, those would be his sounds too—*his* mind, *his* heart, *his* music?

I grabbed my coat, sneaked out of the pew, and ran—down the transept of truth, all the way to the exit doors and the much-needed air on the other side of them.

LIKE EVERYONE ELSE WHO PLAYED the piece, I galloped through *Asturias,* giving my two advisers what Rhys would have called a show-off. A loud torrent of sound. Flamenco played like a Bach fugue.

"Not bad, not bad at all." Wylie grinned in his seat. "Hardly the disaster I was told to expect."

Donnelly blushed, busted. "Well, I didn't go *that* far, Nate. But it's great to see Thea back on track. That was lovely, dear!"

"Thank you." I smiled, politely. "Except this isn't how I'll play it at the concert."

A shock wave went through the room. Wylie reacted first:

"Then what was all this? Warm-up?"

"No. Just a demo, so nobody would worry about my technique. For Friday, though, I want this music to sound the way I . . ."

"Yes?"

I remembered Rhys's hands on the keys, every note charged with passion. "I want to play *Asturias* the way it feels."

"Ah, the sobfest again." Wylie looked even more skeptical than he had been about Chopin. "Very well, then. Show us!"

After pulling all those strings for me, he expected a show. And not just an average show. A tour de force.

I began playing, but this time only for Rhys. Just the two of us, in his cottage, kissing under the sounds of a guitar. *Nothing is ever safe in legends.* Or in music. Or any time you are about to fall in love . . . Then the two of us again—back at school, alone on a terrace. Crisp sky. Gold November morning. I must ask him a question. *Make it a threat. Rip it open.* So—I do. He hesitates—an absolute, breathtaking absence of sound. Until the sadness slams into me, like octave keys hit on both sides of the piano—

There was a handclap. Bracelets jangled from a woman's wrist.

A man chuckled.

Everyone was pleased.

THANKSGIVING TURNED OUT TO BE a big deal: even people I barely knew had invited me to dinner.

"We are thrilled to have you over, dear!" Donnelly smiled, encouraging me to try the turkey she and her husband had been roasting all day. The two had a warm, unpretentious home with topiaries in the front and her beloved herb garden in the back. "Thea is from Bulgaria," she announced to the other guests. "This is her first Thanksgiving."

Fourteen pairs of eyes turned to me around the table, curious what I thought of Turkey Day and how it compared to celebrations in my country. I told stories of food and fetes and folk traditions. But the real comparison I kept to myself. My first holiday in America happened to also be the first I was spending away from my family. Every whiff of freshly cooked food, every burst of laughter or clink of glasses made me wish I were home instead. It was impossible to explain how one could feel so welcome, surrounded by so many wonderful people, yet so alone. And when a guest made a toast ("to all those whose love we will always give thanks for"), it made me miss my parents almost to the point of tears.

After the feast ended, I took a long walk back, but the empty campus only made it worse. The concert was in less than twenty-four hours. I dreaded it. Worst of all was my irrational need to practice—all evening, just in case—as if a few more hours could make a difference.

Don't bother sitting down at the piano unless you're ready to become a wound,

Rhys had warned me. *The music, the song, the dance—everything bleeds, if it comes from Andalucía.*

I had spent the last two weeks trying not to think of him. But now, in a masochistic urge to "bleed" myself numb, I went back to my room and searched under a pile of books for the *Gypsy Ballads*. I wanted to feel the flamenco rhythms again. The rush from his kiss. His voice. His touch. And the sense of being with him, back in that cottage—my happiest days since coming to Princeton. Or possibly in my entire life.

The *Ballads* took up only half the book. The rest was an earlier collection, *Songs*, written shortly after Lorca gave up the piano. It started with a panoply of color, a mix between a schoolyard and a circus. There were merry-go-rounds, horseriders, harlequins, unicorns, and a group of children watching a yellow tree change into birds while the sunset shivered over the roofs and flushed like an apple. After them, in a suite of Andalucían songs, a girl from Seville chose the wind over a suitor who roamed the thyme-scented streets without a key to her heart.

Then I saw a wrinkled page, the only damaged leaf in the book, thickened by what looked like it had been water. Not tears, a larger splash. And all over it—a familiar handwriting. Minuscule rosaries of red ink, suspended on long, slanted loops:

Who else would love you like me
if you changed my heart?

The couplet was repeated obsessively, up and down and diagonally around the printed text, obliterating the entire margins. *Books go through many hands, people scribble,* Rhys had said on Martha's Vineyard, when I had seen the same handwriting in another book. Yet these were no ordinary scribbles. The frantic hand leaving them must have belonged to an Estlin. Not Rhys—his handwriting I had already seen—but someone else in that family. Someone who appeared to have been desperately, hauntingly, in love.

Even more unsettling was the poem itself. Named after Bacchus (the Roman equivalent of Dionysus), it had only six couplets—starkly bare, thrown together like drunken fragments held in place by the whim of the moody god himself:

> *Green intact whisper.*
> *The fig tree opens its arms to me.*
>
> *Like a panther, its darkness*
> *stalks my frail shadow.*
>
> *The moon counts its dogs,*
> *then slips and starts over.*
>
> *Crowned with leaves,*
> *I become black, green.*
>
> *Who else would love you like me*
> *if you changed my heart?*
>
> *The fig tree calls to me, comes.*
> *Frightening. Multiplying.*

I shut the book. What was all this? Moon. Stalking. Fig trees. And these poems—first Orpheus, now Dionysus . . .

"Happy Thanksgiving, babe."

The voice made me jump from the bed. My window was already sliding open, letting the cool air in and with it—cigarette smoke. A figure emerged from the darkness outside.

"Rhys?"

"You've been gone all day. I was starting to think I'd need more of these—" An empty pack of Marlboros landed in the wastebasket. "Odd, isn't it? I'm so wound up you'd think I'll be the one bringing the house down tomorrow night."

"Let's not talk about tomorrow night."

He came in, leaving the window open. "You are still upset with me."

"It's been two weeks, and not a word from you. Did you think I would somehow, miraculously, talk myself out of being upset?"

"Distance isn't always a bad idea. Things between us were getting tense, and that's not what you needed before the concert."

"No, what I needed was your support. But I've been out of luck there lately, so . . . what do you want now?"

"I want you to come with me."

"Of course, that's how you get away with everything: by taking me someplace nice afterward. Spoil her a little and she'll forget, right?"

"It's not like that, Thea. Trust me on this one, even if you don't on anything else."

I decided not to argue, but just go see what he had come up with this time. The ride was quick. He drove as if we were being chased—up to Palmer Square and what looked like an upscale bed-and-breakfast. An American flag hung above the entrance, while all around, in the festive spirit of the season, every shrub or tree was covered in electric lights.

"What is this? Are you taking me to a hotel again?"

No answer. There never was. I had been told long ago that the guy didn't like his surprises ruined.

We walked in, and my already plummeting mood dropped even more. *Nassau Inn.* A gel-haired, eager-to-oblige receptionist greeted Rhys ("Welcome back, Mr. Estlin!"), inquired about our evening, and, with superbly rehearsed discretion, handed him a key.

"Rhys, what do you think you're doing?" It was probably not the best idea to make a scene in public, but at this point I no longer cared. "You book us a room for the night and that's supposed to make up for the last two weeks? Or for being a no-show tomorrow?"

He smiled, took my hand, and slipped the key in it. "I didn't book us a room for the night. Nor am I the one you'll need most at the concert."

"What are you talking about?"

"Miss, I believe you are expected." The receptionist was now smiling too. They were both looking at me. "You will want to go to the Rockwell

Suite, one level up and across the hallway. The lady and the gentleman arrived earlier this afternoon."

I stood there in shock, as a suspicion began to take shape in my mind.

"Rhys, this can't be . . . Who has arrived?"

"I told you: trust me on this one." His entire face was beaming. "You didn't think I'd let Carnegie slip by without your family here, did you?"

Nothing I had experienced until then—not even getting into Princeton or finding out about my sister—compared to what I felt at that moment. I wanted to run upstairs, hug my parents, jump to the sky and laugh and scream, but I also wished this lobby could become an isolated bubble, with just Rhys and me in it, so I could apologize to him, say a million other things (for none of which I seemed to find words), or at least kiss him—which was what I did—and stammer something incoherent, hoping that he would know, as he always did, everything I meant, felt, needed.

The rest of the details I would find out later. How he had done something that had been on his mind for years: establish a scholarship—the Isabel Ríos Music Prize, named after his mother—awarding $5,000 annually to the student with the highest achievement in music. In exchange, the Dean's Office had agreed to let him stipulate how my grant would be spent, and to send everything to my parents on school letterhead (the invitation, the visa paperwork, an entire prepaid trip courtesy of Princeton). Then Rita had helped coordinate the surprise, making sure Rhys could remain invisible. Why go through all this trouble? *Because the reason they are here is your talent, not my money. They shouldn't feel that they owe this to anyone but you.*

"Come upstairs with me, I can't wait for you to meet them!"

He shook his head. "This is your time with them; let's not complicate things. I'll meet them eventually, I promise."

"Does that mean you're still not coming tomorrow night?"

"I want to come, I really do. But I'm supposed to be somewhere on Saturday, and if I go to New York with you, I might not make it."

"You continue to talk to me in riddles."

"I know. That's because it has to do with . . . let's just say it involves a health issue."

"Whose health? Yours?" I remembered Carmela's story. Could he be sick and not telling me?

"We can talk about all this on Sunday, once your parents leave. After that, it will be up to you."

"What will be up to me?"

"Whether we stay together or not."

"Rhys, if what you have to tell me is that bad, I'd rather know it now."

"Bad or not will depend entirely on you." He gave me one last kiss. "If I get my wish, it won't be bad at all."

THE HALLWAY ON THE SECOND floor was brightly lit, almost eerie as I walked toward the Rockwell Suite, still in disbelief, afraid that this would turn out to be a bad practical joke or hallucination. Finally I reached the door. Knocked. Waited a few seconds, then used the key and walked in—

And there they were, both of them. Incredible as it was to see my parents in a hotel room at Princeton, Rhys had made it happen.

CHAPTER 11

From Afar

THE UNAPOLOGETIC, DELIRIOUS red of Carnegie's main hall erupted from the floors, from the seats, and bled along the crescents of the white balconies as if a giant creature had just opened its veins, ready to absorb the music.

Seconds earlier, my name had been called. Someone had held the side door to let me pass. Then the audience had caught sight of a girl and burst out in applause—for a hundredth time that night, welcoming one more teen prodigy to the legendary stage.

Now from that same stage, as I played, a different legend was already taking shape. The soft maple floor had blistered up into a cobbled town square. Red roofs were popping all around. Houses stacked their pale façades on top of one another. Balconies exploded with geraniums. Neighbors peeked out, behind white-laced curtains. It was noon. A chandeliered sun had perched itself in the middle of the sky. And under it, baked in the summer heat, rows of seats had coiled around café tables. People chatted. Glasses clinked. The air buzzed with the anticipation of a spectacle.

A death? Affair? Quarrel? Any pinch of gossip before the day's siesta. Finally, a girl begins to cross the square. All in black, sweeping the ground with the ruffles of her dress. Her walk has the rhythm of a dance, while far across, hidden in the shadow of the darkest wall, a man's eyes flash their fire, follow her every move, watch . . .

The applause came even before the last sounds had died off. A sea of hands clapping, people rising up in waves. Somewhere in the audience, Mom and Dad were probably beyond themselves. Donnelly and Wylie too, savoring their overdue tour de force. But that dark figure watching me from the back—it was no longer there.

Then I saw him. Right in front of me, in the first row where he must have been the entire time. He dropped a white flower at my feet. Or was I imagining this too, just as I had imagined Spain?

"Tesh, that was terrific!" Rita and Dev rushed over as soon as they saw me come out from backstage. The crowds had already left, and those with special invites had stayed behind for a cocktail reception in Carnegie's famous marble-colonnade lobby. "No wonder they saved you for last. Although why didn't you tell me Rhys would be here?"

"Because he isn't."

"The balcony is high, but not *that* high. I saw him leave the flower for you. And front row too—well done!"

The same mistake. I wondered if a single person (except maybe their own mother) had ever known them both without confusing one for the other at least once.

"The flower is not from him, Rita."

"No? But if Rhys isn't the guy dropping roses onstage, then . . . Oh, I see!" She had noticed something behind me and, for a moment, looked transfixed. "I have to say, the clone is just as perfect!"

"Can I join the Thea fan club?" Jake had finally found us and either hadn't heard that last comment or was too polite to acknowledge it. "With a performance like this, you'd think she has Spanish blood."

Rita couldn't help herself: "And with a performance like the one in September, you'd also think she has Polish blood, right?"

He met her eyes, calmly. "Chopin is amazing. Hers, especially. But what she played tonight is often considered impossible to pull off."

"Which is why she had to practice so much. From what I hear, the entire fall break was spent on technique. Day and night."

I was mortified. He smiled—a perfectly controlled smile that almost fooled even me.

"However fall break was spent must have been worth it. Now, before Thea passes out on us, we'd better find her something to eat. Would you like to join us?"

They wished they could, but Dev had to be back at Princeton by eleven. Next we talked to Wylie and Donnelly, then two other professors from the music department, then a few students—everyone came and went, stopping by to congratulate me. Everyone, except the two people I wanted to see the most.

"Jake, I need to find my parents. I've no idea where they are."

"Sure, let's go look for them and then I'll take the three of you out to dinner."

"Weren't you and Rhys supposed to keep your distance? From my family, I mean. He didn't want to complicate things."

"Rhys can decide for himself. I have no reason to keep my distance from anybody."

My heart sank a little, as it did each time I was reminded that Jake might have been the guy for me. Tonight more than ever. We weren't even together, yet he acted more like a boyfriend than Rhys ever had.

Luckily, a man wearing a familiar tweed jacket interrupted my thoughts:

"I don't know who Rhys is, but he certainly missed out. Your performance was truly magnificent."

"Thank you, Professor Giles! I am so glad you came."

"How could I not, after such a thoughtful invitation? And signed in Greek, no less! But just out of curiosity, that piece you were playing—did you choose it yourself?" He seemed surprised when I told him I hadn't. "It's quite astounding, then. I suppose coincidences do happen."

"What coincidences?"

"I suggest you peruse this—" He handed me his playbill. "Once things cool down, of course. You might find the note on *Asturias* most . . . beguiling."

At that moment I didn't care about historical notations, beguiling or not. My parents were coming through the lobby, and although they both looked happy, I could tell my mother had been crying.

"There you are! We didn't think you'd be out so quickly." Dad squeezed me into his signature extra-tight hug that meant he was proud of me.

"Where did you guys go? I was getting worried."

He mumbled something about the restrooms being hard to find, while Mom took her turn for a hug with the biggest smile I had seen on her. I introduced everyone. My parents seemed more nervous than usual, probably because their English wasn't perfect and made them feel out of place. Jake was impeccably polite, charming them both. But when I mentioned Giles's name and that he was my professor, Dad's smile froze in the middle of the handshake.

"So . . . Greek Art? The one class Thea doesn't talk much about."

Actually, it was the class I *never* talked about. Careful not to evoke in their minds any parallels with Elza, I had been referring to it vaguely as "my art history class." Yet if my father knew exactly what Giles was teaching, this meant he still remembered not only Elza's classes but even her professors by name.

"Your daughter is one of my best students," Giles volunteered readily, unaware that my father's heavy accent had just camouflaged a subtle hostility. "Yet I am sure that, when she calls home, she has more pressing things to talk about than the myths of a world many believe to be long gone."

To my relief, the subject of Elza never came up. Giles left eventually, and there was still enough time for my parents to meet everyone before the reception was over. When Jake offered to take us out to dinner afterward, Dad shook his head.

"You kids go celebrate. We'll head back and try to beat the jet lag, so that Thea can show us the campus tomorrow."

I tried to convince them to stay, but they looked overwhelmed and tired. On the way out, Dad pulled me aside and his eyes welled up.

"You were fantastic tonight. We've never heard you play like this."

"Like what?"

"As if you've suddenly . . . grown up, you know?"

"This is college, Dad. One grows up just by breathing the campus air."

"That may be, it may very well be. But try not to grow up too fast, all right? Even though, I must say, this Jake does seem like a great fellow."

I wondered what he might have said if the "fellow" with us that night had been Rhys.

THE HONKING CITY SWEPT US into its lunacy. Limousines and yellow cabs feuded for access outside Carnegie's main entrance, while next to them, on the sidewalk, people elbowed their way through—frantic pins in a box that someone wouldn't stop shaking.

"What kind of a place are you in the mood for?" He looked calm; the pin box didn't seem to bother him at all.

"Something peaceful would be nice."

"How about Asian food?"

"Take me anywhere you want. It's your city."

The restaurant he had in mind turned out to be anything but peaceful: the line started outside, by a heavy wooden door over which a single word— TAO—loomed on a red awning. Just as it had done at Tapeo, the name Estlin worked its instant magic, and a man who looked like he worked for the Secret Service (black suit, shaven head, and an earpiece) came to show us to our table.

Jake took my hand. "Don't let me lose you."

We walked by the bar—an area so crowded we could barely pass through— and, for a few seconds, I had the illusion of being his. His girl. Following him, hand in hand, on one of many Friday nights, our date just beginning.

(*"What kind of a place are you in the mood for?"*

"I just want to walk with you. On the longest, most crowded street in the city . . .")

We were escorted up to the second level, to a table separated from the others at the end of a long glass bridge. Next to it, an enormous stone Buddha presided over the ritual of food, exuding indifference to anything except his own inner peace.

I glanced at the menu but closed it right away, clueless about most of the words on it.

"Is it not what you wanted?" Jake slid to the edge of his seat, ready to leave if I asked him to. "We can go somewhere else. The thing is, though, New York doesn't get much more peaceful than this."

"No, it's perfect. The nicest restaurant I've been to, actually."

"This one?" He looked uncomfortable already—either for my lack of dining experience, or because he had inadvertently outdone Rhys. "Let's get you some food."

"Would you mind ordering for me?"

"Sure. How about sushi?"

"I've never had it."

His eyes widened with disbelief. "Never?"

"It's not that popular in Bulgaria. And I haven't seen it in the cafeteria either, at least not in Forbes."

"Even better, then. You're in for a treat."

I watched him say the strange name of each item to the waitress—without hurry, projecting serenity and the disarming warmth with which he did everything else. The food arrived quickly. Miniature tree trunks of rice and seaweed, arranged on narrow rectangular plates.

I looked for utensils but there were none.

"Have you eaten with chopsticks before? It's easy. Just keep the lower one in place with the thumb, like this—" He helped me adjust my fingers. "And the upper one here, like a pen, so you can use it to lift your food."

The sticks fell on the plate as soon as he let go of my hand. We both laughed.

"Try once more. It's not as hard as it seems."

It was much harder than it seemed. My pulse raced from his touch and I would have dropped anything, even a simple fork.

When the waitress came back to check on us, he pointed at the rose that I had left on the table.

"Could we also get a vase for this?"

She obliged right away.

"Jake, I've been meaning to ask you . . . Why exactly this of all flowers?"

"Because . . ." He stopped himself. Maybe I shouldn't have asked, now that we were under a friendship pact. But it was his fault too—giving me the same flower yet again, in an exact repeat of Alexander Hall. "I figured it might be your favorite."

"Based on what? You didn't know anything about me, back when you and I . . . when we first met."

He tilted his head in disagreement. "I had seen your concert flyers."

The flyers. They had mentioned Bulgaria. And it took just a quick Google search to find out that Bulgaria was famous for its roses—entire valleys of them, feeding the world's perfume industry with rose oil extract. Basically, the rose was a gift of geographical trivia.

"So . . . is it?"

"Sorry, is what *it*?" I tried to focus back on the conversation.

"Is it your favorite flower?"

"No, not really. But it's beautiful nonetheless."

"Well, there was one more reason . . ." His eyes were still fixed on the vase and the stem in it. "Watching you play that night had reminded me of something."

"Of what?"

"A poem I've loved ever since I read it."

So he was into poetry too? Probably handwriting his own lines in books. With red ink, directly over the printed text.

"Which poem?"

He wouldn't tell me.

"Jake, come on. I want to know."

"Maybe you will, one day."

"One day? Meaning never?"

"No. Meaning . . . when it becomes safe to talk about it."

"How is giving me that flower any safer than talking about it?"

"It's not, you're right. I overstepped my bounds. And I shouldn't have."

The obligatory reminder. As if I could forget that this wasn't a date. That he was spending the evening with me only as a favor to his brother.

The drive back to Forbes was just as awkward—sitting next to him in the dark car, mostly in silence. It was a black Range Rover (the exterior, the leather seats, everything black), looking brand new, as if before that night it had never been driven in the busiest city on earth.

"Isn't it a hassle to have such a big SUV in Manhattan?"

"It's not mine. This is the family car and it usually stays at Princeton."

From what I had seen, "family" included just the two of them. "Do you even need a car here?"

"No. I have a bike."

"It's a bit difficult to picture you on a bicycle down Fifth Avenue."

He laughed. "Not a bicycle. A motorcycle."

"I really don't get it. Rhys is the bad boy, yet you are the one living this wild New York life and riding a motorcycle. What do you do with it, meet the other gang members?"

"It's a gang of one, for the moment." His eyes flashed at me, then returned to the road. "Rhys had an accident with his, years ago."

"What happened?"

"Nasty luck. Somebody got hurt and my brother blamed himself. Now he won't come near anything that has only two wheels."

"And he doesn't mind you driving one?"

"He does; he used to go insane with worry. Then the fight turned ugly and he gave up."

I couldn't see Rhys losing a fight, even one against his brother. "You know he's right, though. Motorcycles are too dangerous."

"Not really." He smiled—not to me, not even to himself, but to something in the darkness ahead of us. "The same lightning doesn't strike twice in the same family."

His voice was starting to sound reckless and I looked for a safe change of subject. But there seemed to be no safe subjects between me and Jake—so I said nothing else.

When we reached Forbes, he parked past the main entrance and walked with me down the side road that led to my window.

"I had a great time tonight, Jake."

"Me too."

A huge moon dispersed the darkness enough to let me see that he wasn't smiling. We said good-bye with a hug—a brief one—and I hurried to pull the window open, hoping that its sound would sober me up from the urge to run after him, to be in his arms again.

"You forgot something."

I turned around. He was back. For a moment, I had the craziest thought: that he would kiss me.

"What did I forget?"

But he was no longer looking at me. His eyes were fixed on something behind me, in the room. Something I hadn't seen yet, whose unexpected presence had reminded him not to overstep his bounds again.

"What did I forget, Jake?"

"It doesn't matter."

I wanted to tell him that it did. That few things mattered more and that I didn't want him to leave.

Except he was already gone.

I realized what I had forgotten in the car: his rose. Now in my room, left while I was out, waited a vase of red poppies. In the moonlight, they looked almost black.

*Did you feel me kissing the Albéniz out of you
from across the hall?*

The note had been folded in two and dropped right in the middle of the bursting petals. With just a few words, it confirmed what my mind refused to believe: that silhouette in the back of the Spanish square had been real. Despite letting me spend the entire evening with his brother, Rhys had come to the concert, after all.

I WOKE UP WISHING IT were Sunday. And dreading it. Rhys had promised me answers, but the questions kept piling up. Sending Jake to New York with me, only to then sneak into Carnegie and watch from a distance—who did that sort of thing? Maybe it was a test of his brother's loyalty? Or mine? Not to mention those flowers. How did one go about finding poppies in November?

I tried not to dwell on this and to focus on something I had been dreaming about for months: showing my parents Princeton. They wanted to see everything—my dorm, the classrooms, the libraries, and, of course, Alexander Hall. We even went to the art museum, but I steered clear of the Greek galleries and took them through the main floor instead, where my mother fell in love with Monet's melting Giverny meadows, and my father kept returning to Modigliani's portrait of Jean Cocteau.

After a late lunch in Forbes, Mom's headache forced her to take a nap in my room while Dad and I sat for a cup of coffee on the porch outside. He took in the landscape and, for the first time that day, grew quiet.

"Dad, what's wrong?"

"Nothing is wrong, quite the opposite. It's great to see you settled so nicely here. You seem happier than I've ever seen you."

"Happiness is a complicated thing."

"Even at eighteen?" He shook his head, smiling. "Wait until you reach my age. That's when things start to get really complicated."

I looked at him, more carefully than ever before. My wise, humble, big-hearted dad. Even now, when he was content and at peace, his face seemed resigned to its permanent sadness. I wondered if I should show him Elza's paper. She was his child; he had the right to see it. But what good would it do? His wasn't the kind of sadness that could be lifted by an old memento. He wanted answers. The belated truth. And in the best of worlds—some form of justice.

"Thea, remember back when you were leaving home you promised me not to dig into the past?"

"Of course I do." And I had kept my promise. Mostly. "Why do you ask?"

"Your Greek Art class, for one. Is this how you stay away from the past, by taking the same courses as your sister?"

"I swear I had no idea."

A pause, as his frown deepened. "And what's the deal with that professor of yours?"

"You mean Giles?"

"Yes, Giles. The weird Greek scholar who came out clean in the end because he had no motive. They never have a motive, do they?"

It hadn't occurred to me that Giles might have been a suspect. Yet, given the vanishing of Elza's body, the list of suspects probably included all who had known her.

"Dad, just teaching that class doesn't mean he——" Then I sensed his hostility toward my professor again. "Or is there anything you aren't telling me?"

"Unfortunately, no. Only what you already know."

He pulled out his wallet, and from it—two newspaper cutouts, folded to the size of a dollar bill. When he handed them to me, I recognized the articles I had seen many times over the summer, published in the *Daily Princetonian* three days apart, in December of 1992.

Friday's headline—STUDENT FOUND DEAD, CAUSE UNKNOWN—preceded a brief entry, barely more than an obituary. A girl's body had been found the day before by a jogger, on a hiking trail south of campus. There were no indications of violence, no grounds for alarm in the student community. A memorial service was to be announced shortly. In the meantime the body would remain at Harriet's Funeral Home, until the family made the necessary arrangements.

The second article had a very different tone, and although the weekend had delayed the news from seeing print, the urgency hit you from the start: BODY OF DEAD STUDENT DISAPPEARS, CAMPUS SECURITY ON HIGH ALERT. A staffer had found the empty casket on Friday morning, after unlocking Harriet's premises. This time there was scandal. An implied possibility of a crime. Drugged on fresh gossip, the reporter had dished out the details over several columns, peppered with reports of past death incidents, lists of security measures, and even a critique of the way Harriet's ran its business.

Then there was a name—innocuous, mentioned in passing. A name that had meant nothing to me back in Bulgaria, when I hadn't arrived at Princeton yet:

> *Numerous students and faculty members paid their respects on Thursday afternoon. According to the funeral home's records, the last one to see the body was Vincent A. Giles, professor of the deceased, who signed in with the receptionist at six o'clock and exited the main lobby at six twenty-five, concluding the long list of visits. For the time being, no suspects have been identified. University officials urge the entire campus community to observe an early curfew until the authorities have concluded the case.*

I sat back and stared at the page. *Giles.* All this scholarly chase of cat and mouse over my sister's paper, and not a word to me about his visit to the funeral home. Were there other things he had chosen to keep to himself?

My father stroked my arm. "Don't look so preoccupied. I just want you to be careful, that's all."

"Careful about what, Dad? Of course Giles would go to the funeral home; Elza was his student. That doesn't make him a criminal."

"I'm not saying he is a criminal."

"Then what exactly are you saying?"

"A lot of things were left unexplained, Thea. Including at that funeral home. The day your sister was brought there, someone sent dozens of flowers, in a single delivery."

"What do you mean *someone*? The police didn't track down who it was?"

"They tried. The order had been placed earlier that day, at a local flower shop, by a middle-aged man who asked that the delivery remain anonymous. He paid in cash, so there was no way to trace him."

"And you think it was Giles? Sorry, but I don't see him obsessing over a student that way. Or sending loads of flowers."

"Well, luckily for your dear professor, the man from the flower shop was described as shorter and more formally dressed."

"Then why are you telling me this? And why now, all of a sudden?"

"Your mother and I . . . we've gone back and forth on whether and how much to tell you. At first we thought the less you knew, the better. Maybe it was wishful thinking, to imagine you could come to this school and not have brushes with the past. But seeing Giles at your concert was a reality check. Which is not to say that by now Princeton hasn't become a safe place, it's just . . . I don't think fifteen years is all that long, Thea. Many of the same people are probably still around. So all I'm saying is . . . don't trust anyone, okay?"

AFTER MY PARENTS WENT TO bed, I should have done the same. But this was the post-Thanksgiving party night; I didn't want to be the only person missing.

Tiger Inn was the eating club next to Colonial and clashed with it completely: a white façade crisscrossed with dark brown beams, to evoke the holiday cookie effect of German houses. Rita had texted me earlier that my name would be on a guest list at the door. Luckily, it was.

"Tesh, finally! Are you all right? I haven't heard from you all day."

I said something about showing my parents around, and how I would probably fail at least half my classes.

"You mean Giles isn't cutting you slack after Carnegie? I bet you rock in his class. The man couldn't stop raving about you at the reception."

"He's had better students."

"Really? Some mad archaeologist rubbing genies out of those ancient pots?"

As always, she was spot-on. It gave me a shudder. "The genie would be *A Thousand and One Nights*, not the Greek legends."

"Whatever, that's why I'm a science major. But enough about school. When did you and Rhys break up?"

"What makes you think we did?" She had probably assumed it, after seeing me at Carnegie with someone else. "The guy last night was his brother."

"I figured as much. But if the two of you are still together, how come he wasn't at the concert?"

Or better yet: Why was he there and no one knew about it?

"He's out of town this weekend."

"Did he tell you this himself?"

"Yes, why?"

The answer took a second, but it was enough for the first signs of pity to show on my friend's face.

"He *is* in town, Tesh."

"He is?"

"Dev saw him last night. That's why he had to be back by eleven, remember? The swimmers were having that thing I was telling you about, their monthly . . . well, anyway. But first they partied at Ivy."

"And?"

"Rhys was there with two women, in front of everyone. Apparently, it got pretty bad."

The floor began to slip from under me. She tried to take my hand.

"Tesh, I'm so sorry. Dev didn't want me to tell you but I thought you should know."

I could see Dev across the room, looking at us and then away. "Is he certain it was Rhys?"

"Yes. And also . . ." She decided not to finish. I had never seen Rita change her mind when she spoke.

"Please, just say it."

"Rhys is on the Street right now. At Ivy, with the others."

The rest was noise—noise and heat—as I tried to figure out what to do, how not to break down in front of everyone. Part of me refused to believe it. Although why would my friend be lying to me?

"Rita, I need a favor. Can you ask Dev to take me to Ivy?"

She said something about going back to Forbes, but I wasn't listening.

"Please ask him, if you really are my friend. I have to see with my own eyes, and it will be much easier to get into Ivy if Dev is with me."

None of us said anything as we left Tiger Inn. Ivy was literally across the street: a massive rectangle of sooted brick, thudding with music. Dev knocked. The heavy door opened an inch. Then his face must have been rec-

ognized because the door gave in a bit more, just enough to let us slide past a
security guard dressed in black.

A few steps was all it took. The room was crowded—mostly men, mostly
drunk, and a few strikingly beautiful women—but it wasn't crowded enough
to block him from my eyes. He was in the center, bent over a woman, face buried in her neck, the rest of him weighing down on her until her long hair almost
swept the floor. He lifted her back up, slipped his hand behind her knee—the
same hand holding a beer bottle—and pulled her bare leg up, rubbing his hipbone against the inside of her thigh. She opened his shirt. Traced her nails all
over him. He didn't stop her, poured the beer into his throat, spilling the rest
of it down his chin—his chest—his stomach—until the empty bottle flew at
the wall and shattered against it. Finally free, his fingers snatched her hair and
pulled it back, just long enough for him to take one last look at her face before
he pushed it forward, forcing her mouth into his wet skin—

EVERYTHING IN MY ROOM WAS distinctly visible, strangely alive under the
full moon that had invaded my world through the window. I didn't want to
stay in. I needed to walk. On grass. Among trees. To walk endlessly and
disappear.

In the distance, disfigured like a badly lit stage prop, Cleveland Tower
dominated the entire sky. I took the gravel path in the opposite direction—
past a toolshed, through hills where I had never gone before.

The golf course was drenched in moonlight. Ravenous streams of silver
poured over it, flooding the grass, the trees, and any creature that had moved
until then on its surface. Now everything lay frozen. Wounded. Ready for
a shriek. The night had burst, ruptured like a black pomegranate, and it
bled silence. The same astonishing, delirious silence as the one from another
night, two months ago—

The night in whose dawn I had met Rhys.

It was then that the lies had started. His open shirt in the fog that morning. The messy hair. The flush of those cheeks. His hand, probably still warm
from another girl's skin when he had first touched me.

Not exactly a one-woman guy . . .

I lay down on the grass. The gravel path had ended and I stayed there, letting the moonlight curve around my body and take its shape—a last blueprint from which to re-create me and bring me back, on some future night like this, if I decided to pay those hills another visit. I would be a different creature then. Untamed. Ethereal. Affected by nothing except the moon.

Now I was just a human girl. I felt lost. Scattered. Poisoned by Rhys and everything I had seen at Ivy. Here, far from the crowd, I could sense his breath carried to my skin by the wind, his hand brushing my cheek, as it had done that first morning . . . then the silence of the hills again. And with it—his absence.

By the time I headed back to Forbes, it must have been past midnight. Most of the lights had gone out in the distance, yet a few still glimmered through the trees and I kept my eyes on them as I walked. The outline of something angular startled me. Then I recognized it and kept walking: just the toolshed, clashing with the round shapes of hills and trees. Until a sound nailed my feet to the ground. A voice. Coming from an old pine tree next to me—

Rhys!

It spilled under the branches, too low for any words to come through. Hushed briefly. Spilled out again. Then another voice followed—a laugh— and cut into me. Clear, unmistakable: the voice of a woman.

I turned. Took a few steps toward that tree—

The ragged branches hid nothing, but I saw her first. Her bare back moved slowly, without a single blemish, curving its arc under cascades of golden hair, the shoulders white, ablaze with moon. He was sitting on the ground. Naked. Abandoned to her. Spine pressed against the tree, rubbing hard into the ridges of the bark. His arms were reaching back, gripping the trunk for balance, flexing their muscles each time he pushed inside her . . .

I didn't dare move. But his eyes opened and crashed directly into mine.

A disbelief.

Then fear.

Dread.

Yet he wouldn't stop. His body kept moving, caught in the rhythm of the one above it.

Her porcelain fingers took his chin. Lifted his face. Opened his lips for her impatient mouth. And his eyes—the eyes that had held my world for so long—simply closed, having said their farewell to me.

I ran away.

Back to what? Where?

The grass stifled each sound, but I knew that mine were the only steps on it—he hadn't bothered to come after me.

Then I stopped, terrified. Something else was already happening on that golf course. It was coming from the pond, and I was afraid to look at it, at what my eyes had detected there briefly, in passing:

Ripples. Ripe at first, then slowly thinning. Expanding their dark circles along the surface as the fountain splashed its incessant rhythm out into the night—

But not a sound came from it. Or from anything else.

Like concentric rings on the water . . .

I knew this stillness, and the wild creature about to appear in it.

"Anyone born with the blood of the *samodivi* can summon them," a man who was himself related to me by blood had once warned me. "Just think of these witches at night, and here they come!"

Back by that church in Bulgaria, I had thought of Elza. And she had come—a frail girl in white, ready to dance under the moon. This time I wasn't going to run in fear. I wanted to talk to her, tell her everything. How Rhys had broken my heart, twice in one night. And how all I wanted now was to become like her—a witch, a wildalone—and never be hurt by a man again.

But the hills were empty. Of course they were. Elza was gone, had been for years, and all I would ever have from her were a few faded pages about an old legend and a ritual.

Then I realized I no longer had even this much. To satisfy one of Rhys's many whims, I had grabbed her paper by mistake, with my music scores, and left the whole stack on his piano. The scores were easy to replace. But I needed to get that paper back. And unless I wanted another encounter with him, I had to do it quickly, while I still knew for sure that he wasn't home.

Without wasting more time, I turned my back on Forbes and headed out—toward Cleveland Tower and everything that lay beyond it, waiting for me in the night.

CHAPTER 12

Friend of the Estlins

THE MOON POURED in through the French doors and illuminated everything—every place in the room where he had spoken to me, sat with me, held me.

I knew as soon as I walked in: there was nothing on either of the pianos. But I walked up to the one on the left—his—and glided my fingers over the keys without pressing them.

"Miss Thea?"

The voice nearly gave me a heart attack, until I realized who it was. Elegantly clad, as always, the butler stood at the hallway entrance. Solemn face. Unreadable expression. Just like the first time I had shown up on a whim.

"Good evening, Ferry. I let myself in through the lawn. One of the French doors was unlocked."

He had probably figured as much, but was too discreet to ask about the reason for my untimely drop-in.

"I'm afraid Master Rhys is not in at the moment."

"Yes, I know."

The relentless eyes inspected my face. I knew that Rhys wasn't home and yet had shown up at the house anyway? Unannounced. In the middle of the night.

"Can I be of any help, Miss Thea?"

"I left some music scores on this piano." The word *this* brought relief into the air, as if the piano belonged to no one. "Do you happen to know where they are?"

He nodded but showed no intent to retrieve them. Loyal like a well-trained watchdog, he wouldn't let me take anything from the house until his master returned home.

"I am sorry for disturbing you so late, Ferry. This is my last visit here, and I have no doubt Rhys would be glad to know it as well. I just need my music back before I leave, that's all."

"Leaving at this hour is perhaps rather . . . inadvisable? I can arrange for a taxi, of course, but I suggest you remain here until Master Rhys comes back."

I had to leave, advisable or not. "May I have my music, please?"

He opened the piano bench and took out the scores (in a pile, as I had left them). I checked if Elza's paper was still there. It was.

"Master Rhys cares for you very deeply." His voice had become unexpectedly warm, no longer the voice of a butler. "It may not be too apparent at times. But he does. You might be able to see it, if only—"

"I saw enough for a lifetime tonight, Ferry."

Once again that evening, there was dread in someone's eyes. And this time it didn't dissipate behind closed eyelids.

"Miss Thea, if I may . . ." The sound of him taking a breath filled the room. "I must give you something, if you can spare me a moment."

"Thank you, but I really need to leave."

"What I would like to give you belonged to your family and should be returned to it."

It was as if he had slammed all doors to the house with a single sentence. "How do you know my family?"

"It just so happens." And, pretending that this could pass even remotely for an answer, he headed out of the room. "Come with me, please."

I followed the rheumatic pace of his steps—through the hallway and into the library, where he pointed to a maroon leather couch.

"If you don't mind. I will only be a minute."

The minute felt like ages. My sister. It had to be her. No one else in my family had a point of contact with a Princeton butler. But why wait until now to tell me? Being discreet was a matter of pride for him, I had seen that. And dead relatives were not exactly a topic one broached casually to a houseguest. Maybe tonight, this being my last visit and all, he saw no more harm in mentioning her or giving me an old keepsake—a farewell gift, to soften the blow of what Rhys had just done to me. Yet if Ferry knew Elza, how come Rhys and Jake didn't? Or if they did, why keep it a secret from me all this time?

He returned, carrying a silver tray on which a glass of lemonade balanced its contents over a long thin stem. I wasn't even thirsty. But, clearly, in certain circles the rules of etiquette came first. The glass landed on a side table next to me. The tray sank somewhere, quietly. Then he walked over to a leather-inlay writing desk across the room. Opened a drawer. Lifted the mystery object and handed it to me.

It was a black-and-white photograph in which a girl my age sat at a piano, looking out at the camera, smiling. Next to her, a boy—eleven or twelve, at most—had glued his hands and eyes to the keys, struggling with a tune that had long ago vanished into silence.

I recognized the girl. Her enigmatic smile, the oddly wise depth of her eyes.

"Where did you get this? Did you actually know my sister?"

"She was a friend of the family. A very dear one, even if only briefly."

Elza—a friend of the Estlins. It was impossible to fathom. Who, out of the entire clan, could she have been friends with? Isabel? Archer? Or some other relative I didn't know about?

I took my best guess: "Someone told me once that Isabel . . . I mean, Mrs. Estlin . . . was a famous pianist. Why would she befriend a student from Bulgaria?"

"She didn't, not exactly."

"Then who did? And why?"

"Your sister was a strikingly talented musician, Miss Thea. The Estlins have rarely been able to find a pianist to match their caliber. Even at a place like Princeton."

"Was she really that good?"

"Oh, yes. She could steal your heart with just a few keystrokes." His eyes glided over the scores in my lap. "Although I must say she didn't care much about Chopin. Her taste was decidedly darker, as I recall."

"Dark in what way?"

"In the marvelously complex way of what is often referred to as 'the Slavic soul.' She idolized the Russians: Rachmaninoff, Scriabin, and especially Stravinsky. But, strangely enough, her favorite piece had nothing to do with them. 'Clair de Lune.' She played it every time she was in this house. I used to tell her that once she set her fingers to Debussy, even time itself paused to listen."

I imagined Elza playing in the Estlins' living room, driving the moon in the sky wild with envy at the other, more perfect moon rising from the keyboard.

Then a suspicion crossed my mind.

"Since my sister was such a dear friend, do you know by any chance if someone in this household sent flowers to the funeral home?"

"Certainly. I was in charge of it myself."

Shorter than Giles and more formally dressed. Way more formally, as it was turning out.

"Why did the delivery need to be anonymous?"

He measured his words, the way he had measured that lemonade so it would fill the glass to just below the rim, without spilling.

"Your sister's death was a very delicate matter, Miss Thea. The flowers were meant to express everyone's most sincere condolences. Under the circumstances, however, it was imperative that the family not be implicated."

"Could it have been?"

"I beg your pardon?"

"Was there anything in particular the family was trying to keep private?"

His eyes turned stone-cold. "Given the timing—yes. Any attention from either the police or the press would have been most unwelcome."

"Why?"

"I thought you knew. Master and Mrs. Estlin had just passed, only days prior."

I realized how insulting my insinuation must have been to him. "My apologies, Ferry, I had no idea. And I don't mean to pry. It's just that I'm having a hard time with . . . with all the mystery surrounding Elza."

"That's entirely understandable. Family wounds never heal."

"I wouldn't call it exactly a 'wound.' More of a sense of urgency. As if my own life can't start until I find out how hers ended."

He considered my words, then shook his head.

"Your sister was an astoundingly fearless young lady. Pardon my observation, but from the day you were first brought to Pebbles, I have been certain that lack of fear was something the two of you had in common. Yet the problem with this rare quality, you see, is that it can lead to rather rash decisions. I would never wish for you to go down such a path."

"You mean make the same mistakes?"

"Mistakes are always relative, Miss Thea."

Some were. But others were not—like still being in that house when its owner would come home.

I slipped the photo in my pocket, ready to leave. "Who is the boy at the piano?"

"Master Jake. He was Miss Elza's pupil. She loved the boy to bits, called him 'Miracle Hands.' And that's exactly what he was. The instrument came alive under his fingers, even then."

"Was Jake the only one she gave lessons to?"

The nod was so slight I wasn't sure if I had imagined it.

"But his brother isn't much older. Was he not around?"

"Master Rhys was here, yes."

"Then he must have been so good that he didn't need lessons?"

I had never seen a person so still, as if even the blood in his arteries had solidified.

"You ought to excuse the ramblings of an old man, Miss Thea. At times, I find it difficult to let go of the past. Perhaps you would rather—"

We heard loud brakes outside. Then the front door of the house opened and someone rushed in, calling my name from the hallway.

"THANK GOD YOU'RE STILL HERE! Ferry promised to try and keep you, but I thought I'd be too late."

"As you always are with me, right?"

So much for dreading a face-off with Rhys—the one storming into the library wasn't even him. Now I knew why the butler had served me that lemonade and why it had taken him so long to bring it: he had needed those extra minutes to call Jake, given that the other Estlin was not to be disturbed.

"I can't believe this was all an act, Ferry. Aptly staged, though. And it did keep me in the house, indeed."

"I'm afraid I had no choice, Miss Thea. It was late, and you seemed disinclined to wait. To let you leave unaccompanied would have been imprudent."

"Whereas deceiving me was fine?"

"My apology, if this is how you feel. I assure you that every word you heard in this room was meant with utmost sincerity." Then his face morphed back into the detached mask of a house servant. "Now, unless my assistance is still needed, I will retire for the night."

And with a quick nod to each of us, he left.

"What was that all about?" Jake reached for a hug, as if we were old friends about to enjoy a heart-to-heart. "Deceit, stage acting—not Ferry's usual repertoire."

"But it seems to come naturally to everyone else in this house. And get your hands off me. Or should I say *your miracle hands*?"

The phrase hit him, draining the blood from his face. "What exactly did Ferry tell you?"

"Why? Are you worried that your own version might not check out?"

"There are no versions, Thea. You are my brother's girlfriend. Whatever you need to know must come from him."

"And it did. As a matter of fact, your brother couldn't have been more explicit tonight."

I headed for the door but he stopped me. "Please wait until Rhys comes back. He'll want to talk to you."

"That's highly unlikely, given where he's been all night."

"Where do you think he's been?"

"Seriously?" I couldn't believe he would join in on the act, and pretend that nothing had happened. "Don't lie to me, Jake, okay? Your brother gets high on lying to everyone. And he can do whatever he wants; I guess lying is what makes him . . . Rhys. But I didn't think you of all people would—"

"I haven't lied to you. And I never will."

"Silence can be a lie too, you know?"

He had nothing to say. I asked him to call me a cab and leave me alone—this time he didn't argue.

While I waited for the car, I looked at Elza's picture again. At the girl who had so much—and yet so little—in common with me. She was smiling back at whoever had held the camera, but I liked the illusion that her smile was intended for me. That, in some secret corner of her mind, she had anticipated how one day I would trace her steps all the way to this house.

Then I flipped the image over.

To the most beautiful girl in the world,

♫: Jake.

Made up of the two musical clefs, the tiny heart was unmistakable. Just a doodle, drawn with a quick sweep of the hand.

She loved the boy to bits, Ferry had said. But, as it was turning out, the one in love had been Jake. It didn't matter how young he might have been at the time. Not even a teenager yet, practically still a child. Elza must have become his first innocent (or maybe not so innocent) fantasy. His tragically doomed crush. The kind of crush that stays with you forever.

Many years had passed. Until he had seen her last name on a concert flyer, one September morning. Or it could have been afternoon—late in the day, the light already receding into long shadows, making him think for a second that the whimsical Princeton sunset was distorting the letters, to play a trick on his heart:

. . . the music department's youngest student, Thea Slavin . . . acclaimed pianist . . . just arrived from Bulgaria . . .

No wonder, then, that he had shown up in Alexander Hall. That he had followed me into the museum basement and spoken to me about a musician who lost his love because he was too weak. It wasn't me he had been looking for. All this time, he had been chasing after a long-lost dream—only to realize, in the end, that I wasn't her.

CHAPTER 13

Leap from the Rational

M Y PARENTS' VISIT was almost over. We didn't even have all of Sunday, just a few more hours before they had to leave for the airport, midafternoon, to catch their flight back.

"Cheer up, you'll be coming home in less than a month." Dad pinched my cheek, having no idea that their departure was only part of the reason for my dismal mood.

I was grateful not to have to explain. Let them think that, homesickness aside, I was "nicely settled" at Princeton. Happy. Carefree. Dating Jake. As his brother would say: Why complicate things?

After lunch we stopped by the chapel. While they marveled at the excesses of neo-Gothic architecture, I asked them to imagine being there for a night of organ music—sitting in one of the pews, infinitely small, while thousands of wood and metal pipes howled up against the vaulted ceiling in an attempt to tear open the entire sky. Still, their thoughts seemed to be elsewhere. I walked away, to give them a moment of peace. And as I stood by the exit, watching the two figures sitting quietly, backs hunched, shoulders touching as if chained together by a shared sadness, I realized that to them this wasn't just a school chapel. It was a church unlike any other. The place where, fifteen years ago, they would have been sitting like this, among those same pews, at their daughter's funeral.

Later that afternoon, after we had said good-bye at the hotel and swallowed the tears and reminded ourselves that Christmas was only weeks away, I went back to the chapel. Just hours earlier, my family had been sitting here. And now they were not. It was surreal how loss happened, too fast for the mind or the heart to adjust to it. One minute you had a parent, a boyfriend, a friend . . . and the next you didn't. The only constant was this inescapable sense of loneliness. At Princeton, I would often hear talk about learning to find happiness within one's self and not needing anybody else—a skill I hoped to never acquire. But at moments like these, I doubted that I had a choice.

As I was about to leave, a stream of light filled the nave: the sun had come out. After a day of impenetrable gray clouds, it had finally peeked from the sky, down through the stained-glass windows, spilling their reds and blues like jewels over the chapel's interior.

You need a key, the windows won't speak to you without it, a janitor had told me not long ago, while giving me a tiny object I still carried in one of my coat pockets. Without a clue what a few glass panels could possibly say to me, I found the spyglass and pointed it up, back toward the exit.

At first, all I could see in the little tube was a circle of gray. Maybe it was broken. Or did something block the lens? Actually, I was just holding it wrong, pointed too high up at the ceiling. When I tilted my face a bit—to the left, and slightly lower—things began to slip into view.

Grainy texture. It had to be the wall, falling into focus as it got closer to the light. Lower still—an arched rib, framing the first glass pieces. And from there on down, luminous, bursting in ruby-red, in scarlet, in lapis lazuli and ultramarine, poured a window of astonishing beauty. A delirium of color encaged in stone.

Various faces looked out from the glass, announced by painted trumpets. Apostles. Angels. Animals of sacrifice. All in their own individual rosettes. Below them, in vertical alcoves, bowed those of eternal fame: thinkers, visionaries, writers. But everyone was paying tribute to one man, a man seated in the center.

His right hand was lifted, ready to bestow a blessing. And in his left he held a book—open to where the pages had no text, just a single letter each:

$$A \mid \Omega$$

I lowered the spyglass in disbelief. Was this why Silen had sent me to the chapel that night? I had assumed it was for the *Phantom* film screening. But what if it wasn't? What if he had figured out that these two letters would "speak" to me, just as they had spoken to my sister back in 1992? He must have known her. Or if not, then he probably knew Giles. The reserved art professor and the janitor who went around unlocking doors and sharing odd pieces of wisdom—it was an unlikely duo. Besides, what business would the two of them have, collaborating secretly to send me on a scavenger hunt with clues about Elza's death?

I headed to Forbes, trying to decide what to do next. I could ask Silen about the story he had expected those windows to tell me. But this required finding him first, and our encounters at the Graduate College were so sporadic that I couldn't count on the next one happening anytime soon.

Giles, on the other hand, was just a phone call away. Yet confronting him presented a different problem. If the man had been hiding something for fifteen years, he wasn't likely to volunteer it now. I had to be strategic with him. Provoke him. Say one thing and mean another. He had done it himself at Carnegie, chatting with me and my parents without any sign of a guilty conscience, while dropping hints about "the myths of a world many believe to be long gone." Was he one of those many? Or did he know for a fact that this world was, as of yet, not gone at all?

As I replayed the conversation in my mind, I remembered something else he had said to me that evening: *Miss Slavin, I suggest you peruse the playbill. You might find the note on* Asturias *most beguiling.*

It was the first thing I did when I walked into my room. And the beguiling part turned out to be not the note but the image next to it: the coat of arms of the Principality of Asturias. A blue banner under a royal crown, and a gold cross with a letter hanging from each bar. Alpha on the left, Omega on the right.

My e-mail practically composed itself:

```
Dear Professor Giles,
It was lovely to see you at my concert! I did find
the note on Asturias beguiling. Perhaps you might
find the window over our chapel's entrance even more
so.
If you have some time on Monday, could I stop by your
office?
Thea
```

Within minutes, his reply hit my in-box. Monday certainly worked fine. However, while normally he was not in the habit of coming to campus on weekends, he didn't mind a brief meeting that same afternoon.

"PLEASE, TAKE A SEAT."

He had heard me walk in but wouldn't look up from the book. It had an illustration in red and blue: a stained-glass window.

"I did drop by the chapel today, as you suggested. The Alpha and Omega, quite remarkable. Do you suppose your sister knew?"

"She seems to have known a lot else, so I wouldn't be surprised."

"Neither would I." The oversized volume finally glided shut. "But to get to the point, Miss Slavin, how did you find out about this yourself? The letters are so high up, even I never noticed them in all my years at Princeton."

One of the janitors thought the stained glass would speak to me. He even gave me a spyglass.

I trimmed the answer down to a palatable version: "The window was hard to miss, on my way out of the chapel."

"What were you doing at the chapel? If I recall, you don't practice a religion."

"No, not really. Unless the piano counts."

He stared at me blankly—humor didn't seem to be his thing. I reminded him that the chapel was a Princeton landmark. People went to see it even if they had no intention of praying there.

"Well, of course. But I was hoping that the reason you asked to see me had to do with . . . No, never mind. Was there anything else you wanted to talk about?"

I could tell he was disappointed. Once again, like a big tasty bite, the elusive truth had been snatched from right under the cat's nose.

"Do you play Scrabble, Professor Giles?"

Half surprised and half skeptical, he watched me take a small velvet pouch out of my bag and empty it on his desk: seven wooden blocks, borrowed earlier from the Forbes game room. I turned the letters so they faced him and formed the first word, DAEMON. A spare *A* was left on the side.

"Now, if we remove the Omega and let the Alpha take its place—" I pulled out the *O* and pushed the other six letters toward him. "Can you guess the new word?"

I wished I had a camera: Giles and his jaw dropping, as he spelled out MAENAD. His mouth extended to an oval, the gray mustache drooping over it, curved up at the tips—a perfect Omega of his own.

"How extraordinary! Although it would mean that . . ."

"That my sister wasn't referring to the Bible, but to something else. You said a similar statement was attributed to Dionysus?"

He nodded, looking at the letters while the sentence probably still flashed through his mind:

I AM THE MAENAD AND THE DAEMΩN,
THE BEGINNING AND THE END

"Professor Giles, what if Elza included this because it wasn't just a quote but the ritual itself?"

He looked up, slowly. "Beg your pardon?"

"You know, some sort of chant. The secret words one would repeat, to summon Dionysus. A woman whose lover has just died, let's say. She goes through the ritual and turns into a maenad. The man comes back to life as a daemon. Exactly as you were describing it to me: two lovers possessed by the god, united in him forever. No beginning and no end."

He didn't move, didn't even blink—an oddly scared man, who suddenly seemed desperate for our discussion to stop right there. "How did you come up with all this?"

"Forbes had a Scrabble night; I pulled seven letters and had to play a turn. It happened to be the alternative spelling, with *AI*, but the words were still anagrams—except for the *A* and *O*."

"I see. A perfectly rational explanation."

"Do you think everything has to be explained rationally?"

A pen began to revolve under his fingers, hitting the desk consecutively with each of its ends. "It is hardly a matter of what I think."

"You didn't answer my question."

"Miss Slavin, what anyone thinks is beyond the point. With all due respect to your late sister, if there is indeed an explanation that defies rationality, I don't advise getting involved in any of it."

"Elza is my family. Was, at least. Which makes me involved, whether I like it or not."

"Involvement and curiosity aren't the same thing. For your sake, I sincerely hope you are confusing the two."

I wasn't confusing them, not anymore. "By the way, funny you should say this."

"How so?"

"Back in September, when you asked me to depart from the syllabus, I assumed you were just curious. Now it turns out you were actually involved."

The pen stopped. I handed him a copy of the second article from the *Daily Princetonian* and his eyes scanned the page quickly—he already knew what was on it. His name, printed there all those years ago, had linked him to his dead student for good.

"I was wondering when you would bring that up. As a matter of fact, I'm surprised it took you this long."

"Me too. I came to Princeton determined to find out what happened to Elza, but ended up sidetracked by . . . by everything else at school."

"It was probably the wiser choice."

"Not so much a choice as a mistake—to believe that the past is just a past and I have nothing to do with it. When, in fact, on this campus past and present seem dangerously close to being the same thing. Don't they?"

He stared at me, absolutely still.

"Would you please tell me what happened at the funeral home that day?"

"If you mean what happened to your sister, I am not sure I can be of much help."

"You are the last person who saw her."

"That's what the newspapers claimed, yes."

"Are you saying that someone came to Harriet's after you?"

"She was there when I left. So someone *must* have come after me."

He could very well be telling the truth. But what if he wasn't? It wouldn't be the first time in the history of crime that a culprit looked like a normal person. Respectable member of society. College professor, even. For all I knew, Giles might have been obsessed with the Greek rituals, eager to enact what he believed to be the greatest mystery of the ancient world. And a unique opportunity had presented itself, fifteen years back, with a student from his class. She had been the ideal target: a gullible foreigner, with a predilection for myth and a subtle unrest in the blood. Now, in an almost exact repeat of events, he had come across her equally unsuspecting sister.

"Professor Giles, I need to know what happened."

"Very well, then. I can tell you, if you insist. But, first of all, I have strong doubts that you'd be better off hearing it."

I assured him I could handle my own well-being.

"And second, you must promise me that it will never leave this room." He rose from the chair: a tall and skinny Don Quixote, fired up for a fencing duel with an invisible windmill. "So do I have your word or not?"

"You do."

"Good." A cautious smile, under the mustache. "I think keeping your promise would, ultimately, benefit us both."

He walked over to the window and stood there, looking out at the campus where life followed its usual, undisturbed agenda.

"I was shocked by the news, like everybody else. We hadn't lost a student for many years, and in the whole history of the school there had never been a case where violence was involved or even implied. So the police went to great lengths—very discreetly, of course—but came up with nothing. Or at least nothing that seemed significant on its face."

He paused, as if I was to draw some brilliant conclusion from his last words.

"Naturally, the school conducted its own investigation. Requested full records, all her academic work—which wasn't much, she had been here just a couple of months. The only item in my possession was her paper and I turned in a copy of it. But a unanimous decision was made not to stir up scandal, so I was instructed to neither raise nor answer any questions."

"What kind of questions?"

"From the police, the embassy, the press. As you can imagine, the university could not afford a rumor that a class assignment might have led to the death of a student."

"But your class didn't lead to my sister's death. Or . . . did it?"

"Not technically. Yet there is plenty on these pages, don't you think, that would strike one as odd when, all of a sudden, the author dies mysteriously—and disappears even more mysteriously—shortly after they were written?"

"You mean she wrote about things she was already doing in real life?"

"Already doing. Or about to do. You see, Miss Slavin, I was convinced that your sister's fascination with the Dionysian mysteries was the key to her death and its . . . bizarre circumstances. I regret to say this, but your board game discovery is one more proof that I may have been right."

"In other words, she killed herself, didn't she? By the time Elza wrote that paper, she needed a psychiatrist, badly."

"Mental disease and suicide—that's what I thought as well. Until I went to the funeral home."

"Something changed your mind there?"

"It provided a new . . . angle, shall we say."

"Meaning that it wasn't suicide?"

"It may very well have been. Although someone who has already killed herself doesn't sneak back into town to steal her own body from the coffin, does she?"

"No. But neither does a killer leave the victim's body by a hiking trail, only to bother with breaking into a funeral home later."

"Ah, the break-in theory. I agree with you, a kill-and-kidnap scenario is a bit far-fetched. More likely, it was an unrelated act of vandalism. Not aimed at your sister in particular, her body just happened to be in that room at the time. But tell me, Miss Slavin, why would a thief make sure to lock the doors on the way out?"

"I can't think of a reason."

"Exactly. Yet that article went on and on about outdated security measures, which in the end cost Harriet's its business. It's a funeral home, for God's sake, not a bank vault! But one thing the place certainly lacked was discretion."

"About its visitors?"

"Not only. The receptionist—the one who landed me on the front page of the *Princetonian*—was an extraordinarily chatty lady. What was worse, she had taken the whole case to heart, '*being that girls should never be destined for such a frightful fate.*' " He rolled his eyes, still indignant that the woman had compromised him. "The only redeeming quality of such a compulsive talker is that, occasionally, something useful would slip out. I was given a tour of the premises, a lecture on the prudence of advance funeral arrangements, even statistics of the mortality rates in New Jersey. By the time she took me to your sister, I had blocked the yapping out completely. My God, what a propensity for verbiage! But then it finally paid off. For, you see, there was something in that casket I normally wouldn't have recognized as peculiar."

"Something related to the rituals?" I was already imagining ancient sacrificial paraphernalia. Amulets. Talismans. Poison rings and folding daggers.

"Your sister lay there in a white dress, like a child after First Communion."

"Isn't this typical in America?"

"I don't know about typical, but it certainly fit the mood. There was something so tragic about being in that room, something so . . . *theatrical* (for lack of a better word), that the outfit happened to blend in. Apparently, though, she was found dead wearing an identical ensemble. According to the well-informed receptionist, your sister kept a few of those in her closet. White sleeveless summer dresses, neatly folded on top of her other clothes. In the middle of December."

"The woman just blurted this out? She didn't find it strange?"

"Finding anything strange would have required a brake on the mouth and a demand on the brain. I guess she figured this was exactly the type of outfit someone 'destined for a frightful fate' would wear on a daily basis. And if so, then why not have several? But, to my dismay, the police didn't connect the dots either."

"They knew what was in Elza's closet?"

"Of course. Where do you think the receptionist obtained all her information from? Yet your sister's paper hadn't mentioned a dress code, so the link to the rituals was lost on everyone. When no plausible explanation presented itself, the odd choice of clothing was attributed to cultural heritage—because Bulgaria is full of young women who walk around in long white dresses, as I'm sure you know."

I ignored the sarcasm. "It makes sense, though, to bury her dressed like that."

"This part does make sense. What doesn't is the anonymous flower delivery. You are aware of it, I presume?"

I nodded, seeing no need to tell him that I was also aware of who had placed the order.

"Strange then, isn't it? Your sister had no relatives in the United States, no particularly close friends, no boyfriend of record—yet someone clearly cared enough for her to fill the room with rose arrangements, dozens of them. And I say 'cared' only because I'd rather not imply things that are better left unsaid."

"Things?" I wondered if the butler had been completely honest with me the night before. Being Jake's piano tutor certainly justified some form of condolences. But to drown a funeral home in flowers? "Are you suggesting that this anonymous sender might have . . . that he might have been the one who . . ."

"Stole your sister's body?"

"Yes."

"Miss Slavin, this is what I would much rather believe."

"Rather than what?" His provocative pauses were starting to get to me. "You think he murdered her?"

"I never said she was murdered."

"But there were no signs of an accident, according to the article."

"I never said it was an accident, either."

"Sorry, I don't follow. If her death was not an accident, and not a suicide or a murder, then I really don't understand."

"That's because you are finding it difficult to make a leap from the rational." He smiled, affording me a beat to digest the concept. "Understandably so. Making that leap took me a long time too. Even now, after fifteen years, I can't say in all honesty that I have fully succeeded."

"What leap are you talking about? And why—" I remembered another girl in a white dress, in a churchyard by the sea. "Why would either of us have to make it?"

"Because, to answer your earlier question: yes, I do think there should be a rational explanation for everything. But my wishful thinking doesn't mean there always is. You see, before I left that room, once my effusive tour guide had finally allowed me some privacy, I walked up to the casket to pay my last respects to a student whose rare intelligence and unusual vision of the world I had come to admire. There was so much white in that coffin. The lining, the pillow, your sister's outfit. But there was also a single red spot on her dress, about the size of a penny, under her left index finger. Whoever had folded her hands above the rose bouquet must have pressed them over a thorn."

"That's not possible. The dead don't bleed."

"I know they don't. But I assure you, the stain was very fresh. In fact, a tiny drop had gathered and fell off right in front of me."

My mind took the thought and held it. Not a leap. Just a child dipping a toe in, to check if the water might be warm enough for a swim: *When Giles last saw her, my sister was still alive.*

So . . . no one had come to Harriet's after him. No one had stolen Elza's body and walked out with it, locking doors. She had simply regained consciousness—all alone, in a funeral home. Terrified, she must have found a way out and was probably still alive, in some obscure corner of the world.

My heart began to beat so fast I felt dizzy. I had heard such stories before. Wrong diagnoses. People thought to be dead. Getting buried—in tombs, in coffins—only to be found in a changed position later, if for whatever reason the body had to be exhumed. Chopin himself had feared this, and in the last days of his life scribbled one final wish on a notepad: "If the cough suffocates me, I implore you to have my body opened so I may not be buried alive."

But that was all from past centuries. Modern medicine knew better than to play inadvertent jokes with death. Or did it? Was it possible, even to this day, to pronounce a girl dead and prepare her for burial with her finger still bleeding?

"Professor Giles, I want to believe you. But what did the doctors say?"

"Pardon me?"

"The doctors. How did they react to what you saw in that casket?"

"There were no doctors, Miss Slavin."

"Then the police, or whoever else you told about it."

"I didn't tell anyone."

"You just . . . left?"

Suddenly, everything about that man filled me with dread. His words. His voice. The unshaken calm in his eyes. All these years, the school's mandate for silence had shielded him. But if he had done something to my sister—in the funeral home or afterward—who would have suspected him, given that everyone thought she was already dead?

"Are you all right? You seem a bit—"

"Why did you leave without telling anyone, if you knew she was still alive?"

"I did leave, oh yes. I left as quickly as I could. But, Miss Slavin, *alive* was one thing your sister definitely wasn't." For a moment, he seemed to enjoy the fright on my face. "An autopsy had been performed that same morning.

I saw the report with my own eyes, when I took her paper to the dean earlier that day."

I must have stared at him for some time. He even handed me a glass of water.

"I hope now you understand why I didn't mention anything to the police. Not that I haven't had my moments of doubt, since then. That entire night, I racked my brain how to present the world with a story of bleeding cadavers. I questioned everything, even my own sanity. What if I had hallucinated the whole blood-dripping episode? Not only would I lose my job, but I would also face criminal charges or, at best, psychiatric tests. Of course there was always the possibility, however small, that the coroner's office might have made an error, reporting an autopsy that was never carried out. By morning, I had managed to convince myself that this was most likely the case and your sister was still alive—until I heard the news that her body was missing. It was then that I promised myself never to tell a single soul, a promise I had kept until now."

Neither of us said anything else. Or maybe we did. I was already at the door, pressing the handle down, when a question dropped from my lips almost automatically: "What color were they?"

"They . . . ?"

"The roses."

"Oh, white. Everything in that room was white."

"All of them?"

"Every last one. Why?"

"I just . . . I wondered if this may have been her favorite flower." Then I turned to open the door.

"Miss Slavin . . . Thea . . ." He had never called me by my first name. "Should anything happen—anything at all—that seems out of the ordinary or makes you feel unsafe in any way, will you call me immediately, please?"

Unsafe. As in Jake obstinately giving me the same flower with which his butler had flooded the funeral home back then.

"Will you?"

I nodded, promising him a phone call for which it was already way too late.

CHAPTER 14

Ultimatum

I SKIPPED SCHOOL on Monday and stayed in bed, going over everything a thousand times. Telling my parents was out of the question, at least for now. First I had to make sure Giles wasn't lying or imagining things. And assuming he wasn't, how would I go about tracking down a girl who was neither human nor, strictly speaking, alive? Watch vampire films? Read about witch hunts?

"Is everything all right? We missed you at dinner." Ben was back from Thanksgiving and had stopped by, to hear about Carnegie.

Was I all right? Sure. Except for having just found out that my dead sister was not exactly dead. Maybe the *samodivi* superstitions were true and women in my family just couldn't die? You might kill us, even do an autopsy to mangle up our insides, but by evening we would be up and running again, blood dripping from our fingers and everything.

"Thea, I can see something's bothering you. Is it that guy again?"

"No, not really."

"Are you sure?"

"It's my family, actually. Have you ever discovered that someone related to you is not exactly . . ." I struggled for the right word: *normal? human? properly dead?* " . . . that they aren't exactly who you thought they were?"

"You bet! But in my case, given my view of the clan, that's probably not a bad thing. Last spring, for example, my brother—whom I used to consider a total bore—announced he was quitting his job on Wall Street to go paint rock formations in the Himalayas. Crazy, huh?"

I realized that the cultural gap between me and my friends had just taken on an entirely new dimension. They would continue their unaffected lives, shocked when someone quit a job in finance to pursue a hobby. Whereas my own life had now veered into off-the-charts crazy. The kind of crazy where I should have looked Ben in the eyes, smiled casually, and said: "I know exactly what you mean. A few years back, my sister announced she was quitting her human life to go tear men to pieces in the Balkan mountains."

The next day was even worse. I went to class but couldn't focus. Was I missing any clues? Any leads I had failed to follow? Ferry and Giles had already admitted they used to know Elza, giving me their (supposedly complete) account of events. But what about Silen? He was the oddest of the three. And evasive. And mysteriously absent.

I looked for him that afternoon, on my way to work at the Graduate College. But the courtyard by Cleveland Tower was empty—no one was pruning trees anywhere in sight—so I went into the Porter's Lodge and asked for the janitor.

The woman behind the desk looked at me over her glasses. "Pardon me, who?"

"The janitor. I'm not sure about his exact job title. Keykeeper, maybe?"

This threw her off completely. "Key . . . *keeper?*"

"His name is Silen; I've seen him prune the trees outside. I believe he also keeps the keys to Cleveland Tower and Procter Hall."

"Sweetie, who told you all of this?" She said it slowly, the way one talks to a mental patient. "We keep the key to Cleveland Tower here, in this office. And the only ones who have a key to Procter Hall are the dining hall managers, but I am quite certain none of them work as janitors. Or tree pruners."

"You don't have anyone by that name on staff? Early fifties, always wears black overalls?"

She shook her head but typed something into the computer. "*S-I-L-E-N*, right? I'm afraid there is no such person. We should notify security immediately."

"No, please don't bother. I must have misunderstood." I also must have been out of my mind, to alarm this woman so much she was now on the verge of calling campus police. "It was probably one of the golf course maintenance guys; I often see them around."

"Pruning our trees?"

"Well, I may have been wrong about that. I assumed he was in charge of landscaping because of . . ." *(yeah, right, just try mentioning the shears!)* ". . . because he was dressed that way."

I could already picture the front page of the *Princetonian:* SISTER OF MYS-TERIOUSLY ABDUCTED STUDENT HARASSED BY UNIDENTIFIED IMPOSTOR. I would be questioned by the police. By all kinds of school officials. Not to mention my parents, who would become sick with worry.

The woman was already reaching for the phone. "I doubt that this man you describe is golf personnel. They don't come on our premises."

"Then he must be working at Forbes."

"Either way, we should check with both places."

She swiveled in her chair for a list of phone numbers posted on the wall. It was my last chance to stop her.

"Actually, I was just heading to Forbes myself. And, if you don't mind, I prefer to talk to someone there in person."

"In that case . . . yes, of course. It is ultimately up to you." The chair swiveled back and I sensed a subtle annoyance from behind those glasses. "But I strongly recommend reporting this as soon as you arrive in Forbes. We are fortunate not to have had any incidents of crime around here, yet one can never be too careful."

I said I would follow through, even though I had no intention of asking around for a janitor who wasn't a janitor at all. Everything he had said in my presence was now coming back to me, each line whose poetic beauty I had taken for the wisdom of a man who read a lot in his spare time. And the phrases began to take on a different meaning: *Nymph's music. Job ritual. Ungodly hour. Underworld.* Then there was also his version of my name: *Theia.* The Greek Titan who just happened to be mother of the moon . . .

Tucked in the opposite corner of the courtyard like a minichapel of its own, a library held, among other things, the Graduate College yearbooks. The one I needed was easy to spot—all class years were printed on the spines. While pulling the volume out, I told myself that my suspicions were exaggerated and I wouldn't find proof between those covers. Yet it was right there: a group photograph of the Graduate College staff from 1992.

Silen stood on the side, holding a rake, leaning on the handle with vague detachment. He looked exactly the same as when I had seen him in person: the black mess of hair just as untamed; the wrinkles as deep, framing a pair of eyes that revealed ungraspable wisdom. I could tell that, back when the picture was taken, he had already reached middle age. Fifteen years had passed since then. And for reasons I was scared to even begin to guess, this man—the same man who had called me *ethereal* only days earlier—hadn't aged at all.

"I WILL NOT TAKE A poll as to how many of you have experienced true sadness"—Giles scanned the auditorium, taking an extra second on my face—"because I assume the answer is all of you. Or at least I hope it is."

In my case his hopes were justified. It was already Wednesday, and not a word from Rhys. Not even the courtesy of a good-bye. When Jake and the butler had tried to keep me at the house that night, both had assumed he would want to talk to me. Clearly, they didn't know him at all.

As if to sync the lecture with my mood, Giles turned to the blackboard and wrote that day's topic: Ancient Greeks and the Art of Tragedy.

"Athenian tragedy is often viewed as the highest art form of ancient Greece, surpassing the vases and the sculptures and the magnificent temples. Any guesses as to why?"

The classroom remained quiet.

"A paradox, isn't it? By definition, tragedy is an art based on human suffering but also one designed to give its audiences pleasure."

Someone raised a hand. "Because we can't resist watching the suffering of others? Sort of like the impulse to watch when you're driving past an accident site."

"To some degree—yes. The Greeks, however, were much more interested in their own encounters with misfortune. Every person's individual, visceral experience of it. So, still no guesses?"

None.

"Let me give you a hint, then. In *The Birth of Tragedy*, Nietzsche wrote: '. . . Greeks and the art work of pessimism? The most successful, most beautiful, most envied people . . . Did they really need tragedy? . . . Is pessimism necessarily the sign of collapse . . . ? Is there a pessimism of the strong?'"

He closed the book, signaling our final chance to impress him with an answer. The accident watcher gave it another shot:

"Maybe they figured that by bringing tragedy onstage, they were deflecting it from real life?"

"A clever gimmick. But one can't deflect life, and the Greeks were well aware of it. To *understand* life, on the other hand, was achievable—if done right. To discern the essence of things and live in harmony with them. Which meant accepting also the most terrible, evil, cryptic, destructive, and deadly sides of human existence. You can think of it as a healthy impulse for pessimism. Or, to use Nietzsche's term, a 'craving for ugliness.' This is where tragedy steps in."

I saw the last few days through that prism—predestined, compelled by a cosmic fascination with pain. Suffering as something to look forward to. As the key to understanding life. Maybe instead of Rhys apologizing to me, I was the one who should have written him a thank-you note. For bringing me in touch with the essence of things. With the evil, cryptic, and destructive sides of human existence.

"The question is, how exactly did the ancients do it?" Giles continued his probing. "A pair of opposing forces pulled at the core of Greek tragedy. The first was the world of dreams. Think of an artwork: Isn't it just an expression of something the artist first saw in a dream? The painter, the sculptor, the architect—they dream up beauty and then give it shape. Or voice, because the poet is a dreamer too."

He drew two circles with arrows pointing at each other, and the letter *A* in one of them.

"Apollo. The 'shining one.' God of the sun, of light, and the inner fantasy world. There is so much of him in Athenian tragedy, all his arts gathered into one. Even the Greek amphitheater itself—"

A loud click projected a slide on the screen in front of us: receding ripples of stone under a blindingly blue sky. We were sitting in a diminutive replica. Rows of desks converging toward the center, where a lonely, white-haired actor in a tweed jacket did his best to imbue in us the wisdom of the ancients.

"Imagine coming here for a night of theater, two thousand years ago. Vast open space, descending on a hill. Overflowing with human noise. Vibrant like a fresh canvas. Far down—the stage is set against a backdrop of marble columns, as if a temple has just risen in tribute to the gods. Suddenly sculptures begin to breathe, reliefs come to life: the actors have stepped out. Then poetry begins . . ."

Nothing in the room stirred. I could almost feel a breeze on my face, spilled over from the Aegean Sea or from nearby olive groves.

"And so tell me, which force is opposite to all this?"

Silence again.

"Anyone? Miss Slavin?"

"Opposite to . . . what? To dreams?"

"To dreams, yes. Or let me rephrase: Which art is still missing?"

I realized why he had picked me, out of the entire class. "Music?"

"Exactly! Unique among the arts, music relies on the nonvisual, the nonverbal. Nietzsche defined it as *intoxication*. For the Greeks, however, music was more than a fleeting state of rapture. It offered direct access to the gods, and to the mysteries that we now call rituals. Can you guess whose initial goes in the second circle?"

He looked at me again and I had no choice but to say it: "Dionysus?"

The *D* took its place on the board. I wished Giles and I could switch roles, for once, so that I would be the one asking questions. Right here, in front of the entire class:

"Professor Giles, do you think those rituals still exist?"

Stares at me. Clears throat. "I beg your pardon?"

"Those same rituals which intoxicated the ancient Greeks (and, apparently, modern German philosophers). Do you think they are practiced to this day?"

"Any answer I could give, Miss Slavin, would be . . ."—his eyes shoot me a warning—"it would be, by all means, only pure conjecture."

"Not really, though, given what has happened in the past on this campus."

He coughs, uncomfortably. "Are you implying there could be student practices that I . . . that the school is unaware of?"

"I don't know, I was asking you. Or let me rephrase: Given what you saw in a funeral home years back, do you think Dionysus might be residing at Princeton?"

I had to cut our imaginary interlude, because he was giving out the next homework assignment: " . . . and as I mentioned, this is how music became inseparable from tragedy. The Greek chorus has no equivalent in modern theater: a group of performers whose sole purpose is to comment on the play, directly from the stage and often in song, showing the audience how to react to it. For Friday, I want you to write an imaginary dialogue with Nietzsche about—"

He stopped in front of my desk, staring down at the sheet of paper that had kept me distracted during class: a copy of Silen's yearbook picture. I had no idea what to do—drop it in my bag? apologize? stare back at him and say nothing?—but he continued, his expression unchanged:

"On second thought, why not make that a dialogue with the Greek chorus itself? The creature who made up the chorus was admittedly odd. Fantastic and repellent at the same time. Humanlike but not human. Read *The Birth of Tragedy* to find out who that creature is, then pose questions to him—a Q&A about anything that troubles you in real life."

Except you already know what troubles me, I thought, as he resumed walking. *It's the same question that has haunted you for fifteen years. And if the mystery chorus creature has left you without an answer all this time, why do you think he might now start telling me?*

MY OWN REAL-LIFE VERSION OF the Greek chorus—Rita—had decided not to comment on the latest events. Her only remark came up in the context of Ben:

"Maybe the two of you should hook up," she had said, matter-of-factly. "He really likes you. And you need a rebound, ASAP."

I told her that I liked Ben too—as a friend.

"Too bad, he would have been perfect. I just hope you get over that other tandem quickly."

"Tandem?"

"Mr. Dance Floor King and his rose-dispensing brother. What was the name?"

"Jake."

"Right. He pulls a hell of a smooth act, that one. Just please don't go running to him now, Tesh, okay? From what I saw, he'd be thrilled to have you crying on his shoulder."

"And if I need to cry on it, so what?"

"If you need to cry on it, I'll keep you under house arrest until we find you someone normal, for a change."

Yet finding me someone seemed to have dropped from her to-do list, because when the RCA group went to the Street on Thursday night, the only one conspicuously missing was Rita.

"She's supposed to worry about us, not the other way around," one of the guys told me after I tried her cell phone and it went to voice mail.

Maybe he had a point. It was hard to picture Rita having personal problems after watching her fix everyone else's. But when, later that night, a drunk Dev stormed into the club with his friends and practically looked through me, I knew that something wasn't right. Without a word to the others, I sneaked out and headed back to Forbes.

OUTSIDE, IT LOOKED LIKE IT was raining, but the drops were actually snow. Still two days away, December threatened everything with winter, with defeat, and even though the night wasn't cold, the air smelled of charcoal solitude.

I walked through the deserted campus. Everyone who wasn't at the eating clubs had opted for the safe cocoon of dorms and libraries. An engine whistled, high above the trees—the way to Forbes passed by the local train station, the "Dinky," whose platform snuggled under a heavy, dark-beam roof as if you were stepping into some mystical time voyage tunnel.

The train hadn't arrived yet. There was no one around; a few dim lights drew several parked bicycles and two wooden benches out of the darkness that hid everything else. I tried to walk by faster, but a silhouette detached itself from one of the iron pillars and headed my way.

Jake. Out of nowhere, as always.

"You? On a train?" Why was I surprised? If he had been out drinking, the motorcycle and the Range Rover were no longer options. Still, not a whiff of alcohol came from him. He looked pale, as if he hadn't slept for days.

"I wanted to talk to you. Should have tried calling first, but wasn't sure if . . . I thought you wouldn't take my calls."

"What is there to talk about?"

"You have to see him, Thea."

"Him?" It took me a moment to realize this was not about me and Jake. "So that's the plan now? You try to clean up your brother's mess?"

The train rolled into the station, lugging its cars along the rails with deafening huffs and screeches. A few people came out, walked by us, and scattered away.

"You'll miss your train." The words didn't seem to register. "Jake, your train. It's about to leave."

"I'm not getting on a train."

"Then why are you here?"

"I was hoping to catch you on your way back to Forbes."

The devoted Jake. Ready to track me down, wait for me, stay outside for hours if he had to—so long as it could benefit Rhys.

"Well then. Now that you've 'caught' me, I'll make it easy for you: the next time you get an urge to do your brother favors involving me, don't bother leaving your dorm room."

"I'm actually staying at the house for now."

"Sure. Male bonding?" As if I cared where he chose to live.

"Having me around makes it easier."

"*It* being what?"

"My brother is devastated, Thea."

The laughter burst out; I couldn't help it. "Sorry, that's very hard to believe."

"Because you don't know Rhys."

And you think you do? But I didn't say it. There was no point in shaking his blind loyalty.

"By the way, doesn't your devastated brother have enough of an entourage to make it easier?"

"Rhys has refused to see anyone all week. He's not himself without you."

"And that worries you?"

The question took him aback. "Of course it does."

"Then why don't you teach him how to be fine without me? You seem to be doing it quite well."

Another roll of thunder. The train had taken off and promptly vanished in the distance.

"Talk to Rhys, please. There are things about my brother that I'm sure you would—"

"Your brother is a liar, Jake. And not just that. He is cruel and selfish. I saw him having sex with another girl, right in front of me, and he wouldn't even stop. So I have no intention—none whatsoever—of talking to him ever again."

"Even if this wasn't exactly what you think you saw?"

"Not exactly? Then what was it, his double? Are there three of you now—the sex maniac, the elusive ghost, and the exonerated hero?"

He shook his head. "You have it all backward."

"No, backward would be if Rhys caught *me* having sex and then my sister, out of the goodness of her heart, decided to arrange a reconciliation for us. Except I don't sleep around and Elza happens to be dead, so . . . bummer. Otherwise she might have been quite convincing, don't you think, with her—I believe you called it unmatched—beauty?"

"Me? What are you talking about?"

"About Elza. She's the real reason you came to my first concert, isn't she? And with a white rose, no less!" I could see the fret in his eyes, more eloquent than any answer. "Nothing wrong with that; I take your undying adoration of her as a compliment. Too bad I couldn't live up to it, though, right?"

"Thea, what's gotten into you?"

"Your butler gave me a photo last Saturday. There was a dedication on the back: *To the most beautiful girl in the world*. And a heart made up of the musical clefs. Very clever."

"First of all, I was only twelve back then. I had no idea what I was doing. And yes, I wrote that thing, but . . ."

"But what?"

"It was a world in which you didn't exist."

"Now I do exist, Jake."

We stood there, looking at each other, as if an invisible wall had come between us.

"My hands are tied; you know this. Rhys is my brother, which makes me a brother to you. You have to help me try."

As I walked away, I caught one last glimpse of him. He slid down on the nearest bench and remained there. Leaning back. Motionless. Face turned up toward the heavy platform roof—a grid of beams that could have been sky.

"SORRY, ARE YOU SLEEPING?" I really meant *Are you crying?*—Rita's face was all puffed up, with swollen eyes and a red nose—but I didn't want her to feel ambushed. "We missed you on the Street tonight."

"How was it? Any awkward encounters?"

"Well . . . Dev was there, with a few guys. Dead drunk. Didn't seem too happy."

"Tesh, I was actually asking about Rhys."

I stood by the door, unsure how to respond.

"Let's lie on the floor, it's cozier." She dropped a few pillows on the fluffy woolen rug (her one decor quirk; she claimed to have skinned Chewbacca). "Not that I want you to be running into Rhys or anything."

"No, me neither. By the way, you own some very strange objects." I pointed to what looked like a magnified powder brush, propped on its handle in the middle of the floor.

"Do you like it? It's a lamp." She pressed a button, and a blue luminescent cloud engulfed the spray of hair-thin tubes. "Fiber optics: light conducted by glass. I'll be writing my thesis on this next year. Imagine a fiber capable of transmitting three months of HD video in a single second!"

I loved listening to her talk about things I understood only vaguely. Jake had done it too, in that telescope room under the dome of stars.

She frowned and turned the lamp off. "I really should throw this thing in the garbage."

"Why? It's beautiful!"

"Yes, except it also happens to be a gift."

"From Dev?" It had to be, given how upset she looked all of a sudden. "What's going on between the two of you?"

"It doesn't matter."

"Of course it does. Especially if you spend your evenings on a dorm room floor, with your phone turned off and staring at fiber optics. Please tell me what's wrong."

"Dev and I . . . we had an issue with New Year's. He's going home and supposedly wanted to invite me, but his family would have been outraged."

"What's their problem?"

"That I'm not Indian. Technically, the problem isn't theirs, since he never bothered to mention he was seeing someone. So I told him to take a hike. Now he can go find himself a proper Hindu princess, just in time for the holidays."

"Maybe he'll change his mind."

"He won't. The guy is a total sucker for what others think of him. And even if he did, I refuse to sit around while he does his soul searching."

"I know the feeling."

"Luckily, you don't. Yours is a different kind of beast."

My "beast" was exactly the same: indecisive, paralyzed by family duty. I realized how much I needed to talk to someone. Besides, Rita and I were finally connecting as friends instead of one mentoring the other—so I told her everything. My crush on Jake. How I had mistaken Rhys for him. And how, ever since, he had been stepping aside, leaving me to his brother.

She stayed quiet for a while, then shook her head. "That's incredible! You know I'm not a fan of those two. And I hate to defend either of them, especially after the Ivy episode last week. But I have to ask: What on earth were you thinking?"

"Me?"

"You, yes. First you choose Rhys over him, then the two of you proceed to have this super-intense romantic affair in every house they own on the East Coast. And now you expect Jake to go after you and try to win you away from his own brother? I mean, come on, Tesh, what planet are you from?"

I listened to her, amazed that she would say these things. And afraid that she might be right.

"Frankly, I'm starting to like this Jake guy. To still purr at your feet after all this? Oh, and Tesh, if you're really *that* into him, do something about it. Don't be a wimp like . . . like everybody else. Otherwise some other girl will be spending New Year's with your man, as simple as that."

I left her room and looked at my watch. Past midnight. No way to do anything without breaking social norms.

But none of that mattered. All I wanted was to see him. And Rita was right: I had waited long enough.

HE PICKED UP AFTER THE first ring: "Thea?"

"I want to see you."

"You just saw me. Has anything happened?"

"No, but I do."

"It's almost one o'clock . . ."

"What difference does it make?"

Silence.

"I want to see you."

"Okay, I'm coming over."

It took him only minutes to drive to Forbes. He entered my room but stayed by the door—as far from me as possible.

"Thanks for getting here so quickly." I had no idea what to say to him. How to make up for months of mistakes. Where to even start. "You don't want to take off your jacket?"

The jacket stayed on. "Thea, what is it?"

I want to be with you, I've been wanting it for so long. Saying it to him had seemed possible, earlier, when I wasn't yet in his presence.

"Sorry, that was rude of me." He slipped the jacket off and folded it over the back of the chair, then came nearer. "What's wrong?"

"Jake, I . . ." Our chests almost touched. His shirt was so close, his warmth so palpable under it. "I'm not going back to Rhys."

"We can talk about it again, if you want. But you have to see him."

"I have nothing to say to him."

"That might change, once you give him a chance to explain."

"I don't want his explanations. He's not the one I should be with."

I had finally said it. A hot flush went through me, my face was probably all red—but I didn't care. My fingers slipped under his shirt, over his stomach—

His hands, much stronger than mine even when they hesitated, closed around my wrists and slowly pushed them away. "I would do anything for you. Anything. But don't ask me to betray my brother."

"How are you betraying him? Rhys and I aren't even together."

"That's for the two of you to decide." He reached for his jacket. Then the door.

"Jake—" I was now frantic for a way to stop him. "Fine. If you insist, I'll see him."

His hand froze on the doorknob. "You will?"

"First thing tomorrow. On one condition."

The question smoldered behind the alert blue of his eyes. But this calm was a mask. It had to be.

"Kiss me." *And don't you dare walk out that door, or I'll never speak to you again.* "Not on the cheek, like you almost did once. Really kiss me."

I saw the anger erupt, a dark wave of alarm and pain. Transforming his face. Aging it. He dropped the jacket down. Walked across the room—just a couple of steps, carefully. Stopped in front of me and reached for my face: no hesitation this time, the inevitable had started happening. His beautiful fingers took my chin, lifted my mouth up toward his until we felt each other's breath, then closer, his own lips opening—

I had imagined it so many times, but he erased everything. No one had kissed me before him. No one had touched me, or looked at me, or known that I existed. I began and ended there. He found me. Tasted me. Lost himself in me, as if I was the universe. His lips gave in to mine completely, dissolving me with their warmth, their softness, their incredible way of letting me know they had waited for me always.

I lifted his arms, pulled his shirt off. He left his body to me—its unbelievably smooth skin; the fine hairs on his chest and down his stomach line; the freckles, scattered like shy constellations all over him.

I stood on tiptoes, so my lips could reach his ear. "Take off my clothes."

He breathed faster as he opened my shirt—taking in every inch of skin that was baring itself for him under his fingers—and slipped it off my shoulders, down to my elbows, and then, with one final pull, made it fall to the floor.

"All of them."

I wanted him to hold me naked—completely naked—in his arms. He unzipped my skirt. Pushed it down my legs. Then started kissing me all over, burying his mouth in me until I could no longer breathe.

I moved his hand back to my hips, to the only piece of clothing he hadn't dared to remove from me: "Everything."

I didn't want to tell him that he would be the first. Just to let him feel it,

if it could be felt, once he was inside me. My fingers found his jeans. Unbut-
toned them—

"We can't, not like this." His hands became violent, pushing me away
again. "Not until I know what happens tomorrow."

"Nothing will happen tomorrow. Rhys and I are done."

"Maybe. But I can't take this chance. I need to know."

He threw on his jacket. Didn't even bother with the shirt. Then thought
of something and turned around.

"My heart will always be yours. Either way."

I HEARD THE RAIN AS soon as I woke up—my window was half open, and
the tiptoe of drops down bare branches filled the room with its cryptic beat.
It had come, with one unusually warm morning: the day when I would see
Rhys to say good-bye.

I was ready, in theory. But imagining something and going through with
it were two different things. What exactly was I supposed to tell him, anyway? That I was now switching over to his brother, whom I had wanted from
the start? And that this same insecure brother of his was sending me to break
the news, instead of confronting Rhys himself?

I threw on a sweater and went for a walk on the golf course. There
wasn't much rain by now, just a faint, inert drizzle. Already anemic, the
grass had sunk into the earth, caught in premonitions of darkness and
snow. Yet in one last whim of the dying fall, the rain had trickled through
the blades, filling them up until they appeared—for a few final hours—
fresh and vibrant with life.

I tried to come to terms with what I had seen on these hills. To imagine
taking Rhys back, if he offered enough excuses. He was a guy. He needed
sex. The spontaneous, guilt-free sex that he wasn't getting from me and
that, frankly, most other girls were probably eager to give him. Add to this
the family fortune and the genetic threat of dying young—no wonder he
went through the world like a hurricane. Selfish. Destructive. Entitled to
everything.

The pine tree stood by the gravel path—almost collapsing, weighed down with rain, its ragged bark exposed in the daylight like the wrinkled skin of a man already too old to die. There was no menace under those branches. It was ordinary. Just a tree.

I went back to my room, called Jake and told him I would be at his house in half an hour, to end things with his brother. All I heard was "I'll tell Rhys"—then he hung up the phone.

"Tesh, are you nuts? Where are you going in this weather?"

Rita had just come out from brunch and saw me crossing the Forbes lobby. I looked through the glass doors. She was right: the rain had turned into a downpour.

"Don't worry, I'll be fine."

"How exactly? It's a deluge and you don't even have an umbrella!"

"I'm not made out of sugar."

"Nuts or blind? Hmm . . ." She lifted her hands, palms up, as if measuring on scales the likelihood of me being either. "Sorry, but I have to give you a ride."

"Since when do you have a car?"

"Since I stopped wasting time with Dev and decided to jump-start my life. Now we can hit New York whenever we want!"

The jump-start turned out to be a gray minivan. She had probably picked it for its size, to fit the entire RCA group.

"So where to? Library or practice room?"

"The corner of Springdale and Mercer, behind the Graduate—"

"I know where it is. Although didn't you say Jake had a dorm room?" When I wouldn't answer, she shook her head and started the engine. "I thought you were done with Rhys. It's your own life, of course, but I hope you know what you're doing. I really do."

By the time she dropped me off, the downpour had stopped as suddenly as it had started. I was fifteen minutes early but it was better that way—we could get the whole thing over with sooner.

The house waited on the other end of the lawn, undisturbed, crowned with its own silence. I realized, as soon as I saw it, that to me it would always remain his house—Rhys's, not Jake's—and that I would never want to be in it again.

The wet grass squelched under my steps. I knew that the doors to the living room were closed, that there was no one on the granite stairs. But I saw Rhys as if he were real, rushing out to meet me. To lift me in his arms so that my shoes wouldn't get wet. And to carry me. Carry me and kiss me through the entire lawn . . .

Not this time.

My feet found the stairs, my fingers—the handle of a door. Then I heard the two voices, echoing throughout the house from inside the library.

"—because if that's what you think, Jake, you are out of your fucking mind! It's not why I allow you to live here."

"This is my home. I don't need your permission."

"Stay out of my life, or you'll never set foot near Princeton and you know it!"

"Do whatever you want with your life. But it's her life too."

"And since when is Thea's life any of your business?"

No answer.

"What time did she say she's coming?"

"Ten more minutes."

"You'll tell her that I went out. And that it's better for her not to see me again—now or ever."

"You need to talk to her yourself."

"Are you starting again?" Something hit wood and hit it hard—the windows shuddered. "You'll tell her exactly what I say!"

"Rhys, you broke her heart . . ."

"And you don't think the truth would have broken it? Stop lecturing me, because you have no idea what it's like, being forced to lie to the woman you love."

"Then don't lie to her. You never should have."

"Apparently, you and I differ on what I should or shouldn't do. Especially as it concerns Thea. It's rather presumptuous, actually"—his voice was charging up with anger again—"that you feel entitled to even have an opinion. But either way—you'll do what I say and that's the end of this conversation!"

"What I will do is not your decision."

"Don't make me turn against you, Jake. Or I swear—"

"I don't care what you do to me. She deserves to know and if you don't tell her—"

"Then what—*you* will? Is that it? Is that what my little brother will do for me?"

This time his voice exploded with a rage I had never heard from anyone. The walls could no longer contain it, and it shook the entire place.

"If you tell her anything—anything at all—I want you out of this house! Do not come back!"

A door got slammed. When I came in, Jake was alone, bent over the writing desk.

"Thea?!"

"If you tell me what exactly?"

"My brother is the one who should—"

"Yes, he should. But your brother will never be honest with me; I think by now he's made that more than clear. So please, don't be like him."

He looked crushed. Defeated.

"And don't act like hearing the truth would kill me. I know most of it already."

"You do? How?"

"It doesn't matter how. I know about your family's . . . about the illness that runs through generations. And the way your mom died. I was very sorry to hear it, but I really wish you and Rhys would just—"

"It has nothing to do with my family. It has to do with yours."

He walked up to one of the bookshelves, pulled a large volume and showed it to me. Mikhail Vrubel. The Siberian who had painted the canvas in Rhys's room.

The leaves flew under his fingers. Portraits. Stylized icons. A still life here and there. Then a complete change of course: an obsession with Russian fairy tales. Girls becoming swans. Flying seraphs. Sea kings chasing red-haired maidens. Until a single image obliterated all the others—raw, magnificent, bursting its colors over two entire pages.

Seated Demon. Painted in 1890, after a poem by Lermontov about a demon who fell in love with a human girl on the eve of her wedding.

"He looks like my brother, doesn't he?"

No stretch of the imagination could have prepared me for what I heard next. And, for a while, none of it made sense. As Jake spoke, I kept hoping for a sign that he was joking. But I had never seen him more serious, his voice mechanical, ruthless—the only way he could bring himself to be the one to finally tell me everything—and foreign, the voice of a stranger, heaping up the verdict on me quickly, in seemingly unrelated fragments, too frightening to hold anything but truth.

"The woman you saw with him is your sister. She died years ago, in a ritual, to save his life. In many ways, most of which probably shouldn't matter, he isn't exactly alive himself . . . not in the human sense, anyway. When she sacrificed herself for him, he became bound to her forever. Every month, on the full moon, he has to meet her and be with her the way you saw them—which was never a problem until he ran into you. I warned him, but he had fallen for you hard. You are the first woman he has truly loved. And, knowing my brother, you most likely will be the last. But the one thing he can never do is break his vow. He would be finished. Probably you too. So, since he can't bring himself to go to her after having just been with you, he shuts you off, drinks, goes wild—it drugs the thought of you out. When she's had enough of him, he is free to be with you for another month. That's all."

Then he left the room.

CHAPTER 15

The Guardian of Secrets

*B*EFORE YOU ASK *for the truth, you must be ready for it.*

I left the house right after Jake's hasty exit. I felt unsafe there, alone in the home of someone who had dated me for months and was now turning out to be . . . what exactly? A zombie? Vampire? Some creepy mix of both? A creature whom Giles, in his infinite quest for leaps from the rational, would have called—and please don't turn so pale, Miss Slavin, remember that in ancient Greece this was not considered a malevolent spirit—*daemon*?!

All I needed was one part of the story that didn't fit, one detail Jake had failed to account for, and I could dismiss his entire monologue as a delusion. An elaborate fantasy, triggered by a girl who had messed with his mind many years prior and had remained elusive ever since.

Elza had probably fed him this nonsense back then, filling his head with more than piano tunes and pangs of puberty. She might have told him tales. Legends, you know. Of strange, stunning witches who stole your heart and, with sex rituals, made you theirs forever. But not "forever" as in happily ever after. *Forever.* As in you could no longer die.

It might have disturbed the imagination of that twelve-year-old boy so much that, in the end, playing with death had spilled over into real life. Sneaking into a funeral home, for instance. Dropping blood in that coffin, to spook a few visitors. Then stealing Elza's body and doing . . . God knows what with it. And maybe this wasn't all? Her death continued to be a mystery. No leads. No suspects. But who in their right mind would suspect a child?

I went to class, hoping that the lecture on the decline of Athenian drama would distract me from the drama I was creating in my own head, of juvenile murderers and evil witches. When the hour was up, Giles went around to collect the Nietzsche papers. Mine, of course, was missing.

"I must say I'm a bit surprised, Miss Slavin. It was a fairly straightforward assignment." Fifty heads turned—his own little chorus (except it didn't comment, only watched). "Any particular reason you aren't turning it in?"

I was busy leaping from the rational after breakfast. Instead, I mumbled an apology: personal emergency . . . still catching up . . .

"You have until midnight. I will be deducting half a grade."

His idea of "fairly straightforward" turned out to be a painful crawl through one of the most unintelligible books I had ever read. Luckily, a Web search for "*birth of tragedy*" and "*chorus*" took me directly to chapters 7 and 8—the passages on that fantastic and repellent creature we were supposed to write about.

Satyr. A cross between man and goat. Or to the Greeks: between god and goat. Immortal. Living in a world of myth and ritual. Through the satyr chorus—a group of divine creatures who remained unchanged forever—tragedy offered a much needed consolation that no matter what happened, life would remain indestructible and joyful.

Unchanged forever. I kept on reading. Faced with the absurdity of life, of a tragic world in which action could alter nothing, the Greeks invented satyrs and the wisdom of Silenus, the god of the woods.

It took another second for the name to register, then my eyes flew through the rest of the page:

. . . inspired reveller . . . harbinger of wisdom . . . a sympathetic companion whom the Greeks considered with respectful astonishment . . .

I couldn't believe what I was reading. God of the woods? It was impossible. There was no way.

But it turned out to be all over the Internet. The satyrs (or *silens*, as they were often called) were creatures of pleasure who danced with nymphs to the music of flutes. The oldest and wisest among them—Silenus—was the teacher of Dionysus, said to possess the gift of prophecy. There were many images on vases too, and they all matched: bushy hair, beard, pointed nose, fleshy lips.

I finished the paper quickly and e-mailed it to Giles two hours before midnight. Then I left my room. If there was more than myth to any of this— and to everything else I had been asked to believe that day—then the man who had unlocked Procter Hall for me, the one who had called me a nymph before vanishing mysteriously, was two thousand years old.

Assuming he existed at all, he probably had all the answers I needed. And I was starting to suspect that somewhere, on the other side of those golf course hills, he was waiting for me already.

THE COURTYARD OF CLEVELAND TOWER was strangely quiet. Mute, motionless night bided its time under eaves and arches; even the occasional window seemed dimmer than before. Maybe, with dinner long over on a Friday evening, everyone had escaped to other, less forsaken parts of campus.

Where would I begin to search for him—a man who, for all practical purposes, was a phantom? That clerk at the Porter's Lodge had taken me for a lunatic at the mere mention of a janitor/keykeeper. Now I could imagine her reaction if I added "teacher of Dionysus" to the list. *Oh, and by the way, he doesn't age. Probably can't die either. You might have seen him walking around . . . on hooves. No? Doesn't ring a bell?*

Procter Hall was locked, as always. Then I remembered him saying something about descending down. About labyrinths. *Would your friends descend there with you or would you venture in alone?*

There it was, the small staircase from which he had emerged the first time I saw him. White stone, coiling down so steeply that just looking at it gave me vertigo. I had never checked where it led, nor asked anyone.

You are going to college, not on a ghost chase into the past. It can become a downward spiral very quickly.

Down I went. Somewhere above, my steps echoed farther and farther up against the vaulted ceiling.

Basement. TV lounge with scattered chairs. Pool tables. Dartboard. An old, rust-colored couch. And a sign:

> **DBar**
> **The Debasement Bar**
> **This is your oasis!**

I followed a corridor through a maze of turns, past numerous closed doors until one made me stop. On it, instead of a peephole or a number, someone had carved two ivy leaves in fine detail, down to the web of veins and the tiny stem spirals. Seeing ivy on campus was commonplace, a reminder that Princeton was one of eight schools (the Ivy League) whose names topped the U.S. college rankings. But under these leaves, drawn on the wood in pencil, were six circles stacked in an inverted pyramid.

Grapes.

It had never occurred to me that the leaves of the ivy and those of the grapevine had identical shapes. That the only way to distinguish between them was the fruit.

I reached for the handle—

"You should never open a door through which you might not wish to enter."

My body froze from that voice. I hadn't heard steps. Hadn't noticed when a heavy, dark shadow had sneaked behind me down the corridor. He wasn't supposed to exist, not outside the legends. But when I turned around, he stood right there. Unmistakably real. As if he had been walking by my side, holding the end of an invisible leash.

AMAZING WHAT RUNS THROUGH YOUR head when you are terrified:

So that's how I go? In a basement? Not even a white dress—just jeans and a fleece hoodie? And are those sharp things in his chest pocket . . . darts?

He stares at me patiently. Says nothing.

The guy does have a goat expression. We'd make a perfect horror classic: The Silence of the Goats. *Subtitle:* Stabbed to Death with Darts from the Debasement.

He lifts his hand.

I step back.

Did Elza die in a basement too? Maybe one day, in campus lore, we will be known as "the Missing Slavin Sisters"—

"Don't be afraid of me. I won't harm you."

Nice of him to say. Yet weren't you guaranteed to hear some version of this before you turned up dead in a ditch?

"Who are you, Silen? I mean . . . who are you really?"

"I could tell you. But of what use would it be, if you've already guessed?"

"Then how come your legs are not . . ." I stared down at where his shoes would have been if the overalls weren't too long and almost dragging on the floor.

"More goatlike?" His throaty laughter resonated off the walls. "They could be, if I wished. But that might elicit a few stares, don't you think?"

At the last words, his lower body began to alter in shape and texture, to morph—into that of an animal, black pelt and all—until he stood on hooves, smiling as if none of this had required the least bit of effort.

"So then you are indeed . . ." I couldn't say the name, astounded to be standing next to an actual creature from the legends—a satyr, in flesh and blood—and certain that my world would never be the same once he had confirmed my guess. " . . . the satyr Silenus?"

"Silenus, yes. Although I would much prefer to remain Silen to you. I have been called Silenus enough throughout the folds of time."

The folds of time. He had to have seen many more of them than I could imagine. And somewhere, in his not so distant memory, one of these folds held a secret that was now leaking into my brief human life.

"Did you know my sister?" The possibility made me forget everything else I should have asked (for example, what hid behind that door and why he thought I wouldn't want to enter through it). "I saw you in a yearbook from 1992. You must have known her."

"Only a fool can claim to know the heart of someone like her." He sighed and shook his head. "I was a fool once."

Which meant that even the omniscient satyr had fallen under the dandelion spell, like everybody else.

"Will you tell me about her?"

His body took human form again, gradually, as if a dark and hairy snowman was melting and coalescing back into shape, changing pelt to trousers, hooves to shoes. Then he headed in the direction of the spiral staircase. A slow, gawky strut—feet didn't seem to be his preferred mode of getting around. From behind, he could have passed for any tired, clumsy, slightly overweight man . . . if the sound of a flute didn't follow him. I had heard him play that tune once, and now recognized it: Debussy's *Afternoon of a Faun*. To the Greeks, it would have translated as *Afternoon of a Satyr*. Fragile, dreamy notes rose like incense vapors to the ceiling, as if he meant to enchant the whole building, or at least put it to sleep.

We were still coming up the last few stairs when a door squeaked. Procter Hall had unlocked itself, welcoming us to its vestibule.

He let me go in first. The place was dark, but as soon as we entered, the chandeliers came to life as I had never seen them—the static electric lights turning into tiny flames, quivering inside the glass bulbs. *No sound can escape walls like these.* I had no idea what I was walking into.

"Overwhelmed?" He offered me his hand. I expected his skin to be deadly cold but it felt warm, like that of any human. "I am glad you are no longer terrified of me."

What was the point of being terrified? He had powers beyond anything I could imagine (or comprehend, or escape from). And even though part of me still expected to wake up in my bed any second, I was starting to accept that none of this was a dream. That the hand holding mine was real.

"Real? Things become real only if you want them to be."

He was reading my mind too. And, as if this weren't unnerving enough, he proceeded to lead me through the tables. Literally *through* them. I could see the chairs I had arranged so many times, the wooden surfaces I had wiped at the end of each shift, but now our bodies moved through the vast space as if the dining hall contained only air.

When we reached the other end, he let go of my hand.

"Events from the past should have no place inside the present. And yet you wish to allow them in?"

"She was my sister. Probably still is. Which makes her a part of my present, even if she really became . . ." *A maenad? Some crossover version of a wildalone?* I needed a sane way of saying it: "Is it true that she saved Rhys?"

"Truth is a very malleable thing, Theia."

"But it's still better than secrets. I've been surrounded by secrets, all my life."

"So now you need someone to reveal them to you. And what makes you think I am their rightful keeper?"

"If not you, then who is?"

He pointed to the enormous fireplace next to us. "What do you see?"

High up in the stone, the school's shield was carved within a net of foliage. Dense leaves whose curvy edges reminded me of a tree above a mountain lake, in a legend I had read months ago. "An oak tree?"

"Yes. What else?"

I recognized squirrels. Lizards. Butterflies and birds. But he kept waiting for something more. Then I noticed the face of another animal, peeking through the branches. Only a snout and a pair of piercing eyes: the school's mascot. "A tiger?"

"It is as much a tiger as those leaves on the door were ivy."

They hadn't been, I was sure of it. They were merely disguised as a Princeton symbol if you didn't look too closely.

"Lynx." He glanced up at the carving, as if talking to the animal hidden inside and not to me. "The most elusive of beasts: the guardian of secrets. Comes and goes like a ghost, sees without being seen. One of the god's sacred messengers."

"The god?"

"Dionysus. Only his lynx can reveal secrets from the past. Through the animal's eyes, you can see events obscured by time as if they were happening again, right in front of you. But anyone who seeks out the lynx receives a boon or a bane."

"I don't know what that means."

"A blessing or a curse—this is what the past becomes, once you have seen it. Will you take your chances?"

I told him I would. If the only way to find out the truth was to risk a curse, so be it.

He averted his eyes, back toward the vestibule. Nothing stirred. For a second, even the flickers froze under the heavy rib cage of the ceiling. And there, real whether or not I wanted it to be, the animal appeared—paws touching the floor without a sound, every move flowing into the next with the agility of a young predator. Finally, the eyes poured their odd glare over us: bluish green, like the depths of a lake in whose waters a weeping willow had merged its reflection with that of the sky.

"Now let your cheek carry your question to his ear."

I thought he was joking, but he nodded in the direction of the lynx. *Things are real only if you want them to be.* Numb with fear, I kneeled and reached out, at first only with my hand—

The speckled fur was so soft I could barely feel it, as if my fingers were sinking into just-fallen snow. The ears perked their tufts of black hair. The paws bared their nails, scratching the floor.

I leaned in, reassured by the faint echo of a purr, and whispered my question: a single word. The name of a girl who had the most unusual fate of anyone I knew.

Stung by the sound of it, the lynx jumped back. Stopped a few feet from us, piercing the hall with the sharp wisdom of his eyes. Then something began to change in those eyes, in their hypnotic stare, as if the entire vastness of time was being funneled through them, bringing back events long gone and forcing them to take shape all over again, right here in Procter Hall.

A lawn. Bare trees. Night, drunk on the opulence of moon. And a girl in a white coat, walking quickly. Rushing across the grass, as if her time is running out.

She sneaks in through a French door, careful not to stir someone who has fallen asleep among empty bottles and scattered music sheets. Her face bends over him. A smile. She lifts his hand and slips a ring on it.

The guy wakes up. She tries to kiss him but he sees the ring and all becomes madness: his fury, the flash of silver thrown across the floor, their angry voices (carrying no words, as if muted by the depths of water). Under the girl's calm stare, he gropes among sets of car keys for a missing one, then shoves a helmet at her. But even after she has put it on, after an engine roars off into the night, a chill from her vanished smile refuses to leave the room . . .

The motorcycle ride unfolded in front of us—irreversible, final as only the past could be. But I didn't need to see anything else, I knew the rest already. Jake had said it with just a few words, on our drive back from Carnegie:

"*The same lightning doesn't strike twice in the same family.*"

"*What happened?*"

"*Rhys had an accident, years ago. Somebody got hurt and my brother blamed himself. Now he won't come near anything that has only two wheels.*"

The accident. Rhys dying. And my sister deciding to give up her life for him. Deciding it for both of them—to always own his.

A screech of tires erupted through the hall. Then the air became empty again. Only a four-pawed shadow dissolved into darkness, out toward the vestibule.

"ARE YOU MORE AT PEACE with the past, now that you have seen it?"

I had seen it, yes. But Elza's claim on Rhys was more than just a past. And I could never be at peace with any of this.

"What happened after the accident?"

"I helped your sister go through with it."

"Through . . . with what?"

His mouth opened inside the beard. Closed again.

"Is it true, what they say about those rituals? That Dionysus takes sacrifices—a human life in exchange for immortality?"

He nodded.

"So Elza and Rhys . . . they are no longer human?"

Another nod.

I tried not to panic. Rhys as a daemon. Elza as . . . something I preferred not to think about. Wild creatures, bound to be with each other forever on the deceptively idyllic Princeton campus.

No wonder Rhys had fallen for me so inexplicably and so quickly. Elza and I looked alike. He could have her on every full moon (obviously). But there were new moons, and half-moons, and an entire spectrum of thinner moons dangling their crescents in between. He must have been lonely through all those. Until, finally, her striking double had emerged—right in front of him, in the morning fog. Why would he pass that up?

A boon or a bane.

Silen was looking at me intently. "Our doubts are our strongest enemy, Theia. Whereas, in your heart, you know the truth."

"You mean the malleable truth?"

For once, he had nothing to say. I asked him to tell me the rest, whatever he meant by "helping her go through with it."

"After the accident we had very little time. Only minutes, before the moon would strike the dial."

"Strike what?"

"The moondial. Calling it 'sundial' puts humans at ease, but there is no distinction. Noon becomes midnight, that's all." He took the double flute out of his pocket and placed it on his open hand: one tube lying flat, the other pointing up at a sharp angle. "The moonbeams hit the blade, to cast its shadow. Without this"—his fingers glided along the upper tube—"there would be no moondial, only a garden decoration. The particular one we used that night could have passed for a water fountain, just outside these walls."

I had come across water fountains. There were several around campus and even one at Pebbles, in the garden outside that enormous library. From afar, these things always looked forsaken; I had never seen water coming out of them. But apparently they could quickly become something else: clocks tempting the moon.

"Everything must be done on a full moon, only then is the dial precise. Afterward, the moon's imperfect orbit throws it off by four dozen minutes every night, and the shadow can never align."

"Align with what?"

"With midnight. When the blade receives the full moon exactly at twelve, its shadow is hissed to life. Ignited like a wick by the god himself."

"Dionysus?"

"The very one. Whenever a life has been offered to him, a serpent is dispatched to take it."

"So then . . . this is how my sister died?"

"Died?" A smile curved his lips with its vague sadness. "Death now merely shrivels at her feet. But it certainly became her part of the barter, if that is what you mean."

He stepped over to a niche in the wall opposite the fireplace. A graduate student had once referred to it as an "oriel."

"You are familiar with the legend of the Holy Grail, I am sure. Some believe it to be the chalice from which Christ drank at the Last Supper and which collected his blood after he was removed from the cross. Others see it as a mystical cauldron. In one Welsh legend, King Arthur ventured into the Celtic underworld to steal the cauldron that would restore life to his dead warriors. These lancets"—he pointed at the three stained-glass windows that formed the oriel's semicircle—"tell the story of the knights who went in search of the Grail. One of the more controversial scenes is that of Sir Percival's sister, and how she sacrificed her life to heal a deadly ill woman. It involved a blood-drawing ritual. Hence the name of the glass panel: *Castle of the Strange Custom*."

I looked at the windows. No color yet, just a grid of glass pieces extinguished until dawn. But somewhere up there, hidden among the others, was a scene whose relevance to my sister's death I was already beginning to guess.

"Imagine how much blood must be taken from one human being to replenish the diseased blood of another! A virgin's blood was believed to be more pure and a dishful of it sufficed, but even that could cause anemia and death. Any smaller dosage—say, a chalice—meant that something else had to be mixed in. Something even more potent than blood: snake venom."

"But doesn't venom kill?"

"Not when used properly. You know what the Romans used to say?" He waited, as if it was only natural that I would be hanging out with ancient Romans at school. "*There is no death in the cup.* They administered venom as a medicine, knowing that it could heal if swallowed just as it could kill if received in a wound."

"And my sister received it in a wound?"

"Both, actually. First the serpent delivered death into her veins, then the drink made her immortal. This idea—that one can drink the elixir of life and gain immortality—is as old as humankind. If you look far back in time, the 'grail' would be just a simple skull in which blood and venom were fused to form a substance of unsurpassed medicinal power. In Greece, we use a mixing dish called a *krater.* But even a simple clay chalice will do." He raised his hand and I saw in it a small cup filled with water. "Man can give it names, paint mystery around it, drown it in the perplexity of myth. But in the end the grail is merely a cup. Its only power comes from what we pour inside it."

"I see just water inside this one."

"Water is where you start; it is the source of all life. Then you procure the additives."

I watched him ascend the few stairs to what would have been an altar if Procter Hall served as a church. A massive table stretched under the stained-glass window: the High Table from which Dean West used to say Latin grace and preside over his gown-clad scholarly empire. Now Silen ran his hand along the surface . . . and a figure began to appear, that of a man! Then another—a woman's. The bodies were laid out as if for a wake, covered by a white veil, the two heads almost touching in the middle.

"I thought only the lynx could bring secrets back to life?"

"Secrets—yes. But this is my own past, and I can reveal it to you whenever I want."

He reached under the veil. Lifted the woman's hand. Held the cup under it until the faint splash of a drop against liquid rippled through the hall. I imagined the tiny incision, barely visible on her pale skin. What

Giles had noticed in that casket hadn't been a thorncut at all, but a snake-bite, still bleeding.

"You probably expected to see me holding vials—white and red, the venom and the blood. But with a snakebite, the two are already mixed. And if the fang belongs to Dionysus himself, a single drop is enough to turn a chalice into the miraculous fountain of youth."

He lifted the cup in my direction and I stepped back, terrified that he expected me to drink from it.

"Don't worry, this is not a drink for the living. A sip into one's dead lips, on the other hand, and by the time the next moon rises, life will return to them. This time for good."

"Then how come my sister ended up in a funeral home?"

"It was the only way."

"Why, if there was never going to be a funeral?"

"Because the news of a missing student would have been a disaster for everyone involved. Investigations, media, bounties . . . the search would have been endless. A missing *dead* student, on the other hand, is news that gets forgotten overnight. It offers no prospect of a chase, no possibility of a happy ending. An article hits the front page, then the front page hits the wastebasket, and that is the end of it."

Maybe it was the end for everybody else. But there were two people, in a place I called home, who had never stopped waiting for answers. And who would continue to wait all their lives.

"Did Rhys end up in a funeral home too?"

"No. There was no visible change in him, so he continued with school. The only ones who found out were his brother and that butler—the brother, of course, only years later."

"How come Elza changed and he didn't?"

"Because he had no pact with anyone. When I pressed the cup to his dead lips, he received immortality—and everything that comes with it—but no strings attached, as you humans like to say. He became indebted to *her*, of course, and always will be. But not to Dionysus. Which makes the daemon a beautiful creature, virtually indistinguishable from any mortal man."

"And my sister?"

"Your sister challenged the god to the most formidable of bargains: forcing death to step away from prey already taken. Very few have dared to risk the consequences of that bargain. So she had a . . . reversal, of sorts. A metamorphosis. That night, she went as far from being a human as possible while still resembling one on the outside. It is a place from which she can never return."

Yet she had seemed so human, under that pine tree . . . "Were you the one who stole her body from the coffin?"

"Immortality is the deepest solitude one can imagine. I didn't want her first moments of it to be in a funeral home, all by herself."

"What about Rhys?"

"She was with him when he woke up."

The very thought agitated me—of how Rhys had opened his eyes and seen her; how she had smiled at him, knowing that this time he belonged to her for good. "That's exactly what Elza wanted, right?"

"Well, it was certainly more effective than any ring she could put on his finger. But what she really wanted was to be the girl on whose hand *he* would want to put a ring one day."

"She will be that girl, sooner or later."

The satyr paused, selecting his words. "I believe he has already found that girl. And it isn't the one he sees on the full moon."

"Maybe not yet. But everyone else is in his life only briefly, including me."

"Brevity has nothing to do with it. As you know, love is stubborn. It doesn't end when absence begins."

There was a barely detectable sorrow in his voice, and I wondered how different his heart could be, after all, from those of us humans.

"Now, enough musings for one night. The last shuttle to Forbes will be here shortly." He raised his hand and Procter Hall went back to normal: the two bodies disappeared; the chandeliers froze back to their electric glow. "I can arrange for a much faster transport, but you have probably overdosed on phenomena today."

I smiled, realizing how right he was. "The shuttle will do just fine."

He opened a hidden door next to the oriel and it led us right outside.

"Silen, I would like to see where my sister died." His raised eyebrows corrected me again. "I mean, where she stopped being human. You mentioned it was close by?"

"Quite in the vicinity." He pointed at the adjacent building and I recognized Wyman House, the dean's residence where I had once trespassed by accident. "Trust me, this is a place like any other."

"It isn't. Not to me."

I followed him around the back and through a tunnel of leaves whose dome rustled in the dark, high above our heads. It ended in a garden. Just as he had said: a place like any other. Gravel alleys. Geometric flower beds. Evenly shaped bushes. In the middle, isolated from everything else, a stone water fountain dreamed of summoning back to its throat the voice that had long ago abandoned it.

I noticed no spout, just a bare octagonal surface. "Was this always meant as a dial?"

He nodded and positioned his flute on top, then let go of it. The tubes stayed in place (one lying flat, the other pointing up at the night sky) as if held there by a spell. And the clock emerged. A thin shadow, cast at a harmless angle—about five hours off, a week after the last full moon.

"Your sister was . . . she was remarkably . . ."

By now I had heard it so many times. "Brave?"

"That too." The huge eyes flickered feverishly in the moonlight, each a dial of its own. "But, above all, she was incurably determined."

He must have assumed I would be just like her. Yet I was neither brave nor determined. Even standing in that garden, where a snake had once hissed to life and sunk its fangs into my sister, filled me with such dread that the venom might as well have spread into my own bloodstream.

"I know Elza was brave, but how did she get caught up in this? All this darkness of rituals and sacrifices . . . it had already found her, hadn't it, long before she met Rhys?"

"Darkness doesn't find us on its own, Theia. It is vain. It wants to be invited."

When we returned to Cleveland Tower, the parking lot was empty. The last shuttle to Forbes had probably left.

"Don't worry, we didn't miss it."

I wondered how much more of my mind he had guessed. Or read straight into. Or simply always known. It made being in his presence unsettling and at the same time effortless: for once, there was no point in filtering one's thoughts.

"What am I supposed to do now, Silen? I can't share Rhys with her. No way."

"To share the one you love—the ultimate challenge to a human heart. But what if the girl you are sharing with is your own sister?"

"If anything, this only makes it harder. Elza is so much like me, but . . . better."

"Better according to whom? Don't forget that Rhys has chosen *you*. Everything else is an illusion. Ethereal, like your dandelion whose airy head can so easily be scattered down to nothing."

It was nothing to him. But he wasn't the one who had to live with the thought of Elza. Dread her. Envy her. See her face in every mirror.

"Do you love him?" Anxiety looked grotesque on that face, the last face where I would have expected to find it. "Because if you can break his heart to spare your own a complication, then you don't love him. And you probably never will."

I wanted to tell him that this time mind reading had failed him, but the shuttle's approaching roar distracted me for a second. When I turned back around, there was only darkness. Stretching far in all directions, giggling soundlessly at the girl who had just brought one more nightmare into it.

THE WISEST OF THE SATYRS knew everything. To him, past and future were simply halves of an endless, uneventful, solitary present. But about one thing he was wrong: I would have never hurt Rhys to spare my own heart.

You are the first woman he has truly loved. Everyone had said it—Jake, Silen, even Carmela in her own bubbly way, with hints that Rhys was finally in love after almost falling for someone years ago (as if a girl like Elza would have settled for "almost").

So he did exist, after all, the boy who had broken the ethereal witch's heart. He must have met her in Bulgaria, on that trip he wouldn't talk about. Maybe, because of him, she had decided to go to Princeton. Then, for reasons I still didn't know, things between them hadn't worked out. They had ended up in that fight. The accident. To bring him back from death, she had become something believed to exist only in legends. *Wildalone*. And he, what had *he* become?

According to Giles, the Greek daemon was a toned-down version of Dionysus. Halfway between man and god. Sensual. Temperamental. Prone to madness and even violence. But I didn't want to think of Rhys as inherently dangerous. Silen's description fit him better: *A beautiful creature, virtually indistinguishable from any mortal man*. Did this mean that he fell in love the way mortal men did? That, despite immortality, his heart could still be broken?

Because there was also Jake. Undeniably, unquestionably human. Jake, who was so much more like me—not a demigod but a living person, with fears and flaws and a sense of his own imperfection. Now he needed an answer. My long overdue decision: him or his brother.

Unfortunately, three months of being with someone did make a difference. And with everything bad from those months now flipped on its head—Rhys turning out to be the victim, not the villain—I couldn't imagine leaving him.

I couldn't imagine not wanting Jake, either. People probably lived with this all the time. Dating someone and feeling a connection with someone else too. Having brief fantasies. Uncontrollable crushes. The occasional stolen peck on the cheek. It didn't mean that I would act on any of it, or that Rhys should know. He had said it himself: *Knowing always changes everything. Be with me this way*.

These were still the only words on my mind when I woke up the next day, having slept for twelve straight hours. *Be with me . . .*

Amazed at having waited this long, I ran to his house, but its emptiness hit me from the start: the front door gaped open, as if the place had been abandoned for good. Then it occurred to me that this could be an oversight and Rhys might still be asleep (if daemons slept at all). I went up to his bedroom, knocked—no answer. Just one sound as I walked in: that of falling water.

He stood under the shower with his clothes on, hands pressed against the wall, head bent down as low as the neck would have it. The water poured over him—the indigo of the jeans even darker when wet, the tank top vibrant with the soaked yellow of lemons, and everything else around him white, blindingly white—

Then he turned. Saw me. Reached to stop the water without taking his eyes off mine. His face was ash-pale, but I didn't wait for him to ask.

"Rhys, I know the truth and it hasn't changed anything."

He took me before I had finished the sentence. Took me with his arms, with his mouth, lifted me against the wall, kissing me all over until the space around us vanished and our bodies collapsed into each other through the clothes, oblivious to anything else, wet, exploding, aching.

When he finally slowed down, I realized we had ended up completely dry.

"How did you do this?!"

"I didn't want you to catch a cold."

"Yes, but that's not what I asked."

"You're right. No more secrets." He glanced down—the floor was still wet. Suddenly all the water rose up in a swirl. Accelerated. Began to spin so fast my eyes couldn't keep up . . . until it turned bright red and splashed back down, in the shape of a giant poppy whose petals burst for a second, spilled into a million drops, then vanished through the tiles, leaving them dry and white again.

"You look horrified. Should I not do these things in front of you?"

"I just . . . I need some time to get used to them." Although I wasn't sure that I ever would, or how to even go about it.

"What did Jake tell you?"

I summed it up in a few words.

"That's more or less it. The rest is just details."

"I should probably know those too."

"None of it is good, Thea. I belong to her once a month, that's all."

"It's just sex though, isn't it?"

"It's whatever she wants. She can do anything to my body—that's the deal."

The thought of her even touching him made me feel nauseated. "Were you ever in love with her?"

"Me? Are you serious?" His laughter shattered against the tiles, as that whirl of water had done a moment earlier. "If I were, she wouldn't need this damn arrangement."

"The arrangement wasn't for her sake. She saved your life."

"I never asked to be saved. Besides, she was the reason I had that accident in the first place. So trust me, I'd do anything—anything—to be free of her."

"That's not how it looked."

"How what looked?"

"You saw me standing there, by the tree. And you didn't even stop."

"Stop? Do you have any idea what would have happened if she'd seen you?"

"I've read the legends."

"You've read nothing. This woman is vile; she gets high on killing and would have ripped you to pieces if I hadn't—"

"Rhys, she is my sister."

"Don't ever count on this, okay? She may have been your sister once, but now there's nothing human left in her. Nothing!"

Silen had said the same thing: *as far from being human as possible . . . a place from which she can never return . . .*

We went to the bedroom and he had me lie down, rolling over on his stomach next to me.

"Ask me anything. Anything else you want to know."

I already knew the most important detail, but part of me hoped he would deny it: "What would happen if you stopped seeing her?"

"That's not an option. The rules are simple: I don't object. I don't make her wait. I don't refuse anything."

"And if you do?"

"I tried once. It wasn't pretty." The rage in his eyes filled in the rest for me. "Which is how I discovered the only remedies that worked: alcohol and women. Drinking washed everything from my mind. And the women, they—" He shook his head, as if the irony of it was beyond him. "They compensated for everything she was doing to me. So absurdly, unbelievably willing. All I had to do was pick any one of them—or more than one, whatever—and it was a done deal."

I could see now why my refusal to become the next "done deal" when we first met had exasperated him. "And all this made going to Elza easier?"

"Much easier."

"How?"

"It just did."

"I need to know, Rhys."

"After a few women at Ivy, one more on the golf course doesn't seem such a big deal."

"I see. So you just . . . added me to the mix?"

"You?" He glanced up at the ceiling and smiled. "You were something else entirely. My eyes fell on you in that fog and the world was suddenly at peace. A peace I had never imagined. I knew—before you had said anything, before I had even touched you—that all I wanted was to be near you."

"Even though I looked so much like her?"

"Or more so because of it. I had no idea the two of you were related, of course, but . . . I was drawn to her too, at the beginning. She had that same air of gorgeous, unspoiled innocence that just gets under my skin. Except in your case it's genuine."

"And hers wasn't?"

He chose not to answer. With incidents like the Nude Olympics, "innocent" probably wasn't the best way to describe Elza.

"Did it honestly never occur to you that I might be related to her?"

"Come on, who would have thought? You're fifteen years apart, and she had never said anything about a baby sister. I assumed the resemblance was just a coincidence, some Eastern European look I apparently had a soft spot for. By the time I found out, it was too late. I was already hooked."

"How did you find out?"

"When Jake said your last name at the dinner here. I guess he had seen your recital posters."

No wonder Rhys had driven me to Forbes that night without a word. *Nice to meet you, Thea Slavin*. My name had become Jake's secret revenge—on his brother, for stealing his girl.

"That's when the hell began. I tried to stay away from you, and couldn't. Then I made a pact with myself: we would be together, but not have sex until you knew the truth. Of course, I almost blew it. And I still couldn't bring myself to tell you."

"Why not?"

"Because I thought you'd be devastated. What was I supposed to say? *By the way, babe, I'm banging your sister once a month?*"

"Sure. Just like you told me you could see other girls."

"I never said this."

"No, only that you were not a one-woman guy."

"Because I'm not, Thea. There will always be one other woman in my life. A woman I detest."

I was probably going to detest her too. Once a month, on every full moon.

"And what about everything else?"

"What else?"

"The guys in the jeep."

"I'm done with that. The night when you showed up at my house, I could have killed Evan for the nonsense he blurted out in front of you. I was angry at him. At myself. At the whole fucking world. Then things got even worse, when we had that fight about Carnegie."

"I still don't understand why you said you couldn't come. The full moon wasn't until Saturday."

"Guilt, basically. How was I supposed to face you and your parents, knowing where I'd be the following night?"

"But you came to the concert anyway. I found your note."

"I had to hear you play, one way or another. The plan was to watch from a distance, then drive back here and see Elza on Saturday. It worked—almost."

"Almost?"

"I didn't expect to be jealous of my own brother."

"You. Jealous of Jake."

"No, not that way. I trust Jake more than I trust myself. But I envied his freedom. To spend the evening with you like a normal guy, the kind of guy you need—none of the stuff I come packaged with."

I tried not to think about what I needed, or how things might have turned out if I had ended up with Jake. Rhys was quiet too. High on the wall above us, the painted look-alike sat in peace, guarding his own silence.

"My Greek Art professor mentioned daemons once."

His eyes traced mine up to the canvas. "And?"

"It didn't sound so bad. Definitely supernatural, but not a malevolent spirit. At least not in the Greek myths."

"A hopeful start. What else?"

"Unmatched intelligence and talent for the arts. Is this why you play piano so well?"

He laughed. "I like to think that my playing wasn't terrible to begin with. But you should hear my brother. Apparently, one can be fantastic on the keys even without demonic powers."

Everyone who knew Jake had made it clear what a superb pianist he was—Ferry, now Rhys, and even my no longer human sister who, years ago, had called him "Miracle Hands." But the last thing I wanted was to confirm Jake's phenomenal playing for myself. It was safer for everyone if I never did.

"Speaking of my brother, I need to call him. I lost my temper yesterday." He still didn't know that I had overheard their fight. "Wait for me here; I'll be right back."

The call must have been quick because he returned right away. "It's all sorted out. Jake will be here in an hour."

"Did you tell him?"

"Tell him what?"

"That you and I made up."

"No. Why ruin the surprise? He can find out once he gets here."

We went downstairs, to a kitchen with so many cabinets it seemed equipped to feed all of Princeton. He poured me a glass of wine, but I barely took a sip. Jake—about to walk in, any moment. What would I say to him? How would I look him in the eyes?

Meanwhile, Rhys kept telling me stories about his brother as a little boy: Jake having his first piano lesson at age five; Jake falling from a tree and breaking two fingers, then crying that he would never be able to play again; Jake getting scared by a pigeon that had come in through one of the French doors and flown out of the piano when he began playing . . .

Neither of us had heard his steps. I felt someone watching me—leaning quietly against the door, caught in the darkness of his own thoughts, as always.

My hand began to shake as I lowered the glass on the countertop. *Clink.* The touch of stem against granite. Rhys turned at the sound, saw his brother, and rushed to give him a hug.

"Welcome home! Sorry for what I said yesterday; I can be such an ass sometimes."

There was no answer, just a nod.

Rhys slipped his arm around me. "I've never been happier and I owe it all to my brother. We should celebrate."

Finally, a word dropped from Jake's lips: "We?"

"You, me, and Thea. But we'll skip Ivy this time. The real party is off campus."

"You two can go. I'll see you in the morning."

"That's a joke, right? It's Saturday! Besides, I want you with me on the best night of my life."

Jake continued to look at Rhys, and his face began to soften up. "What time are we leaving?"

"Nine or so. After dinner."

"I'm not hungry."

"Jake, come on! I said I'm sorry about yesterday. Tell me how to prove it to you and I will."

"You don't need to prove anything. It's been a long day and if you want me out later, you'll have to eat without me. Just come get me when you're ready to go."

He said this without taking his eyes off Rhys. Then, leaving them no time to fall on anything else in the kitchen, he turned around and went upstairs.

CHAPTER 16

Rejecting an Estlin

THE PARTY WAS only a few miles from campus. Rhys had assumed we would all go in the Range Rover, but Jake insisted on riding his motorbike—I knew only too well why.

In size and opulence the house was a match for Pebbles, although it lacked the ease with which an impeccable taste mixes old with new, leaving its mark on everything. We walked in, the two brothers on both sides of me (Rhys's hand on mine a subtle reminder which one of them I was with), and heads began turning—the quick eyes of women flashing their envy at me, ready to blaze me down to ashes for the audacity to claim both of these gorgeous men for the evening. And there were many women. Rhys knew almost all of them. He smiled at some, barely nodded at others, but didn't hug or shake hands with anyone. Jake walked next to me like a shadow, eyes lost ahead, not bothering to return a single greeting.

An enormous oval library was converted into a bar for the night. We had just come in when a familiar voice made my stomach turn: "Rhys! Finally, man! We thought you'd bailed on us again." Evan lifted a fist and waited for Rhys to do the same.

"I always show up if I say I will. Thea, this is Evan, the party host."

I couldn't avoid the handshake, but otherwise had nothing to say to the guy. He hurried with an apology that Rhys must have demanded for me in advance:

"Sorry about the last time. My mouth ran ahead of me."

That was a mild way of putting it. I smiled as politely as I could, trying not to encourage further conversation.

After some brief cigar-fumed blather, he left us with one final piece of advice: to knock ourselves out with his dad's booze collection. When Rhys pulled out a chair for me at one of the tables and asked what we wanted to drink, I knew that the moment I dreaded had come. That, for a minute or two, Jake and I would be alone.

He sat down across from me. His body rested on the chair with tired detachment—legs stretched out, elbows propped on both ends of the backrest, head tilted forward. His eyes traced Rhys's steps across the floor, avoiding me.

"I had to go back to him, Jake."

"I knew you would."

"But it doesn't mean that what happened in my room—"

"You don't have to explain. There's no better man than my brother and I am happy for both of you."

A few moments later, without touching the drink that Rhys put in front of him, he said he was going to get some air.

Rhys watched him leave, then shook his head. "We have to find him a woman, Thea."

I couldn't bring myself to risk a reply.

"My brother acts like he's lost the will to live. I've seen it once before and I can't let it happen again. We need to set him up with someone. Tonight."

Once before. He couldn't possibly mean Elza; there had to have been someone else. The thought bothered me and I stopped being careful.

"I don't think your brother needs help. He can have any woman in this room."

"Yes, but the woman who did this to him isn't in the room, and the others don't seem to exist for him. So he needs a little nudge. Preferably from someone hot who'd fuck his brains out."

"That shouldn't be a problem."

He looked at me for a second, dismissing the suspicion before it had taken shape. "No, finding her certainly won't be a problem. But getting him on board will."

The thought of Jake with another woman—one of the many gorgeous women in the room—sent a jab of pain through my chest. It had to be much worse for him. Seeing me with Rhys. Being forced to watch, over and over, while his brother took the girl who should have been his.

"Fine then. How about . . . her?" I pointed to a tall blonde surveying the bookshelves by herself.

"No, not that one."

"Why not?"

"She isn't Jake's type." He said the words slowly, as if struggling with momentary amnesia, and I realized that something else had caught his attention. Something that hadn't been in the room before. "*That* one."

He directed my eyes with the slightest of nods, but I didn't need it: the girl who had just walked in was impossible to miss. She looked impeccable—a sculptor had carved his final masterpiece out of pristine white marble, then brought it to life. A lush copper mane fell in waves down to her waist, lit up the entire place with its astonishing color, and tricked you into believing that a late-summer sunset hid behind her, making its way through the crowd. She smiled at everyone—a benevolent gesture while having to be among mere mortals—and moved with absolute assurance, as if she owned each molecule of air in the room.

"So, what do you think?" Rhys seemed to love every second of it.

I think she makes the rest of us look like pencil sketches. "You know Jake's type. I don't."

He looked at her again until finally she noticed, and her smile shot back an instant challenge: challenge to an equal.

"Ah, speaking of my melancholy brother—there he is, just in time."

Jake sat down. Took his glass and drank half of it in one go. Rhys watched him with a certain spark in the eye he always had when about to ridicule someone.

" '*Not having that, which, having, makes them short.*' Right, Jake?" Then he turned to me and clarified: "Lack of love. Romeo's explanation of what makes his hours long."

"I've read the play."

"Of course you have; I underestimated my woman!" He leaned over and kissed me. Jake's eyes escaped within the crowd. "I was just about to tell our dreamy Romeo that we've found someone who will cut his hours very, very short."

Jake's eyebrows curved up. "We?"

"Yes. Thea and I found you the perfect woman."

"You have *found* me a woman. And what made you think I needed to have one found for me?"

"This morose face of yours. The last time I saw a smile on it was months ago."

"I don't recall much smiling around our house. Not lately, anyway."

"Touché!" Rhys's laughter ricocheted without an impact. "But that's exactly what I mean. You solved my problem, and now I want to do the same for you."

"I can solve my own problems, Rhys."

"With self-imposed celibacy? Never a great solution."

"The greatest solution—for everyone—would be to drop me as a conversation topic."

"Stubborn, just as I told you." Rhys shrugged in my direction, but I could tell he wasn't done yet. "Jake, seriously, you should check this woman out. We were both floored when she walked in."

"Floored at first sight? Always a promising start." His eyes kept trying to catch mine. "And the collective 'we' has decided I should go for the woman it has handpicked for me?"

"Actually, the 'we' wasn't all that collective. Thea picked first, but I had a different choice in mind."

"I see. So I owe this to Thea?" He said it only to me. Watching me.

Waiting for me to look up, to explain it all—but I couldn't. My mind had shut down, terrified of where this was going to end. "And whom did she pick?"

"The one browsing those books. But then the redhead walked in and we both knew she was the way to go. Over there, by the fireplace."

Locating the girl took Jake only a second. In a single swoop, he bent over the table toward his brother, slamming the empty glass down.

"Is this your idea of a joke?"

Rhys backed off immediately. "Sorry. My bad."

"What exactly are you trying to do, get clever with me?"

The fight was escalating so quickly that the trigger had to be something from the past, unrelated to me.

"Forget it, okay? I just thought you'd like her, that's all." Rhys kept retreating. "We should probably head home anyway. Thea seems tired."

"Too late to be leaving now." Jake's eyes returned to the redhead, taking her in, head to toe. "I'm game. After all, what's the downside?"

He walked straight up to her. I watched her eyes fall on him for the first time, watched as he said his first words to her—words I would never know—and she leaned in to whisper something back, reaching for his elbow, a few of her curls dropping over his shoulder to mark their territory without him noticing.

I was desperate to get out of that room. Or for the two of them to leave. To skip this display and take their lovey-dovey chat to some other part of the house where I wouldn't have to see it.

But he brought her to our table. Her name was Nora. She said it to me first, smiling briefly to show a vague curiosity. Then she repeated it to Rhys—measuring him up, savoring the mix of his name, voice, and hand-shake.

"How come we haven't seen you around Princeton before?" He took the small talk upon himself, since Jake seemed unwilling to utter a word.

"Princeton isn't my thing. I just finished school in Europe."

"Really? My girlfriend is from Europe." A tap on my knee clarified the girlfriend reference for her. "Were you East or West?"

"Prague."

"Nice! Czech blood, I take it?"

She shook her head, and the copper waves spilled around her neck as if a lovestruck wind had decided to reshuffle them. "Believe it or not, I'm one hundred percent Irish."

"We're Irish too! Only half-Irish, though." A glance at Jake, who was still silent. "Is your name then a tribute to Nora Joyce?"

Her laughter rang its crystal ripple through the air. "My mother adored James Joyce. When she chose the name, Dad told her that if I turned out half as wild as poor James's wife, he would disown me."

"I don't blame him." Another glance at Jake. "And did you?"

"Did I what?"

"Turn out half as wild."

"No." She beamed her stunning smile at him. "Much wilder." Then her eyes glided over Jake's unreadable face. "The wild gene runs in my family just as the mute one seems to run in yours."

"Don't worry, my brother can be very sweet if given the right inducement. The rest is just veneer. Dark and brooding."

"Yes, I can tell." By now her smile was gone. She seemed fed up, ready to leave.

Finally, Jake's lips opened:

"And by 'right inducement' Rhys means a girl who knows how to handle darkness." He said it so softly that at first I thought he was talking to me. That we were alone again, in a room somewhere. "If she exists, I'd give anything to find her."

Nora didn't lose a second. "Try me."

Her provoking smile again. The quick hair toss, the flushed cheeks.

Rhys rose from the chair. "For that, you two don't need us. By the way, when Jake offers to give you a ride home later, don't get on his motorcycle. Take a cab with him."

"I don't think Jake will be giving me a ride home tonight."

Rhys was reaching for my hand but froze when he heard this. Jake's expression hadn't changed. He watched her, waiting for an explanation.

And she did explain, but not before enjoying her brief moment of victory. It was the only possible outcome, the only leap of logic that didn't involve a woman rejecting an Estlin.

"I'm already home."

"You're Evan's sister?" Rhys tried to clear the surprise from his voice but failed.

"Half sister, although sometimes I think even that's a stretch." She looked at Evan and his friends, whose drunk voices had been knocking the mood out of the room for quite some time. "Anyway, it was a pleasure to have you over. Drive back safely and . . . I promise to cheer up your dark and brooding brother."

While Rhys led me out, I tried not to think about what that promise actually meant.

"I COULDN'T WAIT TO LEAVE that stupid party and have you all to myself. Was it too obvious?"

We were in his living room. He had started to kiss me and unzip my dress when the distant sound of an engine reminded me that Jake hadn't come home yet.

"Rhys, we can't do this here."

"You can do anything you want, anywhere in this house. It's now yours too."

"No, it's yours and Jake's. He might be back any minute."

The notion made him laugh. "You are so adorable when you panic about propriety. That time when you refused to walk across my lawn—it made me want to devour you right there, under those trees. But I think it's safe to assume that Jake won't be sleeping here tonight."

"You don't know for sure."

"Believe me, my brother may be stubborn but men are men. He won't say no to her. No one would. In fact, I bet he's still at Evan's right now, doing exactly this—"

His hand slipped under my dress and everything from that night—Jake's silence, Jake's anger, Jake's unplanned conquest—dissolved like a collage of shadows.

"I want to feel you getting wet . . . Do you like my fingers down there? Or do you want my lips?"

I wanted his lips everywhere. But something wasn't right. "Let's go to your room. Please."

"Not yet. Come, I have a Chopin for you."

Of all things possible—a Chopin . . .

He sat down on the bench, pulled me in front of him, and began playing. It was the one piece that fit him perfectly: the last of the études dedicated to Liszt. I had never attempted its hurricane of sound—not only because of the absurdly difficult technique (after many hours of practice, anything could be learned), but because it exploded with a magnificence that had always seemed beyond my reach.

Under his fingers the étude was unbelievable, a triumph. He played it with absolute ease, knowing that his speed over the keys would charge me with the rush of a roller coaster. His face dived into me—my hair, neck, shoulders—and the rhythm didn't lose momentum for a second. He could no longer look at the keyboard, but having to keep his hands there drove him wild. Until the last chords unleashed his body on mine. He swirled me up from the bench and over the lid of the piano, shutting it with a bang that reverberated through the room. His hands, which he no longer had to control, were pulling off my clothes, and his own, with a violent, blind insistence.

I tried to slow him down—

"Don't." He caught my wrists and held them still. "I can't fight it anymore, Thea. I am yours. All of me. Take me."

His heat invaded my skin. Then the rest of him—the push of his stomach, the speed of his breath, the force of his legs opening mine.

"I've been dying to do this, without guilt or secrets."

His voice. It could convince me of anything.

But I still had my own secrets. Jake's incredible, shy body, so different from the one closing in on me now. His stunning kiss that night, when I had wanted him to be the first one—the only one—to ever be inside me.

My hands kept pushing Rhys away.

"Don't." He won over them again. "They say it always hurts the first time. But it won't, I promise. Thea, look at me."

I did.

"I love you."

The words shot an electric current through me. I wanted to say it back. But my heart kept sinking.

"Trust me, it won't hurt. Just trust me. Open, open for me . . ."

Suddenly my entire body felt him. Pressing, shivering inside me and all over me, forcing the brief pain out then rushing through me, hard, pulsing, making me want to close around him and take him in with every part of me—

When a door was slammed, the sound felt foreign, and at first my mind failed to register what had happened. Then it did. And before Rhys's frown had confirmed it, I already knew.

Jake had walked in on us. He had heard and seen us.

I SLIPPED OUT OF RHYS'S arms and off the piano, wishing I could disappear— from the room, from the house, from the two brothers' lives. And from my own.

"It was Jake, wasn't it?"

"My brother has gone insane tonight. Slamming doors, as if the sacred abstinence of the house has been violated."

"Is he still here?"

"That was the door to his room—so yes. But I hope he won't bother us again, because I'd hate to end our evening with a fight."

"He wasn't trying to pick a fight with you. It's my fault; I'm the reason he—"

"Don't be silly. My brother saw us having sex, big deal. If he can't handle it, that's his problem, not ours."

Except it *was* our problem. Mine, at least. I had to tell Rhys the truth and own up to it. But, once again, the words refused to come out.

"Rhys, maybe I should go."

"You aren't going anywhere. If anyone should be embarrassed, it's Jake, not you." He turned off the lights and took my hand. "Come upstairs. You can sneak into bed while I'm having a chat with him."

"About what?"

"About why he acts like he's gone back to puberty. I wanted your first time to be perfect, and now it's practically ruined."

"Nothing is ruined, you were amazing. I just . . . I wish we'd leave Jake out of it."

He smiled, lifted his shirt from the floor and wrapped me in it. "Wish granted. Besides, technically your first time isn't over yet. I'm considering keeping you up all night, even if it means we will—"

A sound cut him off. He had heard it before I did: an engine again, this time bringing its roar distinctly through the night. A car door closed. The main entrance to the house opened. And a girl's laughter carried her voice through to us, in the dark:

" . . . No, I won't make you beg again. But if you do want me *under* you, then you have to tell me which way to go in this absurdly dark house of yours!"

Nora.

Her steps echoed in the hallway and up the staircase. "My phone is almost dead, so stop saying—" The crystal laughter rippled out again. "Stop saying what you'll do to me, and tell me left or right. Yes, I'm upstairs . . ."

Another sound, barely recognizable: a door opening and closing.

"Finally! My brother has come to his senses. Too bad he had to throw a fit in the process and almost ruin our evening."

Then he went on to talk about Nora. About how he could have sworn, by the way she swooned over Jake at the party, that she was toast even before we left. I pretended to listen, but all I could think of was Jake holding her. Undressing her. Letting her do to him whatever she wanted.

"Hey, what's wrong?" Rhys turned my face toward his. "You don't seem to like the poor girl very much."

"How can anyone not like her? She's clearly perfect."

"I hope Jake thinks so too, although I doubt it."

"Didn't you say she was his type?"

"She isn't, really. There's the red hair and the feisty temper. Otherwise Nora is too much energy, too much physicality in your face—like a well-bred mare. But that's not what gets my brother going."

It had gotten him "going" enough to summon her to his room. "Why was he so angry when you pointed her out to him?"

"Because she reminded him of someone. I should have known not to go there."

"Go where?"

"Jake fell for a girl once, years ago. Lost his head like a madman. The same red hair, but otherwise very frail. Exquisite. She broke my brother's heart, Thea. Just went on and shattered it, like it was nothing."

"How?"

"Fooling around behind his back. I first heard it from someone at Ivy and almost started a fight with him. Thought he was feeding me nonsense, to get back at me for voting against him during bicker week. Then I heard it from someone else. I knew it would crush Jake, so I decided not to say anything until I had confirmed the rumors. In the meantime, he found out from a friend who had run into her at a cocktail party. But you know Jake. He trusted her and dismissed everything."

"What happened in the end?"

"I saw it with my own eyes and couldn't believe it. Couldn't fathom how a woman would have the nerve to be two-timing my brother."

I wondered if what I was doing to Jake qualified as two-timing. It certainly hadn't required any nerve at all.

"He had gone to Seattle, to play at a concert for one of our charities. We were at a party where she drank too much. While I was driving her home, she made a move on me right there, in the car, telling me that Jake didn't need to know." The rage exploded in his eyes. It was frightening and refused to subside. "I told my brother as soon as he came back. He broke it off with her that same day, but walked like a shadow for months. I don't want to think of the damage it did to him. Makes me want to find her and . . ."

It was better not to imagine the things he might have done. "What happened to her?"

"She was sent to Europe."

"Sent?! By whom?"

"I told her to get the hell out of Jake's life. She walked off with a very generous offer. Named her own price, basically."

"You mean . . . you bought her off?"

"Girls like her always have a price, Thea. And thank God they do."

Girls like her. Was I really any better? Only two nights ago, I had been kissing Jake. Making promises to him, naked, in my room.

"You look tired. Let's go to sleep."

"Do daemons sleep at all?"

"It's optional. I think of it as a lifestyle choice, to be as much of a human as possible. If I keep at it, my body starts to need the whole package. Sleep, food, air."

"You don't need to breathe?"

"I could stop if I wanted to. But I've done it for so long that my lungs are used to it, and the illusion is almost perfect. I like needing these things. It gets a bit frightening when I don't." There was a sadness in him when he spoke of what he was. As if, had it been up to him all those years ago, he might have made a different choice. "You, on the other hand, I need no matter what. My only human need that is not an illusion."

We went to his room and soon he fell asleep. I lay in the dark, listening to the house, to its deceptive absence of sound. Somewhere across the hall, Jake was with Nora. Doing to her everything he had been promising on the phone. Everything he had seen his brother do to me. And more.

His type, according to Rhys, was a different—exquisite—redhead. I tried not to think of that other girl and her fatal beauty, but my mind went at it stubbornly. An impossibly frail figure. Devastatingly white skin. Ravishing hair whose red had stolen Jake's heart, the same heart she had ended up shattering.

Now I knew why he had wanted his brother away from me at the beginning. Why all along he had anticipated defeat, certain that I would choose Rhys over him.

My heart will always be yours, either way.

I needed to see him. But the minutes dragged on, and Nora wouldn't leave. Finally, I heard a motorcycle drive off: he was taking her home. When the same sound brought him back to the house, I slipped out of bed and left the room.

Two identical doors faced each other across the stone staircase. One led to Rhys's bedroom; the other had to be Jake's. I pushed it in—it wasn't even fully closed—and saw everything at once.

Clothes, scattered recklessly across the floor. An open pack of condoms, with one torn wrapper left in a hurry next to a stiletto shoe and a dress literally ripped to pieces. That trip on the motorcycle . . . Jake had simply needed a pharmacy run? My eyes stumbled over the bed and the two bodies going madly at each other on it—

I ran away just as his face was lifting off her. Through the open door, I heard her voice: "What is it? Didn't you—" Then his own, cutting her off: "Stay here." I rushed down the stairs but he caught up with me, the jeans thrown on, the rest of him naked, heated up, and whiffs of her perfume—

"Why did you come to me?" He pushed me into a corridor, a part of the house I had never seen. "You wanted to know what I was doing to her?"

"Jake, I had no idea—"

"Now you do: I was making love to you. If I can't have the girl I want, then I'll imagine her in whoever's in my bed. I've imagined so many things with you . . ."

He had backed me up against a wall and I tried to avoid his lips while his mouth chased me.

"Why did you come? To check if seeing Rhys all over you has driven me crazy? It has! That's why I called Nora. Did seeing us drive you crazy too?"

"Stop saying these things to me!"

"I am crazy, Thea, absolutely crazy. I am crazy about my brother's girl. I want her constantly, even when she's not around. And I would do crazy things for her—you know this, don't you?—I want to do crazy things *to* her . . ."

His hand went up my neck and his fingers closed around it. *"I can't betray*

Rhys; that's what I tell myself every time. But then I end up near you and—"

"We should stay away from each other, Jake."

"Wouldn't matter. I see you everywhere, in every girl I meet. I keep hoping one of them will erase you from me, but they all become you as soon as I touch them. Do you ever think of me when you're with Rhys?"

There was no way I would answer him. I tried to move away, but his grip on my throat tightened.

"Tell me. Do you ever imagine it's me and not him?"

"Even if I do, so what?"

"Nothing, I just . . . I needed to hear you say it." His voice kept dropping, lower than I had ever heard it. "I don't want you to be free of me. I want to be inside you every time you breathe, as soon as your lips open . . ." He leaned in so close I could feel his warmth on my skin, over my face. "Breathe, that's all I want, breathe for me—"

I did, and his lips took the air from mine without touching them. Then he breathed out. I could feel it enter my chest: the air that had just left his. Bringing him into me. Filling me up with him until the physical need for him hurt me.

"You make me come just with your breath, Thea . . . I can come just from feeling your breath on my mouth—"

A thousand places burst inside me. I heard my voice say his name and felt weak, numb with ache, terrified of him and the power he had over my entire being.

"Let me go, Jake."

He remained still, hands pressed against the wall on both sides of me.

"Rhys will wake up. I have to go."

"So what if he does?"

"So what? He is your brother, and I am with him. Just let go."

His right hand dropped—away from me, lifeless. I went upstairs without turning back.

CHAPTER 17

Briefly, Like a Thief

I WOKE UP and thought I was still dreaming: in front of me was an explosion of wildflowers, as if someone had robbed a field of its blooms and woven a fabric with them.

"I feel like I should be paying money to watch you sleep. Getting quite addicted to it." Rhys was sitting on the edge of the bed, holding a sundress, smiling. "How's this for a Sunday outfit?"

"Are we staying in today?"

"Definitely not. I'm taking you out as soon as you get ready."

"What about Jake?"

"He's gone. Back to New York, I guess." He handed me the dress, while I struggled with a mix of relief and guilt from Jake's early departure. "Let me see you in it."

"I can't go out in this. It's winter outside."

"It sure is." He went to the window and pulled the curtains. "And it's actually snowing."

The snow floated quietly, in plush white patches. None of this made sense. He wanted me to wear a sundress in the middle of December?

While I was washing up, the rest of the outfit had materialized: a beige woolen coat and matching rubber boots, banded at the top with the same flower pattern as the dress.

He held the coat for me. "That's all you'll need."

The snow had covered everything and muffled each sound, even the one from the engine as we drove through the deserted streets. When he pulled over, the trees by the road were barely visible.

"Come and close your eyes."

We walked through cold silence. Then a sudden warmth enveloped us—heavy, scented of honey like the warmth of summer. He slipped the coat off my shoulders. Lifted my feet out of the boots and placed them on something soft that bent its blades under my toes—

Grass?

"Now you can open them."

All around us—astonishing, bursting through one another up toward the sky, drunk on their own impetuous red—were poppies. Thousands of them. All the way to the trees in the distance where the snow still fell, undisturbed, encircling us in its ephemeral wall of whiteness.

"Do you recognize the place?"

I noticed it only now: the old willow, weeping its sleepy visions down into the ground.

"So it was you, back then? You made the poppies grow?"

"I couldn't resist. Wanted desperately to impress you."

Not that he had to try. The thought of dating an incarnation of Dionysus was mind-blowing enough. And a little bit terrifying.

We sat down among the flowers. I was still hypnotized by the distant line where the waves of red crashed into the snow.

"How is any of this even possible?"

He smiled. "Being a daemon comes with perks."

"Like what? Absolute control over nature?"

"I wish! No, certainly not over all of it."

"What are the exceptions?"

"Humans."

It was the one exception I found hard to believe, given his magnetic effect on everyone. "What else?"

"There are no other exceptions, Thea."

He explained something about alternate dimensions, and his ability to create parallel environments while leaving the rest of the world unchanged. The exact premise eluded me, but I knew what he meant. I had witnessed it, when Carnegie had morphed into a vision during the few minutes while I played. Lush geraniums had sprouted up over the balconies of a Manhattan concert hall, just as countless poppies were now blooming inside a snowy Princeton forest, oblivious to the surrounding winter.

I felt like a child who had found a trove of miracles. "Show me more!"

He put his hands together. Held them briefly. Parted them just a bit, letting a cloud of black butterflies flutter out—as if the wind had blown through a pile of minuscule velvet cutouts and scattered them over the field. When his hands opened all the way, I saw a thin golden necklace: a chain with a poppy bud bending its head over a tiny stem. He clasped it around my neck and kissed the spot where the flower fell, right between the collarbones.

"How come you love poppies so much?"

"The easy answer is that they symbolize resurrection after death."

"In Greek mythology?"

"In all sorts of cultures. Including our good old friends, the Greeks."

"And the noneasy answer?"

His fingers ran through the petals closest to him. "Poppies induce sleep. My mother died from lack of it."

"Rhys, I . . . I know about Isabel."

"You do? Who told you?"

"Carmela. But it wasn't her fault. I may have asked too many questions."

"It doesn't matter. My mother's death is not a secret."

"You think poppies could have saved her?"

He plucked a flower out of the many around us and studied it for a few seconds, then threw it away. "Poppies can't save anyone. They die so fast, how would they possibly undo death?"

"Can daemons undo death?"

"Only one thing can, and you already know what it is. All the rest, this"—his arm stretched out toward the field—"is up to me. Although I try not to mess with reality too much. Not unless I crave something and there's no other way to get it."

"Like the painting in your room?"

"I had to make my own; the one at the Tretyakov wasn't for sale. The two are virtually identical, except mine hasn't been damaged by time. Looks exactly as on the day he painted it."

Better than the original. I thought of that other "original," the one I would always compare myself to. "Rhys, do I resemble her?"

"Whom?"

"My sister."

His body stiffened up, just as it had done months ago when I first mentioned Bulgaria to him, in that same field. "You don't resemble her, no. And I wouldn't want you to."

"Why not?"

"Because you don't . . . claim people. You let them stay in your presence until they want to be claimed—badly. But you don't do it even then. That's why I fell for you."

"And Elza?"

"She had to have what she wanted. I can't tell you how maddening that is." His eyes roamed the field, past the invisible membrane of its warm bubble. "I met her the summer before freshman year, at a piano competition in Bulgaria. We both won and had a drunk night of celebration. When school started, she wouldn't stop writing to me. I think I answered only once—the whole thing was pointless anyway. But then she applied to Princeton and I just . . . I went along with it. She was the hottest girl on campus. And I was vain and stupid, so she decided to make it easy for me. She made it so damn easy, Thea! All I had to do was not say no. Hordes of guys were after her, whereas I didn't need to lift a finger. I had the girl everyone wanted. In my bed. Every night."

He leaned back. His elbows crushed a few poppies, but he didn't seem to care.

"Then her antics started to become annoying. She was constantly after me. I had warned her from the beginning that I didn't want a girlfriend. That it was just sex, nothing serious. But she acted as if I didn't mean it. When I tried to break things off, she went ballistic—cried, begged, threatened. Then suddenly her tune changed and she offered me something entirely different: a truce on my terms. No expectations. No strings attached. Did I want to go to a party with her that night? Sealing the pact, so to speak. And not just any party: 'a forest feast beyond our wildest instincts.' So of course I went. That's how the insanity started. Once I got dragged in, there was no going back."

"Dragged into what?"

"The rituals. You'd never imagine that some ancient pagan shit could survive for two thousand years, right? At first I thought it was a joke. Or some sorority rush—definitely not of American women, that much I could tell. Whatever it was, though, nothing I had ever done came even close. It made me feel invincible and free, and I was fascinated by it. Freaked out as hell. But totally hooked."

"Who were the other women?"

"There were men too, I wasn't the only one. And the men seemed to be normal guys. But the women, they . . ." He looked for the safest way to say it. "There was nothing they wouldn't do, Thea. We drank nonstop— all kinds of 'elixirs' with dubious contents. Plus drum music. Coming out of nowhere, right there, in the forest, while everyone was having sex with everyone else."

"Even my sister?"

"She was mostly with me—but yes. We started going every week. Once, there was even a mock wedding. White veils for the women, wreaths of ivy for the men . . . I was wasted and don't remember much. I think at some point one woman had a snake."

I knew about the snake's role in the rituals, but said nothing.

"After that night, Elza convinced herself that the whole thing had been real and we were in fact married. It was ludicrous. Still, I couldn't get it out of her head. Then she began writing to me again. And not just letters—all sorts of notes on random pieces of paper, creepy messages in books. Left them everywhere, even in my own house! You actually saw one, in that book on the Vineyard."

"Why did you save it?"

"I didn't. I threw everything out years ago, but Jake must have found the Rilke and kept it. My brother, he . . . he lives too much inside his own head. Sometimes I don't understand him at all."

There were things about Jake he would never understand, and this was exactly where the conversation wasn't supposed to go. "Do you remember the library book I showed you once, the *Gypsy Ballads*? Elza left a note in it too. I recognized the handwriting."

"Glad I never saw it. That would have ruined Lorca for me."

"Why do you hate her so much? She was crazy about you. This part, at least, I understand."

"You think you do. But you'd never get on a guy's case the way she did. Two days after my parents died, she came over to give me a book inscribed with more of that nonsense and signed '*E.E.*'—Elza Estlin. Told me she was now all the family I had. Can you fucking believe it? We had the usual fight: me trying to break up with her while she pretended not to hear it. When she finally left, I drank every drop of alcohol in the house. Passed out eventually, only to wake up and see her back in my living room, sliding a ring on my finger. I lost my mind, Thea. Just lost it. I yelled, she yelled back. Then I told her I was going to drive her to Forbes and never see her again. She said nothing—which was odd, but all I cared about was that I'd finally managed to shut her up. We took my motorcycle and I gave her my helmet. Those were my last moments of human life."

"But then your other life began. Which is lucky, because . . . otherwise how would I have met you?"

He managed a half-smile. "She did stop time for us; I guess that counts as a favor."

"How much older than me are you, anyway?"

"Technically, I'm still in my twenties."

"Technically?"

"Let's say I'm twenty-nine."

"This happened fifteen years ago. You can't be that young."

He kept smiling.

"And what do you mean by *let's say*?"

"I can be any age I want."

"You simply decide and your age changes?" This was just as surreal as everything else I had heard that weekend. "Then I'd like to see how you looked before the accident. Can you really do that?"

He stood up, walked behind me, and came around my other side.

The long hair was what I saw first. Falling in waves over the much more fragile shoulders, the much narrower chest. His face was the same: strikingly perfect. Only . . . its cheeks had now sunk in. Its lips were pale. And a sadness—the same sadness I had sensed in him so many times—had muddled up the blue of his eyes, stealing their luster. Below, under the open shirt, his ribs could be counted through the skin, reaching like a skeleton's fingers down toward his stomach.

I came up to him, to this troubled boy my age, and kissed his lifeless lips. When I opened my eyes again, he had gone back to looking older.

"I like you better this way, the way you are with me."

"Then let's forget the rest."

Forgetting Elza. The one thing I would never be able to do. "Rhys, is she good at . . ."

"At what?"

I couldn't say it, but he must have realized I meant sex.

"She isn't human, Thea."

"How about when she was human?"

"You don't want to go there. Trust me. You don't."

"I go there all the time—in my head. And I'd rather hear it from you."

"Then yes, she was good at it." He lay back on the grass, arms folded under his head.

"Just good or fantastic good?"

"Fantastic good."

"And now that she is no longer human?"

His eyelids closed, shutting the sky out of him. "It's like a drug forced into you that you crave while it drains and collapses you. Then you detest it."

"But it's still fantastic good?"

"Better."

Better. A word impossible to compete with, even in theory.

"So much for the proverbial one-to-ten scale, then." I tried to sound lighthearted, but he must have seen right through it.

"Your sister would be a ten for anybody else."

"And for you?"

"Scales are meaningless." He placed my hand on his stomach—below the belly button, where his pulse could be felt through the skin—then slowly pushed it lower. "In my entire existence, your touch has been the only thing to make me feel death would be worth it."

"Then . . . let's not talk about dying."

He smiled and pulled a small book out of his pocket. "We almost didn't get to the real reason I brought you here."

"Did you just make this too?"

"No, this I actually brought with me."

The cover was simple white, embossed in gold:

Arthur Rimbaud: Poèmes/Poems

"The wild child of French poetry. Came up with all this insanely original verse, then quit when he turned twenty and never wrote a line again." He found the page he needed. "This was a hundred and fifty years ago. He must have met you back then—except you were called Nina—and wrote his most beautiful poem about you: 'Nina's Replies.' The rhymes are lost in English, but the rest is all there."

"Read it to me in French first."

"You speak French?"

"Almost none. I just want to hear you read it."

The lines were short and crisp, weaving their rhyming echo through the air: one with three, two with four. He reached the end but wouldn't stop, and at first I didn't realize that the same poem was now in a language I understood. That he was speaking directly into my heart:

—Your breast on my breast,
   Yes? We'll walk
Through fresh sunbeams,
   Our lungs full

Of crisp blue morning, bathing us
   In the wine of day.
Mute and lovestruck,
   The forest bleeds

Green from every branch,
   Transparent buds,
They open and we feel
   Their shiver:

You bury your white dress
   Into alfalfa,
Blushing, blue rimming
   Your big black eyes,

In love with the field,
   Sowing it
With laughter, bubbling
   Like champagne:

Laughing at me, drunk and wild,
   I'd take you
Just like that—by your lush hair,
   How I'd drink

Your taste of berries,
   Your flowery flesh!

Laughing as the quick wind kisses you
   Briefly, like a thief,

Wild blooms tease you
   Laughing, mostly
At the madness of your lover—
   Me!

He whispered the last few words into my lips, having already closed the book. I couldn't have imagined it, the impact someone would have on my body from being the first man to have taken it. Each contact between us now made me want him, only him, and I was unaware of anything else while his hands undressed both of us.

"Rhys"—his naked body shivered at the touch of mine—"I love you."

I had never said it, to anyone.

He made love to me for hours. Whenever we stopped to rest, the silence of the field fell over us—an impenetrable, weightless quilt. But there was one thing neither of us dared to bring up:

The next full moon was only three weeks away.

CHAPTER 18

We Can Change It

"COME, I WANT to show you something." Rhys opened the door to his room but I didn't see anything that hadn't been there before. "It's in here."

"In here" turned out to be the bathroom. The decor was as usual: white marble bathtub, mahogany towel rack propped like a ladder against the wall, crisp towels cascading down its bars. But on the left, under the wall-to-wall mirror, two sinks were carved in the stone where earlier that day there had been one.

"When did you manage to do this?"

My perplexed face made him laugh. "The physical world isn't exactly a challenge for me, remember?"

I did, of course. Yet seeing the nonhuman side of him still startled me every time.

"Some of it was a guess, by the way." He ran his fingers over the empty pieces of a crystal bath set (toothbrush holder, soap dish, tissue box), next to an identical set that held his own things.

"Rhys, that's sweet of you. But I don't mind us sharing a sink when I sleep over."

"We're done with the sleepovers. I want you to live here from now on."

The effect was probably exactly what he expected: I stared at him in shock, couldn't react.

"Come on, say it! Say you'll move in with me."

"Move in . . . how? I have to stay in the dorm, like everybody else."

"Don't worry about the dorm." He took out his cell phone.

"Wait . . . What are you doing?"

"Calling housing before they close for winter break. Since you won't be needing a room next spring, they'll appreciate the heads-up."

"Keeping my room doesn't mean I won't live here."

The phone froze, halfway through the air. "You aren't sure about this?"

"That's not what I meant. The room can be a backup, in case you . . ." I didn't want to say the rest.

"In case I what?"

"Change your mind."

"I'll never change my mind."

He kept looking at me, until I said that I wasn't going to change my mind either. Then he dialed. Asked for a woman by name, thanked her for arranging a dorm room for Jake back in September, inquired about her holiday plans, made small talk about boutique hotels in Rio, before finally informing her that his girlfriend was now moving in with him, so the room in Forbes would no longer be needed. And, yes, Thea would be happy to sign the paperwork, but could they please mail it directly to his address?

"Done!" He hung up and kissed me. "Welcome to your new home, babe."

"That was . . . quick."

"Why waste time? We can also go get your things now, although it's probably better to deal with all of this tomorrow. Or any other day, really. We have the whole break to ourselves."

All we had was a week, but he didn't know it yet. My flight home was the following Thursday, and since he had never asked what I was doing for the holidays, I hadn't brought it up either.

"Rhys, there's something . . ."

"Yes?"

" . . . something I have to tell you."

"Sure, I just need to turn this darn thing off—" A text message distracted him. "Give me a minute. I'll be right back."

He rushed out as if the house was on fire. When I followed him downstairs, I saw immediately why.

Across the lawn, still visible despite the quickly falling darkness, walked six tall figures—lined up like a firing squad, almost identical in their jeans and black bomber jackets. He intercepted them before they could reach the house. The tallest one said something to him (I recognized the face only now: Evan), although Rhys didn't seem to care. The others started saying things too. Then Evan raised his voice. No one moved. Rhys took a step forward, but Evan pushed him back. Another step. Evan pushed him again. A second later, the guy was on the ground, Rhys on top of him, holding him by the collar and bending in for some kind of a warning that probably no one else could hear.

When he came back into the living room, his face was calm and he turned around only once, to make sure the unwanted visitors were leaving.

"Sorry you had to see this. It's not how I meant our evening to start."

"What did they want?"

"The others were brought in for dramatic effect. While Evan, apparently, wanted trouble." His eyes checked the empty lawn one last time. "He thinks the world should revolve around his party hormones. But I am not the world."

The thought of how that guy had looked at me and called me a "snack" gave me shivers. "What did he really want?"

"To convince me to go out with them tonight. And next weekend also."

"Isn't everyone gone by then?"

"Not the swimmers. They practice during winter break and stay at Princeton for most of it. To abandon the team for a woman is the ultimate betrayal."

"You aren't on the team, though."

"I used to be. For all practical purposes, I still am. But now I'm also with you and have a promise to keep."

"Rhys, this isn't about promises." Nor about reluctant sacrifices, which was how he made it sound. "If you want to go out with your friends, you should."

"I'm exactly where I want to be right now: at home with my girl. Unfortunately, Evan wouldn't take my word for it. So I had to give him a friendly reminder that the parties won't evaporate without me."

"Maybe not the parties at Ivy."

"What is that supposed to mean?"

"Ivy isn't the whole story, is it?"

A hint of alarm passed across his face. "Do we have to talk about this? I've put my party life behind. You just saw me do it."

"I want to put your party life behind too. But the secrecy doesn't make it easier."

"I see . . ." He remained quiet for a while, looking through the French doors, as if trying to make up his mind, then turned back to me: "Of course Ivy isn't the whole story. When men are growing up, especially certain men, they need more than just beer and college girls."

"Which is to say . . . ?"

"Which is to say that the team gets together in private, once a month, with real liquor and women who are paid a lot to provide elite services and to be absolutely discreet about it."

"Elite?"

"Top-notch, in every respect. Nothing is off-limits."

His callous tone made me wish I had never asked. "And you're the one who subsidizes all this?"

"You saw Evan's house; the kid has a trust fund. There are others like him. We split the expense." He laid out the rest for me as if it were college admissions: "Being on the swim team gets you in automatically; money is never even mentioned. Everyone else comes by invitation only. We screen them first, to make sure they can afford the tab and know how to keep their mouths shut. Which, by the way, is a rule that applies to everyone, including me. So not a word can leave this room. You know this, right?"

Of course I did. For a bunch of boys trying to grow up, secrecy had to be half of the appeal.

"Come on, Thea, don't give me that look. What I've done in the past shouldn't matter from now on."

"Except you talk about it as if it's the most natural thing."

"How else should I talk about it? This *is* my nature, I'm supposed to be a version of Dionysus. Didn't your art professor mention that about daemons?"

"Yes . . . sort of."

"Well, Dionysus had his retinue and so did I. Imagine me stuck on this campus for fifteen years: raising my brother, fucking your sister, you name it. Pissed off and bored out of my mind. So, because of me, fools like Evan got a taste of the Dionysian, thinking it was just frat parties."

"I understand. But that doesn't mean I'm ready to be part of this."

"Who says anything about being part?"

"If this is your true nature, then sooner or later it will become my life."

"My nature changes when I'm around you. I become human again, and that's who I want to be." He smiled, looking content. Almost at peace. "By the way, you wanted to tell me something when the guys showed up."

"Yes, about the holidays."

"Of course, I keep forgetting! Ivy's winter formal is tomorrow. And we also have a dinner here on Christmas Eve—a family staple that ought to take place, or else evil shall descend upon the house of Estlin."

"What are you talking about?"

"We Irishmen are superstitious folk. An ancestor had too much free time, apparently, and came up with a rule for his progeny: everyone must be present at home on Christmas Eve. It's literally written in stone."

He took me to the fireplace and pointed at a marble tablet inlaid high into the wall. An inscription bent its cursive around a coat of arms:

Tugann neamhláithreacht amháin solitude síoraí.

"What does it say?"

"*A single absence brings eternal solitude.* Dates back to 1649, when Oliver

Cromwell massacred Ireland. The Estlin estate happened to be in Waterford, the first town to withstand a Cromwell siege. Once the troops retreated, the ancestor in question, Thomas Estlin, rushed off to meet with other rebel leaders and didn't make it back home until Christmas Day—only to find that English soldiers had plundered his castle the night before and killed his entire family. So he commissioned this plaque, as a reminder that the death of everyone he loved was his own doing."

"Rhys . . ." I kept looking at the letters, whose crescent rested like a necklace inside the stone. "I don't think I can be at the dinner."

He had been standing behind me but now slowly turned me around. "What exactly are you telling me?"

"I'm going home for the holidays."

"When?"

"My flight is Thursday night."

"We can change it."

"It's too late. Everything to Sofia is probably sold out by now."

"We can change it." His eyes were glued to my face, trying to read it. "Unless that's not what you want."

"I want to stay here, with you. But my parents expect me home for Christmas."

"It's your life. Nobody should tell you how to live it."

"I know, except they—"

"They don't own you."

"They already had one Christmas when their girl didn't come home from school."

He sat down. Rubbed his face for a few seconds, then looked up at me. "Give me your dates. I'll book the same flights."

"Don't change your plans because of me."

"I refuse to be away from you. I'll stay at a hotel and you can see me whenever you want."

"What about the dinner? You said it's a bad omen to break the family rule."

"I don't care about rules or omens. And there's no family left anyway, only me and my brother. Plus Ferry. Christmas is the one time when we can convince him to stop being a butler and join us at the table. Luckily, Irish superstitions run in the old man's blood, so . . ." He took out his cell phone again. "Let's book those tickets. You said Thursday, right?"

"Yes. British Air, through Heathrow."

"Okay, it's the twentieth. Which reminds me . . . I have to check my damn schedule first."

His voice had turned sour at the last words, but it was nothing compared to the change in him only seconds later. His fingers froze. His face became unrecognizably white, as he stared at something on that screen.

"What's wrong?"

He handed me the phone.

A grid of squares, numbered all the way to 31. Inside, spilling from row to row—starting as a crescent, thinning out to nothing, then filling up again—was the moon. Only one full circle. And over it: the number 24.

LATER THAT NIGHT, WHILE RHYS slept, I made up my mind: I wasn't going to Bulgaria for Christmas. He and I would spend New Year's there with my parents. Until then, we were staying at Princeton. Come Christmas Eve, the creature on the hills could have him for a few hours—but that was it. He would meet her with my kiss still warm on his lips. And as soon as her time was up, he would be back. Home. With me.

THE WINTER FORMAL AT IVY became an ordeal while we were still getting ready. Rhys looked me up and down.

"Nice, but this won't do. Too prim for my taste. And too cliché for the occasion."

Earlier, when I had asked him what to wear, he answered vaguely: "Something long and elegant." This was the only long dress I owned—a black halter I wore onstage—and it clearly wasn't going to make the Ivy cut.

"Rhys, maybe inviting me wasn't such a good idea. I don't belong in that world."

"What world? The Ivy crowd? You just brought Carnegie to its knees and now you worry about a bunch of rich kids? They should be trying to fit in with you, not the other way around."

But Carnegie had nothing to do with it. I was never going to walk into a room the way Nora did, and own it.

"Okay, time to improvise a bit." He turned me around and when I looked in the mirror, my dress had changed completely. Peach, turquoise, fuchsia, and cream yellow spiraled in drips over a soft silk jersey, in abstract shapes that resembled orchids. "Do you like it? Women will be dying with envy tonight."

"I think the cause of death might be the man, not the dress. But yes, it's spectacular." While I was saying this, a live orchid on an elastic band slipped around my wrist. "That's the custom, isn't it?"

He nodded, smiling.

"Speaking of custom, how are you allowed at the Ivy formals?"

His eyes widened, genuinely puzzled. "Allowed?"

"The formals are members-only. And you can't be a member if you aren't even a student."

"Ah, that. It's a technicality." As most obstacles probably were, in the Estlin universe. "I'm on the alumni board. Most of the decisions are practically mine."

"No one notices that you stay the same age?"

"Not really, so far at least. All it takes is a little perception management. The members leave once they graduate. And the staff changes every few years. I make sure of it."

"With a generous severance package?"

"More than generous. Complaints aren't even a theoretical possibility."

The nonchalance with which he made such remarks bothered me. Always had. "Does everything really come down to money? One hears things about Ivy, but I thought you of all people would—"

"Some of what you hear is true and some isn't. Ivy gets bad-mouthed all the time, especially by those who bickered and didn't make it. But it's a private club, Thea. They are very good to their members. And if you happen to be from a solid line of Ivy stock, then they go out of their way to be good to you."

They were indeed very good to him. Welcoming him as soon as we arrived, rising from tables to shake his hand. I didn't want to say or do the wrong thing, so I simply followed him through a dining room of dark wood and candlelight, under a ceiling so low it felt as if we had walked into a deftly shaped, mythical cave. The moment we sat down, dishes were placed in front of us by white-gloved hands—perfectly timed, the food still warm and, of course, delicious. Rhys barely touched his, and didn't pay much attention to the others except to answer an occasional question.

Then the postdinner party began, cautiously at first, with two couples braving the dance floor; others gradually followed until the room became packed with people.

"Wasn't this the guy dating your friend Rita, the one who told me you were in Boston?"

I turned and saw Dev drinking by himself, with a melancholic look that didn't last long. A girl grabbed him by the arm and pulled him on the dance floor with overdone giggles.

Rhys shrugged. "Well, I guess that answers my question."

Even seeing Dev at Ivy had already answered it—he wouldn't be at the formal unless a member had brought him as a date. So, Rita had been right. He had replaced her just in time for the holidays.

I tried to forget the encounter, but as soon as Rhys went to refill our drinks, Dev came over and asked if he could talk to me.

"Sure. What's up?"

"It's good to see you here. How are things?"

I wasn't going to make small talk, least of all with him. "What's up, Dev?"

"How . . . how is she?"

"She's fine. Leaving for Budapest, to spend New Year's with her grand-parents." A few seconds of awkward silence. "Honestly, I don't understand why you're doing this."

"Doing what?"

"Giving up on the girl you love, so that some Barbie doll can chase you around Ivy."

"I guess the girl I love forgot to mention that she was the one who broke up with me?"

"Depends on how you look at it, though, right? I'd break up with a guy too, if he didn't stand up for me."

A string of sweat began to gather on his forehead, as I told him how upset I had found Rita that night in Forbes.

"You don't understand, Thea. My family is a nightmare, especially if one isn't Hindu. They would have never let me bring her home."

"Did you at least try? I mean, it's your girlfriend we are talking about, not some random crush. You could have told them that if they shut her out, you might not be going home either."

He stared at the floor, then said, quietly: "When is she leaving?"

"Next week. You still have time. And not to give you any ideas, but I hear New Year's on the Danube is amazing."

He thanked me— twice—and went back to his date, who had been sulking at the bar. Rhys returned with our drinks.

"Ready to dance or shall I give you a tour? Second floor and all that."

"A tour sounds nice."

"Honestly? I keep getting a sense that you don't like the place."

"It's just a bit . . ."

"*Detached and breathlessly aristocratic?*" He pointed to a large portrait at the base of the main staircase. "F. Scott Fitzgerald, Ivy's literary claim to fame. That's how he described the club in *This Side of Paradise*. I don't think there's much aristocratic left in it, though. And certainly nothing breathless."

"Then why do you come here so much?"

"Habit. It's easy to keep doing what you've always done."

We went upstairs and sat by a fireplace in one of the rooms. The walls were covered with photographs, mostly outdated group shots of young men in retro jackets and ties.

"How come there are no women?"

"Because Ivy didn't admit women until 1991."

"That late?"

"You know how it is. People fight for tradition."

"I don't know how it is, no. The traditions I grew up with were somewhat less . . . male centered. And either way, shutting others out of your bastion doesn't seem to require much fighting."

"Except in this case the fight was real. A student sued the club and won, after an eleven-year trial."

I didn't want to argue with him. But what exactly had she won? The right to be at a club that would go to court just to keep her out? There were stories about what girls had to endure during Ivy bicker, culminating in the practice of passing them naked down the same staircase Rhys and I had just climbed so peacefully. *It's a private club, Thea.* And although a judge might have forced its doors open, he had no control over what happened once you walked through those doors. It was all . . . Princeton tradition. A sacrosanct status quo in which the good and the bad coexisted in precarious harmony, often known only to people like Rhys whose families had been on the inside of the fence for decades.

"Is Jake a member of Ivy too?" Somehow, I couldn't picture him enjoying white-gloved service.

"No. Jake had only one parent—me. Which meant he could do whatever he wanted."

"And you couldn't?"

"My father would have expelled me from home if I'd even considered another club."

"Rhys, living in a dorm is not the end of the world. Your own brother is doing it, and he seems to be just fine."

"I meant really *expelled*. Thrown out, with no money. Archer's typical lesson: it was either his way or you could go fuck yourself."

"You don't seem to have liked your dad very much."

"I used to be in awe of him. Everyone was. Until he killed my mother."

"He . . . what?" I knew that Rhys liked to be dramatic, but this was a bit much. "Wasn't your mother very ill, beyond anything doctors could do?"

"She didn't need doctors. I could have saved her myself. For that, she didn't even need to be alive."

Finally I realized what he was talking about. "*Save her* . . . the way my sister saved you?"

"It would have been a different ritual—but yes. My mother was so far gone that we were praying for a miracle. And it happened. Elza with her mumbo-jumbo about eternal love and life beyond death. I thought she was making it all up. But what did I have to lose?"

"Is this why you became involved in the rituals?"

"Actually, what got me involved was sex. But then what hooked me was the promise of godlike power. Of winning over death. First you had to be 'initiated into the mysteries'—which is what the Greeks used to call it, but is just a fancy name for learning how to invoke any ritual you want. For that, I would have done anything. Even married a woman I didn't love."

"But you didn't marry her. Or did you?"

"I almost did. It was planned for the full moon in December, but earlier that week I received a call from a police detective upstate. A sports car had driven off a cliff on the Pacific Coast Highway. Fell over the rocks. Exploded. By the time anyone got to it, there wasn't much left, only enough to track the license number back to a rental agency with my father's name on file."

"That doesn't mean he killed her. It could have been an accident."

"There were no accidents in that man's universe, Thea. You know the last thing he said to me? We were on the phone, they were just heading out of San Francisco, and he said: *I'll be seeing you, son.* My entire life, he had never called me 'son.' Not once."

A piece of wood crackled in the fire. Downstairs, people danced to loud music in a world where accidents did happen, and love was not eternal, and death was invincible. I took him in my arms, but he seemed restless. His lips reached my ear before I could figure out if he was trying to say something to me or kiss me:

"I want to take you home and be naked with you again. Actually, home's too far."

We ran out without saying good-bye to anyone. He parked the car in the thick darkness of a nearby street, pulled me on top of him, and made love to me right there, refusing to stop, whispering into my skin things I wanted to believe, whispering them endlessly. Then he drove without letting me out of his arms, not even when we reached his house and the key came out of the ignition. They held me with the beautiful, strange insistence I had always loved about him, keeping me within him until the last possible moment, and then finally opening to let me out, but not until he had asked me to promise— and I had promised—never to leave him.

CHAPTER 19

A Single Absence

MISS THEA—"

I opened my eyes and saw the butler next to me. An oddly thin figure. Standing still, against the dark frame of the French doors.

"I believe Master Rhys is ready."

Ready. Of course he was. I remembered the rules he had once explained to me: *I don't object. I don't make her wait. I don't refuse anything.*

"Sorry, I must have dozed off. What time is it?"

"Close to nine."

We were alone in the living room. The rest of the house was dark and quiet. "Where is he, Ferry?"

"Upstairs. And Master Jake is on his way. Ten more minutes, perhaps."

His voice was buttery soft. The usually detached face—transformed. Animated by a cautious, almost fatherly warmth.

A knot in my stomach tightened. *Just go upstairs. Smile. Kiss Rhys and let him leave.*

I could barely hear my own knock but he was already at the door when I opened it. Black jeans. A lapis-blue track jacket. Looking incredibly sexy, no matter how much he had tried to downplay the outfit.

"Don't be upset." He pulled me into his arms. "I'll be back before you know it."

"When do you have to leave?"

"I should have left by now."

My eyes were tearing up and I looked down, so he wouldn't see it. His jacket was zipped, but not enough to hide the bare skin underneath. No shirt. And not even buttons. A zipper—the easiest thing to rip open with a single gesture.

She can do anything to my body. That's the deal.

"Thea, I can't leave like this. Talk to me."

Talk? About what? About how I spent countless hours trying to guess the things she would be doing to him, and everything she had done already? Twelve months a year, for fifteen years. It meant 180 full moons, so the scenarios were endless. My obstinate mind started with what I had seen under that tree, then gradually increased the dosage—until there wasn't a spot on him that she hadn't touched, kissed, claimed, fucked.

"Talk to me. Please."

"Just go."

"Maybe I shouldn't, if that's what it will do to you."

At first, the full meaning of his words didn't reach me. "What are you talking about?"

"About taking my chances. I am told she'd come after me and kill me. But there's only one way to find out."

"Don't even think about this. Ever."

I couldn't imagine the world without him. And if his existence depended on it, I would have given him up to Elza—every night, for the rest of my life.

"Rhys, ignore my moods. Just go and come back to me when it's over."

"I won't be long, you'll see. Ivy has a party later. I told Jake to take you there."

"Not tonight."

"Yes, tonight. It's Christmas Eve and you're not staying in."

"I'm fine, don't worry."

"I do worry. And I won't leave unless you promise to go out and have a good time."

I promised. But a party would make no difference. The thought of him with her—holding her, kissing her, practically being her slave the entire night—cut through me as if someone was twisting a knife in my chest.

"Look at me. Thea—" He pushed my chin up. "There is nothing for me outside of you. Nothing. I go to her only because I want another month with you."

Then he kissed me. And in that brief moment, the world was just as we wanted it—with no one else in it.

CHAPTER 20

The Atrium of Pianos

NOLLAIG SHONA DUIT—"

The voice made me turn away from the window: Jake had just walked in.

"—it means Happy Christmas in Irish."

"Hi, Jake."

What else could I say? *Happy* was the one thing this Christmas wasn't going to be, for any of us.

"I know it's hard." His hand pressed on my shoulder. "But Rhys never stays with her long. He'll be back soon, you'll see."

Soon? Only minutes had passed since the dark figure had crossed the lawn and disappeared through the trees. Now the only thing I could detect out there was an ominous silver disk, beaming its stare down from the night sky.

"Thea, come. Let's have dinner."

It was the same table at which I had eaten my first meal at Pebbles. Once again, candles quivered all over it, filling the empty crystal glasses with the illusion of water stirred up by reflected light.

Ferry pulled my chair out. "Merry Christmas, Miss Thea."

"Merry Christmas, Ferry. I'd try to say it in Irish, but that would only butcher it."

"How does it sound in Bulgarian?"

"Vesela Koleda."

"Ah, yes, there is a certain music to it." He lifted the table's centerpiece (a white candle surrounded by holly leaves), and placed it in front of me, together with a box of matches. "In Ireland, we consider this to be the Christmas light. It must be lit by the youngest member of the family."

I looked at him and Jake—the human half of my new family. It was with the other half, Rhys and Elza, that my life had taken a crazy turn.

I lit the candle. Ferry observed, with a ceremonious smile.

"After dinner, we shall leave the light by the window, to guide the lost souls on their path home. But until then, it will bless our Christmas meal."

The meal itself was understated: fish, plum sauce, cream potatoes, and all sorts of salads. After the cutting of the Christmas cake, Jake pulled an envelope out of his jacket and handed it to Ferry.

"Merry Christmas. From all of us."

The old man opened it, glanced through the contents, then slowly folded everything back in. "With all due gratitude, I'm afraid I cannot accept this."

"The gift is more than well deserved, Ferry. And way overdue. You've been running this household for decades; now it's time to have a home of your own."

"My home is with you and Master Rhys. Always has been."

Jake smiled. Took the envelope back and slipped it into his pocket, producing another one in its place, still sealed.

"Plan B, in case you decided that Ireland would be too far. Which, frankly, was what Rhys and I were hoping." Then he clarified for my benefit: "That's the deed to the house next door. Starting tonight, Ferry is no longer in service with us. He'll be our new neighbor."

The piece of paper fluttered as Ferry's hand began to shake. He thanked Jake, excused himself, and came back a few moments later with a gift-wrapped box (for me) and a larger flat package (for Jake).

"These are from Master Rhys. He wanted to surprise you in person, but when he found out that he had to . . . that he wouldn't be present, he asked me to deliver them for him."

"You go first." Jake's eyes flashed in my direction, somehow managing to avoid both my face and Rhys's gift.

I opened the box. Inside was a smaller lacquer box, lined in black velvet, holding a bracelet of golden poppies matching the necklace I had on, and the volume of Rimbaud's poems, this time inscribed:

To my windkissed girl,
Rhys

Jake flipped his own present over. On the other side of the thick brown paper was an address label but no postage stamps—the package must have been delivered by courier.

"That's odd. My brother didn't bother to open it?"

"I believe Master Rhys made a point of not seeing what was inside."

"You mean Rhys bought me a gift without knowing what it is?"

"He considered it a coincidence. 'Lucky aberration' were his exact words. About two months ago, he happened to be home when a phone call was received for Mr. Estlin, extending a second-chance offer to one of Christie's most valued customers."

Jake froze, but his fingers had already ripped the paper. From across the table, I could see a dark wooden frame—probably an artwork.

"They told Master Rhys that the order had been placed in mid-September and then canceled within days. The item in question was among the priciest acquired by Christie's all year—and among the rarest in the market to begin with—so they wanted to confirm the cancellation before putting the lot up for auction. Since Master Rhys had never placed such an order, he figured the only other Mr. Estlin must have really wanted the piece, having been ready to pay a fortune for it. Naturally, he acquired the mystery object on the spot, but requested to not be given any details so that the gift would be a surprise for both of you on Christmas Eve."

"Except the gift wasn't for me. It was for Thea." Jake said it with the even voice of a man resigned to anything, dropped the frame in my lap, and left the room.

Under the glass I saw two pieces, not one. But neither was an artwork. On the left, faded and creased with time, lay a sheet of music. Music written by hand, in clusters of meticulous, tiny notes: the Nouvelle Étude in F minor. At the top was a signature. An *F* directly over the *C*, its vertical line unfolding in ripples below the entire name like the curved trajectory of a whip—

The signature of Frédéric Chopin.

Next to it on the right, completing the symmetry, was a second piece of paper—this one unblemished and white—that Jake must have sent to Christie's, to be framed with the étude. Its thin border in orange and black framed Chopin's name, and my own. Under them was the date: September 14, 2007.

While I sat there in shock, I heard a gasp. Ferry had come behind me and was now looking over my shoulder, lower lip twitching—with anger, or horror, or whatever else hadn't found outlet in his wide open eyes. Then he walked away. Carried the Christmas candle to one of the French doors and placed it on the floor.

"We should go." Jake was standing in the hallway, holding my coat. "I promised my brother to take you to Ivy tonight."

I waited for Ferry to say something. Anything, at least a curt good-bye. But his eyes continued to penetrate the darkness outside, searching it for lost souls who might detect the flicker through the night.

IVY WAS LOUD AND UPBEAT, but it must have been just the swimmers and their friends—everyone else had left for the holidays. People came and talked to us (Jake spoke, I pretended to listen), while the minutes slipped through my mind like mute waves, indifferent, having touched nothing.

"What are we going to do when Rhys comes home?" I asked, once we finally had a moment to ourselves. He didn't answer. "Jake, what are we going to tell him?"

"The truth, what else?"

"But I don't think he'd understand. He'll think we betrayed him."

"Of course he will; that's exactly what we did. I was determined not to let it happen. And I screwed up."

"If anyone screwed up, it's me."

"We all did, including Rhys. He should have come clean with you from the start."

That didn't make me feel any better—Rhys's mistakes were no excuse for my own. Besides, there was something else. Something I couldn't say out loud: that I was blown away by Jake's gift. Not because it was the priciest item acquired by Christie's all year, but because, once again, he had found his way into my heart and Rhys hadn't. Jake was the one who had figured out what I loved and tracked it down. Whereas Rhys, after nearly four months with me, was still giving me what *he* loved. His poppies. His poetry book. An attempt to fix my literary tastes, maybe?

It was past midnight when a large group stormed in and the cacophony became unbearable. I locked myself in the bathroom, staring at the mirror under the fluorescent lights, letting time pass. When I came out, a tall shadow blocked my way and cornered me in the empty hallway.

"Look—at—*that!*" The voice dragged each word through a grin that made me shiver. "The girl who thinks she's too good, just because she managed to spin the head of Rhys Estlin."

"Leave me alone, Evan."

"We've all been wondering about you. Getting Rhys to swear off women? You must be very impressive in the sack."

He waited until I struggled to move past him, then trapped me against the wall.

"Don't play hard to get with me. I see what's going on—he did grow tired of you, after all, and now he's recycled you to his brother. I might as well be next, don't you think?"

His beer-soaked breath was all over my face. I tried to push him away but his body was crushing me.

"Get off me, Evan, or I'll scream for help."

"Scream for help? Girls like you don't do that."

I should have done exactly that, but I still hoped he would let go without humiliating me in front of everyone. Suddenly his teeth sank into my ear, shooting a sharp pain through it.

"I can make you scream in private, if you let me. I've been dying to try you out. Look how hard you've made me already—" He forced my hand down and rubbed it over his zipper, through the jeans. "Come on, promise me that I can try you out once the other Estlin gets tired of you too. I'll be so good to you. You have no idea how good to you I can be, if you keep making me hard like this—"

The rest happened in a flash. He was hurled away from me, a fist smashed into his face and people rushed from all sides, pulling Jake back while a security guard lifted Evan from the floor and escorted him out.

"What did he do to you? Did he hurt you? I hope for his sake that he didn't!" Jake was holding my face and looking into my eyes frantically, as if afraid I might lie to him. "I'm such an idiot, I should have never let you out of my sight! Tell me he didn't hurt you, because otherwise—"

"He didn't, I'm fine."

The crowd had multiplied. Everyone stood and stared.

"Come, I'll get you a drink. Or would you rather lie down?"

"I'm fine, Jake, really. Let's not make a big deal out of it."

He took me to an adjacent room where we could be alone. "You won't have to worry about Evan again."

Something about his tone made me nervous. "What do you mean?"

"He'll be gone from Princeton before school reopens."

"You're joking, right?"

"Far from it. Evan has pulled this shit before; there are files and he knows it. So he'll probably leave on his own, before it goes to disciplinary committee. Otherwise he'll get expelled. Rhys and I will make sure he does."

"Expelled for what? For daring to come near the Estlin trophy girl?"

"He would have done things to you that you can't even imagine."

"Things to me? Just listen to yourself! He's a kid who crossed the line because he drank too much. And you are ready to ruin his entire future over it?"

"I don't care about his future."

"Jake, what's wrong with you? You sound exactly like your brother!"

"I sound nothing like him. If Rhys had seen what I saw, Evan would be smashed to pieces by now. Getting expelled is a treat in comparison, trust me."

"But you realize it's as much Rhys's fault as it was Evan's, right?"

His voice turned steel-cold. "My brother has nothing to do with it."

"Of course he does. Evan considers Rhys a role model, so tonight he tried to do to me only what he's seen your brother do to other girls, even during the so-called Thea phase. And why wouldn't he? I've been with Rhys for months; clearly I must enjoy this kind of thing."

The response took a few seconds. "None of this is up for discussion, Thea. Evan will have to find another campus for his moronic fits."

"And if he refuses?"

"It's not a take-it-or-leave-it deal."

"No, it's the usual Estlin deal. You'll make him name his own price."

"I will . . . what?!" The anger exploded—in his face, his voice, his hands that tightened into fists instantly. "Rhys told you?"

I avoided his eyes, the madness in them.

"What exactly did he say?"

"Jake, I don't think we should—"

"Oh yes, we should. How much did my dear brother dish out?" My silence only fueled his rage, confirming what he had already guessed. "Rhys can be quite the storyteller. Did he give you all the details? How she went after him, and begged him in the car, and told him she had wanted only him from the beginning?"

"Please don't."

"Why not? It's a sexy story. Exactly the kind of story Rhys needs before he sweeps a girl off her feet and onto the piano. Was that when he told you? Or earlier, when the two of you were choosing Nora for me?"

Everything in him was bursting—with fury, with pain, the long accumulated pain of having to step aside. To disappear. To erase himself from everyone's life, including his own.

"Is this how he won you from me, Thea? By telling you that I was once a fool because I let a woman walk all over me?"

"He never tried to win me from you."

"No. He just took you, as soon as he decided he wanted you. Didn't even let you make up your own mind."

"My mind was made up already."

"I don't think so. That night in your room, when we stopped . . . it would have been your first time, wouldn't it?"

I couldn't hear my own "yes." But he did.

"And when I saw you pushing him away on the piano, was it because of me?"

Another "yes," fainter than the first one.

It was all he needed. His arms closed around me, for the first time without guilt, and he breathed me in—deep, as if until now his lungs had been robbed of air.

"Jake, it's too late . . ."

"I don't care."

"But I do. I am with Rhys and we can't—"

"None of this matters now." He took my hand. "I can't believe I waited this long. Come with me."

Come . . . where?

As he led me out of Ivy, I tried to decide what to tell him in the car. That it was too late for the two of us. And that I really meant it. That the only place I needed to go was back to the house. Fast. Because his gift had to be put away until I could figure out how to explain to Rhys why his brother had been trying to buy a Chopin original for me back in September, long before he was supposed to know me. Before Rhys and I had even met.

We passed by the car. He kept walking.

"Where are you taking me? We should go back before Rhys comes home."

"We will, don't worry."

Down another block, just around the corner, was a building whose deserted lobby had a billboard of photos: WELCOME TO PRINCETON'S DEPARTMENT OF ENGINEERING.

"Jake, what are we doing here?"

Without a word, he headed down corridors where ceiling lamps emitted their intense, harrowing light along linoleum floors, as if marking the way to a hospital bed.

Then I saw them. Pianos. Dozens of them, in all shades of black and brown, clustered under the endless brick walls of an atrium whose glass roof must have let the sky in during the day but now closed over us, sealed with night.

"What is all this?"

He smiled, without letting go of my hand. "A temporary rest stop. We're donating these to high schools and small concert halls. They'll get routed from here."

The simple words, the casual tone as always—as if he had shown me the most ordinary thing.

"So this is just storage space?"

"For a week. We asked and the school said yes."

"Who is 'we'?"

"Rhys and I."

He took me past the nearest uprights. A black Yamaha. A mahogany Steinway. A Knabe in rich soft cherry. Then suddenly in the middle, set apart from the others—a white grand piano. Cream white that made you wish for doors wide open out onto a summer field, for insistent sunbeams, for the opium of tiny flowers, and for the touch of lips—unpredictable, like the first notes of music chosen for you by someone else.

He sat down and began playing: softly, as if it was nothing, and without taking his eyes off me, having gone over the étude probably hundreds of times. I had heard so much about his talent, about his magic over the piano—but none of it had done him justice. He owned the keys completely. Every nuance. Every shade of sound that could possibly be drawn from them. The unforgiving fragility of his touch made the music ache for his fingers, seduced into rhythms that were never intended for it, shattered by him ruthlessly then healed back into phrases of absolute beauty. The étude itself was unrecognizable. It poured out of him with the violent sweep of an ocean afflicted by storm—raging, hurling its furious waves of sound—until he decided to hush it back in, console it, lull it with the peace of a few final notes and then end it quietly, distilling into a single last chord the vast darkness of its despair.

When he rose from the bench, I knew what was going to happen and that I couldn't stop him, or myself, even if I tried. In some distant corner of my mind, it felt wrong. But I was hypnotized by his music, by the sadness in his eyes while he played, by his lips that had taken mine once and were now finding them again, erasing everything else, absolutely everything—

"Is this how you take care of my girl?!"

The enraged voice shot its thunder through the building and something hit the piano, smashing it to pieces. The entire atrium shuddered.

"How long have you been after her? Since you ordered your little gift?"

I watched in horror as Rhys grabbed Jake by the shoulders and hurled him against one of the pianos. Jake's body hit the wood and the impact left him bent over, before Rhys grabbed him again.

"Answer me! How long? And did you think I wouldn't figure out where you'd take her? Rushing to get these fucking pianos in here, so you can screw around with her behind my back?"

He hurled Jake once more, against a different piano. I screamed and tried to get to them, but he shouted at me to stay away.

"Why the hell did you do this, Jake? I trusted you with my life!" He snatched Jake one last time and pulled him up, yelling in his face with deafening fury: "You're my brother! Why?!"

Jake didn't fight, knowing he had no chance against a rage that wasn't human. Only his quiet voice made it through: "She was mine before you even met her. I gave her up for you."

Rhys turned around, finding me instantly with terrified eyes whose disbelief demanded an answer but gave me only a second for it. Then they looked past me, and before I could say anything, he was gone.

CHAPTER 21

Underworlds

I N THE HOURS that followed, Jake and I didn't speak. He shut the door to his room while I went into the one across from it—the room that had come so close to becoming my own. Then everything sank in silence, a silence deeper than any I had ever known. And in that silence, each of us began to wait for Rhys.

He didn't come home—not the rest of the night, not the next day. Jake never emerged either, and when the starkly red Christmas sun bled its apathy and vanished through the lifeless trees outside, I threw on my coat and went for a walk.

He was going to show up, eventually. He had to. "Funny how Princeton always keeps me on a tight leash: first my brother, now you," he had said as a joke, once. But it was neither his brother's hand nor mine that held the end of that leash. Something fated and undefeatable had imprisoned him on this campus, so even if he chose never to return to his house, I knew where to find him. Promptly on the next full moon, in one month minus a day.

The rest was less clear in my mind. What should I say to him? Would he even listen? I was ready to explain, apologize, convince, beg, grovel. Yet sometimes in life, if you weren't careful, things could become irreparably broken. Like those Andalucían gypsies—whose blood, I was starting to suspect, filled his own veins with talent and madness and everything else that had doomed Isabel—he probably found it hard to forgive.

A man like that might fall for you, worship you, lay his life and his future at your feet. But once you trigger his jealousy, all bets are off . . .

I shivered. With the sun gone, the temperature was dropping fast. And now there was also wind: the houses on both sides of the road had ended. This far down Mercer, away from the cozy glow of Christmas lights, a vast open land known as the Princeton Battlefield stretched under scattered pines and hueless sky.

A good moment to turn around and go back, it occurred to me. But across the field I noticed the detached façade of a Greek temple. Or what was supposed to look like one: four Ionic columns, shooting their elegant verticals up, each topped with a volute as if a ram had been sacrificed at the base and the horns placed high onto the shaft, in praise of the gods.

It turned out to be a monument. *This is hallowed ground,* a plaque read. *Across these fields in the early light of the third of January 1777, Washington's Continentals defeated British Regulars for the first time in the long struggle for American independence.* And then, farther down: *In the memorial grove beyond you, those who fell in the battle of Princeton, both American and British, lie buried. The historic portico in which you stand was re-erected here to mark the entrance to the tomb of these unknown soldiers of the Revolution.*

Hallowed ground. I liked the sound of it. I also liked the idea of a tomb where enemies were buried together, having finally won peace. In death, all were equal. Feuds no longer mattered. Nor did time. Under that colonnade, antiquity seemed just around the corner. The War of Independence—a blink away. And, somehow, it became plausible that a daemon from the ancient Greek legends could love a girl who was (or, more likely, wasn't) a witch from the Bulgarian ones.

Except Bulgarian legends didn't have happy endings. Certainly not ours, the one about the *samodivi,* in which Vylla marries her shepherd, then falls deadly ill. Homesick for her forest. For her freedom. For moonsoaked nights on the meadow, away from human eyes. Only one thing can save her: to be released as a wild creature back into the night. But it means that the shepherd would never see her again. That he must shut his heart to the world for good.

One quiet evening, when the stars spilled across the blinded sky, he took her hand as if to tell her: "It is time, my love." And back he led her—across ravines and deaf hills and secret mountain paths—up to the lake whose waters had first revealed her to him. There, safely folded, hidden beneath the oak tree's roots, lay a dress of woven moonlight . . .

I ran the entire way back—frantic, out of breath, thinking perhaps that I could outrun fate. Jake was in the living room, sunk in one of the armchairs, staring at the floor.

I stopped a few feet from him. "Any news?"

Instead of a response, I heard the front door open and close. Not a slam. A normal click, of someone coming home on a night like any other.

I rushed into the hallway—telling Rhys that I loved him, that we could fix things, mistakes and siblings notwithstanding—but he wouldn't look at me. Passed at a safe distance and walked into the living room, heading straight over to his brother.

"The two of you are going to Bulgaria. I changed my name on the ticket to yours." A heavy envelope landed on the table. "The flight leaves in the morning."

"Rhys, she loves *you*, not me."

"I'll see if a transfer to Harvard is possible, for both of you. The winter classes start in four weeks. By then, Ferry will take care of the move. All of her things. And yours."

"What are you talking about?"

"Princeton can take papers instead of final exams. So just e-mail them in, no need to come back."

"You know I'd do anything for you, but not this way—" Jake's voice fractured.

"You aren't doing it for me. You're doing it for Thea. And if you break her heart, you will no longer be a brother to me. I'll kill you with my own hands."

He went to one of the pianos, sat down, and smiled at Jake.

"Last playoff?" A brief variation on a Liszt theme, then he tapped on the wood. "Your turn."

No response.

"Jake, come on, don't get all soft on me. It's just a few notes."

Jake slid on the other bench, forcing his fingers to repeat the same tune—mechanically, as if playing in his sleep.

"That's shameful. Try again." Another Liszt, slightly faster.

Jake followed, and the first signs of energy trickled out as he played.

"Much better! How about this—"

The two of them kept playing, racing each other over the keys as they had to have done countless times before I came into their life. With each turn, the strength was slowly returning to Jake. It was probably what Rhys intended, the music being just a pretext, a way of forcing his brother to own up, to shake off the guilt and start a future with me—the same future that Rhys had wanted for himself.

Then he looked at his watch. His hands clutched his knees so hard the skin around the knuckles turned white, and his eyes lifted into mine, letting me know that he wasn't done playing. That the last sounds from his fingers that night would be for me.

A chord slipped out. Cautious, followed by two more, closer together and lower on the keys. Then two more, even lower. And then one final chord—quicker than the others, a hurried question mark. My heart sank as I recognized the piece: the fiercely private Nocturne in C-sharp Minor that Chopin refused to publish during his life. The six chords again, this time charged with force, insistent—not a question but a threat.

Followed by silence. The same silence that the written score had intended to last a mere second had now become merciless in his hands—agonizing, unending, silence in whose grip it was impossible to breathe, in which time itself had vanished until the only thing left was the terrified anticipation of the music that was about to follow. And it did; it finally came. Music as unforgiving as I never knew music could be. Music of absolute, desperate aching.

It began with a single note: high, disarmingly fragile. The right hand took it and curled it into a phrase of crystal beauty, lifting it, letting it drop deep, then repeating the entire move only to reach impossibly high, even higher than before, and roll down a cascade of keys as if a quick venom had drained it of its strength.

Only his hands and arms moved while he played. Yet I could sense the tension in him, in the rest of his body, its hundreds of muscles willing his fingers to deliver this incredible music with a precision I had never thought possible. I wished he would stop halfway through, before the softer middle part—softness I knew he couldn't stand—but he played on, and the harmonies he would have called "saccharine" once were now unfolding into one another with stunning simplicity, until the rhythm broke into syncopated strokes and shattered over the keys, hushing up the higher octaves to a delicate final note—warm and brief, like the touch of a blessing.

Then his silence again. The impossibility of breathing. I imagined him turning around and smiling, letting me go to him. But he sat there without a trace of movement, eyes closed, the eyelids bulging almost imperceptibly until the first tears I had ever seen on him came quietly down his cheeks. Jake sat across from him, bent over in a collapsed heap.

The music resumed—lavishly simple, complete as no music is ever complete. And inconsolable. Hopeless.

I had wondered many times whether Rhys would leave me one day. Now I knew: *this* was his good-bye. This music, which left no doubt of his intent yet made the thought of living without him feel like death. Music with which he was breaking his own heart, giving his brother a chance to mend mine.

I wanted the nocturne to end, so I could tell him that life didn't have to imitate the legends this time. That, for once, we needed to decide our future instead of leaving it up to others or to chance or, worst of all, to fate. But he stopped playing way before the final notes. His shaking hands lingered on the wood for one last second, then he jumped from the piano like a chased animal and ran out of the room—

As if running away could solve anything. I loved him. More than life. More than I feared dying. Which meant that nothing was irreversible, and one day I would get him back—I just had to figure out how.

YOU SHOULD NEVER OPEN A door through which you might not wish to enter.

Yet Silen hadn't predicted that soon, when all other doors of the world would slam shut, this same warning would bring me back to the Graduate College, looking for him.

Or had he?

The vine-leaf door was locked, and I waited—for the familiar voice, for its oddly wise words whose advice I needed now more than ever. But the corridor remained quiet, as I headed back past restroom signs and rows of light switches.

Darkness doesn't find us on its own, Theia. It wants to be invited.

I pushed the switches down, every last one of them. And, finally invited, the darkness became complete.

A STEP DOWN THE PITCH-BLACK corridor.

Then another.

I had walked into the abyss of night so many times, but never like this. Groping for walls. In a basement. Alone. Terrified.

Suddenly a light began to take shape. A faint silver glow, intensifying as I walked, until I recognized what my fingers had felt only moments earlier: the door's handle, shaped like a crescent moon.

This time it opened, and I found myself in a tunnel dug straight into the earth, lit up by dozens of candles hidden inside the wall's crevices. At the other end was a cave unlike any I had ever seen. Whimsical carvings spiraled up in erratic reds and browns, carrying their luminance through the air, all the way to a ceiling whose shoulders bent from the weight of world above. Far ahead, caught in a surreal play of symmetry, a lake doubled everything up. And in the middle, indulged in its own frightening beauty, the strangest of trees cast its reflection—green foliage on the right; bare branches on the left—over a satyr who sat in his usual solitude, waiting.

I followed a stone path across the water, over to him. "What is all this, Silen?"

"The beginning of the Underworld."

"But the Underworld doesn't exist. It's just legend."

"Humans call 'legend' whatever frightens them most. Still, it doesn't cease to exist."

"So you're telling me that this is where the dead . . . that the entrance to the Underworld lies in a Princeton basement?"

"For every world, there is an underworld." His hand swept the air, up toward what lay above us. "These buildings, they all have basements extending far, far deeper than you think. Even your mind"—his index finger touched my temple—"has its catacombs, secret passageways that you can only glimpse, in a single lifetime. And your heart, too; it has the most beautiful of underworlds. Have you noticed that for everything you want or love, something in you always begins to want or love the exact opposite?"

"Yes. That's how I lost them both."

"Lost?" He gave me one of his esoteric winks. "Tonight the fates have cast a choice for you."

"Between a man and a phantom?"

"No, between memory and oblivion. A sip is all it takes."

"Sip from what?"

"These—" He pointed at the water. The stone path divided it in two, with the tree exactly in the middle. "The Lake of Memory or the Lake of Forgetting. A choice given to each soul as it enters Hades."

"The land of the dead? But I'm not dead yet."

"You don't need to be. The tunnel that led you here happens to be the *Necromanteion*, the death oracle of ancient Greece. It allows a communion with the deceased, a brief meeting with your loved ones. For that, many have braved the Underworld. Dionysus himself descended into its labyrinths, to bring back his mother, Semele."

"Dionysus is a god, though."

"Nongods have managed it too. Heracles, Odysseus . . . and, of course, Orpheus." He took a golden sheath out of his pocket. About a square inch, perforated into lace by words that appeared to be in Greek. "This is the first of the Orphic tablets, the one that started them all. Dionysian mystics were buried with them, for the journey to the Underworld, and this one belonged to Orpheus himself. I gave it to him when he decided to venture into Hades."

The thin foil looked so delicate I was afraid to touch it. "What does the writing say?"

"It comes from one of his songs. Instructions for the afterlife."

He recited the contents from memory, in English:

You shall find on the left of the House of Hades a wellspring,
And by its side standing a white cypress.
To this wellspring approach not near.
You shall find next to it the Lake of Memory,
Cold water flowing forth, and a guardian before it.
Say: "I am a child of Earth and Starry Heaven,
I come parched with thirst. I perish."
And you shall be given a drink from the sacred water.

"This means you are the guardian?"

"Me?" He laughed, dropping the tablet back into his pocket. "No, the Lake of Memory is guarded by the fig tree. The sacred tree of Dionysus."

The fig again. Always the fig. No other tree could survive on the barren hills above the Black Sea. But figs did. And it was under a fig tree that my sister had danced, alone with the moon.

"Why are there no leaves on the rest of it?"

"Because the rest is the white cypress."

"Two trees grown into one?"

"We have only one heart. Memory and oblivion both stem from it." He pointed to the left, where bare branches, white like bones, reached down toward the water. "The cypress means letting go. Only a sip from its lake, and you can forget everything that has troubled you until now. Even love. Your mind will be wiped of dark memories just as the bark of this cypress grows immaculately clean."

I imagined forgetting. Quiet. Safe. Earth without a pulse, under the protective snow of winter. I would go back to my life unscathed. Graduate with honors. Conquer the music world. Even date—someone sweet and uncomplicated, like Ben.

"And the other lake?"

"The Lake of Memory will cause everything in your mind and heart to be imprinted there for good. So consider your choice carefully. Once made, it cannot be reversed."

I chose quickly—there was nothing in my mind or heart that I wouldn't want imprinted there. But his voice stopped me: "Not yet. There is something else, something from the past that I must reveal to you."

He looked away, far into the cave, and I noticed her: a white figure sitting among the rocks, bent over a book, undisturbed by our presence. She lifted her face. Waved. Jumped up and began to tiptoe her way along the water.

Ethereal. There was no better word. Even from a distance, her walk stunned with its dreamy lightness, carefree like the steps of a child skipping to the rhythm of a hum. As she came closer, I recognized Lorca's *Gypsy Ballads*—the same book in which she had written a message to Rhys:

> *Who else would love you like me*
> *if you changed my heart?*

Her eyes glided their unforgettable blue through me, detecting nothing but air, and moved on to the Lake of Memory. She reached into the water. Lifted a hand to her lips. Drank, and tossed the leftover drops, spilling a few over the still open book. Then she smiled at Silen—the same cryptic smile that refused to leave a room long after she was gone from it—and with a quick nod to him, she mouthed something before running off into the tunnel.

"What did she say to you?"

He hesitated, and that frightened me more than any lakes or underworlds.

"Silen, what did she say?"

"Until tonight."

It was a simple answer, and at first I saw no threat in it. Elza had known him while still at school. So what? She had come to the cave exactly as I had. Read a book of poems. Taken a sip of water, then walked back out into the unsuspecting world. I would have done it too, only moments earlier, if he hadn't stopped me just in time.

There is something else.

I might have never pieced together the elaborate web of logic—the entire chain of events that had unleashed itself once my sister had set her mind to it—if another line from the same poem hadn't stuck in my own mind. Something about the moon. About how it miscounted its dogs and had to start over. Digit after digit, in a circle, like the hand of a clock thrown off each time until finally the dial would strike midnight, allowing a certain ritual to begin.

"This book my sister was reading . . . it has a poem about Bacchus. About a moon keeping count by a fig tree. Lorca was describing the ritual, wasn't he? That's what Elza was up to that night?"

"Yes."

"And she came here to you first, before she went to find Rhys?"

"Yes."

"How did she know, though? I mean . . . why would she be reading about a death ritual and say she'd be seeing you later, if the accident hadn't happened yet?"

"Because it wasn't an accident."

He had given me the answer weeks ago, when I didn't have a clue what I was hearing: *we had very little time . . . I helped her go through with it . . .* I should have figured it out right then. Rhys dying on a full moon. And exactly before midnight.

"Are you saying that my sister . . . that the two of you killed Rhys?!"

"It was her only way to keep him. He had decided to move to Ireland with his little brother. And with the parents dead, there was nothing left to stop him."

"Nothing, except Elza. With your help!"

He looked down, hunched like the cave's ceiling—a sad resemblance of a man, who had infinite time to atone for what he had done but who probably knew, or at least suspected, that even an eternity wouldn't suffice for him to do it.

"How could you go along with this, Silen?"

"One's concept of right and wrong changes over time. Believe me, I have been trying to make my peace with it ever since."

"Peace with what, exactly? You let her kill him, and then made him a slave to her!"

"Nothing is irreversible, Theia. I can help love find him."

"So that's how I come in? Nice logic: the sister of the one who murdered him will now become his consolation prize. You unlock doors for me, send me to chapels, throw encoded bits of wisdom my way. But whom are you trying to console, really? Rhys or yourself?"

"You are his true love, I have already seen it. Unless I am wrong again."

"When were you wrong before?"

His eyes traced their memories along the shore, as if expecting to see the white figure once more.

"She worried that he was slipping away, that her hypnotic beauty could no longer keep him. So she asked me about the future. Whether, if they were both given infinite time, he might one day love her the way she loved him. Or love her at all. It was a question that carried the doom of its own answer, because time, even an eternity of it, is powerless to let us keep what was never ours. But she needed to know. And to be absolutely certain."

"What did you tell her?"

"Only what I saw. That his future held the most extraordinary thing: a long stretch of oblivion, of darkness, then suddenly within it—love. A love much stronger than her own. Hers wanted and demanded everything, craving with a madness that extinguished every obstacle in its way, even when that obstacle happened to be his heart. Whereas his love was different. It claimed with the abandon of an ocean wave—sweeping you over currents and depths but ready to collapse in on itself, to burst into foam and dissolve to nothing, just so it could deposit you safely on a shore somewhere."

Except I saw nothing safe about a shore that had just cost me Rhys. "Why did you think his love would be for me?"

"I didn't. When she asked me to look into his future, I saw a girl there who had the features of someone I already knew."

And so he had lied to Elza without knowing, promising her a future in which one day Rhys would love her.

"She was going to need my help that final night. And I agreed. After all, why not facilitate what was bound to happen anyway? Besides, back then I would have done anything for her."

"You were in love with her?"

"It wasn't love. Possibly lust, more than anything else. Your sister could be very . . . persuasive. I was her only path to the rituals, so she figured out early on that saying no to a beautiful woman is not in the nature of a satyr."

I had read about the nature of satyrs. And seen it, too, on the more explicit vases. Their obsession with nymphs: chasing them, having sex with them. Some of the images even showed satyrs with erections. No wonder Silen had been calling me a "nymph" all along.

"Don't be afraid, please, Theia. This weakness of mine . . . I assure you, it has been left behind, well into the past. For you I have felt only the most sincere admiration."

"I should hope so. To set Rhys up with a girl and secretly lust after her would have been an odd way of correcting past mistakes."

His eyes flared from my tone, reminding me who he was. But I was no longer afraid of him. Despite his legendary wisdom, he had been a fool: manipulated by a girl into becoming a murderer.

"How exactly did Elza pull it off? Was she as good at killing men as she was at seducing them?"

"The only thing your sister wasn't good at was defeat. She used to pour her heart out to me—mostly darkness, the frantic darkness of a girl about to lose her first love. I warned her to keep him away from the rituals, but she hoped they would intrigue him and spark something in his already absent heart. For a while, it seemed to work. Then he drifted away even faster. So she begged me to arrange the marriage union, *hieros gamos*."

"That ring she slipped on his finger?"

"No, the ring was her idea. Just a sentimental human touch. The ritual itself had commenced weeks earlier, over in the south woods bordering the golf course. I didn't expect him to go along with it, yet she had managed to convince him somehow."

I remembered Rhys mentioning a mock wedding. "Convincing" him had simply meant getting him drunk and telling him that it was a game of no consequence.

"The final rite was supposed to take place on the full moon in December. It was to be her great triumph, her silver-moon wedding night. But he could still change his mind at the last minute—as indeed he did—which demanded a backup plan. She hid his car keys so he would take the motorcycle and give her his helmet. Then a pedestrian had the misfortune of crossing College Road at the worst possible moment. To this day, Rhys thinks he killed a man. When a body was never found, he accused the butler of covering it all up. Spent weeks searching obituaries and missing person records, convinced he could help the dead man's family. At some point, he even toyed with the idea of turning himself in."

"Did Ferry really cover everything up?"

"No."

"Then what happened to the body?"

"There was never a body. The pedestrian who got hit was not exactly . . . capable of dying."

"You?" Of course it had been him. "Why stage all this, if a sip of poison would have been enough?"

"Because it had to be either an accident or a natural death. The rituals don't work with murder."

"Why not? It's a life for a life, isn't it?"

"In essence—yes. But you can't take a life and then offer yours to the god in exchange. So she needed someone else to set the wheel in motion."

And what a wheel it had been! It would never stop spinning, bringing Rhys to her month after month, on every full moon.

"Still, to plan an accident with the intent of killing someone . . ." I forced myself to look him in the eyes. "That sounds like the classic murder case to me."

"Not exactly. She had the criminal intent, *mens rea*. But the guilty act itself—the *actus reus* proper—was mine. A murder has always required both."

"You mean even the ancients got off on technicalities?"

The red flushed his cheeks—another surge of anger he had to swallow, probably because he knew I had a point. "The thing is, Theia . . . an accident meant she could have died too. Then there would have been no life left to offer in a ritual, no maenad and no daemon. Just a motorcycle flying off a curve. I don't know many others who would have taken such a gamble."

"It wasn't a gamble, if you had already revealed the future to her."

"The future is always a gamble. A chance remains, however small, that something might alter the course of events."

"Then why didn't you simply wait for Rhys to ride back from Forbes?"

"Because he would have been wearing a helmet. That way, the odds became unacceptably low."

The odds—of successfully killing him . . .

I didn't know what else to say. I had come for advice, but he was no longer someone I wanted advice from. "Have you considered that the best way to undo the harm, at least in part, might be to tell Rhys the truth?"

"Many times." He looked at the lakes, as if hoping to find there the key to that ever elusive absolution. "But would this really lessen the harm or merely add to it? Once he finds out, he would refuse to go near her."

"And what if he does? He speaks of taking his chances."

"There are no chances to take. She would kill him, you can be certain of it."

He was right. Elza had already killed Rhys once. Why would she hesitate to do it a second time?

"The hour is approaching." He pointed at the lakes. "You have a choice to make."

All along, I had assumed my choice was between Rhys and Jake, when in fact they were now on the same side of the scales. Loving them forever—or at least for the rest of my life—in a world of phantoms where everything was extreme, intense, magnified. Rhys and I would never leave the Princeton campus. I would share his body with Elza. He would share my heart with Jake. And one day, with two of us gone, the other two would continue their unending ritual.

The alternative was to forget. To opt for a normal, human future. Yet, much as I tried, I couldn't imagine myself in it.

"You have chosen with the heart," said the satyr, after watching me drink. "What surprises me most about this world is how little it changes."

"Elza and I are sisters. How different can we be?"

Without an answer, he headed back into the tunnel, turning every now and then to make sure I followed.

"Is this really a death oracle?" I touched the cold, grainy walls. "It can't possibly be real. We are thousands of miles away from Greece!"

"Real? Only if you want it to be, remember?" A smile spread its ambivalence through his face. "The *Necromanteion* is now a jewel of the tourist brochures, but little else. The very notion of a path to Hades—an actual passageway into the Underworld that one could step in and out of—is considered a myth, a curious invention of the ancient mind. And maybe it is better that way."

I expected to see the vine-leaf door. Instead, a patch of sky led us out on a barren hill overlooking an ocean. Or a sea.

"Where are we?"

"At the threshold between two worlds."

"Land and water?"

"No. Past and present."

"What about the future?"

"The future is here—" He pointed at my heart. "You aren't afraid of it, are you?"

I hesitated, and his laughter rolled its hollow echo over the hill:

"The future has many more reasons to be afraid of you than the other way around."

Far below us, waves crashed against the rocks, depositing their last wishes safely on the shore.

"How can I win him back, Silen?"

"If you think of love as a win, you will always lose. Such is the mysterious way of the universe. As for how or when—this I cannot tell you."

"You're the only one who can. You have the gift of prophecy."

"Clairvoyance and prophecy are not the same thing. One is to see the future; the other—to understand it. The last time I presumed to interpret what I saw, my guess turned out to be terribly wrong."

"Then don't interpret. Just tell me what you see."

He kept looking at the sky. In the distance, the sun was starting to rise above the water.

You helped my sister kill him, yet now refuse to help me? I didn't say it out loud, but with him that was just as well.

"My help wouldn't change the outcome for you any more than it did for her. When there's a will, there's a way. Isn't this what you humans say?"

I thought he would leave it at that—vague, as usual. But he added:

"The thing about mankind's wisdom is, it often misses the point. Your sister, for example, had more will than anyone could hope for. And yet she failed to achieve what she wanted."

With that, he turned me around. I saw a familiar building against the silhouettes of trees and distant hills. The same haphazard arrangement of stones, the terrace overlooking the sea: a replica of the Tsarevo church, but older.

"I shall be seeing you again soon, Theia Nymph of the Moon and the Sun . . ."

He held the door open for me. Inside, a familiar table stretched all the way to a stone fireplace from where the vastness of Procter Hall extended out toward the vestibule.

"So this really *is* a church! Only nobody knows it—"

But he was gone. Through the door behind me, all I could see was the golf course, the fence of Wyman House, and . . . night! Everything outside was now dark. How could it not be? While the morning sun was already rising over Greece, here—on a college campus that had become my home halfway across the globe—the night was just beginning.

About the Author

A NATURAL-BORN STORYTELLER, Krassi Zourkova grew up in Bulgaria and moved to the United States to study art history at Princeton. After college, she graduated from Harvard Law School and has been practicing finance law in New York, Chicago, and Los Angeles, where she currently lives. Her poems have appeared in various literary journals, and her essay "Book Collecting in the Absence of Books," about compiling a personal library under Communist censorship, won first prize in essay contests at Princeton and Harvard. *Wildalone* is her first novel.

About the author

About the book

Insights,
Interviews
& More . . .

Meet Krassi Zourkova

by Evonne Dunne

MAGIC IS FOR KIDS. We learn this early on, and it becomes a given, part of the price for growing up. *If you're old enough to drive, it's time to give up fairy tales.* And so, we do.

What's left, then, is a rational, adult existence in which duty erases dreams, logic cancels passion, and our heart is told what it should or shouldn't want, ad nauseam. Magic—if it survives at all—gathers dust on bookshelves, labeled "literature for children" and used sparingly, as a guilty escape.

Wildalone began for me as an extension of this escapism. I envisioned a story very much rooted in reality and in my past, but also one that would contain everything my real life didn't: myths, legends, witch powers and sex rituals, ancient riddles, murderous secrets, and immortal creatures capable of an even more immortal love.

But, as they say, be careful what you wish for. With every page and every plot twist, as I watched my fictional world grow complete, I also felt a certain penchant for magic lodge itself in my mind. I started to look for extraordinary potential in the everyday, to crave intricacies in life's minutiae, and to see each experience through a dreamy prism that earned me concerned headshakes from both family and friends.

Technically speaking, I was writing magical realism: a tale in which the fantastical blends so smoothly with the normal, it becomes impossible to distinguish where reality ends and myth begins. Put more simply, it was a fairy tale for adults. Not the sweeping fantasy recipes I had read as a child, boasting castles and magic objects and superheroes, but a world exactly as the one we live in, except now suddenly transformed by the ability of ordinary human beings to love and dream with an intensity most of us consider to be the stuff of fairy tales.

Over the past few months, as the book has reached its first readers, I have been called more than ever before a hopeless romantic. The "romantic" part I do love. But the word *hopeless* makes my skin crawl. It implies not that the romantic has given up hope, but that he or she is beyond repair. Why is the world so insistent on reforming those of us who dream? And why is romanticism viewed as a liability? Can—and should—we perhaps start speaking of the "hopeless pragmatist" instead?

It could be that finding the magic in our adult lives means reverting to a certain innocence we had while still children. This time, though, it needs to be a conscious choice: to believe in the unlimited possibilities of our inner world. As the saying goes, we are all granted two childhoods, but the second one depends entirely on us. ❧

Behind the Book

THIS BOOK BEGAN AS a whimsical indulgence: a way to revisit the past (my four years at Princeton) not as it actually happened but as I wished it had, with the real and the fantastical going hand in hand.

Imagine being nineteen, having to pack your entire world in two suitcases and move to a strange foreign land. Suddenly the intangibles become your treasures, the only "possessions" you are allowed to bring along in unlimited quantity. Memories. Hopes. Small personal histories that make you who you are. Your family's love, infallible despite the distance. And the richness of a culture— its superstitions, myths, legends—bound to clash with everything you are now supposed to call "home."

What if a girl from Bulgaria came to college in the United States and brought those legends with her, turning one of America's most beloved campuses into a secret home to Balkan witchcraft and Dionysian rituals?

Princeton proved an ideal setting. Hauntingly Gothic and secluded, it seemed somehow immune to time, constantly on the cusp of miracles. Every bit the opulent Hogwarts from *Harry Potter,* it was in fact real—a place one could visit, experience, touch.

It felt only natural, then, that on such a campus mythical creatures could blend in with the eccentric Princeton folk, that deadly ancient rituals might still be practiced there to this day, or that a murder mystery would be solved with clues hidden throughout the campus itself: a Greek vase in the art museum, a stained-glass window at the university chapel, a book of Andalusian poems from the school's library, and a famous Russian painting found in a local mansion.

Thus, Princeton promised both adventure and threat: a world in which everybody was suspect but not necessarily human or, strictly speaking, alive. In such a world, one might expect love to bring solace. But I wanted the story to be, at its core, about a love that is anything but safe. A doomed triangle: a girl in love with two brothers. One a dark and unleashed Heathcliff type. The other mysteriously shy, with the boyish charm of a poet. Can a brotherly bond survive love rivalry? And isn't it better to break one's own heart than to be happy at the expense of others?

The girl, of course, remained the autobiographical anchor of the novel. After a sheltered life of preparing to be a concert pianist, she comes to America itching to *live*—and to figure out what that word even means to her—while carving out her own future instead of the future others expect of her. I wanted to capture the sense of possibility, the surge of self-confidence and courage that Princeton instilled in me. Despite the daily struggles of a foreigner trying to fit in (language barrier, pop culture gaps, clash in habits and tastes), I felt that anything was achievable, that any dream was within reach. Back then, this translated into decisions everyone around me deemed mistakes (such as majoring in art history instead of something more practical, like economics). But even to this day, the optimism about our ability to change our fate has stayed with me— a much-needed center of balance during the last five years while I was working on the novel and juggling a day job in corporate law.

My other hope with this book was to attempt what I had so far merely admired from afar: the long-standing European tradition of lending aura to actual places through works of literature, of embedding ▶

5

Behind the Book *(continued)*

cities or even individual buildings in people's
imagination by creating a legend around
them. In our minds, the Paris Opera
will always have a phantom living in its
catacombs, and a hunchback will forever
hide among the gargoyles of Notre-Dame
Cathedral. This was my most heartfelt
wish when I set out to write a novel set at
Princeton. Because, in the most beautiful
of fusions, a book and a place can collaborate,
enhancing each other's magic. ᅇ

The Oldest Nightclub
in the World

IT WOULD HAVE SAT on a hill, hidden behind
fortification walls, about twelve miles outside
the capital of Greece. Here in the village
of Eleusis—now a major industrial suburb
of Athens—was the place where for two
millennia the ancients came to participate in
secret rituals known as Mysteries, involving
music, dancing, drinking, dazzling theatrical
performances, and . . . something else.
Something unfathomable, inexpressible
in words. An experience both physical and
mystical whose exact nature was kept secret
under penalty of death and of which we know
this for certain: it was believed to be not only
the culmination of one's life, but also
essential to the survival of humanity.

I wish I could say that I had an elaborate
plan to write a modern story bringing ancient
mysticism back to life. In fact, it was the exact
opposite: most of the saga's first book was
already written when mysticism imposed
itself upon it. *Write what you know*, the
advice goes. And so I did. My own life
became a springboard (a Bulgarian girl
comes to Princeton, plays the piano, studies
art history, struggles, makes mistakes, falls
in love). Everything else that I wanted in the
book—the myths and the supernatural—
I took from my country's legends or simply
made up. There is a reason they call it fiction,
right?

Or so I thought. I was sitting on a plane,
reading Wikipedia printouts about Orpheus,
when I felt a chill of recognition: things that
I had made up in the story—an ancient
ritual involving snakebites, demons, and
resurrection from the dead—had eerie
similarities to rites actually practiced in
the Orphic cults. This made me realize for
the first time that the story I had originally ▶

7

The Oldest Nightclub in the World
(continued)

conceived as a modern-day fairy tale could
have much deeper underpinnings. It wasn't
going to be simply about coming of age in
a foreign country, but about the ancient
wisdom of coming into one's own in a
universe that continues to feel foreign
so long as we remain spiritually blind.

For every world, there is an underworld.
This sentence became the core of the novel.
And there are many underworlds for my
heroine, Thea, to discover: the hidden sides
of Princeton, the challenges of living in
America, the dark secrets of her family, and
the treacherous labyrinths of her own heart.
In the more literal sense, there even turns out
to be an underworld beneath the university's
quiet Gothic dorms. For the ancient Greeks,
however, the phrase worked in reverse.
They believed that the reality we live in—
a materialistic reality of confusion, vanity,
fear, and greed—was in fact the underworld,
whereas the real world was inside each of us.
A world of self-knowledge, of wisdom and
truth. A world discoverable through the
Mysteries.

Cut directly out of the rock at Eleusis,
the ritual hall is now an archaeological site,
containing mostly ruins. But two thousand
years ago, it used to welcome the initiates
into its subterranean chamber, preparing
them for the experience of a lifetime. And
there, huddled in darkness on the ninth
day of celebrations, they saw something that
validated their entire existence, breaking the
boundary between the dead and the living,
and affirming the continuity of the cosmos,
of man's place in it.

Or, to put it in *Wildalone* terms, there
might still be a few more underworlds left
for Thea to discover. . . . ❧

Reading Group Discussion Questions

1. *Wildalone* is steeped in mythology, from the Balkan Samodivi to the Greek Orpheus and Dionysus. How did these myths and mythic characters underpin Krassi Zourkova's novel?

2. What are the similarities and differences between the two sets of siblings: sisters Elza and Thea, and brothers Rhys and Jake?

3. What are some of the challenges Thea faces when she comes to Princeton from Bulgaria? How did those challenges and cultural differences enrich the novel?

4. What is the connection between the myths and folklore, and the poetry and music in *Wildalone*? How do music and poetry help create a particular mood and express some feelings for the characters?

5. How would you characterize or describe Thea? Is she naïve? Strong? Is she innocent in the complicated relationships of the novel, or complicit?

6. Did you prefer Rhys or Jake as the better love interest for Thea? Why?

7. The book moves from the psychological to the supernatural. What did you enjoy about either or both aspects of the story?

8. Thea is at the center of a number of complex relationships, though her feelings for Rhys and Jake are at the heart of the story. Why did her love for the brothers outweigh her love of her sister? In what ways was her connection to the Estlins stronger than her connection to Elza? ▶

Reading Group Discussion Questions
(continued)

9. What were your impressions of the character Silen? Did you find him to be benevolent? Did your ideas about him change as the novel went on and his role in Elza's and Rhys's lives was clarified?

10. *Wildalone* has been compared to supernatural romances by authors like Stephenie Meyer and Deborah Harkness. What do you think of these comparisons? What elements of the novel, the romantic or the supernatural, did you enjoy most and why? Why do you think romance and supernatural themes can work successfully together in a novel? ❧

Discover great authors, exclusive offers, and more at hc.com.